A Ms. Adventures at Sea Novel

The Shadows of the Sea

(Las Sombras Del Mar)

———◆•◆•◆———

by

Christine L. McKellar

authorHOUSE®

AuthorHouse™
1663 Liberty Drive, Suite 200
Bloomington, IN 47403
www.authorhouse.com
Phone: 1-800-839-8640

First published by AuthorHouse 11/28/2007

ISBN: 978-1-4343-4842-5 (sc)

Printed in the United States of America
Bloomington, Indiana

This book is printed on acid-free paper.

FOREWARD

So many of my faithful readers have said they see me as my fictional protagonist, Quinn. Not so. Certainly there are hints of my personality in the character, but Quinn is actually a composite of the many women I've met in my colorful, diverse and peripatetic life. Again, the *MsAdventures at Sea* series is purely fiction and after having written nonfiction for so many years, I can't begin to describe the delight I get in letting my imagination run free.

Just as with my two previous novels, *A Port of No Return* and *The Devil's Valet*, there were so many helping hands on deck, I hardly know where to start. As always and I hope forever, my former husband, James A. McKellar, Jr, has been unstinting in his support and unfailing in his encouragement. He even helped me devise a solid plot.

A major thank you to Helen Margulis, for printing out the three-and-a-half pound rough draft of not only this novel but *The Devil's Valet* as well, to proof read. Your input has been invaluable, little buddy. (Also, thank you big time, cha-ching, for handling the finances at the book signings, so that I can do the badda-bing!) I owe a high five to Gordon Margulis for blessing his wife and me as we set sail to the Western Caribbean, then to the Panama Canal, to research this novel and also promote the previous one.

I'd like to thank Marty Cole, Bay Club marina master, for taking Helen and me on yacht tours to refresh my memory of deck plans and rigging. Thank you to the crew at the Red Sails Inn Restaurant; Jack Dargitz, Captain Bobby, Charlie, and George. Also, I salute Captain Ann Kinner of Seabreeze Books and Charts, Shelter Island, for taking my book on faith and consignment. Same with Jim Spain at the La Jolla Shores Market in La Jolla, California.

Transiting the Panama Canal has been a dream of mine ever since I first set foot on a sailboat. I had to settle for a cruise ship excursion, but our tour guide, Melvyn Oller, proved to be an invaluable asset once again when my crew on the *Vanora* set forth through the canal. Mel responded immediately via email to any questions I had and made clear certain particulars only a captain would know about going through the Panama Canal. Muchas gracias, amigo!

Aside from my dogs, Sultan and Noelle, music has been my daily muse and sole companion. I can honestly say that all three of my novels were written to the strains of guitar maestro, Ricardo Griego's CD, *Sombras (shadows)*. I even took inspiration from the title of his CD for the title of this book. Ricardo's original compositions and mastery of the guitar embody the mystery and beauty of flamenco/Latin music.

I'd like to thank editor/author Jarret Keene for including me in the *Las Vegas Noir* anthology of short crime fiction stories (publication 2008). When I initially protested that I'd never written crime fiction before, Jarret boosted not only my morale but my ego when he said, "I've read every word of your first book and I believe you can write anything." I believe he's as happy as I am with the result; a 6,000 word crime fiction story, *Bits and Pieces*.

To my readers, well, what can I say? I can only hope my stories take you to the place all readers want to go, along the path of "somewhere else," the place that keeps the world at bay for an hour or two. I hope my stories entertain you. I also apologize for how tardy I am in bringing Quinn and Noah back. However, I think you'll forgive me when you embark on your latest adventure aboard the *Vanora* across the Gulf of Mexico, through the Panama Canal, and along the coast of Central America and Mexico.

In closing I would like to express my pride in my son, Matthew. When our standard poodle, Noelle, was diagnosed with fibrosarcoma cancer earlier this year, Matt spent hours researching the disease and he spends even more hours ensuring Noelle receives the best holistic treatment available. His love, loyalty and devotion to his best friend of nine years is certainly part of the reason Noelle is not blind as predicted, and as I write, she remains as frisky, adorable and gorgeous as ever six months after her initial diagnosis. Matt gave me hope and a peace of mind that allowed me to finish this book. Good job, son. We love you.

So now, mates, let's set the main and raise the jib. It's time to go sailing!

-Christine

July 2007

CHAPTER ONE

Quinn Anne Carrigan awoke to the sounds of Guns and Roses, "Sweet Child of Mine," pulsing in her ears. Groggy, she rolled out of bed and nearly tripped over a large duffel bag that lay packed on the floor.

"Cyndi! Turn that damn thing down, would you please?"

The heavy scent of marijuana hung thickly in the air as a grumpy and tousled Quinn stalked out from behind the curtain that separated the bedroom from the rest of the tiny studio apartment. Her petite roommate was sitting on her boyfriend's lap on the couch; both looked at Quinn in stoned indifference. The irony between the song blaring on the stereo and the thoughts beating in her brain wasn't lost on Quinn, but it was the almost bovine look on Cyndi's face that made Quinn want to start screaming and throw a real tantrum.

Today was Quinn's last day in Miami. She was scheduled to set sail early the following morning on the seventy-six foot luxury sailboat, the *Vanora*. Her employer, Hank Somers, had hired her and three others to deliver the yacht to a new owner in Mexico, then stay on as permanent crew. This would be Quinn's second voyage as a hired cook on yacht deliveries; her first one three weeks ago had been a six-day delivery to Negril, Jamaica, aboard the forty-foot sloop, the *Zephyr*.

"It's not even noon yet, you two. Can't you take the party someplace else?"

Cyndi struggled to her feet. She was off the crutches she'd had to use for a turned ankle, but she still walked with a slight limp.

"Jeez, Quinn, what *EV* er! You sure have been a grouch lately, you know that?" She pouted as she clung to Joey's arm. Too disgusted to bother pointing out that Cyndi and Joey's drug-induced antics of late would be enough to make a saint sling some oaths, Quinn pressed her lips shut and went back to bed. Cyndi had been driving Quinn mad with her constant clinging to her Italian boyfriend. "Like eel skin on a handbag," Quinn muttered. The hotheaded construction worker had all but moved in on the two young women while he weaned himself off of harder drugs.

As Quinn lay curled up on her side, she heard the glass patio door slam shut. Her anger passed as swiftly as it had come only to be replaced by a sense of apprehension. Quinn had to force her body to relax as she mentally reviewed the ten days that had passed since an excited Hank had tossed pictures of the *Vanora* under her nose. Ten days that had been the most topsy-turvy days of her life. Like riding a tsunami, Quinn had risen to heights she hadn't dreamed of, then plummeted into deepest despair.

The six-day crossing on the *Zephyr* to Negril with Captain Tommy, the ill-fated Chip, and the heart-throbbing handsome Noah had instilled in Quinn a deep love for blue water sailing. The frown on her face eased into a sleepy smile as Quinn remembered how she'd met Hank and the crew of the *Zephyr* a mere month ago. She silently blessed the tipsy blonde, Gail, whom she'd met at the Sur de la Mar restaurant on the day Quinn had gone in to pick up her last paycheck.

Gail had just come off a yacht delivery from Mexico and at Quinn's request, she'd taken Quinn and Cyndi on a tour of the 57-foot yacht, *The Sapphire II.* One thing led to another and Gail had introduced Quinn to Hank Somers. Hank was so impressed with Quinn, he practically hired her on the spot to help sail the *Zephyr* from Miami to Negril, Jamaica.

The unpleasant set of circumstances that had led Quinn to quitting her job as a cocktail waitress at the popular seafront restaurant had paled into insignificance after the thrilling adventures she found aboard the *Zephyr.* Now half asleep, Quinn grimaced at the memory of setting the galley on fire her second day out to sea. She groaned, lost somewhere between sleep and wakefulness; she could almost feel the flames that had seared the top and bottom of her right hand.

Caught up in her memories, Quinn saw again Noah's oar swing through the air before smashing down into the sapphire Caribbean Sea where she and Chip were helplessly floating. In her disembodied state Quinn imagined she could see droplets of water like sparkling diamonds flying off the tip of the oar. Her body jerked as she subconsciously relived the moment the oar hit the water behind Chip's head, sending up a blood-tinged back spray that seemed to blot out the sun.

Restlessly, Quinn tossed and turned. Jumbled images of Chip's limp and bleeding body being dragged over the transom of the *Zephyr* mingled with a dull sense of terror that the shark that had attacked him was about to attack her too. Quinn struggled to awaken from her semi-slumber but the heavy heat in the apartment, and an all too familiar sense of ennui, kept her trapped somewhere between reality and illusion.

The light ocean breeze flowing through the louvered bedroom windows off of Biscayne Bay did little to ease the afternoon humidity. Quinn thought she heard the comforting resonance of Dr. Felix Templeton's deep voice. With a little whimper she let go and let her imagination take her deeper into the shadowy reaches of her memories.

The muffled bleating of a car alarm in the distance began to register in Quinn's brain. Dreamily, Quinn felt Noah's full lips tracing the curve of her jaw. She could feel his heavy dreadlocks brushing against her bare shoulders. "Quinn, Quinn, why did you run away? I feel you like I feel the air I breathe... I feel you belong to me and I belong to you."

Quinn sensed a deep stirring inside of her; the restless ache that had never really gone away since the day when Noah had sneaked up on her in the lagoon outside of Negril. They'd made love in the warm, undulating tropic waters, and both had been awed by the intensity of their union. Now, Quinn arched her back to press closer to Noah. The seductive, exotic scent that always surrounded him filled her nostrils. Her need for him was so intense that she began to breathe in hard little gasps as she struggled to envelop him with her arms and her long legs.

Quinn could feel Noah's hard body moving against hers and he was growling deep in his throat. A sudden, sharp pain in her lower abdomen caused Quinn to stiffen and look up in alarm. Her mouth opened in a soundless scream when she found herself staring, not into Noah's arresting topaz-colored eyes, but into the red eyes of a hideous creature—its hairy snout curled into a snarl. Strings of saliva dripped from long, yellowed fangs. "She's having his baby," the beast's hot breath huffed in waves over her face. "Lydia is having his baby."

"Noooooooo!" Quinn's wail of anguish rang in the small apartment. Jerking fully awake from the nightmare that had kept her nearly paralyzed, Quinn leaped from her bed and looked wildly around. "No, no, no!" Sobbing, she ran into the bathroom and began splashing her face with cold water. Moments later, she raised her head. Red-rimmed green eyes looked back at her from the mirror.

"That crazy witch! Oh, *please* don't let it be true. Please, God, not Lydia pregnant with Noah's baby! He already thinks she's put some kind of a stupid curse on him." Quinn almost spat out the words, "The chupacabra! As if that wasn't insane enough, now she says she's having his baby?"

Face still damp, Quinn grabbed a bottle of water from the refrigerator and wandered out onto the tiny gated patio. She sat down at a shaded table and pressed the chilled bottle against her swollen eyes. Quinn shuddered and thought, *isn't this peachy. Now I'm having major nightmares about Noah and Miss Psycho Nymphomaniac. And let's not forget the chupacabra! Oh, what has happened to my Noah?*

Quinn heard footsteps striding purposefully down the sidewalk between the two rows of studio apartments. She sat straight up in a moment of short-lived panic, debating whether to stay put or bolt inside and pretend she wasn't home if the footsteps were headed to her unit. Before she could make up her mind, the darkly handsome face of her newfound friend, Marcus, popped up over the fence fronting the patio.

"Yo, Quinn, hope I'm not bothering you. I tried to call but your phone went right into voicemail. Just thought I'd drop by and wish you a bon voyage."

Quinn waved him onto the patio. He was carrying a small gift bag that he set down on the table between them. "Brought cha a little something. Where are Joey and Cyndi?"

"I have no idea. They were up and partying early this morning, *again*. I got a bit cranky about it and they left."

She looked inside the bag and saw a small jewelry box. "What's this? Are you getting serious on me?" Quinn's tone was light and teasing. They both laughed. Marcus was a diehard and outspoken player, but he was also a fun date. He and Quinn had fast developed into good friends—not lovers—after the fabulous party Cyndi's boss had thrown the previous week. Opening the box, Quinn was touched by what she saw inside. Carefully she pulled out a bronze and silver St. Christopher's medal on a long, gold chain.

"Oh, Marcus, how thoughtful!"

He grinned broadly as she clasped the chain around her neck.

"I got one too, Quinn, my mom gave it to me when I left home. St. Christopher's the patron saint of travelers, you know."

"Well, he was until the Church decided that it was more myth than reality that he carried Jesus across the river." She shrugged. "Who cares what 'they' believe? It's what's in our hearts that matters." She stood and went around the table to give Marcus an affectionate hug and a kiss on the top of his head. "Thank you, buddy. I'll wear it all the time."

"Hey, wanna take a spin on my bike?" Marcus was referring to the true love of his life; a black 1984 Harley Davidson Shovelhead low rider. After a mere second's hesitation, Quinn agreed. Getting out of the stifling apartment, she thought, might help dispel the sense of gloom that was hanging over her. She'd pretty much finished packing two duffel bags for the six months she'd contracted to sail on the *Vanora*.

"Give me a minute. I need to change into something more appropriate."

"Sure you wanna change?" Marcus's tone was light but there was an appreciative gleam in his eyes as he looked Quinn up and down in the tank top and boxer short ensemble she was wearing.

"Sure I'm sure, I don't think this lime green would go too well with road rash," she joked. "Come on in and get something cool to drink. I'll only be a minute."

True to her words, Quinn was ready before Marcus finished the cold Corona he'd gotten from the refrigerator. She'd changed into jeans, boots, and an embroidered denim shirt.

"Oh, great. You're going to drink and drive?" Quinn frowned at the stocky body builder.

"It's only a beer, Quinn. You need to loosen up a bit. C'mon let's go."

Marcus decided they should head down to Key West. He knew of a family-owned fish house along the way where they could stop for a bite to eat. The hot June sun seemed to have chased away the scattering of clouds, taking the humidity along with it. Sitting behind Marcus on the Harley, Quinn's spirits lifted as the wind whipped around her.

Traffic was fairly light and before long they were past Marathon Key racing toward Key West along the seven-mile white ribbon of bridge that rose over the aquamarine ocean. The scenic drive over various bridges and through tourist towns was still as enthralling to Quinn as the first time she'd cruised down to Key West by car with her ex-flame, Don Ford.

Quinn had met Don soon after moving from her parents' home in Boston to take a stab at a modeling career in Miami. Her sometimes ditzy but goodhearted friend, Cyndi, was a fashion designer for Olga's Exotic line of bathing suits and cover-ups. Cyndi's cousin, Mike, had introduced

5

Quinn to the visiting Cyndi at a rock concert in Boston and the two young women became friends. So much so that six months later, Quinn abandoned her dream of becoming a physician's assistant—much to the dismay of her conservative mother and the disappointment of her physician father. She moved to Miami to live with Cyndi in her one-bedroom apartment.

Cyndi had made arrangements for Quinn to model a custom line of bikinis and beachwear for Olga's annual catalog. The trendy little designer was outspoken about how easy it was to work with Quinn. "Girl, making you look good is a piece of cake. I'm telling you with your long legs and great figure you've got it all!"

As it turned out, Quinn *didn't* have it all. Despite the cajoling of the professional photographer, Sebastian, Quinn couldn't relax and get into the swing of things. She couldn't shake the years of her Catholic upbringing. She remained wooden and uncomfortable in front of the camera. Desperate to get enough photos for the catalog and in need of the money, Quinn went along with Sebastian's suggestion that she do a couple shots of the sweet liqueur he carried along with him. Soon she was taking a few tentative puffs of the potent hashish he also offered to her. By the end of the three-week session, Quinn had gotten over any qualms she may have had about smoking organic drugs.

However, she hadn't loosened up enough to follow Sebastian's suggestion that she take off her bathing suit top for him during the final photo shoot. Quinn fled his studio in mortification. She decided it was time to find a respectable job where she could keep her clothes on and function without the use of drugs. Cyndi had met her Italian boyfriend, Joey, and Quinn saw less and less of her size-one, pierced, and trendy roommate. Quinn answered an ad in the *Miami Herald* for a receptionist at a yacht brokerage and was hired immediately.

There she met Don Ford, the firm's handsome and super successful salesman. Don was older and far more sophisticated than the young men Quinn was used to dating. He began hitting on Quinn immediately. Before too long he had her convinced they were destined to be married. Within a few months, she moved in with him at his Biscayne Bay Yacht Club condominium. It was the beginning of a string of lies and deception for Quinn. She lied to her family and said she was only dating Don. Thanks largely to the convenience of her unchanged cell phone number no one back home even knew she'd moved out of Cyndi's apartment.

It was also the beginning of the end of Quinn's innocence. Don was a constant partier and a heavy cocaine user. Quinn spent nine months trying to keep up with him, an effort that included her snorting cocaine. She started doing a line or two at parties and nightclubs, then she began occasionally doing some early in the week to get revved up and back into her work mode. Quinn suspected Don was cheating on her, too. It all became too much one weekend when he showed up at the condo with a scantily clad, collagen-enhanced blonde whose large, immobile breasts boasted of major implants. Don tried to forcefully get Quinn into the hot tub with him and his new friend. The woman had taken off her clothes and Don was already naked. Quinn left, never to come back, with Don's whacked out laughter ringing in her ears and the unforgettable image of the blonde's head bobbing up and down in the swirling water.

Marcus down-shifted the motorcycle and Quinn sat up straighter to pay attention to where they were going. He'd cut across to an exit and the bike rumbled to a stop at a red light. Quinn was anxious to take her helmet off and shake loose her long, wavy brunette hair. The aroma of fried seafood in the light air made her realize how hungry she was. When the signal turned green they swung left, and a few minutes later Marcus pulled into a small dirt parking lot.

Once they were seated on Momma Joe Po-Po's outside patio, Marcus began grilling Quinn. "So, you're leaving for Mexico tomorrow. Is Hank going with you and the crew?"

"I know he wants to. He's working on it. I guess he has to clear it with Loomis Grady. They work together. Loomis sells yachts then refers Hank to the new owners to find delivery and maintenance crews for them. Hank is kind of like a commodore, I guess. He's got a stable of captains and crew working for him. Loomis gives me bad vibes for some reason. He's fat and mushy-looking and always kind of sweaty. Eww!"

The two were laughing when the waiter came to take their order. While they waited for the food, Quinn relayed as much information as she knew about the crew and the captain she'd be sailing with on the *Vanora*. "The captain must be Hispanic. I haven't met him but his name is Diego Reyes. There's this little hard-body, older chick named Marnie who I think is a lesbian. Loomis swears she's gay, anyway. She's going to meet us in Mexico. Hank says a crew of four is all that's needed to get the *Vanora* across the Gulf and through the Panama Canal."

The drink orders arrived. Feeling more relaxed and carefree than she had in days, Quinn decided to heed Marcus's admonishment to lighten up and she'd ordered a banana daiquiri. Marcus was having a Red Stripe Beer.

"So, Quinn, there's you, this captain, and Hank—if he can get away. You're shy a sailor there, girl, until you hit Mexico."

"Ouch! I just got a brain freeze." Quinn set the tall goblet down with a bang on the table and squinted at her lunch companion. Marcus chuckled sympathetically, then turned to greet the waiter who was bearing down on them with platters of food. Quinn's spasm passed with the usual quickness associated with that peculiar anomaly. The conch burger before her smelled tantalizingly delicious and she decided to reserve the daiquiri for dessert. Marcus was busy dipping calamari strips into the variety of sauces he'd ordered.

Halfway through the crispy, tender conch sandwich, Quinn paused and asked Marcus how his marinated Cuban pork tasted. He smacked his lips and, over her protests, put a good size portion on her plate. Quinn retaliated by giving him most of the sweet potato fries that had come with her order.

"Construction's slow for us right now," Marcus sat back in his chair. "I think that's kinda why Joey's so in your face with Cyndi right now. The company we work for is going through some kind of insurance hassle over a hurricane last year and the damage it did to a major high-rise project. It's turned into a legal mess."

Although his next words surprised her, Quinn had a sense almost of déjà vu; a feeling of rightness in the air, when he said, "Whaddya think this Hank dude would say about hiring me on as one of the crew? I been sailing Hobie Cats for years."

"It certainly wouldn't hurt to ask," Quinn leaned over and gave the body-builder's huge bicep a pinch. "You spend too much time working out at the gym—I imagine you could use some fresh air and a different kind of work out."

The two friends split the bill when it arrived, then got back on the Harley Davidson. When they arrived at the little island of Key West the streets were crowded with tourists. As they strolled along Duvall Street, Quinn giggled and commented to Marcus on how the unmistakable smell of sunscreen from the passing crowds mingled in the air with the aroma of food. "It's like cologne around here and everyone's wearing it."

They browsed through shops for a couple of hours and visited the home of Ernest Hemingway. The afternoon passed swiftly and soon it was almost time for the sun to set.

"We'd better get over to Mallory Square, Quinn," Marcus moved her firmly through the throngs heading in the same direction. The famous locale and its expansive view of the setting sun drew enormous crowds three-hundred and sixty-five days a year. Quinn knew from past experiences that the square would be teeming with arts, crafts, and entertainers. There would be a non-stop show featuring jugglers, fire-eaters, human statues, and even tightrope walkers.

"What a zoo, huh?"

Quinn nodded in agreement as a gold-painted Elvis strolled by. "Did you know that Duvall Street is probably the longest city block in the world? It runs from the Atlantic Ocean to the Gulf of Mexico. Pretty cool, huh?"

His reply was lost in the wail of bagpipes cutting through the noise of the jostling, festive crowd. Quinn could see the silhouette of the player dressed in a kilt near the edge of the wharf. The sun was making its descent and suddenly cameras of all types were being pulled out as tourists began clapping and snapping. The Scotsman's chanter and pipes skirled on in the background, before slowly fading along with the shrinking sun.

A crescent moon hung over the darkened waters as Quinn and Marcus sped back to Miami over the forty-three bridges that linked the tiny islands to the mainland. Quinn was drowsy. She laid her head on Marcus's broad shoulder as she watched the shimmering water sweep by. As always, when her mind was still and her hands weren't busy, her thoughts turned to Noah.

Noah's "mojo" that Hank had given her when she met him at the Village Pub to sign the crew contract for six months on the *Vanora* was secreted away in her lingerie drawer. Not meeting her eyes that day, Hank had pushed a little sealed box at her from across the table.

"Noah wants you to have this. He still thinks Lydia's out to get him and anyone close to him with that voodoo crap. I don't know what his aunt had those obeah people do to him but, the dude's hurtin'.' I can see it." Hank sighed. There was a strained silence while Quinn fumbled with the packet, then tucked it deep into her purse.

"Noah's a changed man, Quinn, I doubt you'd recognize him if you saw him walking down the street." His tone was cryptic. Quinn could tell he didn't want to talk further on the subject.

Marcus maneuvered the motorcycle smoothly around a slow-moving pickup truck. Quinn raised her head, then tilted it back to let the cool wind sharpen her senses. The sickle moon riding in the sky brought to mind one of the odd objects she'd found when she opened Noah's package. Quinn was home alone at the time. Inside the battered little box was a drawstring leather pouch. Within the pouch were what looked like handmade charms. Quinn shook the bizarre-shaped items out into the palm of her hand and immediately a nasty, crawly feeling swept over her. It was as though the very shadows in the corners of the room were creeping in on her. Instinctively, Quinn bolted into the kitchen and tossed the knotted and twisted pieces of metal and twine into the garbage can under the sink.

After turning on every light in the apartment and pacing around the little living room for several minutes, Quinn decided to retrieve the odd ornaments. She'd felt a hollow little ache in her chest when she realized the leather pouch and its contents were the only physical mementos she had to remember the handsome Jamaican by.

They were in the city now and soon Marcus was pulling into the parking lot at Quinn's complex. He idled the bike and asked Quinn if she'd like for him to walk her to the door. "No thanks, it's late and tomorrow is the big day. I don't know if Hank got a full crew together but if not, I'll ask him about you coming along. Could you be ready to go if he says okay?"

Marcus shrugged. "Hell, yeah. I don't have much by way of responsibility. I'll leave money with my roommates for at least a month's rent and utilities. It'd take me all of ten minutes to pack a bag. I'm not as high maintenance as you are," he smiled as he took the helmet from Quinn and strapped it to the back of the motorcycle.

"Right on," Quinn gave him a quick hug. "One way or the other, you'll be hearing from me as soon as I know something, okay?"

She glanced around the parking lot looking for either Cyndi or Joey's car before heading down the sidewalk to her studio apartment. Neither vehicle was there so she assumed the couple was partying over at their friend Chad's house. *Fine by me*, she thought, *maybe I'll get a good night's sleep. They'll be at it all night once they get started.* Quinn had severed most of her ties with the old crowd. Her last encounter with Darrell Simmons, the former head chef at the Sur de la Mar, had scared her. He had looked and acted like someone coming down off of crack cocaine or methamphetamines. His anger and resentment toward her had been evident in his voice and facial expression.

Quinn winced as she recalled the two times she'd gotten so stoned and drunk that she'd gone to bed with her coworker. Darrell had become so possessive and demanding after the second time, Quinn had taken a week's vacation home to Boston to get away from him. A week that proved to be near disastrous for Quinn. Bored with the sedentary lives of the few friends who had not gone off to college, Quinn had gone out one night by herself. An unexpected urge to do some drugs led her to leave a nightclub with two guys from the nearby university.

Instead of the promised university dorm, Quinn found herself in the parking lot of an abandoned warehouse doing a line of coke with Andy and Eric. The private party turned into a nightmare fifteen minutes later when the two fraternity brothers decided to exact payment from Quinn—as in attempting to rape her. After a violent struggle, Quinn managed to break free and run off into the night, blindly stumbling through alleys and down side streets. She finally spied a lone taxi and frantically hailed it down. Her parents never knew about the incident. Quinn had sneaked quietly into the house and to her bedroom.

On the flight back to Miami the following afternoon Quinn could almost physically feel the shift her life had taken during her vacation. She fully realized there would be no going home—she'd outgrown the family nest. She dreaded her future, however. The thought of going back to the endless rounds of partying and, most likely, the chance that she'd succumb once again to Darrell's advances and end up having meaningless sex with him, made her want to run far away somewhere.

Rather than run away, Quinn did something that surprised even herself. Darrell had prearranged to meet her upon her arrival at the airport. In the car on the way to her apartment he kept up a running monologue on everything that had happened with their crowd since she'd been gone. The stories Darrell had regaled her with were all about drugs. He and Raoul were going to start dealing cocaine. Joey had wrecked Cyndi's car after a wild party then slapped her in the face when she'd protested.

Once inside the studio apartment, Darrell made himself at home; lying down on the king-size bed and firing up a joint. The evening news filled the small area with stories of terrorism, serial killers and out-of-control gangs.

The surge of disgust that suddenly swept through Quinn wasn't centered entirely on the oblivious Darrell. There was the sanguine expression of a news reporter as she calmly faced the camera with a report about a five-year old boy shot down in a drug deal gone bad, there was Darrell's story about Joey slapping her best friend Cyndi, and there was the memory of Andy and Eric's laughter in Boston as Quinn had fled sobbing into the dark and empty night, struggling to pull up her jeans as she ran.

Quinn turned to Darrell and, with steel in her voice, ordered him out of her apartment—and out of her life. Dumbfounded, he left—after calling her a few choice names and accusing her of using him. He threatened to get back at her as he stalked out into the darkness.

The next day Quinn quit her job at the Sur de la Mar.

Life certainly has a way of working out sometimes, she mused to herself as she pushed open the gate that guarded the darkened patio. Quinn hadn't turned on the outside light when she'd left earlier that day. She'd assumed Cyndi and Joey would be there when she got home. *If I hadn't quit, then gone in for my last paycheck, I might have never run into Gail again, met Hank, and got hired on the Zephyr. God only knows what I'd be doing!"*

Quinn was putting her key into the lock of the sliding glass door that served as the sole entrance to the apartment when a soft rustling from the far side of the patio made her freeze. She strained her ears to hear over her suddenly pounding heart. For a moment, she thought maybe Darrell had come back to carry out his threat of revenge. All was quiet.

It's only a rodent or something in the palm trees, she thought with a sense of such relief her hand started shaking. As she was turning the key, she heard her name spoken from the darkened recesses of the patio in a low, almost guttural voice. Quinn could feel the fine hairs on the nape of her neck rise. Her knees went weak as she slowly turned to face the intruder.

CHAPTER TWO

Quinn's clammy skin stuck to the cotton shirt she was wearing as she pressed her back against the glass door. Peering into the shadowy corner of the patio she could see what looked like a disembodied white object moving slowly back and forth as though beckoning her. Again the low voice spoke to her. "Quinn, you and I. We must talk."

"Noah?" Quinn whispered into the darkness. "Noah? Is that you?" A jumble of emotions washed through her. Yearning and desire, then a piercing sense of loss and sadness. She pushed herself away from the door and walked toward the seated figure whose outline she could now discern. "Are you all right? I've been so worried about you! Why don't you come inside?"

"Not yet. You sit here with me for now." He gestured at a nearby chair. Quinn noticed with a jolt that the floating white object was Noah's arm; it was wrapped in what looked like a cast or a bandage from his shoulder to beneath the elbow. There was a moment of awkward silence after Quinn sat down. She was near enough to catch the familiar and deliciously musky, semi-floral trademark scent of Noah's. She wondered briefly if perhaps it was a pomade that he used on his heavy mane of dreadlocks.

The silence was broken by a heavy sigh. "Quinn, I must explain some things to you. Things I know you will not be having an easy time understanding. There are some things I do not even understand—or believe myself."

Her eyes had grown accustomed to the dark and Quinn leaned closer to Noah. She noticed with some surprise that he was wearing one of the trademark Jamaican knitted caps. In the brief but intense ten days that she'd spent around Noah, she'd never seen him wearing any kind of hat or even a headband. He seemed thinner, too, somehow diminished. She could clearly see now that it wasn't a cast on his arm but a heavy bandage.

"I'm so happy to see you, Noah. I've been so worried. I heard about what happened after I left Negril. That whole voodoo thing with Constance and your Auntie Sharmaine. The drugs. I knew how sick you were. Hank kept me updated and I also talked to Dr. Felix. So much has been going on here, too. I'm glad you decided to come and talk to me."

"I miss you, Quinn. I miss you from the top of my head to the bottoms of my feet. When you left me after we made love in the lagoon, I did not know what to do. What to think. It was as if you took a part of me away. I left a piece of my soul there that day!"

Noah leaned forward and his light eyes looked like pools of liquid gold floating beneath the heavy cap. Quinn drew in a sharp breath when she realized unshed tears were causing the illusion.

"Noah, I am so very sorry. I—it, well, it was all so overwhelming. I've never experienced anything like that before." Even in the cool night air, Quinn's cheeks and body flushed with a deep heat. "Then when I realized how stupid we were to not think of birth control…" She stopped, suddenly aware that she'd never told Noah about her epiphany regarding him and Gail on the *Sapphire II*. How utterly shocked she'd been when she realized Noah had in the past had one or more sexual encounters with the promiscuous woman.

Quinn couldn't help the moan of anguish that slipped from her lips when right upon the heels of *that,* came the truly devastating memory of the phone call from Dr. Felix that had rocked her to her knees. *I wish I could tell you this in person, Quinn. You're not going to like this at all. I seriously hope you're sitting down. Noah had some visitors early this week. One of them was a detective. Detective Hector Caballero…Lydia Caballero's father…I'm so sorry, Quinn, but her father claims she's carrying Noah's child and they want him to be held accountable for it. The prenatal expenses and then child support…*

"To have us a child? That could only bring us joy, Quinn-nay!" Noah's voice, loud and thick with emotion, interrupted her memories. "You did not, you *do* not think I would leave you or forsake you for that? Woman, tell me that is not what you were thinking!"

Stunned by the ferocity of his words, Quinn shrank back into her chair. Noah was visibly agitated. When Quinn finally spoke the words spilled out, and so did the weeks of pain, anger, and remorse.

"Wait just one minute there, Noah. You have *no idea* what I've been thinking! What am I supposed to think? You seduced the living daylights out of me. You told me all about some crazy Puerto Rican chick named Lydia who, you claim, not only *seduced you* but put some freaky, bizarre curse on you. She branded you, and had you tattooed with the image of some supernatural, blood-sucking creature. Now she says she's pregnant with your baby!" Quinn would have jumped up and bolted into the apartment right then but she was shaking so badly she didn't think her legs would carry her that far.

Noah, however, leaped to his feet. "It's not true! It cannot be true that the child she carries is mine! She lies! You know, Quinn, that she lies. Only you know what she had done to me. How she had me branded personally like some slave she owns!" He grabbed his groin as he spoke. "She is crazy. Insane. How can you believe that what she says is true?"

The cloudless night and a faint light from the apartment across the way allowed Quinn to see Noah's silhouette clearly. There was something odd about it—something seemed to be missing or off balance. Her eyes traveled from his face, down to the bandage on his arm and back to his face again. Then it hit her. The woven cap he was wearing fit snugly on his head—no heavy dreadlocks fell from beneath its edges.

As if sensing her scrutiny, Noah started to walk past Quinn toward the gate.

"Noah, wait! Come inside and talk to me, please." She grabbed his right arm, the one without the bandage.

"No, Quinn, I cannot go in there with you. I know that you are leaving with Hank on the big yacht tomorrow morning. I come to ask you to believe in me for a little while longer. Until I can prove to you that I am not the father of the child of that wicked *skettle*. I will deal with her. She has caused me and you too much sufferation." In his distress Noah used Jamaican slang.

"What's happened to you, Noah? What did they do to you? Forget Lydia for now. With DNA they can prove whether or not you're the father. I know she's evil. I know she tricked you. What happed to your arm? Your dreads?"

"I have been cleansed, Quinn. I was taken through purification. They shaved my head. Even my body." Noah took Quinn's hand. Quinn felt a sharp stab of anticipation; strangely it disappeared as quickly as it had come. "There is much you don't know about me and my family."

He ran her hand along the rough ridges of the bandage on his left arm. "They removed the curse. The mark, the tattoo of the chupacabra is gone."

As if answering her unspoken question, Noah added, "The other marking. There is nothing to be done with that."

The phone inside the apartment began to ring. Quinn and Noah were mere inches apart. She noticed for the first time how high and broad his forehead was. His amber eyes with their thick spiky lashes, and his dark arched eyebrows seemed more pronounced without the distraction of the mass of dreadlocks he had when she first met him. If anything, Noah was even more handsome than before. His nose ring was gone. The only jewelry he was wearing was a silver symbol on a short leather thong around his neck. The design looked to Quinn like something a chicken would scratch into the dust.

The phone, which had stopped ringing, started to ring again. Quinn sensed something almost insistent in its ring. "I'd better get that, Noah. Are you sure you don't want to come in for some tea or coffee or something?"

"You go, Quinn. There is still much left to be said. But, another time. That is something I have seen to, that we will have time. You have those things I left with Hank for you?"

Quinn nodded, even as a little shudder swept over her. She wanted to ask Noah what he meant with his cryptic comments about time. The phone had gone silent again. Noah took her by the waist and pulled her close to him, until they were nose to nose, their lips almost touching.

"Be careful, Quinn. There are things in this world you don't know of. Keep your eyes open and listen from here," he put the palm of one hand over her heart. "Take the mojo with you," his hand moved caressingly across her breast. He paused for a beat as though he wanted to linger, slowly rubbing his thumb along the full curve of her skin. Quinn could feel her heartbeat accelerate and she pressed closer, leaning into his touch. With utter tenderness, Noah pressed his lips softly against hers, then pushed her away.

"When next I see you, all things will be irie," he said. Without looking back, Noah strode out of the gate—and was gone.

Quinn stood motionless, heart still beating rapidly. Those few moments of intimacy with Noah had left her more aroused than any foreplay with any man before him. "Will it ever end?" She spoke aloud into the empty night. "What's gotten into me? Why me?"

Quinn slid open the patio door and went into the airless little apartment. She opened the louvered windows in the bedroom and turned on the living room fan before checking the caller ID on the telephone. Like she'd figured, the caller was Hank.

Worried that something had happened to delay the departure of the *Vanora* in the morning, Quinn hit the callback button and stood anxiously gnawing on her lower lip. *Please, God, please don't let anything mess this up. I want out of here!*

Hank's voice when he answered sounded normal. Quinn breathed a sigh of relief. "Whaddup, Captain?"

"Hey, Quinn, I've been trying to get a hold of you all night. Did you lose your cell phone or what?'

"Oops, sorry, Hank. I forgot it today. I've been having problems with the battery keeping a charge. Guess I need a new one. Are we still on for tomorrow?"

"We are...and we aren't."

Quinn's heart sank. "What's wrong? What happened?"

"Nothing's really wrong except we're short a deckhand. I can take time off to get the *Vanora* as far as Cozumel, where we'll pick up Marnie, but not through the canal and over to the west coast. The kid I was going to hire didn't show up today. So far right now it's you, Diego, and me. Not that we can't handle it but I'd feel better with someone along who's planning to stay onboard for the duration."

The wave of relief that swept over Quinn made her almost feel giddy.

"I know someone who could go, Hank. Remember Marcus? Cyndi and Joey's friend?"

There was a long moment of silence. Then Hank said, "Sure I do. The party animal. He's the guy that was passed out on your floor last week when I stopped by to take you to check out the *Vanora*. Right?"

Quinn's heart sank. She clearly remembered that afternoon. The look of disgust on Hank's face as his eyes swept the room. Cyndi and Joey were passed out on the couch. Marcus was snoring on the living room floor. Marijuana roaches littered the ashtrays and wine bottles were scattered about. She recalled the sinking feeling in the pit of her stomach and the tone in Hank's voice, *I was going to ask you to come with me to check out the Vanora, but I can see you're in no shape for that right now. Why don't you call me when you sober up?* With that he'd left abruptly, leaving Quinn to wonder if her sailing career was over before it had even really started.

"Hank, listen. I've gotten to know Marcus better. He's become a good buddy—almost like a big brother to me. I can promise you he's a hard worker. What's more important, he's got a really deep loyalty streak. He knows how to sail, too. Marcus smokes a little pot and likes to drink, but he doesn't do hard drugs like Joey and that crowd."

"I thought Joey was off the hard stuff?"

"He says he is but if he keeps hanging out with the same old crowd, I imagine he'll start it up again. Especially now that he's got Cyndi back in the palm of his hand."

Hank chuckled at the mention of her roommate's name. "Yeah, Cyndi's a little handful." His voice grew stern, however. "I'm in a bind, Quinn, so I'm going to have to take your word on it with this Marcus dude. You need to make it clear, and I'm certainly going to make it clear—no drugs of any kind on the *Vanora*, got it? No pot, not even any downers like Xanax."

Quinn promised she'd relay the message loud and clear to Marcus. As she was about to hang up, Hank about knocked her for a loop with one last question.

"So, what did Noah have to say tonight?"

Quinn's jaw actually dropped. There was a long, drawn out silence as she struggled to come up with a good answer without lying to the commodore. Before she could reply, Hank assured her in a dry tone, "I'm not stalking you or following Noah, Quinn. He called and asked me if I knew the directions to your apartment. Said he had something important to discuss with you in person before you set off sailing to Mexico. What's between you two is between you two but I was wondering if he's getting you all worked up over this hoodoo voodoo crap."

"Jeez, Hank, you seriously don't think I believe in that stuff, do you?"

"I don't really know. I know Noah certainly does. I don't want any of that superstitious bullshit on the boat, though. I've seen people wig out and lose it at sea after hours on watch in rough weather. It's strange what tricks your mind will play on you under certain circumstances."

"I'm a dyed-in-the-wool, baptized Catholic, Hank. I'm not into black magic or anything. Noah came by to make sure I got that package from you. And there's nothing between us." Quinn groaned inwardly at her white lie. "We *all* got close to each other as you can imagine on the *Zephyr*. Me, Chip, Tommy, and Noah. It's not every day one of your mates gets attacked by a shark and almost dies."

Hank laughed. "Okay, Quinn, okay. We agree then. No drugs and no voodoo, right?"

"Absolutely right!"

"I'll see you at the yacht club dock tomorrow. Diego won't be in until late tonight on the red-eye from Mexico City. We won't be setting sail until at least noon. Get a good night's sleep."

Quinn actually did get a good night's sleep. She called Marcus before going to bed, and grinned at the boyish excitement in his voice. He was a good guy. Quinn was comforted at the thought of him coming along. Cyndi and Joey didn't show up until the first light of early dawn. Quinn was already brewing a pot of coffee and reading the morning newspaper when the pair came stumbling in. It was obvious they'd been doing more than drinking and smoking pot. Joey's eyes had glassy look to them and he didn't seem the least bit tired or sleepy. Cyndi kept repeating herself as she moved restlessly about rearranging knickknacks and pillows.

Quinn mentioned that she'd be leaving in a few hours for her six-month tour on the *Vanora*. "I'm going to take a spin on my bicycle. You guys need anything from the store?"

"Not me, I'm heading back over to Chad's." Joey was picking at the skin on his arm. "Unless you got some vodka here. I could really use a Bloody Mary."

"Joey!"

Even Quinn cringed at the petulant tone in her roommate's voice.

"You're staying here with me." Cyndi was furious. Her pale face only enhanced the almost maniacal glare in her bloodshot eyes. "I don't like those girls staying over there at Chad's. They're a bunch of cheap-ass strippers!"

"Oh, brother, you two. I thought you were cleaning up your acts." Quinn's face had a grim expression. "I'm out of here for six months in a couple of hours, but the lease is in my name, Cyndi. Don't think for a minute I won't have my dad get you evicted—and him." She pointed at Joey. "You're here like twenty-four-seven, Joey. You need to get a job and get a life. You're both out of your minds, out of control, and I'm sick of it!"

Quinn dragged her two duffel bags out on to the patio and slid the patio door shut behind her with a bang. A door that still had a crack in it from one of Joey's previous outbursts of jealousy over Cyndi's imagined flirtations. *Well, she **was** all hot and bothered over Hank for awhile,* mused Quinn as she set off on her bicycle. *Good thing he didn't buy into the simpering, helpless female ploy. I can't even imagine Cyndi on a sailboat.*

As always, the physical exertion of pedaling her bike calmed Quinn down considerably. The morning was still cool enough to make the ride enjoyable. Earlier, she'd checked the weather conditions in the newspaper.

This month, June, was the beginning of the hurricane season that would run until October. From what she'd read it looked like clear sailing for the next week at least. Little was Quinn, or the meteorologists for that matter, to know that the Atlantic and Caribbean coasts were about to suffer through the worst hurricane season in recorded history.

The well-manicured lawns of the homes in the upscale Coral Gables suburb swept by in a blur. Quinn was caught up in the rhythm of her pumping legs and steadily beating heart. Her thoughts turned to the early morning a month ago when she arrived at the dock to sail to Jamaica aboard the forty-foot sloop, the *Zephyr*. The heavy smell of diesel fuel had hung in the air in contrast to the crisp and biting aroma of freshly brewed coffee.

Quinn heart lifted and she began humming as she recalled the surge of adrenalin that shot through her when Noah had tossed her the springer, or dock line, to cast off. She began pedaling even faster as she relived the sensation of the rolling, almost sensual, rhythm of the yacht as Tommy steered the *Zephyr* out into the harbor swells.

Quinn stopped at a convenience store for a doughnut and a cold drink. The sun had moved above the horizon and she was sweating. She finished her snack and decided to head back so she could take a shower before going to the *Vanora*. All was quiet when Quinn rolled her bike onto the patio. The door was unlocked and there was no sign of Joey and Cyndi. The message light was beeping on the telephone.

"Hi Quinn, this is Shelly at Dr. Peterson's office. I know you're leaving for Mexico soon. Please give me a ring before you go, okay?"

This was the phone call Quinn had been half-dreading. Ever since she'd had unprotected sex with Noah in the lagoon at Coral Cove, Jamaica, she'd been plagued with worry. Her worst fear, of course, was that she might be pregnant. Simply thinking about how that would have adversely affected her pursuing a career as a sailor, much less impact her entire life, still gave Quinn the shivers. Once she'd gathered her wits after the encounter, she put two and two together and was stunned to realize how sexually active Noah was.

He'd slept with the notorious Lydia, who he'd first met as the cook on a yacht delivery a couple of months before he met Quinn. Noah actually had sex with Lydia again, even after her bizarre and dangerous behavior onboard the forty-five foot yacht he, Chip, and Lydia were sailing across the Gulf of Mexico. Then there was Gail from the *Sapphire II*. The heavyset blonde had regaled Quinn with stories of the men she'd had sex with in the course of her sailing career. And Noah was one of them.

Quinn sighed. Granted she'd come home from Jamaica with burdens on her mind. Her concern for Noah, who'd gone on a drug and alcohol binge the last night she was in Negril, weighed heavily on her. Then there was the development with Hank and Cyndi, her confrontation with Darrell, and Joey's out of control drug abuse. When Quinn's parents came into town for a medical convention, Cyndi let too many cats out of the bag at a dinner one night about Quinn's experiences during the week she was on the *Zephyr*. Viviane Carrigan's maternal instincts went on high alert and Quinn had to contend with her parents' outspoken disapproval of her continuing on as a hired deckhand.

The only relief Quinn had was on the morning she'd awakened with a sure knowledge that she wasn't pregnant. Hank had secured a six-month contract with the new owner of the elegant, 76-ft luxury yacht, the *Vanora*. With all the drama building up around her, Quinn couldn't wait to get out on the open sea and away from Miami. The only nagging issue left was—what if Noah had given her some type of sexually transmitted disease? For days Quinn had felt bloated, tired and listless. There was an underlying current of unease that flowed inside of her. The tension and drama alone of Joey and Cyndi's on again, off again, volatile relationship had her in a constant state of watchfulness.

Unable to bear the uncertainty of perhaps having a physical condition that was draining her and sapping her energy, Quinn had made an appointment with a clinic. She did so under the pretense that she'd be traveling outside the United States. She wanted to be sure she was current with all necessary vaccinations. She'd asked for a complete physical.

Quinn was about to find out the answer, she hoped, to whatever it was that was dragging her down. The electronic menu seemed to drag on forever as Quinn punched numbers on the phone. When Shelly finally was put on the line, Quinn had steeled herself for the worse. If playboy Noah had infected her with some STD, she'd have to cancel, at the last minute, her voyage on the *Vanora*.

"Hey, Quinn. Sorry it took so long to get back to you. Everything looked good except for one minor thing."

"What do you mean, Shelly? I'm leaving in a couple of hours. What's wrong?"

"We aren't saying anything's really wrong. Your pap test came out fine. It's just that in the blood panel you've got a slightly elevated white blood cell count although your kidneys, liver, and heart all look good. Dr. Peterson would like for you to come back for another test at your convenience."

"What does that mean?"

"You might have some kind of secondary viral or bacterial infection or something. An amoeba you picked up in Jamaica. Again, it's nothing to get all stressed about. We simply don't want to ignore it, okay?"

"Sure, fine. Whatever. When do you want me back?"

"Check in with us in a few months."

Quinn hung up the phone and sat down. Coming from a medical background like she did, she'd been a part of many a dinner conversation with her pediatrician father to know that she most likely wasn't faced with anything serious. Rather than get all worked up, she decided to deal with it later. Right now she had to get to the yacht harbor. She called for a taxi, then scribbled a note to Cyndi. *You and Joey were gone when I got back. The door was unlocked. I hope you two stay out of trouble. I'll call as soon as I can. Quinn.*

The cab driver arrived within twenty minutes. Quinn met him in the parking lot; the two oversized duffel bags at her feet. He had a turban on his head and spoke in broken English. On the short ride to the yacht club, Quinn managed to convey to him that she was going sailing on an extended journey. His enthusiastic response touched her. She took his card, promising to call for his cab when she got back to Miami.

"Rajid is my name. You call me and I will look after you."

The morning had turned glorious. Regardless of all the minor upsets Quinn had experienced in the last twenty-four hours, her spirits lifted as she strode down the long pier toward the berth where she knew the *Vanora* would be. The anticipation of what lay ahead started the adrenalin flowing in Quinn's veins. By the time she reached the yacht she was almost running.

Quinn had spent two days shopping for provisions earlier that week. The *Vanora* already seemed like home to her. The yacht's towering mast was bobbing gently side-to-side in rhythm with the incoming tide. Quinn looked with pride at the flowing white fiberglass hull and the burnished brass on the round portholes that lined the vessel. Blue sail covers and an expansive blue canvas bimini beckoned to her. Quinn tossed her heavy bags on the deck. She grasped the handrails of the plank leading to the main deck and hoisted herself aboard.

"Hank?"

Quinn could feel the deck humming smoothly under the power of the two idling Caterpillar diesel engines. The distinctive chuff chuff of water pouring out of the engine exhaust in the stern was like a pulse beating. No one was in sight so Quinn started down the few steps into the main salon. She tossed her bags ahead of her. The sudden descent from bright daylight into semi-darkness temporarily blinded her. At the base of the companionway she was startled by a figure in white.

"*Quien es? Quien esta aqui?*"

Flustered Quinn halted abruptly. "Hello? I'm Quinn Carrigan. The cook. And you are?"

"I am Diego Reyes. The captain of the *Vanora*. Welcome aboard, *cocinera*."

Quinn's brain registered two things immediately. One; she didn't like the condescending tone of the man in front of her. Two; her entire being resonated to the atmosphere of the yacht. The mingled scents of freshly varnished teak and the earthy smell of diesel fuel called to something deep inside of her. Still, her hackles rose as she braced her feet and faced her new captain.

"It's a pleasure to meet you, sir. Are Hank and Marcus here yet?"

The captain circled about her. There was something almost sinister in the way his body moved. Smooth and calculated. Quinn instinctively retreated from his scrutiny. Diego Reyes was lean and rangy. His close-cropped black hair was thick and curly. He was handsome in a saturnine kind of way. High, well-defined cheekbones and an aristocratic, haughty nose enhanced his arched brows and close-set eyes.

The wiry captain stopped in front of Quinn.

"So, *senorita,* I have heard many admiring things about you. It seems our commodore Hank would like to know you much better."

Embarrassed by the man's leering glance and the sneer in his voice, Quinn tried to move around him, but he blocked her escape. "*Momentito, mujer,* let me make one thing perfectly clear. There will be no favoritism on my ship, *comprendas?*"

Quinn decided to hold her ground and she looked the captain of the *Vanora* right in the eyes. What she saw startled her so that she couldn't help but do a double take. Diego Reyes had eyes indigenous to his Hispanic background. More than that, while his left iris was a light brown, his right one was solid black. Midnight black. Like a bottomless pool it had neither depth nor reflection. *Is he blind in one eye? Is he wearing one of those tinted contact lens? Am I seeing things?* Quinn was truly stumped for one long moment. She didn't know what to do or what to say.

Suddenly, a thought so bizarre and off-the-wall flitted across her brain that before she could stop herself, Quinn started to giggle. *Oh I get it. Instead of a patch over his eye, this captain has a patch IN his eye.* The cocky captain seemed thrown off balance by Quinn's sudden change of demeanor but before he could say anything there was a slight rocking of the *Vanora* and a loud male voice sounded out.

"Ahoy mates! Anyone aboard?"

"Marcus? I'm in here." The relief in Quinn's voice was evident. Diego moved swiftly away from Quinn toward the navigation station on the other side of the cabin. Marcus's stocky body filled the doorway. He was balancing a large canvas bag over one shoulder and grinning from ear to ear.

"Now this is a yacht!" He whistled in admiration as he gazed around the spacious wheelhouse. Diego turned and came over to introduce himself. The men shook hands and Quinn noticed how cordial the captain had become. *Great. I can already see he's one of those macho Latin types that think women don't amount to anything. How I wish Captain Tommy were here!*

"Come with me, *amigo*. I'll give you a tour of the boat." Marcus followed Captain Reyes out into the sunlight.

Quinn went forward to stow her bags in the roomy forepeak cabin she'd claimed for herself. The only entrance to the vee-shaped area was through a hatch on the foredeck. There were two good-sized bunks; one on the port side, one on the starboard side. She was thrilled that she had her own private bathroom and shower. There were two portholes to allow a flow of fresh air and Quinn planned on leaving the heavy entry hatch open, weather permitting. The owner's cabin was in the stern. There were two guest cabins with private baths, a captain's double cabin, and another crew cabin amidships near the washer and dryer.

After she'd unpacked and placed a few personal items around; a framed picture of her family and some scented cachets and soaps; Quinn climbed up the steps onto the deck and made her way back to the galley. She was pleased to find Hank had come onboard. He and Marcus, it seemed, were getting to know one another. They were sitting at the mahogany dining table sipping on sodas.

Quinn gave a Hank a mock salute. "Anybody ready for some lunch?"

Hank grinned at her, nodded, and went back to his conversation with Marcus. Captain Reyes was nowhere in sight but Quinn made him a hot pastrami sandwich also. When Quinn brought the men two plates heaped with thinly sliced beef brisket and melted cheese, cole slaw and Thousand Island dressing on French rolls along with potato chips, Hank told her to leave Diego's food in the microwave. "He's gone to take care of some last minute paperwork. Sit your butt down and let's eat. We've got some work ahead of us."

"What do you think of your new captain, Quinn?" Hank popped a chip into his mouth.

"Well, he's certainly not a bad looking guy. What's with the eye, though? I've seen people with one blue eye and one brown eye, but never with one brown eye and one black eye." Quinn had already decided it wouldn't be prudent to voice her instinctive dislike of the man before they'd even left port. She figured she should at least give him the benefit of the doubt. For now, anyway.

Hank shrugged. "I dunno. He can see out of it though, that I know for sure. Must be some hereditary thing. Other than that, he's very qualified. I guess he's somewhat of a ladies' man, Quinn. You'd better watch out." He said the last with a broad wink.

Marcus snorted. "Not to worry, Hank. I think Quinn's about done with men for the time being, aren't ya?" He gave Quinn a sympathetic glance.

"Poke me with a fork, guys, that's how truly done I am." Quinn stood and picked up the woven plate holders. As she busied herself in the galley, she reflected on the leather pouch she'd tucked beneath the mattress of her bunk in the forepeak. *Let's hope whatever weird magic Noah thinks he's got going on, it'll ward off el senor Capitan Diego Reyes. He gives me a real bad case of the creeps. Although,* she mused as she put assorted flatware into the dishwasher, *with those strange eyes he is kind of sexy…in a freaky sort of way.*

CHAPTER THREE

———— ◆•◆•◆ ————

Captain Reyes was back at the *Vanora* one hour before the scheduled castoff. Hank was taking Marcus around the huge yacht getting him familiarized with his duties. Quinn trailed behind the two men. She happened to be lingering near the wheelhouse when she spied Diego striding down the dock toward the yacht. He was gesturing with sharp, angry jabs to an overweight, swarthy man who was striving to keep up with the obviously irate captain. The two men were speaking rapidly in Spanish. Although Quinn could hear their voices as they neared the *Vanora,* she didn't understand a word they said.

With a condescending gesture of his hand, Diego dismissed his companion and climbed up the steps and onto the yacht. Quinn had darted into the wheelhouse, hoping the captain hadn't noticed her on the deck. His eyes were obviously as good as the next person's, maybe even better, she discovered.

"I see, *cocinera,* that you have an interest perhaps in the business of Diego Reyes?" His odd eyes traveled up and down her body.

Quinn's face flamed. "My name, *Captain,* is Quinn, and what you do is entirely your own business. You mind yours and I'll mind mine." She was startled by her own boldness. There was something about this arrogant man that had Quinn's dander up. Her gut feeling was that if she didn't maintain equal ground with him from the beginning, the crossing to Mexico was going to be hell for her. *Even with Hank and Marcus onboard they can't be with me all of the time,* she thought with a slight shiver. *It's a big boat after all.*

26

Diego laughed, his white teeth in contrast against his olive skin. *"Muy bien,* Quinn. *Muy bien…por el tiempo."* He headed toward the sound of Hank and Marcus's voices.

As large as the *Vanora* was, Quinn soon found out that the exercise of heading out to sea was pretty much the same as on any other boat. She and Marcus were put in charge of dock lines and fenders. Hank hovered about keeping an eye on the two deckhands. He nodded his approval at Quinn as she moved forward to stow her lines and fenders in the forepeak locker. Marcus stowed his in the transom.

Diego handled departing the dock with practiced ease. Quinn felt a grudging respect for the captain as they cruised smoothly out into the harbor channel. Soon everyone converged in the wheelhouse. Salsa music was pulsing from the state-of-the-art *Bose* speakers. Quinn went over to sit by Hank.

As she walked by Diego, he reached out and grabbed her arm. "Are you serving lunch today, *senorita?*" He never took his eyes off the long deck and gleaming expanse of water before him.

Quinn jerked her arm out of his hand. "We've eaten. I left a sandwich for you in the microwave, Captain. I can see you've got your hands full. I'll go get it."

"You guys want a beer or something while I'm in the galley?" Both Hank and Marcus said yes. Diego added that he'd take a Coke.

Quinn absolutely loved the galley on the *Vanora*. There was plenty of counter space and all the appliances were gleaming and state-of-the art. Best of all, two large square windows offered natural light and an expansive view, unlike the tiny portholes she'd grown accustomed to on the *Zephyr*. And unlike the *Zephyr*, this galley was open to the spacious main salon, which also had similar windows.

The whole environment was efficient and cheerful. Quinn danced around between the refrigerator and microwave, grabbing beers and gently nuking the captain's sandwich in the microwave. "Thirty seconds on, thirty seconds off, thirty seconds on again," she sang to herself in time with the salsa music.

When she removed the heated sandwich, she put a paper towel over the top of it, then stood stock-still for a moment. *He's damn lucky I'm not one of those restaurant workers who don't get mad—they get even—and spit in a nasty customer's food,* Quinn snickered to herself. *The cook is one person he shouldn't be messing with!*

"Just kidding," she said aloud as she walked the few steps up into the wheelhouse, two beers and a Coke tucked under one arm; the plate of food balanced in her hand.

"Talking to yourself?" Marcus raised a quizzical brow as he helped relieve Quinn of her provisions.

"Well, you know, being the only girl onboard, I need someone sensible to talk to," Quinn winked.

Marcus and Hank seemed to think her little joke was pretty funny. Diego snorted and muttered something in Spanish. The overall mood turned festive as the *Vanora* rode easily out of the busy harbor. Even Diego seemed to lighten up after he'd finished eating. It was a clear, beautiful day. White clouds were piled like cotton puffballs on the far horizon and the blue water sparkled beneath the hull of the seventy-six foot yacht.

Quinn marveled at the architecture of the city of Miami as the *Vanora* swept by. On Quinn's first sailing adventure the *Zephyr* had sailed at dawn. She'd missed seeing the gleam of the bright tropical sun on the pristine white buildings and the almost blinding reflection off of countless windows.

"So what's our heading, Captain?" Lulled into serenity, Quinn thought she'd attempt to soften the arrogant man's attitude toward her.

Rather than answer her directly, the captain addressed Hank. "Are we staying with the original plan, amigo? Cozumel, then through the Canal and up along the Mexican Riviera?"

Hank nodded, but there was a thoughtful frown on his face. "I've got to head back to Miami once we get to Cozumel. Loomis has been on a roll this year with sales and contracts for me. I've got a big race coming up in February that I need to start focusing on. I'm short of decent crew lately for some reason. You'll be picking up Marnie in Cozumel. Between her, Marcus and Quinn, you shouldn't have a problem going through the locks."

He walked over to the captain's station and pulled out a logbook. "The buyer's phone numbers and information are all right here. He's the owner of a pharmaceutical company in Guadalajara. His name is Rafael Santiago. It seems he wants to keep the itinerary open once you get to the Mexican coast."

Hank grinned in his usual disarming way. "I imagine he's got a gaggle of beautiful senoritas he wants to bring onboard to entertain. And I doubt he wants his wife, if he has one, to be tracking the *Vanora's* whereabouts."

Diego laughed and nodded in agreement. Quinn could tell by the salacious gleam in his eyes that he was looking forward to the idea of the yacht owner using the *Vanora* as a floating bordello. That was one scenario she hadn't entertained when she agreed to sign a six-month contract binding her as a fulltime crewmember. Even Marcus looked somewhat delighted at the prospect. Without comment, Quinn collected empty cans and the captain's lunch plate and went back to the galley.

Quinn spent a couple of hours going through the staterooms and organizing the heads, putting in fresh toilet paper, clean towels on the racks, and soap in the showers. She was relaxing with a book in her forepeak stateroom, when there was the sound of footsteps on the deck, then a tapping on the open plexi-glass hatch. Before Quinn could get up off her bunk, Hank poked his head down inside the cabin.

"Ahoy, matey, permission to enter?"

She grinned up at him. "Sure, sailor. Come on down."

Despite herself, Quinn couldn't help that little quiver of sexual attraction she always felt around the gray-eyed, blonde-haired Hank as he descended backward down the steps. He was tall and had a surfer's body; tight glutes, long muscled thighs, lean torso and broad shoulders. The feeling of being traitorous to Noah when she responded to Hank's attractiveness had faded a bit over time. It wasn't that her desire for Noah had faded; it was more like she'd finally managed to put him into a separate compartment in her mind.

"Nice job, girl," Hank looked around the cabin that now reflected Quinn's personality. "Looks almost cozy."

She thanked him and offered him a seat on the starboard bunk.

"Where is everybody?" Quinn asked.

"Marcus is fishing off the stern. We're on the outside in open water. Last I saw Diego, he was going over some charts. We're on autopilot for a while. Both of them are keeping watch."

Quinn offered Hank a bottle of water and they chatted idly for a few minutes. Hank seemed perfectly at ease, leaning on one elbow, long legs stretched out on the bunk. He sat up, patted the mattress beside him and said, "Come here for a minute, Quinn."

For a moment Quinn could only look at Hank in shock. Hastily, she recovered and moved over to sit at a cautious distance from him. Hank must have sensed her surprise and uneasiness. He laughed and patted her on the shoulder. "I only want to talk—for now, anyway." He added teasingly. Quinn blushed a deep red, then she laughed too.

"I'm sorry, Hank. All that talk about topless women, and Captain Reyes attitude"— she stopped abruptly. The last thing she wanted to do was complain about the captain. Or any crewmate for that matter. Her experiences on the *Zephyr* had deeply imbedded in her an appreciation of how important it was to have loyalty and camaraderie on a crossing.

"That's kind of what I wanted to discuss with you," Hank said. "I wouldn't worry too much about the wild women. You might have to put up with some topless broads running around the boat, but I doubt Senor Santiago will be hosting orgies or anything like that."

He looked at Quinn with a grin that could only be described as impish. "Hell, who knows? You might even loosen up enough to take your top off once in a while."

Quinn scowled and jabbed him in the arm. "Don't hold your breath, buddy. My momma didn't raise any fool."

They both laughed, then Quinn added primly, "Anyway, I'd simply hate to ruin my tan lines."

"Oh, really?" Hank's eyes gleamed. "Mind if I check them out?"

"You cad!"

"Okay, okay. Let's get back to business." He lowered his voice. There'd been footsteps on the deck a few minutes ago. They'd faded away but Hank was cautiously alert.

"I've picked up on the vibe between you and Diego. He is a bit arrogant, I admit. He comes from a well-to-do family in Mexico City. You know in Mexico you're either rich or you're poor, and generally the rich tend to be snobs about it. On top of that, he's got a lot of macho in him. I understand he's a real lady-killer."

"Great choice of words there, Hank." Quinn rolled her eyes and faked a shudder.

Hank patted her knee reassuringly. "Not to worry, kiddo. He'd have to be blind as a bat not to find you attractive, but he's a really good captain and very professional. Aside from a little bit of attitude, I doubt that he'll be bothering you."

He rose from the bunk. "I'd better get out of here. We don't want to give our crewmates the wrong idea, do we?"

"Marcus could care less, Hank. We're truly just good friends. As for Captain Reyes, if you want my opinion, based on what he said when we first met, he thinks I've got some type of special favoritism with you. That's what his problem is. I doubt he finds me attractive. I don't get that vibe. Jeez, I certainly hope Marnie doesn't find me attractive!"

Hank was still laughing when he went topside. Quinn followed him shortly thereafter. It was getting close to dinner time. She was anxious to get into her spotless galley and prepare a mouth-watering meal for her mates. Amidships she was startled when Diego Reyes rose up suddenly from behind a sabot that was strapped to the deck. He had a beach towel in one hand, a beer in the other, and he was wearing a champagne-colored *Speedo*. His sculpted bare torso rippled with muscle, his smooth skin glistened with suntan oil.

Whatever material that Speedo is made from, it doesn't leave much to the imagination, Quinn thought, as she quickly averted her eyes from the revealing swimsuit. The sun was making a majestic descent toward the purple and gray horizon of the Atlantic Ocean. Looking east, Quinn's eyes were caught by the spectacular seven-mile bridge that spanned the gap between Marathon Key and Bahia Honda. The curving white expanse gleamed in the sunlight and contrasted sharply with the deepening blue of the water. Cars raced across the bridge, their windshields reflecting the setting sun's rays like laser-tag beams.

"So, *chiquita,* you don't waste any time. Already you have Hank climbing in and out of your stateroom." Diego laughed. A rather high-pitched laugh, Quinn noticed, for such a machismo kind of guy. "Did he climb in and out of your bed as quickly?" He eyed her boldly up and down. "I for one would have taken more time, much more time."

Quinn was rendered momentarily speechless. She could only shake her head as without a word she hurried aft to the galley, leaving Diego to stand alone, muscled thighs taut as he braced against the steady motion of the *Vanora,* a knowing look in the eyes that followed her.

Safe in the galley, Quinn began to prepare an inaugural dinner for the crew. Marcus came bounding in and grabbed her around the waist. "What's cookin'? I'm starving." He swung her around, then planted a big kiss on her forehead. "This rocks, babe. I owe you big time for getting Hank to hire me."

"You don't owe me anything, you big galoob. And, if you don't let me go, there won't *be* any dinner." Quinn smiled at the boyish Italian. Marcus was big-hearted and genuine. Quinn counted herself lucky to have him onboard. She had no doubt that in a pinch he would prove himself to be fearless. She also had no doubt that he would defend her to the bitter end under any circumstances.

Quinn marveled again at the difference in the *Vanora's* galley compared to the out-of-date and cramped galley of the *Zephyr*. Gleaming stainless steel appliances, granite and teak counter tops, and the sub-zero freezer had her dancing and singing as she prepared carne asada tacos, refried beans and Spanish rice for the evening meal. Quinn had marinated the flank steak all day in aromatic spices, now she sliced the meat and began to cook it in chili pepper oil. She put canola oil in another pan to get ready to fry the fresh corn tortillas.

Hank had put on a CD and Soft Cell's *Tainted Love* began to pulse through the cabin speakers. He danced his way into the kitchen, a rum and Coke with a twist of lime in one hand. Hank handed the cocktail to Quinn and asked what he could do to help. She put him to work slicing avocados for guacamole dip. Then she had him mash garlic and grate jalapeno jack cheese to put into the refried beans she was ready to bake. The Mexican-style dinner was a salute to their destination and the country she was to call home for the next six months.

Quinn rightly assumed Captain Reyes was at the helm so when Marcus wandered back into the galley, she sent him to the bar in the salon to make a batch of Margaritas. The night was full upon the *Vanora* by the time dinner was ready. Quinn set the table in the wheelhouse with a red-checkered tablecloth and napkins. She placed an earthen pot with an aloe vera plant and little Mexican flags decorating it on the table as a centerpiece.

A sliver of moon shone in the cloudless sky as the *Vanora* sailed along the Florida Keys. The yacht was on autopilot and the crew of four sat down and began to eat with gusto. Everyone piled their plates with the crispy meat-filled tacos topped with fresh chopped lettuce, cilantro, juicy tomatoes, diced onion, and cheddar cheese. Hank in particular liked the refried beans that he'd help prepare. Quinn had instructed him to blend in pico de gallo and sour cream along with the garlic and cheese before popping the dish into the oven.

Quinn saw a different side of the captain during the meal. Rather than arrogant, he seemed almost gracious, complimenting her on the food and telling the crew stories about his family's background and the history of the capitol of Mexico.

"Originally, Cuidad de Mexico was called Tenochititian. It was built by the Aztecs on an island in Lake Texcoco, high in the plateaus of the Valley of Mexico. They were ingenious, these Aztecs, and built artificial islands and dams to allow for growth. The waters of the lake were salty so the Aztecs even built aqueducts to channel in fresh water from surrounding rivers."

Diego Reyes lifted his chin, and Quinn could see a gleam of the usual arrogance in his eyes. "I, myself, can trace my ancestry back to the Aztecs, on the side of my mother. My great, great grandfather is from Spain."

Curious about the captain's background, Quinn asked about his family; if he had brothers and sisters and what his father did for a living. Diego's face went blank for a moment. When he finally looked at Quinn, she involuntarily drew back in alarm. Both his eyes looked blacker than the pits of the olives she'd used to garnish the Spanish rice. Quinn had never seen eyes that looked so flat yet so full of some dark, dangerous emotion.

"I am the only son. I have one sister who is at a university in Spain. My father is a professor of mathematics at the University of Mexico. My mother died when I was young. Is there anything else you would care to know, *cocinera*?"

Quinn's face flamed at the sarcasm in his voice and the derogatory way he addressed her. "No, not really, Captain. Thanks for entertaining us during dinner."

She rose abruptly and began to clear the empty plates from the table. Not one morsel of food was left. Quinn's heart lightened a bit that her mates had enjoyed the dinner she'd so happily prepared. Marcus rose, too, and began to gather up the other remnants. Quinn couldn't help but hear him growl at Diego as he passed by, "I may be only a deckhand on this ship, but, dude, lay off of Quinn. She doesn't deserve it."

Hank must have thought the same thing. When Quinn went back to retrieve the tablecloth and napkins, he and Diego were deep in conversation. Hank motioned for Quinn to take a seat. "You two haven't even known each other for one day and I can see already you're butting heads. What gives? I'd just as soon turn back around then have any tension on the *Vanora*. Marcus is even copping attitude. Why don't we get to the bottom of this right now?" He looked expectantly at Quinn.

"I—I don't think it's *me* with the attitude, Hank," Quinn sputtered. "It seems my mere presence is annoying to Captain Reyes. He's as much as said so."

Diego looked at Quinn with hooded eyes, a slightly sardonic smile on his lips. "My apologies, *senorita*. I've explained to Hank that I don't approve of favoritism on my ship. I've been under the wrong impression with you, as Hank has explained to me."

He puffed on the long cigar in his hand and a wreath of smoke floated over his head.

"However, I must confess," he tapped the ash from his cigar into an ashtray, "I believe females on boats are *malo suerte*, in general."

"Bad luck?" Quinn snorted. "That's kind of an ancient superstition, don't you think?"

"Hey, wait a minute," Hank held up a conciliatory hand. "What about Marnie, Diego? You've sailed with her before."

Diego laughed, and said with a broad wink. "Marnie, I do not consider a female."

Hank laughed, too. Marcus came walking along the side of the cabin and asked what was so funny. Quinn replied that it was a guy thing. Hank invited Marcus to sit with them so Captain Reyes could outline the current course of action. Diego informed the crew they would round Key West near midnight, then head out into the Gulf of Mexico. He said he would take the eight to midnight watch, Quinn and Marcus would have the midnight to four, then Hank four until eight in the morning.

"I know that you, Quinn, have had some experience." The captain's tone was neutral. "However, I prefer to get us out into the open sea before you and Marcus take the watch. When Marcus is more familiar with his duties at sea, he will have a watch of his own."

Quinn busied herself cleaning the galley and laundering the dinner linens before she went forward to her cabin for a few hours sleep. Being so near to the bow she could noticeably feel the rise and fall of the yacht and hear the water breaking along the fiberglass hull. They were still running on the two diesel engines; there wasn't enough wind to push the seventy-six foot boat under sail.

Quinn braced herself against the sink in the head as she washed her face and brushed her teeth. After donning a pair of terrycloth pajamas she crawled into her bunk. She left the main hatch open so she could enjoy the cool, fresh air. Her last thought before falling sound asleep was, *if we hit any storms on this crossing, sleeping here could be quite a sleigh ride.*

Chapter Four

The crew settled into a simple routine on the crossing to Cozumel. Diego's attitude toward Quinn wasn't exactly warm, but it was tolerant. Marcus adapted to life at sea as though he'd been born to sail. Day by day, Hank and Quinn's friendship deepened. The gray-eyed commodore was respectful and easy to talk to. Quinn knew Hank had brought his laptop along with him and was in touch with Captain Tommy and Chip; Quinn's friends and former shipmates from the *Zephyr*. Hank mentioned that he'd emailed Noah several times but had gotten no response.

The skies became overcast and gloomy halfway across the Gulf of Mexico. It seemed to Quinn that the closer they got to Cozumel the more Diego's attitude seemed to reflect the sullenness of the weather. Quinn also detected uneasiness in the captain's demeanor. He was constantly monitoring the weather and sea conditions and she said as much to Hank. Hank shrugged.

"Seems to me like these swells we've been riding are bigger than usual. On one hand that's kind of good. We'll get to Cozumel before the five days we reckoned at this rate. Diego's a pretty seasoned captain so I imagine he's being cautious and keeping an eye out for tropical storms or depressions. I'd better start paying attention myself, now that you mention it."

Hank took the time to show Marcus how to use some of the navigational equipment. Quinn already knew most of the basics but she wanted to know more. It became a morning ritual that after Hank's watch, and after Quinn served breakfast, the three Americans would spend an hour together poring over charts and working on the laptop. Captain Reyes usually kept the *Vanora* on autopilot. He spent a lot of time prowling the yacht from bow to stern, always looking out for other ships, his odd-colored eyes sweeping the horizon at regular intervals.

One morning, Quinn left the nav lesson earlier than usual. She had a slight headache and was headed to her cabin to get some aspirin. The sun was shining and for the first time in days there were no heavy clouds in the sky. The wind was beginning to freshen, too. The crew of the *Vanora* had only had the sails up about half of the time they'd been at sea. Quinn looked around at the shining sea and breathed a deep sigh of contentment. She was looking forward to hoisting the sails.

Quinn was climbing backwards down the steps into her stateroom when a loud bang reverberated from the bow, causing her to lose her footing. She could have easily fallen and been injured if it weren't for a pair of lean, hard arms that caught her around the waist. Quinn struggled to turn around and found herself face to face with Diego Reyes. He was slightly taller than Quinn. Her green eyes were mere inches from his black and brown ones.

"What are you doing in my cabin?" Her voice was shaking in indignation. Quinn was breathless from the close call; her chest rose and fell rapidly. Diego tightened his grip around Quinn's waist and pressed against her heaving breasts. His odd eyes moved down to her lips and for one sickening moment Quinn thought he was going to kiss her. She was ready to claw at his face when the captain laughed, then released her.

"Technically, *chiquita*, I am not in your cabin. I was in there," he pointed to the forward sail locker, "pulling some canvas. When I shut the door it must have startled you."

It took Quinn a good moment to get her breathing, and her temper, under control. *Technically*, Diego was right. One third of her cabin was the storage locker for spare sails. Quinn hadn't thought about that when she decided to bunk there. Still, she believed Diego had no right to enter her personal space without some prior warning or asking her permission. Quinn moved as far away from the captain as she could in the limited area of the cabin.

"Next time you could give me a head's up, don't you think?" Her tone was brittle. "I'm entitled to some privacy on this boat."

"But, of course. You were too busy with your boyfriend, Hank, and the other one or I would have begged your permission, *senorita*." Diego's voice dripped with sarcasm.

"He's not my boyfriend!" Quinn said hotly. "I made that mistake once and I won't make it again!" Too late, she clapped her hand over her mouth.

The last thing she wanted Diego to know about was her affair with her former shipmate, Noah. Diego raised an eyebrow and moved past her toward the stairs.

"No? Then what is this?" He tossed a heavy necklace at Quinn, then moved up and out of the stateroom with limber ease. Quinn looked at the chain and medallion she'd caught in her hand and groaned. She'd brought along the necklace she'd purchased for Hank in Montego Bay. Quinn was planning to give it, and a thank-you note, to Hank before he left for the States. She'd left a draft of the note and the necklace out on her vanity table that morning. Obviously, Diego had read the note.

"None of this is his damn business," Quinn muttered as she dug out the aspirin, then rummaged in a drawer for a bathing suit. One thing Quinn had a lot of was bathing suits from her short-lived modeling career. Most of them were sexy and flattering since Cyndi had custom-designed them expressly for Quinn.

"I certainly don't want to look sexy with Diego around, that's for sure." She sighed as she tossed aside one bikini after the other. Finally, Quinn settled on a modest navy blue and lime green two-piece. She chose a plaid cotton cover up, pulled her hair back into a ponytail, and grabbed a paperback book before going topside. The men were getting ready to set sail. Hank called to Quinn to help Marcus raise the forward jib. Soon the *Vanora* was heeling gracefully to the starboard side.

Quinn arranged herself on the deck near her cabin and lost herself in a sailing adventure classic, *Two Years Before the Mast*, by Richard Henry Dana, Jr. She'd just rolled over onto her stomach when Marcus came up and plopped down beside her. He offered her a cold beer. Marcus was wearing a pair of baggie shorts and it seemed every muscle on his body was cut and well-defined.

"I saw our revered captain coming out of your cabin earlier, Quinn, what gives?" Marcus's eyes were covered by Oakley sunglasses but Quinn could hear what she couldn't see—a smoldering anger beneath his casual tone.

"He was getting out one of the lighter sails, that's all. It was a bit of an unpleasant shock to find him in my cabin, though. Kind of like finding a hair in your food." Quinn laughed and so did Marcus. "However, I *did* tell him he needs to give me notice next time. Or, he can ask me to haul one out for him."

Marcus nodded, then patted his flat stomach. "Speaking of food, isn't it about lunch time?"

"You're *ab*-solutely right," Quinn punched him lightly on his torso. "Let's go round up some grub. And, I promise, no hairs."

Quinn made tuna melt sandwiches on sourdough bread with pickles and onion rings on the side. Hank had been napping all morning. He must have smelled the food, since he showed up just as Quinn was setting placemats on the cockpit table. The wind had picked up and the seas seemed rougher but the crew was enjoying the sunshine. After trimming the sails, everyone sat down to eat. Several times Quinn had to grab at her mug or a condiment jar as the *Vanora* strained restlessly against the ocean current and winds.

Quinn had stood up to begin clearing the table when one particularly large swell hit the *Vanora* broadside, sending Quinn, plates, and utensils flying across the slanted deck. Her head connected to the main boom with a loud crack. She must have been knocked out for a few seconds because the next thing Quinn was dimly aware of was someone picking her up. Her vision was blurry and she couldn't see who was carrying her. There was a strange thrumming in her ears that seemed at the same time to permeate every cell in her body.

"Whoa, now, that's a nice goose egg."

Quinn was lying on her back on the big sofa in the main salon. Someone was pressing a cold compress on the side of her head behind her left ear. She could hear Hank and Diego talking. Their voices faded and she opened her eyes to see Marcus's anxious face looming over her. Moments later the engines rumbled to life and she could tell by the noises on the deck that the men were taking down the sails.

"You all right, Quinn? Man, you hit the boom *hard*, girl."

"I have a mean headache, Marcus, but other than that I think I'm okay." Quinn pushed the ice bag away from her head. "Sorry, but you're giving me another one of those brain freezes."

"Yeah, well, you're lucky you didn't hit your temple. You got a nasty bump there. Stay put and I'll clean up the galley."

"No, Marcus, I need to get up and—"

"You will not go anywhere." Diego's voice, full of command and sharp as the gusting wind, cut through the cabin. "You will stay where we can keep an eye on you. You are not to go to sleep. You may have a concussion."

Quinn did feel drowsy and it was with great effort that she managed to stay awake the rest of the day. Hank and Marcus kept checking on her at intervals and tried to keep her entertained. Right before dinner, Quinn got up to use the head and a wave of dizziness swept over her. Fortunately,

Marcus was right there in the galley making spaghetti and salad for the crew. He helped her to the nearest toilet, the one in the master stateroom.

Rather than sleep that night in isolation in her forward cabin, Quinn slept on the couch in the main salon. Her sleep was punctuated with odd, almost hallucinogenic flashbacks. Jumbled memories of her childhood mingled with images of her life in Miami. She saw her older brother Greg tumble out of a tree in the yard of their Boston home. Eleven years old at the time, he'd suffered a fractured collarbone. Then, Cyndi was there, laughing and chanting some strange, garbled incantation over his prone body.

Quinn tossed and turned, muttering as the images in her mind shifted to the island of Jamaica. She was in the lagoon again with Noah. The normally clear waters were swirling around their naked bodies in a whirlpool of dark intensity. Riding on the edges of the cresting ocean were hideous sea creatures; half shark and half scaly beast. One of the mutants stretched out a long, snakelike appendage and grabbed Noah by his thick main of dreadlocks.

Quinn began thrashing around. She tried to scream but all that came out was a long, harsh whisper. "Noah, no, don't take Noah. Take me." As if in answer to her prayers, hard claws dug deeply into her shoulders. Quinn's eyes flew open. In the dim light of the main cabin she could see the satyr-like features of Captain Reyes mere inches from her face.

He was sitting beside her on the sofa. Quinn could feel his hip pressed intimately against hers. The weather had deteriorated and the *Vanora* bucked and heaved in the heavy seas. Diego's body moved with an easy grace next to Quinn, in tempo with the motion of the yacht. To a casual observer, they could have been lovers, intent on the foreplay that precedes the ultimate intimacy. Quinn struggled to sit up but Diego pressed her shoulders firmly down into the pillow she'd been sleeping on.

"Don't try to get up, *cocinera*. It wouldn't be good for you right now. The weather is bad and we would not want you to fall and hit your head again, *si?*"

Quinn was suddenly aware that she couldn't have gotten up easily even if she tried. She was cocooned on the sofa with a wide, mesh harness normally used in berths to keep sailors from being tossed in their sleep to the deck during high seas. Someone had taken her security a step further than the norm and had fitted the harness snugly over her, then clipped it to the bulkhead wall.

"What do you want?" Quinn shifted her body so her hip was no longer touching the captain's.

"You were having *uno malo sueno*—a bad dream. I came to rescue you from your nightmares." Diego removed his hands from her shoulders and reached over to unclip the harness. "You see, Quinn, I am not such a bad person." He moved so that Quinn could sit up.

"So, who is this Noah? Is he the one you were sleeping with on a different crossing?"

"Oh, puh-leeze! What does it matter? You certainly don't have to worry about me sleeping with anybody on this trip." The annoyance in Quinn's voice was obvious.

Diego stood up. "What matters, *chica,* is that everyone stays loyal to the captain. I have seen too many times how closeness between the crew can cause problems. One thing I demand is complete loyalty, *comprendas*?"

The brass clock over the navigation station began its mellow ringing. It was midnight, and Quinn heaved a sigh of relief. It was time for Marcus to come on watch. Moments after Diego disappeared up the stairs to the wheelhouse, Marcus came up from his cabin. He stopped to check briefly on Quinn before reporting to Diego.

"Glad to see you're up," he said. "Man, it's kind of rough down there. I couldn't fall asleep for a while." He left before she could answer. Quinn used the head, then went topside, where she assured both men that she was well enough to sit through her watch with Marcus. They were motoring steadily through the rough seas. Basically, all the two crewmates had to do was keep an eye on the radar and monitor the weather conditions.

Sheltered in the enclosed bridge, Quinn snuggled into a corner with a blanket wrapped around her while Marcus went to the galley to get some tea and cinnamon rolls. While sipping on the sweet, hot beverage, Marcus brought Quinn up to date on the progress of the seventy-six foot yacht. According to Diego's reckoning they were about sixteen hours away from Cozumel. Hank had expressed some concern that afternoon over a high-pressure system brewing to the southeast, near Jamaica.

"High pressure meaning tropical storm or hurricane," he elaborated to Quinn.

"Oh, that's just hunky dory," Quinn frowned. "But, if it's that far behind us we don't have to worry about it, right?"

"I guess not. Diego doesn't seem worried about it. He knows more about Mexico's climate than Hank does. It's hurricane season in these parts right about now, you know. Diego says it runs June through November."

"Marcus, it seems something's bugging Diego. He prowls around like a cat and he's always checking the radar." Quinn sat up straighter. "Hey, maybe he's uptight about Marnie coming on board when we get to Cozumel?" She mimicked the sneer in the captain's voice. "Another *female*. Such bad luck, *senor*!"

At Marcus's urging, Quinn dozed for most of the three hours remaining on their watch. Hank's appearance at four o'clock woke her up. Quinn felt rested and the throbbing in her head had subsided. She was hungry and decided to make an early breakfast. Quinn could tell Marcus was tired; she promised him she could whip up a hot meal in no time.

True to her word, before long the three of them were hunched over blueberry pancakes, sausage patties, and scrambled eggs with biscuits and gravy. Long, rolling swells had replaced the choppy seas and were pushing the *Vanora* along. Some of the swells were so big the large yacht seemed to slide down their faces.

Marcus went to his cabin right after breakfast. Quinn tidied up the galley then went topside to sit with Hank. The sun was beginning to rise and Quinn commented on the odd cast to the morning sky. The horizon had a sullen, brassy look to it. It seemed to Quinn that the very air was trying to condense and hold the sun still in its orbit. There were no clouds, and no wind to speak of.

"We're making damn good time with these following seas," Hank said, as he smoothly turned the wheel to guide the yacht through the water. "You'll like Cozumel, Quinn. There's a Senor Frog's there at the main market place. You can grab a taxi and go to the Mayan ruins about fifteen minutes out of town, too."

"Sounds good, Hank. Too bad you have to get back to Miami." Quinn had a sudden thought. "Hey, wait a minute. I've got something for you."

She worked her way carefully forward to her cabin. She'd decided to take advantage of being alone with Hank and give him the necklace. There was no telling how hectic things would be once they reached Mexico. They'd need more provisions and Marnie would be coming onboard. Quinn hurriedly scribbled a new note that she tucked into a small pouch along with the chain and medallion.

By the time she got back to the wheelhouse, the sun was up and already the air was humid and sticky. Hank put the *Vanora* on autopilot and, with a quizzical look at Quinn, he untied the strings of the pouch and emptied the necklace out onto his palm. He whistled.

"Nice, Quinn. Really nice. Thank you."

Quinn blushed, then hurriedly explained how she'd bought the piece of jewelry in Montego Bay as a token of her appreciation for Hank hiring her as cook on the *Zephyr*.

"You've opened up a whole new world to me, Hank. I can't tell you how much I appreciate it."

Hank smiled and slung an arm around Quinn's shoulders. 'You don't have to thank me, girl. I consider you an asset." He kissed her lightly on the check. "And I consider you a good friend, too, you know."

Quinn was about to say something when she felt the vibration under her feet of the water pump starting up. "I guess *El Capitan* is awake. I'd better go warm up his breakfast."

By the time Diego emerged, his hair still damp from the shower, Quinn had his breakfast and a fresh pot of coffee ready. The rest of the day was uneventful except for the big dolphin fish, or Dorado, Quinn hooked later that afternoon. It had been Hank's suggestion that they troll some fishing lines behind them. Quinn was actually nodding off when her line began to sing. It took two of them to pull the fighting fish in.

Even Diego was delighted at the catch. Quinn, however felt a twinge of sadness as she watched the scales of the flopping creature change from yellow into a rainbow of colors. The blunt head, with its tiny mouth and sharp little teeth, banged up and down on the deck; at one point coming perilously close to Quinn's bare legs and causing her to leap backwards in alarm.

"Yummy, yummy," Hank smacked his lips. "Fresh mahi-mahi for dinner tonight." He explained to Quinn that mahi-mahi was the Hawaiian name for the fish. "It means strong-strong. Even though people call it a dolphin fish it's not related to the real dolphin. Dolphins and porpoises are mammals."

Quinn nodded and a wave of nostalgia washed over her as she remembered how one afternoon on the *Zephyr*, Chip had given everyone a lesson on the difference between dolphins and porpoises. It was only hours after that little lecture that she and Chip were dumped unceremoniously into the ocean and he was attacked by a black-fin shark. Quinn shuddered at the memory and excused herself to go to her cabin for a nap while the men cleaned the now dull-colored fish.

CHAPTER FIVE

T he dinner Quinn prepared that night was five-star. She'd decided to simply brush the Dorado filets lightly with olive oil, then broil them with a touch of dill and squeezed lemon juice. She melted butter in a pan with fresh chopped garlic and crushed rosemary and let it slowly simmer before adding the mixture to potatoes whipped with one part buttermilk, regular whole milk, and salt and pepper.

As a side dish, Quinn made steamed green beans with toasted slivered almonds, French-fried onion strings, a dash of Worcestershire and a garnish of freshly shaved Parmesan cheese. She baked a batch of croissant rolls to serve with herbed butter. Quinn set the table in the main salon with clean linens and candles. She placed a bottle of Chardonnay in an ice bucket on a side table.

This would be Hank's last night on the *Vanora*. They would be reaching Cozumel sometime in the early morning. In honor of the occasion, Quinn asked the crew to dress for dinner. She chose a black, scarf-hemmed halter dress with a bold parrot design in green, tangerine and scarlet patterns. She placed a black lace snug over her shoulders and put her hair up with clips made from abalone, then donned a pair of sequined sandals with a medium wedge heel. Quinn even splurged and applied eye makeup that accentuated her green eyes and thick, black lashes.

Marcus and Hank showed up clean-shaven and dressed in slacks and collared shirts. Diego, however, surprised them all when he entered the salon in a crisp, white captain's uniform. He bowed formally, then removed his cap and sat down at the table. The *Vanora* was still bouncing around a bit, but in the warm, candlelit salon, redolent with the aroma of fresh bread, garlic and rosemary, the quartet could have been dining in an intimate restaurant.

Once everyone was served, Diego said a blessing in Spanish, the words flowing in a beautiful cadence from his tongue. For a few minutes there were only murmurs of appreciation from the diners. Quinn was enjoying the food as much as the men. She knew she'd reached a culinary plateau as far as her cooking career went. The Dorado was delicately flavored and broiled to flakey perfection. The garlic and rosemary mashed potatoes complimented the fish and the green beans added a crunchy, pleasing texture to the whole meal.

The bottle of wine was passed around a second time before Quinn noticed that Hank was wearing the pendant she'd given him. Her eyes darted swiftly from his neck to Diego's eyes and she wondered if the captain noticed the expensive gift. He was looking straight at her. Even in the dim light the difference of color in his irises was obvious. A chill went down Quinn's spine.

"So, *amigos. Mis compradres.*" Diego raised his wine glass. "We will all miss our first mate, Hank, no?"

"*Si, si,*" said Marcus, as he passed his plate to Quinn for a second helping.

Hank leaned back and rubbed his stomach. "And I'm certainly going to miss Quinn's cooking."

Quinn smiled at him, then Captain Reyes spoke again.

"You may have been surprised at my uniform this evening. I must make clear that it is the custom for me to wear the proper clothing when the owner is onboard. And so it should be with you," he nodded to Quinn and Marcus. "*Con permisso*, Hank, I think it is better to make this clear to Quinn and Marcus before you leave the *Vanora*, so that there is no misunderstanding."

Marcus beat Quinn to the punch. "You mean we gotta wear *uniforms?*" The disgust in his voice was evident.

"No," Diego sounded amused. "*I* wear the uniform of a captain but you two as crew must dress, how do you say? Uniformly? In a manner that will distinguish you from guests onboard."

Quinn was flabbergasted. "What does that mean? I doubt Marcus and I have similar outfits in our wardrobes."

"Shit, man," Marcus slapped his big hands on the table making the plates rattle. "I didn't sign on to be no freaking butler or a servant here."

Hank spoke up. "Hold on there, dude. I don't think Diego's saying you're a boat slave or anything. I kind of see his point." He looked at the captain. "Can you be a little clearer? This is news to me, too."

Diego calmly helped himself to more food before he spoke. "It is more professional that as the crew of the *Vanora* we all stand out and distinguish ourselves. What if we have eight new guests and a fire breaks out or we run into a storm at sea? The peoples must know who to look to."

He patted his mouth with a napkin. "I did not say you must wear uniforms. I am saying you must be noticeable. You could have t-shirts made in Cozumel with *Vanora* printed on them, perhaps." He looked pointedly at Quinn's low-cut dress. "Both of you should wear either white or blue pants, or shorts, while on duty."

"That sounds reasonable to me," Hank looked at Quinn and Marcus. "You guys good with that?" His tone implied he was making more of a statement than a question. Quinn nodded. Marcus shrugged, "I guess so." Then he stood up to help Quinn clear the table.

Quinn's head was beginning to throb a little and she grimaced as she bent over to load the dishwasher. Hank and Diego had gone to the wheelhouse. Quinn straightened up and said to Marcus, "This 'owner' business," she hooked her fingers into the air, "is beginning to sound like a monarchy. Every time Diego says 'the owner' I feel like he's saying 'the king' or 'his highness' or something."

Marcus laughed. "Yeah, I get the same feeling. The good news, Quinn, is Hank asked me to stay on for six months. I signed the same contract as you this afternoon."

Delighted, Quinn gave him a big hug. "Fabulous! At least I'll have one friend on board. Marnie seemed okay the one time I met her, but it sounds like she and Diego know each other pretty well."

Any further conversation was interrupted when Hank entered the galley. "We should be arriving in San Miguel de Cozumel early in the morning. We'll need all hands on deck so why don't both of you rest up until midnight. Diego and I are going to split this watch, then we'll take turns on deck with each of you as we get closer to land.

"You guys need to really keep your eyes peeled tonight for fishing boats, cruise ships, and other craft, okay?"

Quinn and Marcus murmured their assent, then each went to their separate cabins. The weather was still blustery. Quinn had to hang on to the steel halyards as she moved along the deck to the bow. Safely inside her stateroom, she secured the hatch above her and got ready for bed. She decided to wear a comfortable pair of drawstring pants and a t-shirt that she could sleep in and also wear topside when the yacht got into Cozumel.

The rhythmic bouncing of the yacht was soothing to Quinn. As a precaution she hooked up the safety netting alongside her bunk. There was no way Quinn was going to risk getting another bump on her head. Before long she was fast asleep. The only sound in the vee-shaped cabin was the echo of the ocean sweeping by and the sound of waves slapping the long, sleek hull of the *Vanora*.

Quinn must have slept more soundly then she realized. A loud pounding on the plexi-glass hatch had her sitting up and groggily looking around before she realized where she was. She undid the security lock. The heavy hatch flew open to reveal Hank's worried face peering down at her from out of the gloom.

"Are you all right? You had me worried, Quinn. I've been banging on the glass it seems like forever. I was beginning to wonder if your head injury did you in or what?"

"I'm fine, really. Sorry, Hank. I was out like a log. For a minute when I woke up I didn't know where I was. Give me five minutes and I'll be right up."

Quinn brushed her teeth, grabbed a hooded jacket, and pulled on a pair of deck shoes. Hank was waiting for her, and he escorted her to the wheelhouse. Marcus was there with Diego. Quinn was surprised to see how close to land they were. She could see lights along the shoreline and flashing maritime beacons. The engines were rumbling and the radio crackled in the background.

"We'll pull up beside the fuel dock," Diego's lean face looked sallow in the green light of the radar console. "We'll clear customs and quarantine in a few hours. No one leaves the *Vanora* until that happens. I'll bring her up to the dock along the starboard side. So, now is the time to bring out and secure the springer lines and the fenders."

Quinn and Marcus scurried about the deck getting the *Vanora* ready to dock. Luckily, there were few boats cluttering the area. Diego expertly brought the big yacht up and around, then backed it in alongside the long dock. The smell of diesel fuel was thick in the air. A fine mist of rain began to fall, which quickly turned into steady downpour. By the time Quinn and Marcus had secured the heavy dock lines, they were both soaking wet.

Back onboard the *Vanora*, Quinn stood shivering in the wheelhouse. Marcus was checking the cleats on the deck. Hank had apparently gone below to get his duffel bag in order for his departure later that morning. He'd be taking the ferry across the 12-mile wide Yucatan Channel to Playa del Carmen on the mainland, then a taxi to the airport.

"So, *chiquita*, you will miss your close friend, Hank, *si*?" Diego's eyes met Quinn's, then traveled boldly down to linger on her chest. Quinn was suddenly and uncomfortably aware that due to the damp chill her nipples were erect and pressed tautly against her cotton shirt. Quickly, she pulled her jacket closely around her, her cheeks flaming in embarrassment.

"You look nice all wet, *cocinera*," Diego's pointed tongue darted out and he ran it along his lips. "Perhaps later today I can show you where the best snorkeling is on the island."

Before Quinn could respond, Marcus popped up from the main salon. "Did I hear snorkeling? What about diving, you guys? Some of the best reefs in the world are right around here. You know, the black coral and all."

"We can do that, too," Diego didn't take his eyes off of Quinn. "I would be happy to take you both to where only the locals go."

"I'm going to make breakfast," Quinn couldn't get away from Diego's scrutiny fast enough. When Hank joined her in the galley, Quinn saw he was still wearing the jewelry she'd given him. Her heart was heavy at the thought of him leaving. In one sense, Hank was her last tie with Noah. She thought back to the day she, Noah, and Gail had gone to the Village Pub. Her first glimpse of Hank when he walked in the door had her almost choking on the beer she'd just swallowed.

If it hadn't been for me leaving with Noah, Tommy, and Chip for Jamaica, I wonder if anything would have happened between Hank and me? Quinn couldn't help but think as the two worked companionably side-by-side, making cheese and mushroom omelets.

As if sensing her mood, Hank set the microwave timer to cook strips of bacon, then grabbed Quinn by the wrist. "Hey, I was thinking I might be able to get back here after all. I'd like to go through the Panama Canal with you guys. Diego's been on the radio with the owner. He says Senor Santiago wants to keep the *Vanora* here for a week. He's planning on flying in to do some diving."

"Oh, Hank, that would be awesome!"

Hank chuckled and brushed her cheek with one hand. "Well, we'll see. Keep your fingers crossed."

Marcus and Diego came down and Quinn served breakfast buffet style. The rain had stopped and everyone took their plates to the wheelhouse where they could watch the sun rise through the broad windows. The town of San Miguel was on the west side of the flat island of Cozumel. In the early morning light Quinn could see in the distance the outline of the Yucatan Peninsula. Slowly the harbor came to life; small boats began chugging out to sea. The occasional beep-beep of a mo-ped or car horn cut through the air.

The customs office opened, the inspection of the *Vanora* and her crew went off without a hitch. Quinn noticed how deferential the government officials were in the presence of Captain Diego Reyes. She had to admit to herself that he exuded an air of aristocratic authority. His immaculate white captain's uniform only added to his commanding demeanor. Diego was smilingly confident as he dealt with the two customs agents, then ushered them off the *Vanora*.

It was time for Hank to go. Quinn walked with him down to the busy port terminal of San Miguel. Two huge cruise ships, the *Star Princess* and the *Disney Magic* apparently had come in overnight. Throngs of tourists were milling about. Taxis by the score lined the streets waiting for fares. The drivers were either leaning on the vehicles smoking cigarettes, or actively trying to cajole people into hiring them.

Hank got in line to buy his ticket to the mainland, then came to stand by Quinn.

"What's with the long face?" He slung a casual arm around her shoulder.

"Oh, nothing, although, I *am* going to miss you. I'm really glad you hired Marcus. I like having a friend onboard. "

"Not to worry, if all goes well, I'll be back at the end of the week. Anything you want me to bring you from Miami?"

Quinn shook her head. "Will you let me know what's up with the old crew? And swing by my apartment to make sure Cyndi and Joey haven't trashed it?"

"No problemo. I was planning on doing that anyway."

The two friends hugged, then Hank strode off and disappeared into the crowd boarding the ferry. Quinn wandered around the nearby shopping plaza, where she bought a couple trinkets, a sundress, and some chocolates before heading back to the *Vanora*. She could hear the throbbing beat of salsa music coming from the yacht before she was halfway down the dock.

The blue bimini was up, shading the cockpit from the hot mid-day sun. There were a number of people on the yacht. Quinn could see them in the cockpit, and moving about on the foredeck. When she climbed onboard, her heart sank. Two women were sitting with Diego Reyes, who was wearing his trademark Speedo. One was blonde, rather stocky and had broad, coarse features. The other woman was much younger. She was a pretty brunette with a lush but slender figure. Both were wearing g-string bikinis.

Marcus came out of the galley, an ice chest in his arms. He greeted Quinn with a huge grin. "The bar's open, *senorita*. Get on your bathing suit, grab a margarita, and join the party!"

"Yes, please. You must join the party, Quinn. You've worked hard in *la cocina* on this voyage. Now, it is the time for fun and reward." It seemed to Quinn that Diego's tone held a touch of mockery. Before she could answer, a wiry familiar figure rounded the wheelhouse. It was Marnie.

Marnie went straight to Quinn and stuck her hand out. "Say, whaddup? I'm surprised you haven't jumped ship. Diego can be a real hot dog. But, I'm sure you know that by now."

Marnie was smiling but the smile didn't reach her eyes. Reflexively, Quinn shifted the bags in her arm and took the proffered hand. She mumbled something about putting her purchases away and went forward to her cabin.

Two men and a topless woman were sunbathing in front of the forepeak hatch. One of the men was straddling the woman, rubbing suntan oil on her bare back. The other lay on his back, a straw hat over his face. Quinn murmured an apology as she stepped around the threesome. She climbed down the steps into her cabin, and closed the heavy hatch above her. Quinn suddenly felt like a total stranger aboard the *Vanora*.

CHAPTER SIX

The last thing Quinn wanted to do was mingle with the group topside. But it was hot and stifling in her cabin, even with the portholes open. She changed into a one-piece swimsuit and pulled on a short, white knit cover-up. *I'll have one margarita to be sociable, then I'm going to give the galley a good going over,* she promised herself as she climbed up the stairs and out into the sunlight. The sunbathers were nowhere in sight.

Quinn was heading toward the galley when the deck began to rumble as the twin diesel engines started up. She hurried to the wheelhouse. Diego was at the helm, a cigar clenched between his teeth; one hand was on the wheel and with the other he motioned for her to come closer.

"What's going on? Where are we going?" Quinn looked out the windows and saw Marcus on the dock uncleating the dock lines. The two male guests were stationed one at the bow, one at the stern, ready to catch the lines when he tossed them.

"We are going out to sea. There is a reef for good diving and my friends are eager to go there." Diego laughed as he turned the big wheel and slowly inched up the throttle. The *Vanora* began to move smoothly away from the dock. "At sea, the captain's word is law, *cocinera*. Now that Hank is gone, perhaps it is time you become more *simpatico, si?*"

Without a word, Quinn left the wheelhouse and went to the galley. She halted abruptly and stood for a moment in total dismay. Grocery bags lay everywhere. On the counters, in the sink, some tilted and spilling their contents all over the floor. Marnie and the formerly topless woman, who was now wrapped in a sheer pareo, were poking through the bags.

"Hey," Marnie looked at Quinn. "Where do you want this shit? This is your domain, isn't it?"

Quinn flinched at the woman's crudeness. "Marnie, you know what? If it's shit it belongs in the sewage tank. If it's food, I can show you where to put it."

Marnie looked at Quinn in surprise, then she laughed. "Okay, girlie. Fair enough. So, where do you want this—stuff?"

Quinn directed the women on where to place the groceries. The *Vanora* was fully underway by now, the deck beneath Quinn's feet gently rolling. Marnie and her helper, Carmen, offered to make sandwiches for everyone so Quinn went in search of Marcus. She was determined to avoid Captain Diego at all costs. He was drinking heavily today. She intuitively knew that he could be an ugly drunk. There was something evil lurking beneath his polished veneer. *Too bad I can't hook him up with Lydia. They're two of the same tribe. Things that make you go hmmmmm.* Quinn smirked.

Marcus was in the cockpit entertaining the heavyset blonde. His arm was around her bare shoulders, one hand lying casually across her breast. The woman didn't seem to mind. She was laughing; a hand on the inside of Marcus' thick thigh. She was feeding him grapes with the other; teasing him as she rubbed the ripe cluster across his lips before allowing him to grasp one grape at a time with his teeth.

Diego was in the wheelhouse steering the vessel, an arm around the waist of the shapely brunette. The wind was brisk and the seas were choppy. Quinn couldn't imagine any of the passengers wanting to snorkel or dive in such rough water. She certainly didn't want to. That they were all drinking made her nervous. If something went south, Quinn had a feeling she would be the only one sober enough to deal with a crisis.

She slipped quietly away to her cabin, where she spent an hour straightening everything up after the crossing and writing in her journal. Quinn fell asleep on her bunk, pen still in hand. She didn't wake up until the rumble of the forward anchor chain being dropped broke her slumber. She could hear shouts and laughter. When Quinn pushed open the cabin hatch, she found herself looking at a pair of brown hairy legs.

"Sleeping beauty has awakened, heh?"

A strong hand grabbed Quinn beneath the arm and pulled her easily up the stairs and onto the deck. "Time to join the party, *cocinera*. Soon it will be time for food. Perhaps we'll be dining on some conch or crab."

Diego was smiling. His tone of voice was pleasant; almost playful. Rather than antagonize him, Quinn smiled back. "Conch would be nice. Where's Marcus?"

Diego motioned toward the rear of the boat. "He is preparing to dive. I have extra gear for you, too."

"It's too windy for me, Diego. Anyway, I'm not certified. I prefer to snorkel."

Diego pushed his sunglasses down on his nose so he could look directly at Quinn.

"We must fix that. I will need the three of you to clean algae from the keel and hull after we get through the canal. You must be better-rounded to crew on my ship, *chica.*" All the joviality had left the captain's voice.

Silently, Quinn marveled at how Diego Reyes' moods could shift like the wind in a spinnaker sail. She'd come to the conclusion that the man was unbalanced, and she wondered how he would react under any real stress. It was as though he had a burr or something on his soul that was constantly irritating and digging deeper and deeper into his very being.

"I don't have a problem with that, Diego. I understand there are a couple of dive shops in Cozumel where I could take some beginner's lessons."

Quinn smiled brightly at Diego, then began to move toward the rear of the boat. She was on a mission to talk to Marcus before he went diving. She was just in time. He was starting to climb down onto the diver's platform. The two male guests and Marnie were in scuba gear waiting to follow Marcus into the ocean. Quinn motioned for him to come back on the deck.

"What's up, Quinn? You want to buddy dive?" There was a puzzled expression on Marcus's face. He'd taken off his fins and pushed his mask up on his forehead.

"No. I might snorkel a bit, though, if the wind dies down." Quinn had noticed they were anchored off a small sandy cove. She could see people scattered about on the beach, and splashing in the surf. Diego had set anchor about a quarter mile offshore. Quinn spotted a number of bright blue, yellow, and black snorkels bobbing at various intervals through the water.

"I hope you haven't had too much to drink today," Quinn tried to not sound too judgmental.

"Aw, c'mon. I'm not *that* stupid. Or careless."

Quinn quickly apologized. "I know, Marcus, but if anything happened to you, I don't know what I'd do." She pulled him out of earshot of the other divers. Marnie had already dropped backwards into the water. The two men were about to follow.

"That Diego is something else." Quinn lowered her voice and moved closer to Marcus.

"Now he's insisting I get scuba certified so you, Marnie, and I can clean the bottom of the boat. I think he's forgotten about the matching t-shirts or whatever." She frowned. "He has such mood swings! It makes me wonder if he'd snap under certain circumstances."

"Is this why you interrupted my dive?" Marcus was grinning at her.

Quinn shook her head. "I wanted to ask you not to leave me alone up here with Diego for too long. He's got those women to entertain him, but he's been drinking and he went all jiggy on me again a few minutes ago."

Marcus put his arm around Quinn's shoulders. "Not to worry, little buddy. I wasn't planning on making a day of it. I'm on a mission to find us something really good for dinner. A couple crabs, a conch, or something."

Quinn watched as Marcus pulled the mask over his eyes. He climbed down the few steps to the dive platform, then pulled his fins back onto his feet. He turned around and waved before falling backward into the choppy water. Quinn stood for a moment watching the bubbles on the water's surface disappear.

The *Vanora* moved restlessly up and down. Quinn could feel the tug of the anchor. The yacht seemed to be pulling impatiently against the restraint of the metal and rope that kept her stationary. Quinn suddenly realized how quiet it had become. No music, no laughter. Diego and his lady friends were nowhere in sight. She presumed they were forward sunbathing.

Quinn was in the galley scrubbing out the microwave when she heard a dull thudding sound. Startled, she ran up the steps and out onto the deck to see if another boat had hit the *Vanora*. No other vessels, aside from a few kayaks and a cruise ship in the distance, were nearby. Relieved, she went back to the galley and finished wiping out the microwave.

Quinn was opening the refrigerator to inspect the contents when the strange reverberation began again. More curious than afraid at this point, Quinn listened closely, then followed the sound down the steps that lead to the amidships cabins. The noise stopped, and Quinn was about to turn around when she heard whimpering. The captain's cabin door was open and the noise seemed to be coming from there. The whimpering turned into quiet little sobs. Cautiously, Quinn crept closer, then peeked into Diego's quarters.

The large blonde woman Diego had brought onboard was naked and straddling the equally naked and prone captain. The younger woman was nude, too; she was curled up in a fetal position beside the perspiring couple. Quinn could see Diego had one hand on the brunette's breast. His other hand was clutching the plump derriere of the woman he was urging on. "Har-dah! Har-dah!" Diego's voice was harsh. He was breathing in short, heavy gasps.

Quinn could only stare, open-mouthed, at the pornographic display. Diego and his companion were oblivious to their surroundings. The woman's broad back blocked Diego's view of the hallway where Quinn stood frozen in shock. The heaving woman began to grunt, then wildly grind her hips, trying to please the demanding captain.

The brunette whimpered again, and Quinn managed to remove her eyes from the interlocked couple. She could see why the girl was crying. Diego's hand barely covered her ripe breast and he was squeezing it so hard his knuckles had turned white. His fingernails must have been gouging deep into the tender flesh. A wave of anger washed over Quinn with such force that she felt dizzy.

With great effort, Quinn pulled herself together. She was about to rush in and drag the girl from the hellish situation when, as though sensing the heat of Quinn's anger, the woman stopped whimpering and looked right at Quinn. The look of pain on her face vanished, only to be replaced by a look of abject fear. She shook her head from side to side, then mouthed the word "no." She took Diego's hand and removed it from her breast, then placed it between her legs, all the while signaling for Quinn to not get involved.

Quinn bolted down the hall, up the steps, through the galley and out into the sunlight. She was unaware of the tears streaming down her face, but she was totally aware that her entire body felt as though it were covered in slime. She stumbled to the transom, grabbed a pair of flippers, a mask and a snorkel, flung off her cover up, then leaped into the sparkling blue and purifying salt water.

Quinn used one arm to hang onto the dive platform as she pulled on the flippers. She spit into the mask to prevent the glass from fogging up and pulled it over her face, then adjusted the snorkel. She'd snorkeled before, but not in the tropics. Her stay in Jamaica had been brief and too packed with drama to allow time for water sports.

The late afternoon sun seemed to have been carrying the wind along on its majestic descent to the west. The waves had subsided and the water temperature was perfect. Quinn pushed off from the *Vanora* and headed toward land. When she submerged her head in the water all anger and disgust fled. The temporal world seemed to fade as Quinn's eyes opened wide in wonder at the seascape unfolding beneath her.

Coral reefs teeming with sponges and anemones invited closer inspection. Quinn took a deep pull of air through the snorkel and swam down to examine the incredible beauty of the ocean floor. Schools of brightly colored fish darted about among the waving arms of sea plants. The rich hues and shades of the coral, sponges and crinoids made Quinn feel like she was floating in a fantasy land worthy of Lewis Carroll.

Quinn surfaced for air, then began swimming toward a group of snorkelers who were closer to the beach. Quinn spent a good hour exploring the reefs in silent companionship with those around her. The setting of the sun brought her back to reality. It was getting too dark to really see much. Quinn swam quickly out to the *Vanora*. When she reached the transom, she was relieved to hear voices and the sound of rock music playing. Dive gear was scattered about on the aft deck.

Quinn was shivering after being in the water for so long. The heat of the day was evaporating from the land as the sun went down. Marcus was coming out of the main salon when he spotted Quinn. He rushed over to her and placed the towel he'd been wearing around his hips over her shoulders.

"Damn it all, Quinn! I've been worried as hell about you. You didn't leave or note or anything. For all I knew, you could have fallen overboard! Diego didn't know where you were, either."

Quinn winced at the mention of the captain's name. The vision of his disgusting ménage a trois came immediately to her mind. She apologized to Marcus and said she'd gone into the water looking for him. A white lie, but in Quinn's mind, anything was better than the truth.

"Did you catch us any dinner?" Quinn hoped to distract her upset buddy. It worked.

"Did I? You bet I did! I got us a good-sized conch and Aldo speared a decent halibut." Marcus was grinning from ear to ear. "You up to another one of your fish feasts, Quinn?"

Quinn assured him that after a hot shower she'd be up to almost anything, then she hurried forward along the outside deck to her cabin. She was sure the other divers were taking showers, too. Diego and his partners were nowhere in sight. Quinn had no doubt she'd be seeing them soon. She wondered how she could ever look at the degenerate captain again without her disgust being obvious. *You'll have to grin and bear it*, Quinn scolded herself. *Don't think about it. Do your job. Mind your own business. Who knows? Maybe Hank can cut my contract short?*

Safely back in her cabin, Quinn spoke aloud, "Better yet, maybe Captain Diego Reyes will fall overboard and get eaten by a shark."

Quinn was suddenly more homesick then she'd ever been in her life. As clear as a photograph, she saw Captain Tommy at the helm of the *Zephyr* with his red hair, steady blue eyes, and unflappable demeanor. She wondered how Chip's wounds had healed from his unfortunate encounter with the black fin shark. And Noah—Quinn drew a deep and shuddery breath. Their passionate lovemaking so far transcended the animal coupling of Diego and his companions that Quinn couldn't even reconcile the two in her mind.

She hurried through a shower and towel dried her hair before donning a lavender sundress and a pair of sandals. Quinn knew Diego was planning to sail back to the port of San Miguel after dinner. The owner of the *Vanora* was due onboard in the morning. Diego wanted the yacht washed down and the bright work polished before *Senor* Santiago's arrival. Quinn had no doubt the lascivious captain had taken a nice long nap following his strenuous afternoon. She couldn't help the sneer of disgust that temporarily disfigured her normally pleasant features.

CHAPTER SEVEN

T he sun was beginning to set in earnest splendor as Quinn moved around the galley preparing dinner. Marnie volunteered to help and the two women finally had an opportunity to get to know one another.

"Quinn, you ever prepare conch before?" Marnie was holding a small wooden mallet in her hand. Quinn shook her head.

"You gotta beat the sh—er, I mean the crap out of it to tenderize it," Marnie demonstrated, as she began to pound briskly on the slab of white meat in front of her. She asked Quinn for a sliced lime so she could squeeze the juice on the conch.

Quinn had already prepped the halibut. She was going to bake the fish in a cilantro, habanera and tomatillo sauce. The conch was going to be broiled and served as an appetizer. Quinn learned a lot about Marnie during the hour the two crewmates spent together in the galley. She'd been born in the borough of Queens, New York. Her parents were German and middle class. Her dad was an ironworker and her mother worked at the local library. Marnie had four brothers; Quinn could tell by the inflection in the tough woman's voice that she adored all four of them.

"So what's the deal with you and Hank, Quinn?" Marnie was slicing the white conch meat into one-inch strips. Quinn was slicing red potatoes. She had two pounds of freshly washed spinach leaves draining in a colander. She was going to parboil the strips of potatoes, then roast them in the oven along with the fish.

The spinach would be sautéed at the last minute with garlic and lemon juice in one tablespoon of oil and two tablespoons of soy sauce. A Chinese chef in Boston had taught Quinn that particular trick. The oil and soy sauce combination somehow made the spinach taste like it had been drenched in butter.

"Me and Hank?" Quinn stopped cutting the potatoes. "What makes you think something's going on? We're *friends*, Marnie. Jeez, first Diego and now you."

Marnie shrugged. "Well, it seems like a no-brainer to me. You're both single and good-looking. I think you'd make a great couple." She spread the conch bits out on a cookie sheet and turned on the broiler. "As for Diego…" Marnie slid the tray into the top oven. "I'd watch out for him. He's completely heartless."

"Believe me, he is so *not* my type." Quinn grimaced as she arranged the potatoes around the halibut and placed the dish in the bottom range. "I'm going to get a cocktail. Can I get you anything?"

"Thanks, but I'll grab a beer when I bring the appetizer out."

The *Vanora* was bobbing gently under a cloudless, starry sky. The cockpit was well lit and the strains of Spanish guitar music floated in the air. Marcus looked dashingly handsome in a white cotton shirt and a pair of jeans. He introduced Quinn to the two men who'd come onboard early that day; Aldo and Cesar. Diego's female companions introduced themselves. The blonde held out her hand and said her name was Marta. The brunette ducked her head and mumbled, "*me llamo Serena.*"

Moments later, Diego and the third woman, Carmen, entered the cockpit. He looked rested, indeed, she noted with a twinge of contempt. Diego was talking animatedly with the smiling woman, one arm around her waist; the other waving in the air. He led Carmen over to where Marcus was sitting, then he placed himself between the two women he'd spent the afternoon with.

"Ah, *cocinera*," Diego stared at Quinn. "How did you spend your afternoon? Your friend, Marcus, thought you had fallen overboard." He smiled, white teeth glistening against his dark skin. "Or, perhaps he was worried something upset you, and you had jumped ship, *si?*" Diego caressed Selena's shoulder. Quinn had the sudden and distinct impression that the captain knew she had been a witness to his abuse, and he wanted her to know that he knew it.

"I went snorkeling, Diego. It was magnificent. Too bad you missed it." Quinn kept her voice noncommittal.

Marnie appeared bearing a platter of the succulent conch and passed it around the group in the cockpit. Quinn excused herself to go check on the main entrée and start the wilted spinach side dish. The potatoes had browned nicely and the red sauce was bubbling, so Quinn shut off the oven and began to heat oil and soy sauce in a large skillet. When she turned around, she was surprised to find Selena standing behind her.

The brunette smiled shyly at Quinn and asked in halting English if she could help.

"Sure, you can set the table on the deck." Quinn showed her where the placemats, napkins, and flatware were kept. Marnie came into the galley and set the emptied platter in one of the sinks. When she brushed by Selena on the way, Quinn noticed how the younger woman winced at the contact on her right breast.

"That pig man!" Quinn spoke out loud as she slammed the colander on the countertop.

Marnie looked at her with a raised brow. "And which pig man might you be referring to?"

Quinn was about to answer when Selena returned with Carmen. The four women busied themselves with the final dinner preparations, then carried plates to the cockpit where the men were waiting in anticipation. Quinn handed a plate to Aldo and seated herself beside him. Marcus had opened a couple of bottles of chardonnay, which he decanted with a flourish into the multiple wine glasses on the table. Lights twinkled along the shoreline like a string of brilliant baubles. A gentle breeze flowed around the large yacht. The expanded crew of the *Vanora* ate with leisure and obvious enjoyment.

After dinner, Diego announced they would be setting sail for San Miguel as soon as the women had the galley put back into order. He raised his half-empty glass of wine. "The ladies have done such a wonderful job of feeding us men and keeping us entertained. I salute you. All of you."

He rose and walked around the table to stand behind Quinn. He put his free hand on her shoulder. "You must relax, *cocinera*. All work and no play is not good for you. Perhaps you could join us," he motioned with the wineglass to Marta and Selena, "after we get into port."

As if sensing her disgust, Diego squeezed Quinn's shoulder hard, then set the wine down and spoke to the men. "Let us prepare to pull the anchor."

It only took twenty minutes to clean up the galley. Marnie let Quinn know that she wanted to speak with her in private. Quinn suggested they meet at Marnie's cabin amidships. It would be too obvious if Marnie went to the forepeak. Diego would most likely stay on deck with the other men for the two hours it would take to get to the harbor.

Marnie's cabin was smaller than Quinn's, but at least there was an open porthole. The bed was neatly made. Quinn noticed a framed picture on the small vanity table. It was Marnie with her arm around the waist of a tall, spare-boned woman with shoulder length red hair.

"That's my gal, Rhonda," Marnie said. "She might sail with us from Puerto Vallarta to Cabo."

Quinn knew she meant Cabo San Lucas, a booming resort town on the tip of the Baja Peninsula. "That would be nice. She'd fly into P.V., then out of Cabo? Where does she live?" Quinn took a seat on the only chair.

"We both live in Fort Lauderdale. Didn't Hank tell you? He and Rhonda went to high school together. That's how I met Hank. Rhonda works for Princess Cruises."

Marnie perched on the edge of the bunk. "I've only crewed for Diego once before on a delivery to Belize. He was okay, but compared to how he's acting on this trip, it's like apples and oranges."

She eyed Quinn. "And, he's certainly got a hard on for you, girl. I can tell. He wants you *bad*."

Quinn flinched. "That's disgusting. He doesn't do a thing for me." She thought for a moment, then decided to take Marnie into her confidence. There was something about the mannish woman that made Quinn feel that she could trust her. Marnie truly seemed more like a man than some silly woman who would spill her guts to just about anyone. Quinn told Marnie about the scene she'd accidently witnessed.

"He's vile. He was really hurting Selena and he didn't care. I think he knows that I saw them. I think he's getting some twisted kind of a kick out of it."

Marnie nodded. "He's seems to be that kind of guy. My older brother, Ray, and his wife own a restaurant in Cozumel. She's a native. That's why I hooked up with you guys here. I was visiting them for Ray's birthday." Marnie stood up and walked around the little cabin.

"What's weird is Diego was here about a month ago. Nothing goes on in San Miguel that practically everyone knows about. The small town thing, you know?"

Quinn nodded. She was listening intently. There was a weird sensation in the pit of her stomach. It was similar to the feeling she had in Jamaica on the way to the airport with Dr. Felix when he was telling her about Noah's Aunt Sharmaine and the Obeah voodoo experience. It was a feeling of premonition—coupled with a sense of real dread.

"Diego comes here often. When he's not working for Hank, he works for one of the private charter boat companies. Diego loves the big life and he usually keeps a high profile. You know, hitting on the tourist chicks at Senor Frog's. Taking two or three women to dinner at some of the better restaurants. The trashier the women dress, the better he likes it. I don't think he has to work, I think he really loves the sea. I heard he made some good investments in Google or something. One thing you've got to give the man; he's a damn good captain."

Marnie went to a small locker in the corner. "You don't mind if I get ready for bed while we talk, do you? It's been one helluva long day."

Without waiting for a response, she casually stripped down to a pair of Jockey briefs, then pulled a man's chambray shirt out of the locker. Quinn couldn't help but note there wasn't one ounce of fat on Marnie's body. She was lean and wiry, and had no breasts to speak of. Her body was like that of a teenage boy.

Marnie resumed her perch on the bunk and went on with her story. "So, here's Diego in San Miguel. But, he's not staying at his usual hotel. He's not out partying and picking up stray broads. As a matter of fact, the only reason my brother knew he was in town is because Diego got into an accident out near the Mayan ruins of San Gervasio. Diego wasn't hurt much, but the fellow with him was. He didn't have on a seatbelt and I guess he went through the windshield."

The *Vanora* was now underway on a steady port tack. Quinn shifted in her seat and braced her feet on the floor. Marnie lay down on her side, her head in her hand. She patted the edge of the bunk. "You can sit here, if you'd be more comfortable."

Quinn declined the invitation with a quick grin. "I'm fine, Marnie. I kind of like the isometrics."

"Suit yourself," Marnie smiled back.

"Ray's brother-in-law was one of the paramedics on the scene. The weird thing is this other guy, the injured dude, was none other than Luiz Montoya. He's what they call the 'glimmer man' around here. He's the man behind a lot of the crime on Cozumel. Prostitution, drugs, hell, you name it. Murder, even. But, he never gets caught at anything. He's always right around the corner. Or has an airtight alibi. The whole island is afraid of him. Nobody messes with Luiz Montoya. I bet he even has the *policia* in his pocket."

Quinn was really listening now. She'd caught Marnie's drift. Why would the proud and arrogant captain be cruising the island with a low-life drug dealer? Diego Reyes, with his starched white captain's uniform and his highly developed sense of aristocracy?

"Damn, Marnie. You don't think Diego's thinking of smuggling drugs from here to San Diego, do you? Why would he do that? Like you said, he doesn't need money!"

Marnie shrugged. "I don't know what to think. Diego is definitely a sly one. He strikes me as being edgier now for some reason. It's like he has a grudge against the world. I wouldn't put it past him to try to smuggle drugs. It'd be like a thumb in the nose to all the rest of us peons if he got away with it. And his contempt for women, is something else, wouldn't you say?"

Quinn nodded in agreement, then rose from her seat. "I'd better get to bed. With the owner coming in tomorrow, Diego's going to put us all to work. Marcus and those other guys can handle docking the *Vanora* tonight. Thanks for the head's up."

Marnie walked with Quinn to the door. "Let's keep this to ourselves, okay? I mean, don't tell Marcus. For all we know nothing's going on. Luiz could've been taking Diego to some kinky sex circus or something."

Quinn made a face. "Okay. How about we pinky swear on it?" She held out her hand and crooked her little finger. For a moment, Marnie's face went blank, then she laughed. "I almost forgot about that. Okay, pinky swear it is." She wrapped her little finger around Quinn's. "*Hasta manana.*"

Once the *Vanora* had moved out of the lee of the cove, the wind caught her sails. Quinn paused along the high side of the yacht on the way to her cabin. She held onto a halyard and leaned against the safety line that ran the length of the vessel. Quinn drew in deep breaths of the clean salty air. She marveled at the moon as it drifted among the ever-shifting nebulous clouds in the midnight sky. Quinn pulled off the scrunchie holding her hair in place and let the wind lift the heavy tresses. Motionless she stood, mesmerized by the gentle rhythm of the *Vanora,* and the sensuous feel of the air current passing over and caressing her face, hair and body. Finally, with a sigh, Quinn released the halyard and went to the forepeak cabin.

CHAPTER EIGHT

T he *Vanora* seemed like almost a different ship by noon of the following day. Gone were all traces of revelry. Diego had unceremoniously hustled his guests off the yacht early in the morning. He roused the crew and, as Quinn had predicted, put the three of them to work. He helped Marcus lower the dinghy with the automated winch into the water, then set him to wiping down the hull. Quinn and Marnie were assigned the task of polishing the teak and bright work on the deck. Diego straightened out the chart table and navigation station, then paced around supervising the crew's work.

He surprised the sweaty and tired group when he left the yacht for an hour, then returned with bags of hamburgers and French fries. "When you are finished eating, be sure to remove the garbage to the dock. I want the galley as clean as the rest of the ship for *Senor* Santiago's arrival."

"What an ass," Marnie muttered to Quinn as they sat in the shade of the big mainsail boom. "Here I thought he was being generous for a change. He just doesn't want to mess up the boat."

Quinn laughed. "It'll be kind of fun, though, don't you think, to see Diego suck up to someone he obviously thinks is better than he is." She took a healthy bite from the burger she was holding.

Diego had one more request for his crew after they'd finished with lunch. "You must all make the best first impression. After your showers, please put on these along with shorts. And be sure to wear your deck shoes." He handed out generic white *Izod* shirts to each of them. "I'll deduct the cost from your pay."

Flabbergasted, Quinn could only stare at the medium-size shirt in her hand. Marcus snorted in disgust. "We'll see how long this lasts," he said, as he headed off to take a shower. Marnie commented that she rather liked the idea. "Makes it easier to decide what to wear." Then she left, too.

Quinn was alone with Diego. There was a challenging look in his eyes, and a sly smile on his lips. "You have a question for me, *cocinera?*"

"No. Not really. Not anymore."

"No more? Why do you say that?" Suddenly, Diego didn't look so sure of himself.

Quinn shrugged. "Because, Diego, I realize that you're never going to accept me. You're always going to find fault with me. Not only that, you're out to make everyone around you miserable. As miserable as *you* are. If Hank will allow, I might leave the *Vanora* once we're through the canal."

She turned and headed toward the forepeak. The humidity was intense. The odd brassy sky Quinn had noticed a few days before was back. The world seemed to be in some kind of a vacuum. It was as though the air itself was condensing; drawing the moisture off the ocean and absorbing all of the sun's rays. She was oblivious to the historic low-pressure system that was building several hundreds of miles away off the coast of Jamaica.

The arrival of *Senor* Rafael Santiago was in a sense anti-climatic in Quinn's eyes. She, Marnie and Marcus were in the main salon when they heard Diego's welcoming salutation to the new owner of the *Vanora*. The man who walked into the air-conditioned salon with the captain had a duffle bag slung over one shoulder.

Rafael was of average height and medium build. He looked to be in his early thirties. Where Diego's features were sharply defined, the owner of the *Vanora* had a truly aristocratic face. Rafael Santiago had a high forehead, finely arched nose and eyebrows, and a mega-watt smile. He sported a closely trimmed mustache and beard that enhanced a generous mouth.

"Greetings, *amigos!*" Rafael pushed his sunglasses atop his long black hair. Quinn noticed immediately the color of his eyes; they were as green as her own. As the crew introduced themselves, Rafael shook each of their hands. His grasp was firm and he made eye contact, a warm smile on his lips. Quinn could tell Marcus and Marnie were as impressed as she was. Suddenly, the words "the owner" didn't sound so ominous.

"I can see you have all taken good care of my investment. Now let's take the *Vanora* out and see what she has in her."

Without further ado, the crew went to their stations. Diego already had the engines warmed up and in record time the seventy-six foot yacht was headed out into the Yucatan Channel. The wind was blowing briskly in the slot between Cozumel and the mainland. Rafael took the helm and ordered both the main and the foresail up. Once the sails were set, the *Vanora* seemed to leap through the water.

Quinn had finished grinding the winch to trim the main. She was looping the tail of the mainsheet around her elbow and hand to keep it from tangling once she set it on the deck. The yacht was practically on her side; the toe rail that ran the length of the deck seemed to be almost in the frothing water. Quinn had to brace her body to complete her task. She felt a thrill of exhilaration as the *Vanora* swept along, cleanly slicing through anything the ocean could throw at her: Exactly like Quinn had imagined she would, when Quinn first saw a picture of the expensive yacht.

In the cockpit, Rafael was standing at the wheel. His head was thrown back and he was laughing in delight; long black hair flowing behind him. Marcus and Marnie were sitting on the high side of the cockpit. Diego was inside at the nav station.

"This is something else!" Quinn exclaimed as she plopped down between Marcus and Marnie. The yacht was heeled so far over that, with her legs braced against the binnacle, Quinn was practically standing up.

Rafael grinned. "She is everything I expected her to be. Let's let her run for another half hour or so. Then we'll tack and have lunch. Sound like a plan?"

There was a chorus of agreement. For the next forty-five minutes, the crew of the *Vanora* sat in the cockpit and watched the mainland grow closer and closer. Quinn noted that Rafael was an expert yachtsman. He seemed sensitive to every move the yacht made. He adjusted the big wheel with ease to accommodate the sails and the shifting wind.

Quinn was thirsty and her stomach began growling. As if sensing that the crew was getting hungry, Rafael nodded to the trio. "Let's tack. Take down the jib. We'll use the main alone on the way back."

He fell off the wind and Quinn and Marnie went forward to lower the smaller sail. After the sail was stowed in the forepeak locker, Quinn went below through the amidships entrance and into the galley. Diego was getting a beer out of the refrigerator.

"*Cocinera*, how do you like your new owner?" The sneer in the captain's voice was obvious.

"He seems like a nice enough man." Quinn waited for Diego to move so she could get cold cuts from out of the crisper. "He owns *the boat*, Diego. Not me. I'm only the hired help."

"Ah, but a man like him, Quinn? He is rich, he is handsome. And he is single, I understand." Quinn was surprised that Diego had used her Christian name. A rare occurrence indeed. "I think a man like that could easily have a woman like you. If he so wanted, that is."

"Diego, what is your problem?" Quinn moved around him to get into the refrigerator. "Not every woman is a slut or a prostitute, you know."

Diego laughed that odd, high-pitched laugh of his. "Oh, we shall see. We shall see."

He deliberately brushed against her as he headed toward the wheelhouse. Quinn had to suppress a shudder, then she got busy making a variety of deli sandwiches. She made turkey with Swiss cheese, lettuce and tomato, shaved ham with cheddar and tangy mustard; and salami with pepperoni, mozzarella cheese, lettuce, and red onions topped with Italian dressing.

Marnie came down to get a soda. "Yum!" She grabbed a slice of salami and stuck it in her mouth. "Hurry up, we're all starving. Here, let me give you a hand."

The two women took a platter of sandwiches, bags of chips, and several cold Root Beers to the cockpit. The *Vanora* was cruising smoothly at an easy seven knots. After passing around the sandwiches, Quinn and Marnie seated themselves at the table. Rafael had put the boat on auto-pilot. He thanked the women for the meal, then asked each of the crew to tell him something about themselves.

Marnie pointed at Quinn to go first.

"I was born and raised in Boston. I was planning on going to med school—my dad's a pediatrician, but instead I moved to Miami. That's where I met Hank and got hired for my first yacht delivery on the *Zephyr* to Negril, Jamaica. This is my second voyage, and I certainly hope not my last." Quinn smiled at Rafael. He kept his eyes locked on hers for a long moment, a smile playing at the corners of his lips. *Oh, man. This guy is certainly sexy, charming and handsome!* Quinn couldn't help responding to Rafael's natural magnetism.

Marnie spoke next. She was brief and to the point. "Born in Queens, New York. Dropped out of high school to go work on a fishing trawler. Moved to Fort Lauderdale and started crewing on the sailboat racing circuit. Met Hank through a friend...and, tah-dah! Here I am."

Everyone chuckled at the flourish Marnie added to the end of her succinct bio. Marcus was equally as brief. "Military brat here. Moved around most of my life until I decided to move to Miami by myself a few years ago. I've been in construction; I *was* in construction, until Quinn here turned me on to sailing." He raised his soda and winked at her.

"Such a diverse crew," Rafael sat back in his seat. "I myself live in Guadalajara, Jalisco, Mexico. I deal in drugs." He laughed at the startled group around the table. "Legal drugs. That's a small joke that I enjoy making sometimes. We are owners of a pharmaceutical company."

He turned his attention to Diego. "And you, el Capitan? I understand your home is in el ciudad de Mexico? Are you of a relation to Professor Reyes at the Universidad de Mexico?"

Quinn detected an odd look that passed between the two men. Diego finally spoke. "He is my father."

"I see." With that cryptic remark, Rafael rose and stretched. "I think I'll take a small *siesta*. Diego knows a place for us to anchor for a few days. Tomorrow I would like to do some diving. *Buenos tardes*, my friends."

The three days with Rafael onboard flew by. The *Vanora* was anchored off a quiet cove on the southeast end of the island. Rafael was an avid diver and spent hours in the water. When he learned that Quinn wasn't certified to dive, he gave her several lessons. He was patient and Quinn was not only grateful for that, she was also grateful for not being left alone too often with Diego.

One day Quinn and Marnie were suiting up and Marnie made a reference to Diego's seemingly insatiable sexual appetite. "He's bound and determined to do you, Quinn, I can tell by the way he looks at you."

"Now *that* is disgusting, Marnie. I'd jump ship first!"

"You would jump from my beautiful ship?"

Startled, Quinn spun around. Rafael was climbing down onto the dive platform.

She blushed. "I was joking. Marnie and I threaten the guys all the time that we'll abandon ship if they don't behave." Behind Rafael's back, Marnie nudged Quinn, and with a wink, gave her a thumbs up.

It was almost like having a vacation with the owner of the *Vanora* onboard. He was fun-loving, easy going, and had a good sense of humor. Each night was like a *fiesta*. Rafael enjoyed his cocktail hour before dinner. He would make margaritas and mojitos for everyone. The stereo boomed, and he even got the crew dancing on the deck. There was an abundance of fresh seafood harvested from the ocean by the divers; including lobster, since Rafael had gone night diving for the delicacy.

Quinn noticed a serious side to the Mexican millionaire. He was often on his cell phone. The third night at anchor, he received a phone call that cut short his stay on the yacht. Quinn was busy in the galley. Rafael was in the master cabin behind the galley and main salon, where he'd gone to shower. He'd left the cabin door open, which was understandable given the heat and humidity in the still air.

Quinn heard his cell phone ring. *"Bueno?"* Rafael answered with the standard Spanish greeting. He had a distinctive tenor voice; it carried easily through the air. There were several moments of silence. Then he spoke in a rapid string of what could only be commands. His voice was firm and steely. There would be no room for insubordination from a man who spoke in that manner.

When Rafael came up from the cabin, he asked Quinn if she'd seen Diego. She said he might be in his cabin. Rafael walked into the galley and reached for one of the freshly cooked shrimp Quinn was preparing to make into a cocktail. He was mere inches away. Although Quinn could see the tension simmering behind his green eyes, he smiled at her and winked.

Rafael was wearing a floral silk shirt that accentuated his eyes. He'd put on a pair of tan slacks, and he wore his loafers without socks. His combed, shoulder-length black hair was still damp and lay along his shapely skull. Quinn was mesmerized. His charm was magnetic.

"Tomorrow I must leave to take care of my business. I think you should wait until I return to continue with your scuba lessons. I'm not so sure the dive shops in Cozumel would be good for you."

Rafael was standing so close to Quinn that the scent of his cologne, light and spicy, filled her nostrils. He reached for another shrimp and his hand brushed over hers. "I would not want anything to happen to you, Quinn. I would not like that at all."

The stereo erupted into music, startling them both and saving Quinn from having to respond. Diego waved a hand to them from the entertainment center, a cold smile on his face. Rafael motioned for the captain to join him on the deck. After one long, direct look into Quinn's eyes, Rafael left the galley.

The night was filled with revelry. Quinn skipped making dinner in favor of a variety of hot and cold appetizers, chips and dips. Rafael outdid himself at the bar, then insisted on teaching the crew some classic Latin American dance steps. Marcus, with his natural ability, was quick to master unfamiliar moves. He took a reluctant Marnie in his arms and began traversing the deck with her.

Rafael bowed formally to Quinn, then swept her into his arms and began a sinuous tango. Quinn felt like she was in a dream. The pulsing beat of the music, the heady thrill of dancing in the arms of a handsome man across the broad deck of the *Vanora* under a starlit sky, combined with the soft caress of her summer dress as it swirled around and between her legs, created a feeling of sensual surrealism.

Rafael's arm was firm on Quinn's back. In tempo with the music he moved her farther and farther away from the lighted aft deck, until they were dancing alone in the semi-darkness near the bow. With practiced assurance, Rafael dipped Quinn backwards in one arm. Grasping her exposed thigh with his free hand he drew her leg up across his hip, then twirled around in a slow circle. Quinn could feel her loosened hair brush along the teak deck. Between her half-closed lashes, Rafael's face appeared to be no more than a dark silhouette against a spectacular star-studded palette.

Rafael pulled Quinn up and drew her supple body against his. It was obvious he, too, had been aroused by the combined romantic elements of music, the embrace of the dance, and an evening sky that seemed designed expressly for lovers.

"Oooooh, that was *lovely.*" Quinn spoke without meaning to.

Rafael laughed. "Oooooh? I like that. Yes, I do. You are quite a dancer, *querida*," his voice was soft and caressing.

Quinn could see his face clearly now. She was hypnotized by his eyes. In the dimness of the night they were like deep, dark, and deliciously dangerous tidal pools. His lips were accentuated by the dark growth of beard surrounding them. Rafael was holding her so close Quinn could feel his warm breath caressing her cheek.

"I've never danced like that before. You're quite a leading man, Rafael."

Quinn couldn't suppress the slight quaver in her voice. She was feeling a heat inside of her that she'd only experienced with one other man, Noah. Quinn suddenly felt confused, then a wave of guilt washed over her. She took a deep breath and a step backwards. Slowly and reluctantly, Rafael released her from his arms.

They were standing mere inches apart. Rafael tilted his head and smiled at her. "I see no reason to rush into anything, Quinn. Obviously, I am very much attracted to you. And I believe you feel somewhat in the same way?"

His smile turned into a naughty grin. He looked so engaging that Quinn smiled right back at him. She nodded.

"Very well, *querida*. Come," he held out his hand. "Allow me to escort you to your cabin."

Quinn took his hand. They both laughed since her cabin was a mere few feet away. Rafael held open the heavy hatch while Quinn climbed down the steps. She paused at the bottom and looked up. Rafael gave her another of his long, measuring looks, then he blew her a gentle kiss and carefully lowered the hatch.

CHAPTER NINE

M uch to Quinn's mixed sense of disappointment and relief, Rafael had already left the *Vanora* by the time she woke up the next morning. Diego was nowhere in sight, either. Quinn more than welcomed the captain's absence. She needed time to prepare herself for what she knew was coming. If Diego had issues about her friendship with Hank, he most certainly was going to want to see her head roll over this flirtation with "the owner."

"He'll probably make me walk the damn plank or something," she grumbled aloud as she loaded the coffeemaker basket.

"Yeah, I imagine he will." Marnie's voice so startled Quinn, she spilled a tablespoon of coffee grounds onto the counter.

"Jeez! Marnie, don't *do* that! I'm a wreck as it is."

"Well, you should be. It was obvious to one and all that *Senor* Rafael Santiago has got the hots for you. What's up with that?"

Marnie's wiry hair was plastered onto her head and she was wearing her trademark chambray nightshirt and jockey briefs. "I mean, yeah, you're a real baby doll and all, but, what*ever*. Hank, Diego and now Rafael?"

She snickered. "Maybe you wouldn't be getting all of this attention if I weren't just some darling little dyke, huh?"

"I don't think it's funny." Quinn was wiping furiously at the spilled grounds. "Who knows what Diego will do now? I guarantee he's going to do his best to make my life utterly and completely miserable from here on out. I can only hope and pray Hank makes it back—and soon."

"Yeah, me too. Are you gonna make some food or what? Marcus and I stayed up partying last night. I woke up before anyone else with the worst hangover. I was tossing my cookies over the transom when Rafael and Diego got up."

Marnie reached into the plastic band of her underwear. "Here. Don't leave this lying around, either. Rafael asked to me to give it to you. I imagine Diego would literally hang you from the yardarm if he found it. I need some fresh air." She left Quinn holding a square, embossed envelope.

Quinn tucked the missive into the pocket of her cut-off jeans with plans on reading it later in the privacy of her cabin. Marcus came up from the crew quarters looking almost as gnarly as Marnie. His eyes were bloodshot and the morning light seemed to bother him.

"Breakfast will be ready in a minute," Quinn said, with a sympathetic grin. "Why don't you go topside. You look like you could use some fresh air, too."

Marcus nodded and stumbled up the steps. Quinn quickly scrambled eggs, heated sausage patties in the microwave, and toasted bagels. She could hardly wait to read what was inside the envelope. An hour later she was in her cabin; the overhead hatch safely secured. The heat was almost unbearable even at such an early hour. There was no breeze and the open portholes only served to allow in the oppressive humidity.

Quinn pulled out the envelope and looked at it thoughtfully. Don Ford, the yacht salesman, had seduced her at nineteen. Smoothly, expertly and without fanfare, he had taken her virginity under the guise of love and marriage. Noah, on the other hand, had truly gotten under her skin and awakened a dimension of sexual passion unknown to Quinn.

Rafael Santiago was an enigma. Rich, handsome, sophisticated; but without pretense or false airs. He was mature and intensely romantic, too. For a moment it seemed as though the world around her was split into two dimensions. It was as if she was holding both yesterday and tomorrow in her hands.

"So what does Rafael see in me?" Quinn broke the seal on the envelope. "I guess I'm about to find out."

She unfolded the thin sheet of paper. In bold black strokes, Rafael had written:

Quinn= Querida,

I have three recommendations for you. A) DO NOT JUMP SHIP. B). Do not give anybody any "ooooohs." C). Love the eagle that soars over your head and wishes to carry you along on his wings.

Rafael

"Oh, my."

Quinn reread the note.

"Oh me, oh my."

She looked around the cabin, then rummaged in the dresser for her *Spanish/English* dictionary. The four years of Spanish she'd taken in school had left her with a rudimentary grasp of the language. But living in Miami and now traveling in Mexico had driven home the old adage; if you don't use it, you lose it.

She thumbed through the pages until she came to the "q's:"

Querida (ker ri-da) n.f. 1, darling; dear. 2, mistress.

Quinn repeated the definitions. "Darling, dear, *mistress?*" She sat down.

Diego's words echoed in her mind. *I think a man like that could easily have a woman like you. If he so wanted, that is.*

Apparently, Rafael Santiago does want a woman like me, Quinn thought. She read the note one more time, then searched for a hiding place. She'd forgotten about Noah's mojo that she'd tucked deep beneath her mattress. She put the envelope beside the leather pouch.

"Oh, Noah. Where are you? How are you? Will I ever see you again?" Quinn spoke aloud; hot tears welling up in her eyes. There was a sudden banging on the top hatch. Quinn hastily dabbed at her tears. Diego was waiting impatiently for her when she came up on the deck. He thrust a wad of dollars and a piece of paper at her.

"You take Marnie and go into the village for supplies. Here is a list of items. There is a marine store at the south end of town. You will need fresh foods, too. Sometimes we must wait at sea for two days for our turn to go through the Panama Canal."

Quinn was surprised Diego didn't take a shot at her regarding Rafael. The captain seemed preoccupied. She could tell he had other things on his mind. There was a nervous little twitch around his thin lips that she hadn't noticed before. He surprised her even more when he said, "You and the crew may have off the rest of today once you return, and tomorrow, also." She couldn't see his eyes behind his sunglasses.

It took two hours for Quinn and Marnie to shop and restock the boat. Some of the items on the list Diego had given her struck Quinn as odd.

"Why in the world would he want ten rolls of duct tape?" Quinn said to Marnie as they wandered through the cluttered marine supply store.

Marnie laughed. "Maybe he wants to tape you to the bow of the ship. You know, like a modern-day keelhaul."

"Very funny, Marnie, very funny."

Mid afternoon found the crew of the *Vanora* freely wandering the streets of Cozumel. Diego had disappeared again. The women shopped and Marcus trailed around behind them. Finally, he grew bored and suggested they stop at Senor Frog's for some food and refreshments. "I could use a Margarita. Damn, it's humid here."

It was four p.m. and even with two cruise ships in port, the spacious upstairs bar/restaurant appeared to be nearly empty. There were a few tables of older tourists, and groups of college-age young adults doing shots of tequila and dancing to the loud house music. Quinn, Marnie, and Marcus found a table by a window overlooking the busy downtown district.

Quinn watched as scantily clad waitresses walked around with shots of tequila. Anyone willing to do a shot had to also be willing to have their ears pulled, their breasts grabbed, and their butts smacked.

"I think I'll pass on the shooters," Quinn said, the memory of a sex-crazed Diego squeezing Selena's breast still fresh in her mind. Marcus ordered a round of Margaritas on the rocks and a combination appetizer platter.

"Will you look at that?"

Quinn followed Marnie's eyes over to the bar. An overweight girl who didn't look old enough to even be drinking had wrapped herself around her boyfriend's leg. It was obvious they were tourists; and it was obvious they were really drunk. A small crowd of onlookers were urging the girl on as she rubbed her crotch up and down along the guy's thigh. Her face was screwed up in a grimace of concentration as she moved her hips in tempo with the techno music blaring from all corners of the room. Her boyfriend had his hands on her breasts, a sloppy grin on his face.

"Good Lord!" Quinn averted her eyes. "Where do you think her parents are? Why would a girl want to do something like that in public?"

"I dunno," Marnie said. "But, I think she just got what she was going for."

Quinn glanced over and saw that the girl had ceased her restless activity. Her face was slack and her eyes closed. She was slumped onto the chest of her boyfriend. He had one hand on her ample rear, and with the other he was doing a shot of tequila. The onlookers seemed to have melted away once the show was over.

Marcus was grinning from ear to ear. "Either one of you ladies care to give ole Marcus here a lap dance?"

Quinn simply rolled her eyes. Marnie snorted in outright disgust. "Not even, dude. Nothing personal, of course."

The waiter brought the drinks. When he came back with the food he asked the group if they were from one of the cruise ships.

"No, we're on a private yacht," Marcus told him.

"Well, you'd better keep an eye on the weather. I heard there's a kick-ass hurricane brewing near Jamaica. It must be something because one of the crew from the Princess ship said he'd heard they might skip their next port of call. It'd be too dangerous for the big ships to be at dock or near land. They're all better off out at sea." He took the empty platter and some plates with him and left.

"Hurricane? I wonder if Diego is aware of it." Quinn had a worried look on her face.

"I'm sure he'll find out about it soon enough if he already doesn't know." Marcus put a reassuring hand on Quinn's arm. "Hurricanes change course all of the time. I'm sure there's nothing to be worried about."

It was dusk by the time the three friends got back to the *Vanora*. After such a late snack, everyone agreed they'd feed themselves if they got hungry. There was still no sign of Diego. The crew spent a relaxed and quiet evening together, playing cards and drinking wine. Quinn was sound asleep before midnight. Sometime in the early morning hours, she was awakened by a hollow echoing sound. It seemed to be coming from the waterline of the hull close to her bunk in the forepeak.

She listened intently for a few minutes, then dozed off. Her sleep was uneasy. It was too warm in the cabin. Mosquitoes and flies were irksome in this part of the world, she'd discovered. Even with bug spray to protect from being bitten, their very presence was annoying.

Diego was already in the galley drinking coffee the next morning when Quinn entered. His appearance surprised her. The normally immaculate captain looked like he hadn't shaved in two days. His eyes were bloodshot.

The hand holding the coffee mug shook ever so slightly. He looked exhausted; like he hadn't slept a wink in the past forty-eight hours.

"Good morning," Quinn eyed him cautiously.

Diego grunted and took a gulp of coffee. "Did you get all the supplies?"

"Yes, I put the boat stuff in the laundry area."

"Good. After breakfast, you all may go."

Diego went up to the wheelhouse, leaving Quinn to gape after him. It was obvious Diego wanted the *Vanora* all to himself for the day. *Gross, he's probably planning a* real *orgy and he doesn't want us around,* Quinn shook her head. She decided to make waffles, eggs and bacon and serve the meal buffet style.

Quinn was loathe to sit with only Diego for company while she ate, so it was with a real sense of relief that she greeted Marcus who came yawning out of the crew quarters. Marnie followed him shortly and soon all four of the *Vanora's* skeleton crew were eating on the deck.

Marcus brought up the waiter's comments about a hurricane brewing in the Caribbean. Diego looked at him blankly for a moment, then shrugged. "I have heard nothing. These things change all of the time. I will tell you if, and when, there is something to worry about." He stood up, empty plate in hand. "We leave for the Panama Canal in two days." Diego walked toward the companionway entrance to the main cabin.

"Have you heard from Hank yet?" Quinn blurted out. "Is he coming back to transit the Canal with us?"

Diego stopped and looked at her. There was a trace of the familiar sardonic sneer in his voice when he replied. "*Cocinera,* you will have plenty to keep you busy during the transit. You must be exhausted with all the attentions you've been receiving of late. It might be best you take this time to relax, then focus yourself on your *real* job."

"Damn," Marnie broke the silence after the captain had disappeared. "He didn't answer either question, did he? Dude looks like an all night poker party, too. I wonder what's up?"

"I'm going to ask around about the weather," Marcus got up from the table. "You gals want to take the ferry across to the mainland? Or stay here and go to those Mayan ruins outside of town. We could hire a taxi and split the cost between us."

It was agreed to save the ferry ride for another day. The taxi driver they hired was cheerful, spoke excellent English, and was informative. He kept up a running monologue on the history of Cozumel on the short drive to the ruins of San Gervasio, eleven miles outside of San Miguel. The small island had been a popular hideout for pirates in the late fifteenth century, he informed them. Out of the 40,000 or so Mayans that once inhabited the island, only thirty ended up surviving the smallpox brought by the Spaniards in the mid-1500's.

It began to rain, and rain hard, as they pulled into the large dirt parking lot at the tourist attraction. From what Quinn could see through the pelting rain, there was one lone tour bus and a few other cars scattered about. She could see the dim outline of several buildings; no doubt curio shops and a food court. The driver, Jorge, suggested they wait a few minutes. Tropical showers had a tendency to disappear as fast as they arrived. Marcus took advantage of the moment to ask Jorge if he knew anything about an impending hurricane.

"*Si,*" the driver looked at Marcus in the rear view mirror. "Some of the locals are preparing for the storm. But, then, it could change its mind and not come to Cozumel. As with all things, this is in the hands of God."

The rain abated and Quinn, Marnie and Marcus picked their way through mud puddles as they followed the taxi driver to the entrance to the national park. While still photographs were allowed, they were asked to check in Marcus's video camera. The trio was heading down a path into the jungle when they encountered a middle-aged couple who were on the way back from the ruins.

"You'd better go back to the gift shop and buy some bug spray," the woman warned them. "I've never seen anything like this."

Her husband agreed. "There's a guy wandering around with a canister and spray gun who'll squirt you for a dollar, but I have my doubts as to what's in the canister."

Marcus volunteered to run back and get the spray. Already, Marnie and Quinn were slapping at the pesky insects. Even the flies were biting. Upon Marcus's return the trio wandered along the rocky paths that wound throughout the jungle and crumbling ruins. Quinn shared some bits of the history of San Gervasio with her companions from a brochure she'd purchased at the gift shop.

"This site was dedicated hundreds of years ago to the Maya goddess of fertility and medicine, *Ixchel.* Apparently, it was like a Mecca to Mayan women from the mainland, too. At one point in their lifetime they would make a pilgrimage here."

"Fertility?" Marnie eyed Quinn up and down. "You'd better be careful with your boy toys from now on, Quinn, after coming here."

"Don't say that!" Quinn slapped her on the shoulder with the brochure. "I'm not planning on putting myself in that kind of position with anyone."

Marcus and Marnie erupted into laughter at Quinn's unintended double entendre. She ended up giggling, too. The heat and the insects were increasing exponentially, so after a quick tour and one stop at the Temple of the Hands; a curious structure with numerous little red hand prints painted on the wall, the three sailors headed back to the taxi and to San Miguel de Cozumel.

Diego was waiting on the deck of the *Vanora*, and the crew could tell something was wrong by way he began frantically waving to them the moment he saw them. All three broke into a run. Once they were near the yacht, they could see what had disturbed the captain. A tidal surge had caused the protective rubber fenders to displace. The *Vanora* was straining at the springer lines, her hull was scraping against the cement dock.

Half an hour later, the fenders and dock lines had been adjusted and secured. The crew could easily see in the distance that another squall was fast approaching. What they couldn't see was the massive low-pressure system that was following rapidly upon its heels. Hurricane Cecelia was about to make meteorological history.

CHAPTER TEN

The high-pitched keening of ninety-knot winds ripping through the halyards of the *Vanora* had at first sounded like an off-key funeral dirge reverberating in Quinn's ears. The eerie noise produced by the tremendous force of the wind had nearly driven her mad. Now, she was tired. More tired than she'd ever been before in her life. She was soaked to the bone, and black and blue from head to toe.

The large yacht bucked and reared and slid sideways down huge troughs of ocean as the crew struggled to keep the *Vanora* from capsizing in the monster seas caused by Hurricane Cecelia. All four of the sailors were queasy. It was the sudden rise of the ship on a towering wave, then the seemingly bottomless drop that had their stomachs roiling.

The intensity of the storm and its consequences had forced everyone into the wheelhouse. *May God damn Diego Reyes to hell*, Quinn thought as she huddled miserably between Marnie and Marcus. Diego was clinging to the huge wheel using all of his body weight to try to keep the yacht from rolling onto her side—or worse yet, pitch-poling bow over stern. *But don't damn him yet, not yet, Lord, not until we're safely out of this and into port*, she added prayerfully.

It seemed so hard to believe that fourteen hours ago the *Vanora* was docked securely in San Miguel. It was even harder to believe that Diego, knowing full-well a hurricane was bearing down on the island of Cozumel, had deliberately delayed their departure until well past the safety zone.

He'd also ignored the advice of other captains to find a "hurricane hole" or a protected marina where the *Vanora* could possibly ride out the upcoming storm if well-enough secured. Diego's argument had been that as flat as the island was, it would be nearly impossible to find adequate shelter. He insisted it would be wiser to take a yacht the size of the *Vanora* out and try to skirt the storm. Yet, still he delayed their departure.

There had been no word from Hank. In desperation, Quinn had decided to check with the harbormaster's office to see if he'd left a message. It was the harbormaster who advised Quinn that the *Vanora* should set sail immediately. According to meteorological reports, the huge storm was growing rapidly as it swiftly crossed the warm, open waters of the Caribbean. It was heading straight toward Cozumel.

Quinn hurried back to the yacht and relayed the information to Diego. He merely looked at her blankly and said, "We leave tomorrow as planned," then he disappeared below.

Marcus seemed as apprehensive as Quinn. "This explains that weird high tide yesterday, I imagine. It's done nothing but rain the past twelve hours, too. I'm about as waterlogged as an alligator."

The weather began to deteriorate rapidly throughout the day. The wind increased and the tide grew higher and higher. Quinn became really alarmed when she noticed shopkeepers boarding up their windows. The two cruise ships had left the day before and oddly, no other liners had come to replace them. By nightfall the rain had increased to frenzied sheets of solid water. There were times when Quinn couldn't even see the dock it was coming down so hard.

The *Vanora* was bouncing around and rising higher and higher beside the dock as the storm surge grew stronger. The last time Quinn had gone to her forepeak cabin she'd wisely decided to grab her toothpaste, toothbrush, and some dry clothes. If they were headed into a hurricane she realized there would be no way to access her cabin. She'd be sleeping in the main salon. Quinn secured the glass hatch on her cabin as tightly as she could.

Conditions worsened throughout the night. By morning Quinn, Marcus and Marnie were definitely alarmed and on edge from lack of sleep. They pleaded with Diego to set sail and get the yacht out to sea and away from land. Marcus reasoned there still might be time to outrun the hurricane that was bearing down on Cozumel with explosive speed.

The city center was being evacuated, as Quinn discovered when she checked with the harbormaster one last time in vain hope that Hank had tried to contact the *Vanora*. As she struggled against the elements to get back to the yacht, a gust of wind literally almost blew her off of the dock. The sky was dark, almost black with immense clouds; the heavy rain unremitting. Marcus had to grab Quinn by both arms to lift her on to the heaving deck.

Diego emerged from the hold. He'd been checking on the engine fluids and the bilge pumps, he said. Finally he gave the long-awaited command, "Cast off! *Apurarse! Pronto!*"

The crew sprang to action. Diego fired up the engines and turned on the spreader and mast lights. As Marcus prepared to jump onto the dock to undo the lines a vague shape appeared in the rain. It was the harbormaster, he'd come to release the dock lines for the crew of the *Vanora*. Quinn saluted the thoughtful man as Diego gunned the engines to push the heavy yacht away from the dock and send her out into the swelling, angry sea.

Once the bumpers were stowed and the crew was assembled in the protected wheelhouse, Diego outlined a course of action. The hurricane was traveling northwestward from Jamaica; his plan was to head south through the Yucatan Channel. This tactic would keep the *Vanora* on the leeward side of Isla de Cozumel. Diego hoped to outrace the storm while continuing along a course to the Panama Canal.

Since Cozumel was only ten miles east to west and thirty miles north to south, the captain figured the land would only offer a small respite from the fury of Cecelia. The tallest natural point of the island reached only fifteen meters above sea level—or about fifty feet; the height of an average four-story building.

Diego ordered everyone into safety harnesses. Out of necessity, they'd already donned bright-yellow foul weather gear. He sent Marcus and Marnie amidships on the deck to raise the main with all reefs in place. Quinn was sent below to make sure anything movable was secured. Diego even had her stow the cushions in the wheelhouse and cockpit.

It relieved Quinn somewhat to see how thorough the captain was. She was as puzzled as Marcus and Marnie as to why he'd delayed any proactive measures to deal with the hurricane in the first place. Now that they were inexorably caught up in it, Diego was all swift and decisive action. Still, even he couldn't control the raging elements surrounding them.

The *Vanora* had handled well under the reefed main for the few hours it took to clear Cozumel. From what they could pick up on the marine band radio the hurricane, however, seemed to be moving with maniacal speed. Diego's plan was to follow the coast line of Central America south, staying a good twenty miles off shore. If Cecelia stayed her course the *Vanora* would only be subjected to the outer edges of the immense storm.

Once around the tip of the island, Diego called for a southeasterly tack. For several hours they would be beating toward the storm trying to put a safe distance between the *Vanora* and land. It took Quinn, Marcus and Marnie fifteen minutes to complete the normally routine task of tacking the boat. It was nearly impossible to see more than a few feet ahead, and the wind seemed determined to rip their very bodies off of the deck. The winch handles were slick with salt and water. With the rough seas and zero visibility, the trio had to act on instinct.

Quinn gave silent thanks for the safety harness she was wearing. As she laboriously worked her way back to the wheelhouse she had to clip the sturdy nylon line attached to the harness to a lifeline, inch her way to a steel stanchion, unclip the line, then repeat the same process again on the next section of lifeline. The stanchions ran at four-foot intervals along the deck.

She'd almost made it to the door of the wheelhouse. Quinn knew Marcus and Marnie were somewhere close behind. She turned and squinted into the blinding rain. The darkness seemed to get darker. Quinn let go of the nylon line and cupped both hands around her eyes to help clear her vision. Then total darkness fell in the form of a huge wall of water. Quinn was slammed to the deck. Something heavy landed on her ribs, momentarily knocking the breath out of her.

The *Vanora* rolled slowly onto her side as tons of saltwater spilled off the deck. Quinn rolled, too, swept helplessly along in the surge. The nylon straps of the safety harness cut deeply into Quinn's flesh, even through the heavy plastic slicker she was wearing, but the strong straps kept her from going over the side. The weight on her chest shifted. Quinn suddenly realized it was Marcus; he'd been flung against her by the force of the wave.

"Where's Marnie?" Quinn tried to scream out over the noise of the wind and the pain in her side. Her voice came out in choking gasps. Marcus pointed to the stern. A patch of yellow showed through the thick veil of rain. Slowly, the shape became more solid as Marnie began to crawl toward her crewmates. Quinn realized with a prayer of thankfulness that all of them were still attached to the yacht by their harnesses.

The *Vanora* had recovered from her near capsize, yet she was still bouncing erratically in the storm-tossed sea. Quinn and Marcus held hands and formed a human chain, barely reaching Marnie as another wave caused the *Vanora* to heel to the other side. After fumbling with Marnie's safety clasp, Marcus managed to unclip it from the life line and drag the drenched, shaking woman into the wheelhouse.

Marnie was groaning through clenched teeth. "My shoulder, there's something wrong with my right arm and my shoulder."

Diego was wrestling with the helm. "Strip her!" He ordered without taking his eyes off of the tempestuous seas surrounding them.

After removing Marnie's harness and foul weather gear as gently as possible, Quinn could see why her crewmate was so uncomfortable. Her right arm was twisted outward at an unnatural angle. For a moment, Quinn feared the worst. She was certain that when Marnie's shirt was removed, she'd be looking at a compound fracture. Quinn steeled herself as she undid the first few buttons; determined not to show any emotion when faced with bare shattered bone protruding through torn flesh.

Quinn nearly sobbed in relief when she gingerly peeled the damp shirt off Marnie's shoulder and down her arm. Having worked for six months in her father's pediatrics office, Quinn instantly identified the injury. She'd aided Dr. Carrigan in treating more than one little boy who'd fallen from a tree for a dislocated shoulder. She patted Marnie's other shoulder.

"Hang in there, kiddo. Your shoulder's dislocated. I know it hurts like heck right now, but you'll be surprised at how fast most of the pain goes away once we get the humerus back into the scapula socket."

Marnie grimaced. "Talk English, would you, Quinn?"

Quinn motioned for Marcus to come help her. "Contrary to what you see in movies, you don't put your foot into someone's neck, then heave on the arm until the shoulder pops back into place. I'll need you to hold her, though, so I can get enough leverage to try to *slide* the joint back in. We don't know if there's any nerve or blood vessel damage, either."

Quinn helped Marnie lay down on the unsteady deck, then she instructed Marcus to kneel behind Marnie's head so he could hold her shoulders. The wiry-built woman didn't seem in the least bit self-conscious that she was nude from the waist up. Quinn grasped Marnie's right arm right above the elbow with one hand. With the other, she manipulated the area around the injury with her fingers for a few minutes. Suddenly, and without warning, Quinn pressed all her weight onto Marnie's shoulder using the palm of her hand.

Marnie yelped in pain, and Quinn sat back on her heels.

"*Shit!* Man that hurt!" Marnie sat up with the help of Marcus. She was rubbing her shoulder, but smiling with genuine respect and gratitude at Quinn. "You were right. It's as sore as hell now but doesn't hurt *nothing* like it did before." Even Diego couldn't hide the grudging smile on his lips and the quick gleam of respect in his eyes.

Quinn helped Marnie to her feet. "Hang on. I'll get you a dry shirt. I brought spare clothes with me from my cabin to the main salon before we left the dock."

Diego released the helm to Marcus. He was obviously fatigued; he looked like he'd aged ten years. His weariness appeared to not affect his prickly tongue, however.

"How impressive. Perhaps I should now call you 'Doctor Quinn, Medicine Woman'?" Diego laughed. "For now, how about simply Doctor *Cocinera*? Is it possible you could medicate your captain with some caffeine? Some hot coffee?"

While the drama inside the cabin had subsided, the drama outside continued. Quinn had to battle her way to the galley. The large urn of coffee she'd made much earlier was strapped to a bulkhead hook with bungee cords. Diego had gone to the nav station where he was trying to tweak the radar screen and monitor the radio.

Quinn poured steaming coffee into four spill-proof mugs. One by one, she took Diego a mug, then Marcus, then Marnie who was now sitting in the wheelhouse wearing one of Quinn's t-shirts. After Quinn had made her way up with her coffee, she helped Marnie struggle back into her harness and foul weather gear. Diego emerged shortly thereafter and suggested the women get some rest.

"You may sleep in the master stateroom. In the event we have to abandon ship, we four need to stay close together." With that ominous pronouncement, Diego dismissed them with a wave of the hand and bent his head to discuss something with Marcus.

Although she was truly drained of all her resources, Quinn was certain it would be impossible to fall asleep under the present circumstances. She helped Marnie down the steps into the master cabin. Quinn detected the faint scent of Rafael's cologne as she rearranged the large berth with blankets and pillows as a cushion against the pounding of the ocean on the *Vanora's* hull. Lying beside Marnie in the darkened cabin, Quinn's limbs slowly began to feel like lead. She sank into a mindless stupor.

CHAPTER ELEVEN

T he darkness was all enveloping. What startled Quinn awake wasn't any motion, rather it was a lack of motion: A lull in the ceaseless pounding of a maddened sea and the mournful creaking of a sailboat in dire distress. Quinn felt like she was smothering. Frantically, she began to claw at the heavy bedspread and pillow covering her face.

It took her a full minute to realize where she was. She was lying on the starboard bulkhead of the master cabin. Not in the bunk. *Oh dear God, we've capsized. We're sinking!* Frantic, she began searching for Marnie beneath the bed covers.

"Quinn!" Marnie's calloused hand wrapped around Quinn's ankle. "Shit, oh shit. I think we're going over."

"We've got to get topside, *now*." Quinn was groping her way to the cabin door.

"Where are Marcus and Diego?" Marnie's voice was breathless. "Why didn't they come get us?"

Quinn didn't have any answers. Stumbling over fallen objects, the terrified women made it to the slanted cabin door. Quinn let out a long breath of relief when it became obvious that the main salon wasn't flooding with seawater. Slowly, the *Vanora* began to right herself. At the sound of hoarse shouting from the deck, Quinn's knees almost gave way in relief. She and Marnie struggled up the companionway to the wheelhouse—and into a worse nightmare.

The broad glass windshield of the *Vanora* had a huge crack running down the center. Diego was struggling with the helm, but Marcus was nowhere in sight. The sea conditions were pretty much the same. The wind was lifting the spray right off of the water. What little sunlight that filtered through the massive clouds was creating an eerie glow. The atmosphere around the *Vanora* had an odd yellow cast to it.

"What happened? Where's Marcus?" Before Diego could answer, Quinn saw where Marcus was. He was alongside of the deck and so was part of the one hundred foot main mast.

Diego spoke through clenched teeth. "We lost the mast. It snapped in two. Broke the windshield. The sail became like a drogue. It was pulling us over. Marcus had to cut it loose."

Quinn watched anxiously as Marcus made his way back to the wheelhouse. She realized the men had to be completely exhausted. It was time for her and Marnie to take over so the captain and Marcus could rest.

"Where are we?"

Diego responded that the rain was so intense it seemed to be interfering with the radar. There was no way to tell how near or far the ship was from land. Even worse, there was no sure way to tell if other vessels were in the area. Quinn shuddered as a vision came to mind of sliding down one of the immense waves into a deep trough, then broad siding an unseen cruise ship.

"We should be getting clear of the hurricane in the next few hours. We are on the fringe of it right now."

"If this is only the fringe of Cecelia, may God spare me from ever being *inside* a hurricane. This is hell." The look on Quinn's face was grim.

Marcus entered the wheelhouse along with a gust of wind and a splatter of rain. His face was grey with exhaustion, his eyes bloodshot. Quinn handed him a towel to mop the water off his face. "Marnie and I will go make you guys some sandwiches. I can boil some water for tea in the electric teapot. Then I really think you and Diego should rest a bit. We girls can take over the helm."

Within the hour everyone had eaten. Marcus went below to take a nap in the main salon. Diego insisted on staying in the wheelhouse but he was fast asleep in a corner seat. Quinn had the helm. Thankfully, there seemed to be a lull in the ferocity of the weather. The seas were still running high but the over-sized waves seemed almost orderly after the nightmare of the last several hours.

Night had fallen. Diego had instructed Marnie to shine a mega-watt searchlight at intervals across the heaving seas. Quinn concentrated on simply trying to keep in rhythm with the *Vanora*. There were several occasions when Quinn could actually feel when the rudder was out of the water. The bow of the yacht would disappear for a breathless moment into the face of a wave and the stern would rise for a few shuddering seconds, before sinking back down into the ocean.

Every muscle in Quinn's body ached from the strain of manipulating the helm. Her ribs were still sore from the impact of Marcus's solid body earlier. Marnie, Quinn was learning, was steadfast, dependable and fearless. She was an adept sailor and had a lot of nautical miles under her belt. The two women took turns at the helm and with manning the searchlight. Quinn's stomach quaked every time she crouched outside of the wheelhouse trying to shine the light over the water. The mass and power of the ocean seemed monumental, unconquerable, and utterly merciless in the path of the light's beam.

After three hours, Quinn and Marnie decided to wake up the men. Both women were mentally and physically fatigued almost beyond endurance. The constant adrenalin coursing through their systems and the physical demands of combating the relentless tossing and pitching of the *Vanora* was taking its toll. Diego awakened almost instantly. Quinn gave him a report of the current conditions. The captain excused himself for a moment to use the head and rouse Marcus.

When Diego came back to take over the helm, Marcus was right on his heels. Quinn was numb. She promised herself she would sleep for a week once they were safely at a dock somewhere. Calling on the last ounce of her reserve, she offered to go below and get more sandwiches and hot tea for the crew. Flashes of lightening were jaggedly cutting through the darkened sky.

Just as Quinn stood up to head into the galley, she felt the deck of the *Vanora* rise with her. Quinn grabbed onto the binnacle and instinctively braced herself. The seventy-six foot yacht rose up the face of a huge wave. Barely cresting the top, the *Vanora* slowly spun with the grace of a ballerina in a complete circle as she slid down the back of the wave. Quinn heard Diego curse, "*Madre de Dios!*" She saw the wheel spin in his hands. Diego began frantically to try to regain control of the helm.

White as a ghost, Quinn sank down between Marcus and Marnie. Marcus put an arm around her shoulder. Everyone was hanging onto something; as much out of fear as necessity. A spark of anger ignited in Quinn's breast, burning through the fear and total weariness that had been the only emotions she'd experienced for hours. She had a curse of her own to add. *May God damn Diego Reyes to hell,* Quinn thought as she huddled miserably between Marnie and Marcus.

As she mentally reviewed the captain's procrastination at getting his ship and his crew safely out of the destructive path of the hurricane, the spark of anger grew into a flame.

"Dammit, Diego!" She shouted above the noise of the elements beating on bulkheads. "We wouldn't be in this situation if you'd given the order to leave Cozumel one day earlier!"

Diego had managed to get control of the helm. His face was dripping with sweat. He snarled at Quinn without looking at her. "This is my ship. I am the captain. I know that I'm doing, *cocinera*." He turned the wheel hard to starboard to keep the *Vanora* from broaching a wave. "No one knows the value of the *Vanora* as I do. I will not let her go down."

Almost as if satisfied at having scared the living daylights out of the four mere mortals aboard the luxurious vessel, the seas seemed to flatten out somewhat and the wind and rain began to slowly abate. The horizon became distinguishable as the morning sun struggled to break through towering storm heads in the distance. Quinn stared out over the water in wonder. She could see rolling mountains of waves but gone were the frightening white caps and the wind no longer blew the spume like stinging darts off the top of the water.

As a whole, the crew drew deep breaths of relief. In the dawning light, Quinn looked around at her companions. *What a sorry looking bunch. I must look like hell, too*, she thought. The men's faces were covered in stubble. Their eyes sunken in exhaustion. Marnie had deep circles under her eyes and her skin looked mottled and pale. All of them had crusts of sea salt riming their facial hairs and their heads.

Wearily, Quinn stood up. She felt like an old woman. Her muscles, her joints, even her bones ached. She mumbled that she'd be making the crew a hot meal and some coffee. It was still rough below, but with the guard rails and clips in place on the stove, making breakfast was manageable. Quinn made a bacon-sausage-and-egg scramble with toast; and she made a lot. None of them had eaten a decent meal in the last two days.

Marnie came down and offered to help. The two friends were mostly silent. They'd endured a harrowing experience together. Their relationship had been tested to the utmost—and had endured. Quinn smiled at Marnie, a hint of tears in her eyes. "Guess we're a pair of real survivors, aren't we?"

Marnie looked soberly into Quinn's eyes. "I'd crew with you any time after this, Quinn. I'm sorry if I ever misjudged you." They gave each other a brief hug, then served up breakfast.

Diego posted the two women at the helm while he and Marcus moved carefully along the outside deck assessing the damages to the *Vanora*. Aside from the cracked window and the broken mast there was no real structural damage that they could see. The radar was operating at full capacity again. After plotting a course, Diego split the crew into watches. The low pressure system had pushed them closer to Panama than he'd anticipated. He wanted Quinn and Marnie to rest first.

"Take four hours of sleep. Then, Marnie and Marcus will have a three hour watch. "You," he smiled thinly at Quinn, "you and I will then have a three hour watch. When everyone is rested up, we can go back to our regular watches."

Marcus told Quinn she could sleep in his cabin, rather than in the main salon. She thanked him, then followed Marnie to the crew quarters.

"Oh joy. Three hours alone with Diego," she grumbled. "I think I'd rather be riding out Cecelia." At the look on Marnie's face, Quinn exclaimed, "Forget I said that. I take it back!"

After straightening up Marcus's cabin, Quinn washed the salt off of her face, thoroughly combed her hair, and brushed her teeth. It was still too rough to attempt taking a shower, but not so rough that Quinn was asleep almost before her head hit the pillow. It seemed like only minutes later, Marcus was gently shaking her. "Sorry, little buddy. The captain wants you on deck for your watch."

When Quinn went on deck the difference in the weather momentarily stunned her. Gone were the screaming winds. The heavy skies had patches of bright blue sky showing through. The ocean had ceased its destructive rampage. The *Vanora* rode smoothly over tall, rounded swells. Diego had transferred the helm operation to the cockpit wheel. Quinn sat down on the port side, a mug of hot coffee in her hand.

"It's beautiful, isn't it?" Her voice was soft and reverent. Diego let his eyes travel across the broad expanse of water, then he nodded in agreement. Scattered shafts of sunlight streamed from the sky causing the tops of certain swells to glisten in varying shades of luxuriant green dappled with silver and hints of deep violet blue. A strong, steady breeze blew across the deck.

Quinn thought Diego's eyes had a haunted, distant look in them. His usually arrogant features seemed to droop. For a moment he looked unutterably sorrowful in the rapidly shifting light. Quinn caught her breath and without thinking, stretched out a comforting hand. Diego stared blankly at her, then shook his head. When he spoke his words were cutting, but somehow empty of his usual venom.

"Understand, *cocinera*, that you are not to argue with or shout at your captain. Especially in front of others." Quinn dropped her hand into her lap. Restlessly, Diego shifted his body to better accommodate getting the helm to agree with the sea. "You are aware there is such a thing as mutiny?"

Quinn was certainly aware of classic tales such as *Moby Dick* and *Mutiny on the Bounty*. Secretly, she thought Diego Reyes was over-reacting to her mini-meltdown. Her gut feeling was that he was still determined to intimidate her. Their entire relationship, she realized, was based on a tug-of-war between dominance and submission. As tired and debilitated as Quinn was, she wasn't even close to being psychologically diminished by Diego.

Quinn had personally witnessed how Diego enjoyed demeaning females. But, she'd discovered an inner strength over the past few harrowing days. Quinn had crossed a threshold. Instead of being afraid of life; the memory of melding with the universe when Noah made love to her in the lagoon in Jamaica—when all of life centered into the very heat, heart and soul of her in one glorious union with all things created, and conversely afraid of dying; the force and might of Hurricane Cecelia had made Quinn, if anything, more resilient, and damn near fearless.

She didn't even flinch when Diego added with his familiar sneer, "Even taking the owner of this yacht as your lover makes no difference. You work under my command, *comprendas?*"

Diego released the helm to Quinn and went below. Over the next three hours she managed to keep contact with the captain to a minimum. Diego spent quite some time in the engine room and the hold. He mentioned at one point that the *Vanora* had sprung a leak near the propeller shaft, but said it was nothing to worry about. He'd put some temporary caulking in the crack that should hold until they got to a shipyard in Panama.

Diego seemed preoccupied. Quinn speculated it might have something to do with when he'd have to answer personally to Rafael Santiago as to why he had risked losing the multi-million dollar yacht. It never crossed her mind that Rafael's main concern hadn't been for his beautiful yacht. She would discover later that the handsome entrepreneur had been livid with anger at Diego and near paralyzed with fear that Quinn and the crew would end up dying in the horrific hurricane. He'd gone so far as to try to send his own jet in search of the *Vanora*, but the intensity of the storm had made such an attempt impossible. Rafael had waited impatiently with a troubled heart until he finally heard from the captain of the *Vanora*.

CHAPTER TWELVE

The radio squawked incessantly the closer the *Vanora* got to Panama. *"Querida,"* the caress in Rafael's voice sent delicious shivers down Quinn's spine. The surprise on her face had been genuine when Diego summoned her to talk on the radio with the owner of the yacht. The look on the captain's face, however, boded no good. His eyes were glittering slits in a face as hard as a mask. Quinn had no idea the tongue lashing Rafael had laid on Diego.

"Querida, I have been so worried about you! Are you well? Did you get injured? Did anyone get injured? Were you frightened, Quinn?"

"I'm fine. We're all fine." She glanced at Diego's retreating back. "Diego was in full command. He kept us from capsizing." Her tone relayed true respect for the captain's capabilities. Her personal feelings she was keeping to herself.

"Rafael, that's so kind of you to ask about us." She laughed. "You wonder if I was frightened. That's really sweet."

"You have no idea how frightened *I* was, *querida*. I couldn't eat. I couldn't sleep wondering if you were all right." His tone was serious.

They chatted for a few minutes, then Rafael mentioned how the *Vanora* would be at a dock for repairs for a few days.

"My business detains me. So many people need their drugs." They both laughed. Quinn had picked up on how much Rafael enjoyed making jokes about his pharmaceutical business. "I would have liked to have sailed the Panama Canal with you, but it seems that's not going to be possible."

Quinn's heart had done a little triple leap at the thought of having Rafael on board again. The disappointment seeped into her voice. "Oh, that would have been wonderful. I'm so sorry you can't make it."

His next words had the hairs on her arm standing at attention.

"What I would like to do, Quinn, is have you fly here to Guadalajara for those few days the *Vanora* will be repaired. I can send my pilot, Donald, to pick you up in the corporate jet."

Quinn was momentarily speechless. That would go over like a hot balloon with Diego, for sure. What would Hank think? What if I go and then Noah finds out? Her thoughts were jumbled and confused.

"Are you still there?" Rafael sounded amused.

"I'm here. I'm thinking. I'm not sure if Diego—"

"Do not worry about Diego!" The steel was back in Rafael's voice. It was the same tone Quinn had heard him use in Cozumel when he was talking to his office on the cell phone.

"Think it over, *querida*. You have a few days until you reach Panama. I promise you that I will behave as a perfect gentleman if you agree to be my guest."

Quinn thanked him. As she was about to hang up, Rafael asked if Marnie had given her his note. "Yes," Quinn smiled. "And I'm trying to follow your recommendations." Rafael laughed, said something in Spanish that had a romantic ring to it, and disconnected the call.

Quinn went to the galley in a daze. She wondered if the giddy sensation pulsing through her mind and body was what romance writers meant when they referred to a character as "walking on air." She moved as though she were in a trance as she began making a ham and spinach lasagna for dinner. As she blended freshly minced garlic, chopped spinach and raw egg into the ricotta cheese mixture, a troubled frown replaced the dreamy expression on Quinn's face.

Diego had finally gotten hold of Hank Somers. He, too, was unable to make the transit of the Panama Canal aboard the *Vanora*. To say that Diego looked peevish when Hank asked to talk to Quinn was an understatement. However, Quinn reflected with a nervous glance up into the cockpit where Diego sat brooding, *that* look was nothing like the enraged mask after his conversation with Rafael.

"All kinds of shit is going on over here, Quinn." Hank's stress was evident even over the static of the connection. "Some major law firm has been checking into Noah and Loomis Grady's background. Mine, too. This isn't good."

Disturbed, Quinn asked why someone would want to investigate Hank or Loomis. The words were barely out of her mouth when she suddenly remembered her last meeting with her parents at brunch in Miami. Viviane Carrigan had again expressed her misgivings about her only daughter's new career... *before you go sailing off into the sunset again, dad and I would like to know a little bit more these men. I think this Noah and Hank could bear some scrutiny.*

Dr. Carrigan had chuckled and patted Quinn's hand reassuringly. *You can't blame your mother for her concern, Quinn. If everything is as 'shipshape' as you say, then you have nothing to worry about. I'll just have Cedric & Fenn run a quick background check on them. You know, credit, police reports. That sort of thing.*

Rather than ruin the last morning with her parents, Quinn had wisely chosen not to inform them she was already booked as full-time crew on the *Vanora*. Unwisely, she hadn't protested her father's interference. Now, Hank and Noah were embroiled in some weird investigation. Loomis Grady, Quinn could have cared less about. The obese and crude man had always given her the creeps.

Hank didn't seem to care to elaborate. He had cut short the conversation and promised to call again in a few days. Quinn didn't even get a chance to ask about Noah's health. What was bothering her, as she began to layer the lasagna in a deep pan, was the apprehension in Hank's voice. What could the handsome and engaging commodore possibly have to hide? Quinn sighed in exasperation at her parents' interference. She was an adult now. Couldn't they respect that?

Quinn had to giggle at the thought of what Viviane Carrigan would say if she knew her daughter had recently survived one of the worst hurricanes in Caribbean history. All the news reports of the destruction wreaked by Hurricane Cecelia were pouring in. *I'd better call home. Mom and Dad must be freaking out!*

Quinn hurried through the dinner preparations. As soon as she had the heavy lasagna pan in the oven, she washed her hands and steeled herself to approach the sullen captain with a request to radio her parents in Boston.

Diego had passed by the galley several times on his way to the bar in the main salon, but he chose to completely ignore Quinn. She approached the captain in the cockpit with a sense of dread in her heart. He was well on his way to being drunk; she could tell by the look in his bloodshot eyes. Diego fixed his brown and black eyes on her with menacing intensity. Quinn had no idea where her crewmates were but she fervently wished they would appear.

"And what can I do for you, *cocinera*? I can see by the look on your face that you desire something from your captain." He patted the cushion beside him. "Sit here."

The last thing Quinn wanted was to be in close proximity to her nemesis. She had no doubt his state of mind had a lot to do with her—and Rafael Santiago. Quinn perched nervously on the cockpit seat.

"I need to call my parents, Diego. I imagine they're worried about me. They know our itinerary. I called them before I left Miami." Quinn felt a twinge of guilt as she recalled the disappointment and resignation in her mother's voice when Quinn finally got the nerve to phone home and let her parents know she'd signed on to the *Vanora* for six months.

Diego took a long swallow from a highball glass. Quinn was near enough she could smell the bourbon whiskey. The evening sky was rich with the colors of an incredible sunset. Quinn had no idea how green the melding of ocean and sun made her eyes look. Diego leaned forward. He took her chin in one hand and tilted her head so that she was looking directly into his own unusually-colored eyes.

"Is that all you want from me, Quinn? That's it? A phone call?"

His grip on her chin tightened. His fingers were like a vice. Quinn tried to pull back. Diego set his glass down with such force on the cockpit table that an ice cube jumped out. He stood up, pulling her along with him. He released her chin and took her by the shoulders. The sun had done its usual magician's prestige, slipping below the horizon with startling speed.

"What is this? You don't think Diego Reyes is good enough for you? Daughter of a doctor!" He all but spat out the words. "You have no idea the history of the Reyes family. None at all." Both of them were swaying in rhythm with the swells of the ocean. "We have a long history of professors, and doctors and—martyrs."

Someone below, most likely Marcus, flipped on the mast and running lights. Lights came on in the main salon. Diego dropped his arms to his side. "I do not need to be in the employment of Rafael Santiago, *cocinera*. I choose to do so. But, I will not be driven from my post because of a spoiled and silly little *gringa*. I will not be a sacrifice as my brother was."

He lurched slightly, and grabbed Quinn by the nape of the neck, pulling her close to him. With his lips against her ear, he hissed, "You do not want to suffer the consequences of being disloyal to Diego Reyes." He pulled back, then caressed her cheek with his palm. "Or do you...*querida*?"

Diego laughed, sat down, crossed his legs and picked up his highball. With a dismissive wave of his hand, he told Quinn to go ahead and call her parents on the ship's radio. She couldn't get away from him fast enough and almost stumbled over the lip of the companionway door. Quinn was now totally convinced the captain of the *Vanora* was not only imbalanced but delusional as well.

Quinn kept her conversation with her parents brief. She assured them all was well. She wasn't lying when she told her mother that they had managed to outrun Hurricane Cecelia. *Just barely,* she reminded herself. After asking about her brother and his family, Quinn made the excuse that dinner was ready and she had to get busy. She promised to call again in two weeks.

Diego had disappeared and he didn't show up for dinner. Quinn ate with Marnie and Marcus in the cockpit under a half-moon sky. The lasagna was baked to perfection; hot, cheesy and redolent with garlic. Quinn served it with an antipasto, and warm crunchy garlic toast.

Marcus smacked his lips. "Diego doesn't know what he's missing. He's not a happy camper. I saw him earlier and he said for us three to split the first two watches. We'll be in Cristobal by tomorrow morning."

Not knowing where Diego could be lurking on the big yacht, Quinn waited until Marnie came into the galley while she was loading the dishwasher to pull her fellow crewmate aside. Quinn related most of what had transpired between her and Diego earlier.

"Do you think he's getting paranoid? What's with the 'martyr' and 'sacrifice' business?" She looked thoughtful. "Now that I think about it, I don't recall Diego saying that he had a brother. He said he had a sister."

Marnie shrugged. "I guess we'll have to keep an eye on him. I'm as sorry as you are that Hank won't be back soon. Now we're short a line handler, which means we'll have to hire one at the Cristobal Yacht Club."

This was news to Quinn. Marnie had to explain that the Autoridad del Canal de Panama, or the APC, required all captains to have four line handlers on any vessel up to eighty feet in length. "Generally, the yacht club is the hangout for wannabe's. Problem is," Marnie yawned, "you never know what you're gonna get. I'm off to bed."

It had been with great relief that Quinn had moved back into her forepeak cabin once the *Vanora* was clear of the bad seas associated with Hurricane Cecelia. Now, as she made her way forward, she spied Diego on the opposite side of the deck. As quietly as she could she maneuvered her way to the cabin so he wouldn't see her. Her heart was pounding as she slipped through the open hatch. Captain Reyes sounded like he was arguing, and he was gesturing with both hands. What disturbed Quinn was—he was talking to thin air.

CHAPTER THIRTEEN

The Cristobal Yacht Club sat on the Atlantic side of the Panama Canal close to Gatun Lake; at one time the largest manmade lake in the world. Diego had appeared on the deck of the *Vanora* around three that morning. He seemed completely sober and alert. As the *Vanora* neared the opening to the Panama Canal, Quinn could see scores of shipping vessels of all sizes and nationalities waiting in the open sea for their appointed time slot to transit the canal.

Diego briefed the crew on what to expect. "We will dock at the yacht club. I need to make arrangements to repair the damages to the *Vanora* after we clear customs. Once the boat is cleaned up, you all may have some time off."

Marnie and Quinn exchanged glances. Quinn had confided to her two friends that Rafael had invited her to fly to his home in Guadalajara for a few days. Marcus had been really impressed. "A private jet? How could you say no?"

Marnie agreed. "You go, girl. May as well enjoy the perks."

The only person who was unaware that after much soul-searching Quinn had decided to take Rafael up on his offer was Diego. To her knowledge the yacht owner hadn't contacted anyone onboard the *Vanora* since the day before yesterday. *Maybe Rafael got too busy and forgot about me,* Quinn thought with a mild sense of relief as she wiped down the fiberglass cockpit.

Rafael had done no such thing. Shortly after lunch, a stocky blonde man wearing aviator glasses showed up on the dock. He looked to be in his late twenties. He introduced himself as Rafael's pilot, Donald. Marcus invited him aboard. Diego was at the yacht club letting the staff and other captains know he was in need of a line-handler.

"Mr. Santiago sends his apologies, Miss Carrigan, for not giving you much notice. He's a busy man and has a tight schedule. I can stand by for only two hours while you pack your things. I'll be back." Donald smiled at her, then jumped off the yacht and strode down the dock.

Quinn was thrown completely off guard. "What made Rafael so sure I'd go? What if I'd decided not to?" Marcus and Marnie looked at each other, then at Quinn.

"Seems like you're obligated now," Marnie said. "You'd already made up your mind to go, anyway. Maybe the man's psychic on top of everything else."

Quinn hurried through a shower and packed enough clothes and toiletries for three to four days. She quickly blew dry her hair. *What if Diego isn't back before I leave? Do I dare simply leave him a note?* Unfortunately, she wasn't allowed that luxury. Diego was on the deck when Quinn emerged from her cabin with a canvas overnight bag on one shoulder.

"Going somewhere, *cocinera*? Perhaps on a little vacation to the lovely city of Guadalajara?"

He moved closer and took off his sunglasses. Again, Quinn was struck by his unusual eyes. There was something both repelling and oddly attractive about the contrast of the brown iris and the solid black of the other. Diego began to circle around her; much like he had when they first met. Quinn could feel his eyes creeping over her entire body. She knew he was undressing her in his mind.

"Diego, I was going to tell you. Actually, I was debating whether or not I should go. Then, when Donald showed up unexpectedly an hour or so ago, I realized it would be rude of me to *not* go at this point."

Diego stopped his prowling. He was again face to face with Quinn. "You were going to *tell* your captain? Should you not perhaps have said, '*con permisso, mi Capitan*'?"

At this point, Quinn was backing away from Diego. There was an intensity about him that she didn't like one bit. "You gave all of us time off, Diego. I don't think my contract states I have to answer to you about what I do in my free time."

Before Diego could respond, Donald called to Quinn from the dock. "Miss Carrigan, it's time to go."

Diego grabbed Quinn's arm hard enough that a bruise developed later. "You will answer to me on your return." She fled.

The ride to the Panama City airport in a taxi was mostly scenic, definitely bumpy, and a real hair-raiser. More than once, Donald laughed and patted Quinn reassuringly on her arm or knee as the driver careened with inches of a beat up delivery truck or another car. The rural countryside reflected a level of poverty that was surprising to Quinn. The amount of litter along the way saddened her for some reason.

At the airport, Donald led Quinn into the private terminal where her bag was searched and her passport scrutinized. The Astra 200 Air Jet he led her to was gleaming in the afternoon sun. Donald gave Quinn a hand up the steps and into the main cabin. Six leather executive seats lined each side of the aluminum frame. Beside each chair were leather covered armrests with cup holders. Donald showed her how to pull out the mahogany tables recessed inside the armrests.

Donald introduced Quinn to the co-pilot, Ruperto, then asked Quinn to please fasten her seatbelt and prepare for takeoff. Quinn noticed that directly behind the cockpit was a well-stocked wet bar. *Oh, man, what am I thinking?* Quinn groaned inwardly as the jet taxied down the runway, then rose smoothly into the bright blue sky. *What in the world does Rafael want with me? I'm only the 'cocinera'—the cook on his yacht. What am I getting myself into?*

Quinn dozed throughout most of the four-hour flight to Guadalajara. At the airport, a driver in a Mercedes was waiting for her—along with a dozen magnificent white roses and a note:

Dinner at nine. Mi casa es su casa. Besos, Rafael.

The driver was all smiles but he didn't speak much English. Quinn bid Donald goodbye, and before long, she was being driven through a tree-lined, upscale neighborhood in the suburbs. Rafael's two-story Spanish style house was covered with ivy. A profusion of flowers and manicured shrubs added an almost European flair to the grounds. Quinn was greeted at the door by a stooped, gray-haired man who introduced himself as Pablo. His English was as bad as her Spanish, but Quinn understood his hand gestures.

Pablo led Quinn to an airy, comfortable guest room. The over-sized canopy bed, the dresser, and the vanity table were obviously antique and made from exquisitely carved Spanish oak. White lace drapes that matched the bedding graced the verandah doors. The scent of roses wafted in from the garden right outside.

"This is absolutely lovely!" Quinn exclaimed. Pablo smiled at the obvious delight in the young woman's voice. He set her bag down near the closet and spoke, motioning with his hands. Quinn understood he was asking if she'd like for him to unpack her bag. She shook her head no. Pablo bowed, then quietly left the room.

Pablo apparently was Rafael's personal valet. Over the next few days, Quinn would discover he cooked, cleaned, took care of the laundry and ran errands. It struck her as a bit odd there were no women servants in the house, until Rafael explained three women came in weekly to do the serious cleaning.

Quinn spent an hour or so wandering around the gardens surrounding the house. She was sitting in a shaded gazebo with the paperback she'd brought along when Pablo came out with a pitcher of iced tea and a glass. He also carried a pair of shears and two vases. Pablo mimed that Quinn was allowed to cut the flowers. She thanked him. Within the hour she'd collected two large bouquets in a riot of colors.

When Pablo came out to collect the pitcher and her glass, Quinn followed him back into the main area of the house. The interior was cool and dark. The living room and dining room furnishings were as elegant and expensive as the guest room. Quinn spied a place for one of the floral arrangements on an entry table in the formal living room.

She noticed a silver filigree picture frame and peered closely at it. A stunningly beautiful blonde woman smiled back at her. One arm was around a handsome young boy who, judging by the missing teeth, must have been around six years old when the picture was taken. Perched on the woman's lap was a little girl who appeared to be three or four years old. Both children had exquisite olive skin. The boy's eyes were light green like Rafael's. The little girl had long blonde hair and deep dark eyes fringed with thick lashes.

Quinn looked up from examining the picture and found the old valet's eyes were fastened on her. "Who are they, Pablo?"

"*La familia de Senor Santiago.*" His eyes were mournful. "*Pero, no mas.*"

"No more? What do you mean? They're not dead are they? Is he divorced?"

Pablo simply shook his head and left the room.

Nine o'clock came and went. There was no sign of Rafael. He hadn't telephoned either. Quinn had only nibbled on the light dinner Pablo laid out on a buffet table in the dining room. She was ready to go to her bedroom and call it a night when the front door burst open.

"*Pablo! Donde esta mi vida?*"

Rafael strode into the dining room.

"Quinn, *querida. Lo siento mucho.* I so apologize. You must forgive my tardiness."

He took her in his arms. Quinn would remember the kiss that followed for the rest of her life. It was The Kiss; the one that transcended all others. It was the kiss of a passionate and sensual man who'd found everything he'd ever desired. Quinn could feel the pulsing of Rafael's heart in the full warm lips that covered hers. When he slipped his tongue between her lips, Quinn's mouth flooded with heat. Her mouth was literally watering at the taste of him.

It was Rafael who broke the embrace. Quinn could feel the muscles in his arms trembling. She felt weak and powerless. If one kiss from this man could leave her feeling so aroused and so vulnerable, what if--? Almost tripping over her own feet, Quinn moved to the buffet table.

"You must be hungry, Rafael. Shall I fix you a plate?" Her voice was shaking as badly as her hands. Rafael stepped in close behind her. Wrapping his arms around Quinn's waist, he nuzzled her neck. "I am a man who is starved, *querida*. I have never known such hunger before."

The sonorous clang of a doorbell rang throughout the house. There was a babble of voices, then Pablo ushered two men and a woman into the dining room. Rafael greeted his guests with hugs and introduced them to Quinn. She couldn't help but notice how attractive all three visitors were. Where the men's features were strongly defined and patrician; the woman's face was delicate and hauntingly beautiful. It was as though they'd all been bred from the finest Latino gene pool.

Rafael made introductions all around. Felicia, Geraldo, and Frederico spoke excellent English and were obviously delighted to meet Quinn. The group ate, drank wine and listened to music until nearly two in the morning. Before leaving, Felicia promised to take Quinn shopping the next day, Friday, since Rafael had meetings scheduled for most of the day.

Quinn could tell by his drooping eyelids that Rafael was exhausted. He walked her to the door of the guestroom. "I'm freeing up my schedule so we can spend the whole weekend together. Do you ride, *querida*? Do you like horses?" Quinn nodded. She loved horses, although she'd only gone horseback riding a few times.

Rafael took Quinn in his arms and kissed her gently on each eyelid, then her nose, then on her mouth. After a long embrace, Rafael caressed her face with his hand, his fingers lingering for a moment on her lips.

"*Buenas suenas, mi amor,*" Rafael turned, and disappeared down the long dark hallway.

Chapter Fourteen

Guadalajara was beautiful. Everywhere Quinn looked there were flowers and tree-lined streets. Original architecture abounded, even among the more modern shops and malls. Felicia proved to be a personable and charming companion. The two women shopped for a couple of hours, then stopped for a bite of lunch at a seafood restaurant.

Felicia told Quinn that her family and Rafael's family had been close friends going back several generations. "Mama and Papa for years wanted a marriage between the families and all eyes were turned to me and Rafael." She laughed, dark brown eyes sparkling. "But, we are too much like brother and sister. We grew up together. We argue too much."

The attractive woman glanced at the large diamond on her ring finger. "I married someone I met at the university. He now works for my father. We are very happy together. What about you, Quinn? How did you meet Rafael?'

Quinn was a little relieved that Rafael obviously hadn't broadcast to his friends and family that she'd met him as a deckhand on his yacht. *Actually,* she thought, *I work for Hank and not for Rafael.*

"I crew on sailboat and yacht deliveries," Quinn explained to Felicia. "Rafael bought a seventy-six foot yacht, the *Vanora,* from a yacht brokerage in Miami. A friend of mine hired three of us and a captain to sail it to San Diego for Rafael."

Felicia clapped her hands. "How fun! Tell me more!" So Quinn spent the next hour describing the trip to Jamaica aboard the *Zephyr.* She told Felicia about the galley fire and Chip's shark attack. Quinn even found herself sharing parts of her disastrous romance with Noah. It wasn't until after the bill arrived that Quinn finally got a chance to ask Felicia the question that had been burning in her subconscious ever since yesterday.

"I saw a photo of Rafael's family in the living room. Pablo wouldn't say much about them except that they're 'no mas'. I presume that means they're divorced"?

Felicia nodded, then looked down at her coffee cup. "It's been a few years since Elise left and took the children. Rafael was devastated. Not only by her leaving, but that she took his children. Her father is a Supreme Court Justice in the States."

Felicia's voice grew hard. "I think she had a plan the whole time. They were married here in Mexico. She wouldn't have the ceremony where she lives in La Jolla, California. Rafael has bought a condo there so he has a home for the children when he visits them."

Quinn was bursting with questions, but Felicia changed the subject. She also insisted on picking up the bill. Still, Quinn wanted to know everything. How Rafael and Elise met. How long they were married. What happened to their marriage. When Felicia dropped Quinn off back at Rafael's house, she had one final thing to say.

"I wouldn't bring up the subject of Elise. If I were you, Quinn, I'd wait until when, and if, he mentions it. Rafael was so devastated over losing custody of the children he got himself fixed. He said he would never be put in a position where he could lose one of his own children again. For a Latino man to do something like that, well, that says a lot." With a wave, she drove off in her Mercedes SUV.

Rafael made it home before seven. He'd phoned Quinn an hour earlier to tell her they'd been invited out to dinner with some customers from San Diego. He and Quinn would have time for one cocktail together at the house before leaving for the restaurant. Quinn thanked her lucky stars she'd brought the best of the few dresses she kept on the *Vanora*.

When Quinn heard Rafael shouting for Pablo, she flew down the hallway to the study. The Mexican millionaire was wearing a green silk suit with a lavender shirt and matching tie. He looked so handsome that Quinn's breath caught in her throat. He was holding a martini glass in one hand. He stretched out the other to her.

"Come to me, *querida*. I have missed you today."

Slowly, as if in a dream, Quinn walked toward Rafael, the silk dress whispering against her thighs. He set down the cocktail and put his hands on her bare shoulders. The halter dress Quinn was wearing was backless.

Rafael's face was mere inches from hers. His hooded green eyes looked deeply into hers as he moved his hands from her shoulders and lightly traced the curve of her spine with his fingers. Quinn's skin tightened as a shiver pulsed over her entire body.

Rafael murmured something beneath his breath, then he put his hands on Quinn's slender hips and pulled her close to him. His kiss was gentle at first. Unable to resist, Quinn put her arms around his neck and pressed even closer. Her breasts were full and ripe and she ached for Rafael to take each one into his mouth. Her nipples were like hard little buds straining against her dress.

With a groan, Rafael took Quinn's lower lip between his teeth. He moved her so that her back was pressed against the wall. His hips undulating, Rafael cupped Quinn's right breast in his hand and began rubbing her nipple with his thumb. He dropped his head and ran his tongue slowly down her neck. His breath was hot on her sensitive skin.

Quinn was beyond caring that Pablo might enter the study unexpectedly. When Rafael's mouth closed over her breast and his tongue darted at her nipple through the silky fabric, Quinn was completely at the mercy of her lover. As if sensing Quinn's surrender, Rafael pulled her dress up to her waist. He fumbled briefly with his trousers, then gently pushed her thighs apart with his knee.

The moment Rafael glided inside of her, Quinn experienced a spasm of absolute pleasure. She groaned aloud and began moving her hips in tempo with his. Rafael took her wrists in his hands and held them over her head against the wall. He was vocal in his pleasure. *"Ah, amor de mi vida,"* he repeated over and over again. His thrusting became more urgent, then Quinn's whole body jerked as she crested on the wave of not one but two orgasms. With a loud cry, Rafael emptied himself inside of her.

The rest of the evening was almost surreal to Quinn. Rafael was tender and attentive to her every need. He couldn't stop touching her. He caressed her knee and thigh under the table at dinner. He would lean in and whisper in her ear, sending spine-tingling chills down her back. The two couples from San Diego were loud and seemed determined to get as drunk as possible. They downed shot after shot of tequila. It was with relief that Quinn and Rafael bid them goodbye shortly before midnight.

Back at the house, Rafael took Quinn by the hand and led her silently up the stairs to the master bedroom. From there she followed him up a small spiral staircase that opened onto the rooftop. The moon rode high in the sky and the lights of Guadalajara twinkled around them. Potted trees and flowers decorated the concrete slab. In the dimness, Quinn noticed a telescope in one corner.

Rafael led her to a broad sofa. There was a bar nearby and he handed her a snifter of Benedictine and brandy. Still not saying a word, Rafael slowly untied the neck of Quinn's dress. They made love several times that night on the rooftop. Rafael explored every inch of Quinn's body with his tongue, his mouth, and his hands. He would tease her to the brink of orgasm, then let the heat subside, only to start all over again.

The night was beginning to lose its hold on the lovers when Rafael finally released Quinn in a crescendo of unbridled passion. Completely spent, Quinn lay in Rafael's arms; her head nestled against his smooth chest. Dreamily, Quinn heard the sleepy chirruping of a cricket stirring. The trees began to rustle as birds began their daily activity. In the distance, Quinn could have sworn she heard the lonely howling of a coyote or a wolf. "*El lobo*," she murmured softly, before falling asleep.

The following two days with Rafael were filled with laughter and adventure. Rafael took Quinn out to a gated equestrian estate area near Lake Chapala where he owned a townhome and boarded his three thorough-bred horses. Just like when he was giving Quinn dive lessons in Cozumel onboard the *Vanora*, Rafael was a monument of patience as he taught Quinn how to ride English and jump hurdles. They made love in the townhouse, in the stables, and even by a stream out in the meadow where they'd ridden the horses.

Rafael was an experienced lover. He was thoughtful and considerate and seemed to delight in Quinn's very presence. He was also the perfect host; charming, laughing, entertaining. *But,* she reflected, as she packed her bag on her last day in Guadalajara, *it's like there's something missing in him. He truly is an enigma. He's holding something back from me. He hasn't once mentioned his children. He's never even asked if I was on the pill and he hasn't volunteered that he's had a vasectomy.*

Rafael was unable to accompany Quinn to the jet at the airport. He called for his driver, then took Quinn aside. "*Querida,* I can't tell you how much I have enjoyed having you here with me." He squeezed her tightly and whispered into her hair. "You give me life. You give me reason to live."

It wasn't until Quinn was in the air that she realized Rafael hadn't made any mention of whether he would be back on the *Vanora* soon, or if he would invite her back to Guadalajara. *Neither of us has once said the "L" word. Am I in love with Rafael Santiago? Is he in love with me?* Quinn reflected as the small powerful jet soared through the twilight sky. As brief as her time had been with Noah there had been an intensity and emotional connection with him that was definitely missing in her relationship with Rafael.

Quinn was extremely attracted to the owner of the *Vanora*. She knew his feelings were reciprocal. There was an underlying tenderness in the way he made love to her. But, something was lacking. Some essential sharing and bonding. She and Noah had grown close on their night watches. They'd shared intimate knowledge of each other long before they made love in the lagoon.

Oh, boy. I sure hope this weekend was worth the hell I know I'm going to go through when I get back to the boat. Quinn stirred restlessly in her seat. *Diego is going to be fit to be tied.*

Diego was in no shape to torture Quinn—or anyone else for that matter—when she boarded the *Vanora* that evening. A stranger was sitting in the cockpit when Quinn tossed her bag onto the deck, then climbed up the steps. She noticed immediately and with relief that the mast and windshield had been repaired. Quinn could hear Marcus and Marnie talking in the galley; the clatter of pots and pans told her they were making dinner.

The thin, slightly built man rose to pick up Quinn's bag and hand it to her. "Hey, how you doing? You must be the cook." His eyes were restless in his smooth, bland face. "I'm Yoshua. Diego hired me as a line handler for the transit." He had one of those smiles that never reached his eyes, Quinn noticed. She introduced herself, then said she'd better check in with the captain and crew. Quinn suddenly realized she was having an experience she'd never had before. For the first time in her life, she'd met someone that she instinctively disliked on sight.

"Hey gang," Quinn greeted Marcus and Marnie. "What's for dinner?" She laughed. "Now *that's* a switch!"

The sailors hugged her with enthusiasm. "Glad you're back," Marcus was grinning from ear to ear. "I'm no gourmet chef, but," he gestured to Marnie, "she's even worse."

"Where's Diego?" Quinn wasn't eager to confront the captain but she figured she may as well get it over with.

"Oh, man, you missed the shit." Marnie suddenly looked grave. "Why don't you stow your bag and we'll fill you in after dinner."

Dinner was nothing more than bean and cheese burritos with sides of rice and beans. Quinn doused her plate with hot salsa to add flavor to the unimaginative and unseasoned meal. Yoshua ate pretty much in silence, then excused himself to go into Colon to take care of some last minute business.

The *Vanora* was scheduled for a morning transit. They'd be up after one of the cruise ships that regularly sailed the canal. Marcus mentioned that the toll for the *Vanora* was almost eight hundred dollars. "I understand the cruise ships have to pay upwards of $180,000 in tolls each time they sail through." Quinn whistled through her teeth.

Once the three original crew members were alone, Marcus clued Quinn in on all that had transpired in her three-day absence. "You knew we had to hire another line handler. So Diego hired this Yoshua dude he found at the yacht club. A pilot will be coming onboard in the morning, too. Can't transit without one."

"We've been busy." Marnie interjected. "Men were crawling all over for a couple days. They repaired the mast and replaced the windshield." She took a long drink from a bottle of beer, then glanced sideways at Quinn. "I am dying to hear about who's been crawling all over you and how was it?"

Quinn's face turned red. She glared at Marnie in mock disgust, then urged Marcus to carry on.

"Diego's been busy with the APC paying fees, booking a pilot and getting us scheduled in, so we weren't really worried when he didn't show up the night before last. He wasn't here yesterday morning either, but Marnie and I went into Colon with some other crew members we met at the club." Marcus shook his head. "Man, that place is wild, Quinn. Don't even bother."

Quinn stirred impatiently in her seat. "Well, what happened with Diego? Where is he now?"

"Diego got mugged. Or so he says. He ended up with a concussion and was in the hospital overnight. He looks like someone beat the living crap out of him. I guess he's got a couple cracked ribs, too."

Quinn expressed her shock. As much as she didn't like the captain, she certainly hadn't ever wished something like this on him. "Where is he now?"

"Oh, he's in the owner's cabin nursing his wounds with a bottle of bourbon. I'm hoping he's going to be sober enough to get us through the canal tomorrow. At least we'll have a pilot onboard."

Later, after Quinn had whipped her neglected galley back into shape, she asked Marnie what Marcus meant when he insinuated Diego might have lied about the mugging. Marnie shrugged. "Marcus was thinking that Diego actually might have gotten on the bad side of a pimp. Sounds like something he'd do. Get a piece of ass, then not want to pay for it."

"Oh, that's bad," Quinn grimaced. Just thinking about Diego's sex life made her feel slightly ill. "What do you guys think about Yoshua? He seems kind of slick to me. He never looks you in the eye."

Again, Marnie shrugged. "He's an odd one. But, he's only going to be onboard for two nights. Tonight and tomorrow night. It takes an average of ten hours to get through all six locks—providing there isn't a lot of traffic."

"Has anyone checked on Diego lately?" Quinn was worried. What if the doctors had given him prescription pain pills and he was mixing alcohol with them? The crew needed Diego Reyes to get to the Pacific Ocean. They needed him to get through Central America and safely to San Diego.

Marnie snorted. "Be my guest. I'm going to go help Marcus get the extra dock lines ready for tomorrow. See ya in the morning, glory."

Quinn tiptoed to the door of the aft stateroom. She wasn't ready to face Diego quite yet, but she wanted to make sure he was all right. Carefully, she opened the door a tiny crack, then sighed with relief. She could hear the captain's loud and sonorous snoring. Quinn closed the door and made her way to the forepeak.

The familiar cabin felt like home. Quinn scribbled in her journal for over an hour before taking a quick shower and crawling into her bunk. She wondered what Rafael was doing. Was he asleep in his king-size bed? Was he on the roof gazing at the stars and remembering their smoldering, steamy lovemaking? Or was he in his study brooding over the loss of his wife and children, a snifter of brandy in one long, elegant hand?

What if I never hear from him again? What if he simply has us deliver the boat to San Diego and that's it? Quinn fell asleep, a troubled frown on her face.

CHAPTER FIFTEEN

The sight of Diego's battered face the next morning made Quinn wince. His bottom lip was broken and scabbed over. The left eye, the brown one, was puffy to the point where it was a mere slit. This was doubly disconcerting since now he was looking at the world with one solid black iris. He had a dark bruise on one high cheekbone. Quinn could tell his side was bothering him by the way he carefully lowered himself onto the captain's chair in the wheelhouse.

Silently, she brought him a mug of hot coffee and a plate of scrambled eggs and sausage. Diego's expressionless midnight eye bored into her. "Welcome back, *cocinera*. You look as though you thoroughly enjoyed your stay at the hands of *Senor* Santiago." He leered at her.

Quinn changed the subject. "I heard about what happened, Diego. I'd like you to know I'm glad it wasn't worse. You could have been killed." Her sincerity must have been evident in her voice. Diego gave her a measuring look, then nodded his head in appreciation.

The *Vanora* motored into position to enter the three locks leading to Gatun Lake. The pilot had joined them shortly after breakfast. He was a portly and cheerful fellow who really seemed to enjoy his job. His name was Roger. He explained the working of the canal locks to the crew as they approached. Long, steep locomotive tracks ran along the outer sides of the two-lane locks. The locomotives were used for the larger container and cruise vessels. Cables were attached from large ships to the locomotives to keep the massive boats aligned and tow them to the next lock.

"As you might know, the French began construction of the Panama Canal in 1881. However, their attempts failed and the United States Corps of Engineers took over from 1904 to 1914. If you were to tour Panama by auto, you would see many barracks and housing projects built during that time for the workers. Many are used as homes still to this day."

There was a break in his narrative as he assigned each of the crew a line to handle. Quinn and Marnie had the bow lines and Marcus and Yoshua the stern. There were two other yachts that were rafting up side by side with the *Vanora* to go through the locks. After the fenders were set and the lines from the thirty-seven foot sloop next to them were cleated to the *Vanora's* deck, Roger made sure the crew was ready to catch the half-inch leader lines the dock workers threw down at them. He instructed them to tie their respective lines to the leader line which the canal workers hauled back to the top.

As the fresh water from the lake was pumped into the chamber, the *Vanora* and her two companions rose until they were even with the next lock. It was the crew's responsibility to keep the tension tight on the lines attaching them to land. The heavy steel gates were opened and the yachts moved into the next chamber. After reaching the third, they were level with Gatun Lake. They would reverse the whole process on the west side of the Isthmus of Panama. The *Vanora* would be lowered until she was level with the Pacific Ocean.

It took almost an hour for the *Vanora* to go through the Gatun locks. The crew had to maintain their stations and Quinn chatted with the family on the sailboat to the starboard side. A sizable catamaran was rafted up on the other side of them. Quinn only had glimpses of four or five darkly tanned and long-haired crewmen.

Once out in the lake, the respective crews freed the lines connecting their yachts to one another. Diego had Marcus take over the helm as the *Vanora* began the seven-hour motor journey through the Panama Canal. Quinn offered Roger some snacks and refreshments. Everyone but Yoshua and Diego sat in the cockpit and listened to the pilot as he explained the dynamics of the locks.

"On the Atlantic side the water pumped in from the lake lifts the ships twenty-six meters above sea level until they are even with the lake and the land. On the other side, the Pacific, the ships are lowered again to meet the sea. Only gravity is used to drain the water to the lower levels. Each lockage uses about one-hundred and ninety-seven million liters of fresh water, which is flushed out to sea."

"Why don't they use ocean water?' Quinn wanted to know.

Roger smiled. "Good question, *senorita*. The salt water would have to be pumped up from the level of the sea, 26 meters to the level of the lake. To install such a system would be costly indeed. Also, the salt water would continually corrode the lock mechanisms and destroy all this vegetation that you are seeing."

The weather was perfect. Not too humid and the sun was shining. Quinn knew how suddenly that could change. The first day in Panama, she'd felt rain drops when she could have sworn there wasn't a cloud in the sky. She gazed across the lake at the lush foliage that surrounded the famous waterway. The jungle was thick and dense and Quinn had a mental image of how easy it would be to get lost in its tangled and smothering grasp. She shuddered.

Roger yawned hugely. "Enjoy the scenery, *amigos*. If you don't mind, I'd like to find a spot where I can take a nap."

Marcus, in his usual big-hearted fashion, offered the pilot the use of his cabin. Quinn and Marnie decided to take an hour or so to sunbathe. They settled on the foredeck near Quinn's cabin. Quinn brought out pillows so they could get more comfortable.

"Dish it up, girl," Marnie was on her stomach, leaning on her elbows. "I'm *so* dying to hear about your trip to Guadalajara. And I mean *all* about it."

Over time, on watches, Quinn had pretty well told Marnie all there was to tell about her relationship with Noah and about the gorgeous, but psycho, Lydia who claimed she was carrying his baby. Marnie in turn had shared bits and pieces of her life with Quinn. She'd been brutally raped at seventeen and as a consequence had a hysterectomy.

"Not that the rape had anything to do with my sexual orientation. I was raped *because* of it by some gang-bangers in Harlem. And, I was hanging with the wrong crowd. That's when I escaped to the sea."

This disclosure had led to Quinn telling Marnie about her own near rape experience in Boston with the two frat brothers, Andy and Eric. "All because I had this weird urge to do some coke. I got so sick of drugs and the consequences. My friend Cyndi's life is a mess now because of her druggie boyfriend, Joey. What's up with that? What's the attraction?" For a moment Quinn looked frightened. "One of the cooks at the restaurant where I used to work started doing meth. Now, that stuff scares me. It alters people."

Marnie agreed. "I read about a woman whose kid went ape shit on it and killed somebody. She said she truly believes meth is one of the plagues the Bible predicts will cover the earth in the last days."

Quinn arms prickled with gooseflesh. "Let's change the subject, shall we?"

As they lay basking in the tropical sun, Quinn reflected that she and Marnie had a lot more in common than Quinn ever thought they would. She was glad. It was nice to have a female friend in the sailing circuit. Even if the friend was gay. Again, Quinn's conservative parents flashed through her mind. She giggled.

"That good, huh?" Marnie sat up.

"I was thinking of something else, but, yeah. It was that good and then some."

Quinn was reserved on the sex part but she told Marnie everything else about her trip to Guadalajara. About Rafael's many homes, his horses, his friends and of course, Quinn told her about his former wife and two children. Marnie was as puzzled as she that Rafael never mentioned his family or that he could no longer sire children.

"So where does it go from here? Do you want kids someday? Would you ever consider living in Mexico with Rafael?"

"I love children! Someday, when I settle down, I'd like to have two; a boy and a girl." Quinn grew thoughtful. "I'm not sure I'm in love with Rafael. I'm totally infatuated with him, I guess. But, then, there's Noah. Something's got to be resolved there before anything happens."

She would have elaborated more if Marcus hadn't come forward to join them.

"Well, you missed all the action." He tossed a beach towel on the deck beside Quinn.

"Yeah, what?" She scooted over to make room for him.

"I guess Diego isn't too fond of that Yoshua, either. I heard him go off on him just now. I don't understand Spanish but it sounded like he was giving the dude a real reamin'."

Marcus was interrupted as a Turkish freighter ship passed slowly off the port bow. Several deckhands were leaning over the rails, whistling and calling to the women on the *Vanora*. Two of them held video cameras. It was obvious they were filming Quinn and Marcie in their bathing suits. Quinn laughed and blew a few kisses at the men. Marnie casually flipped them the bird.

"What'd he do to make Diego so mad?" Quinn was curious.

"I dunno. I think he was pissed because he saw Yoshua coming out of the master stateroom. Yoshua's been kind of roaming around on the boat. Exploring, I guess. Can't blame him, I was curious, too, when I first came onboard."

Quinn sighed. "Diego at his best isn't the most pleasant person. His injuries have made him more irritable. Although, I don't want that Yoshua anywhere near my cabin. He definitely gives me the creeps."

"Yeah? You've at least got to give the little guy some credit. Sounded to me like he wasn't at all that bothered by Diego's attitude. He kind of blew him off."

The cruise through the lake and through the canal toward the Gaillard or Culebra Cut, and the Pedro Miguel Locks, was smooth and uneventful. The scenery was green and restful after the heaving and tumultuous ocean. Quinn did notice a difference in Yoshua's demeanor. He seemed almost defiant. Diego didn't show his face much. When he did he was even more sullen than before.

The pilot woke up around four in the afternoon while they were motoring through the Gaillard Cut. Roger explained that this stretch of the canal represented fifteen percent of the waterway's total length.

"The cut was the most challenging of all the engineering marvels that went into constructing the Panama Canal. There were many mud slides and the heat and disease certainly took their toll on the laborers." Roger was enjoying a mug of root beer and an egg salad sandwich Quinn had served him.

"Rock drills, dynamite, and almost one hundred steam shovels were used to remove over ninety-six million cubic yards of earth and rock to lower the floor of the site to within forty feet of sea level. If all the material that was removed in the construction of the canal was placed on railroad cars it would circle the earth four times."

Quinn shook her head in wonder. It was at that precise moment she made up her mind. She was going to sail her way around the world. She remembered reading how sailors who sailed across the Equator would get their left ear pierced as a sign of their accomplishment. Sailing the Panama Canal struck her as a similar goal any true sailor would aspire to.

Roger continued. "Of great interest, as you will see once we get closer to the Pedro Miguel Locks, is how the canal dissects the great Continental Divide. It will be obvious to the eye as we cruise by."

In an effort to keep things simple for the crew since there was one more set of locks to negotiate, Quinn baked a chicken noodle casserole for dinner. She tossed a green salad and set out some rolls and butter with paper plates and napkins. Anyone could help themselves to something to eat at their convenience.

It was almost dark when the *Vanora* entered the first lock on the Pacific side. This time the yacht was being lowered to sea level. A tour boat was rafted to the port side. The only occupants were the smiling captain and his plump, dark-haired daughter. As the *Vanora* slowly sank with the water draining from the chamber, Quinn let her hand slide down the cool bumpy cement wall. She closed her eyes and thought of the countless men and women who had made enormous sacrifices to build this man-made wonder of the world. She marveled at how in less than ten hours, the *Vanora* had crossed from the Atlantic to the Pacific Ocean.

Roger interrupted her reverie. "Be sure to pay attention to the last gates. These had to be the tallest and heaviest of all the miter gates in order to handle the extreme tide fluctuations of the Pacific Ocean. They are twenty-five meters high and each one weighs seven-hundred-and-thirty tons." He added that all six locks had a total of forty pairs of miter gates and each set had to undergo maintenance every ten or fifteen years. They were removed and taken to a dry dock on the Atlantic side.

The Control House on the center wall of the highest chamber was well lit. Sound carried easily over the water and Quinn could hear the line handlers along the wall laughing and joking. Forty minutes later, they were through the last lock. The *Vanora* was heading toward the Bridge of the Americas, then out into the Pacific Ocean. Diego had topped off both fuel tanks at Cristobal. There were plenty of provisions and fresh produce onboard from when Quinn and Marnie had shopped in Cozumel before the hurricane.

A small cutter had picked up the pilot, Roger, once the yacht was past the last lock. With a wave and an "adios" he'd jumped easily from the deck of the *Vanora* onto the bobbing power boat. There was only one more stop to make. Quinn knew from Marcus that Diego had prearranged to pay Yoshua a hundred dollars, then drop the freelance line handler off at the Balboa Yacht Club at the end of the transit.

Much to the surprise and consternation of the crew, without a word, Diego motored right past the yacht club. Yoshua was in the galley getting a plate of food.

"What gives, Diego? Aren't you dropping off what's-his-bucket?" Marcus didn't sound too happy.

Diego took his sweet time answering. The lighted arch of the impressive Bridge of the Americas was glowing larger and brighter. The skylight of Panama City on the port side looked like something from a cosmopolitan fantasy. Diego fiddled with the helm, then spoke in a voice that brooked no argument.

"The decision is mine. I can use him." He eyed each sailor individually for a moment. "There will be no discussion, *tambien*. You got that?"

It wasn't too much longer before the crew of the *Vanora* got it. They would understand Diego's mindset and motivation once and for all. It would prove to be the most harrowing experience of any of their lives. It would also set into motion a whole new series of events for Quinn and her two buddies. Just as the core of Hurricane Cecelia had grown exponentially; fed by a series of meteorological events, so too had a bitter seed thrived inside Diego Reyes. Fed by circumstances out of anyone's control and fueled by his pride and arrogance, Diego had made decisions without regard to the consequences.

In his mind the lives of his crew were, if not dispensable, as meaningless as the many women he had used and abused in a lifetime of self-indulgent vengeance. Diego Reyes hated the world. In particular he had a deep hatred of his own country and of the United States. He was out to prove that he was superior to the two governments that had caused him unmitigated grief and bitter loss. Nothing was going to get in his way. Not Quinn, not Marnie, not Marcus. And most certainly, not the shifty-eyed line handler, Yoshua.

CHAPTER SIXTEEN

◆•◆◆•◆

Morale aboard the *Vanora* plunged within the next few days. Diego became more tyrannical and hostile. Yoshua seemed unfazed by his lack of popularity. He had a smug air about him that disturbed Quinn. "Do you think Yoshua's got something on Diego?" Quinn was on watch with Marcus. "Something he's maybe blackmailing him with? It's obvious the two can barely tolerate one another."

"Who knows? I'm just waiting to see who tosses who overboard first." Marcus was manually steering the yacht under the bimini in the cockpit. It had been raining quite a bit but it was a warm precipitation. "I wonder why Yoshua keeps disappearing. He says he's keeping an eye on the engines and that slow leak next to the propeller shaft. Diego's making himself scarce lately, too."

"Maybe they're trying to avoid each other." Quinn sighed. "Too bad we can't afford that luxury."

Marnie had proven earlier that she was as tough as she looked. The *Vanora* had cleared the Gulf of Panama and was about ten miles offshore heading north to Costa Rica. The crew had been lucky. The wind was abundant but not blowing so hard they had to reef the main. They were cruising comfortably on a starboard tack at an average of six knots. Lunch had been served and the galley cleared when Quinn heard a commotion from the crew quarters.

Marnie was shouting and it sounded like someone had kicked or slammed a cabin door shut. Quinn raced across the main salon and down the amidships stairs. She skidded to a stop. Quinn could hardly believe her eyes. Marnie had Yoshua pinned to the bulkhead with one hand around his

116

throat. In the other hand was a knife. Marnie was waving it under the scared line handler's nose.

"You wormy little prick!" Marnie pressed closer to Yoshua. "You sneaky piece of shit."

"Marnie!" Quinn stood a few feet away. "What are you doing? Put that knife away, for heaven's sake!"

The knife Marnie was wielding was a small but potentially deadly rigging knife. The crew carried them on watches in the event a line got snagged or tangled. Each knife was also equipped with a screwdriver and a long, pointed marlin spike. It was actually the marlin spike that Marnie was holding perilously close to Yoshua's eye.

"I've about had it with this guy. Sneaking around. He was in my cabin for freak's sake!"

Marnie snarled at the cowering man, "And I *really* don't like your attitude, dude. You act like the cat that's swallowed the canary. I want to know what's going on."

Before Yoshua could respond, Diego's voice filled the small hallway. "Release him, Marnie. *Now!*"

Reluctantly, Marnie let go her vice-like grip on Yoshua's throat. She still held the marlin spike pointed at him. "Why is this scum still on our boat, Diego? It's no secret you can't stand him, either."

Diego's bruises had begun to fade and his injured eye was almost back to normal. The fading yellow discoloration around his eyes and nose somehow made him look even more feral. He was standing so close to Quinn in the crowded corridor that she could smell his musky cologne and the faint odor of perspiration. It suddenly crossed her mind that the captain of the *Vanora* didn't dislike Yoshua; he was afraid of him.

"Really, Diego, Marnie's right. Why is he onboard? We didn't need an extra deckhand after the canal."

"I will not be questioned by the likes you. Either of you." Diego was livid. "And you," he spat at Yoshua, "you come with me."

Yoshua pushed himself away from the wall and stepped around Marnie. His face was pale but he had a half-smirk on his lips. Silently, the two women watched as he followed the rigid back of Diego Reyes up the stairs to the main salon.

"Marnie, jeez. I thought for a minute you were going to take out his eye." Quinn looked troubled.

"Naw, I only wanted to scare the little wuss." Marnie snapped the rigging knife shut, then pocketed it. "But if I catch him sniffing around my cabin again, I may just cut off his damn balls." Quinn laughed, then shook her head and went back to the galley. She could hear Diego and Yoshua arguing in the master stateroom.

Later, when Quinn went topside, Marcus stood up and stretched. "I could hear Diego and Yoshua yelling at each other after that little encounter with Marnie today. Diego seems to have moved into the owner's cabin for this leg of the trip. I could hear them through the open hatch back here. No love lost between those two, none at all. Well, I'm going to check the radar. Keep an eye out, okay, Quinn?"

Quinn laughed as she took the helm. Yoshua had certainly come close to literally having to keep an eye out. Marnie came around the side of the cabin right then. She'd been on the foredeck checking on the lines and shackles. She sat beside Quinn, then glanced around to make sure no one was in earshot.

"I don't like one bit what's going on around here. I was thinking we need to make up a story so that Diego has to take us into port. We could call your new buddy, Rafael, from shore and ask him to do something about Yoshua being onboard. It wouldn't be a bad idea if you could even get him to replace Diego. I wonder if Hank's available now. He could certainly handle this boat."

Quinn was silent for a moment. "Right off the bat, I don't know Rafael's cell or home phone number. You realize what you're talking about is real life mutiny, don't you?"

Marnie was caught off guard. "That sounds a bit extreme, baby doll. What we've got going on here is a crazy-ass captain and a squirrely stranger onboard. I'd call getting rid of them common sense—not mutiny."

Marcus came up with a pair of binoculars and went to the stern. He scanned the horizon several times before joining the women in the cockpit.

"We've got a few blips on the screen. Looks like there are two boats a ways behind us. One of them is moving pretty damn fast. There's what looks like a container ship about even with us off the port side. Everybody keep a sharp lookout tonight. We don't want to get run over."

It was dark by the time dinner was ready. The yacht was on a different tack and the wind had died quite a bit. Diego started the engines to recharge the batteries. He had the main dropped and they were cruising along at a good clip. For the first time in two days, the entire crew sat down to dinner at the same time.

Quinn had made chicken and dumplings with spinach salad and cornbread. Diego and Yoshua seated themselves at opposite ends of the table. Quinn sat by Marcus and across from Marnie. The food was delicious but the conversation lagged until Marcus mentioned that he thought there was a high amount of traffic in the area.

Diego was immediately alert. "Why didn't you notify me about this earlier, *amigo?*" Yoshua quit shoveling the food into his mouth and stared at Diego; his usually restless eyes fixed steadily on the captain's face.

"I was going to mention it, Captain, but I haven't seen you until now. I logged it and I'm on top of it." Quinn could feel the tension building between the two men.

"How about I make some dessert?" She tried to change the subject.

"Not tonight, *cocinera*," Diego stood up from the table. "Make some coffee, and make it strong. I want all of you as alert as possible."

The night air was cool and the rain heavy but intermittent. The seas were medium with rolling swells. Diego assigned Quinn and Yoshua to the first watch; Marnie and Marcus the second. He showed Quinn the blips on the radar and told her to keep an eye on them. The larger blip, the container ship, seemed to be running parallel with the *Vanora*. Two smaller green dots were trailing behind the yacht.

"These bother me," Diego pointed at the dots. "This area is known for its drug smugglers and even the rare pirates. A yacht like the *Vanora* would be a prize indeed. Her electronics alone would be worth an attack." He motioned with his hand at the impressive display of navigation, communications, and media equipment.

"There is also the threat of kidnapping and holding crews for ransom. I do not believe you would want to fall into the hands of such people as these. You would be a prize indeed, *gringa*." He glanced sideways at Quinn with a look that made her want to get outside and away from him immediately.

Standing watch with Yoshua was wearing. He was fidgety and kept asking Quinn to repeat herself. He spoke fairly fluent English so Quinn, in an effort to keep Yoshua focused and also entertain herself, asked him to refresh her Spanish vocabulary.

Throughout the watch, Quinn made a conscientious effort to keep track of the other vessels in the area. She checked the radar every ten or fifteen minutes. She also asked Yoshua to periodically scan the dark, rain enshrouded night surrounding them with the binoculars. Quinn went to monitor the radar one last time before her watch ended. She noticed that the larger blip had moved well past the *Vanora* and was no longer a concern.

One of the two smaller vessels seemed much closer; well within the three mile range denoted on the radar screen. Quinn was debating on whether to alert the captain when a hand closed around the nape of her neck. Quinn spun around. Marcus pressed a finger to his lips. He motioned for Quinn to follow him into the galley.

Under the guise of helping Quinn prepare hot beverages and snacks for the next watch, Marcus expressed his unease. "I did a little snooping of my own, Quinn. I checked the bilges and the engine room. I also checked the propeller shaft." He reached around her for a croissant. "Unless I'm sorely mistaken or just plain old blind, there's no leak back there and it doesn't appear there ever was one, either."

"Oh, I don't like this one little bit." Quinn bit her lower lip nervously. "I guess it's time I shared with you what Marnie told me in Cozumel." Quinn related the story about how Marnie's brother had found out Diego was in Cozumel earlier on the sly. She also told him about Diego's seedy companion at the time; Luiz Montoya.

"Something's definitely up and it stinks to high heaven. I wish you would have told me earlier." Marcus had a hurt look on his face.

Quinn gave him a contrite hug. "It was Marnie's idea to say mum about it for a while and I gave her my word. I'm sorry, Marcus. It's not that I don't trust you. I'd trust you with my life, ole buddy."

"How touching!" Diego had somehow sneaked up on them.

"All of this talk about trust." His hair and clothes were damp; he'd obviously been out on the deck. "Isn't that the lesson I have been trying to teach you all along? That you must trust your captain?" Diego shook his head. Droplets of water fell from his hair onto his prominent cheeks. For an eerie moment Quinn thought they looked like teardrops. She blinked her eyes to rid herself of the illusion.

"May I ask what has caused this moment of deep sincerity?" He looked from Quinn to Marcus. Both of them remained silent. "But, of course. I didn't think you would let me in on your little secret." Diego shrugged. "It is of no consequence to me." With that, he turned and went up the stairs to the cockpit.

"I'd better get Marnie up." Marcus poured two mugs of coffee. "And you'd better get some rest. My radar's up. I think the three of us need to stay on our toes."

Quinn agreed, then mentioned that Marnie had an idea Marcus might be interested in hearing. "Tell her we talked. I'm sure she'll be open to telling you what she's thinking."

There was a light mist in the air when Quinn made her way forward to her cabin. She took a hot shower and washed her hair. She was bone weary and filled with unease. Quinn blew dry her hair, then updated her journal. Still restless, she pulled out Noah's amulets and Rafael's note from beneath her mattress.

The two men, *my two lovers?* Quinn thought with an air of odd detachment, were as different as the separate cultures that defined them. Noah, with his carefree, boyish charm was steeped in generations of superstition. He was one of four illegitimate children of a Canadian businessman who had a legit family in Canada, but who also supported and spent time in Jamaica with Noah's family; his mother Beatrice, his sister and twin brothers. The Canadian family had no idea the West Indies family existed.

Noah's Aunt Sharmaine was an obeah priestess. She'd been instrumental in putting her nephew through a cleansing ritual to eliminate the curse of the chupacabra that Noah believed his former lover, Lydia, had placed upon him. When Noah tried to break up with the insanely possessive and jealous Puerto Rican woman, Lydia had gone so far as to have her brother drug Noah and brand her initials on his penis. At the same time, she had Angel tattoo a crude rendering of the mythical chupacabra on Noah's forearm; hence the curse.

Rafael Santiago believed he soared above the common ilk, Quinn reflected as she read again,

Love the eagle that soars over your head and wishes to carry you along on his wings.

A millionaire many times over, Rafael did indeed live in a rarified atmosphere; private jet, luxury yacht, multiple homes and condos spread across two countries. He was an aristocrat through and through. His grandfather had founded one of the largest pharmaceutical companies in the Americas. His mother was a respected professor of geology and ancient artifacts.

Rafael exuded charm and confidence. He was handsome and articulate, and a master equestrian. He was also a passionate and demanding lover.

Quinn's face grew warm at the memory of the first time they made love in the study of his Guadalajara home. Yet, there was something emotionally elusive about him, something that Quinn couldn't quite define. She shook her head, then tucked the two mementos back beneath her mattress.

The motion of the cabin began to increase. *A squall*, Quinn thought as she climbed into her bunk. Just to be on the safe side she hooked up the security webbing. "Rockabye, baby," she hummed to herself with a little giggle. Before long Quinn succumbed to the undulating motion. She would never in her life sleep as well anywhere else as she did in the arms of her beloved ocean.

CHAPTER SEVENTEEN

"I didn't mean for it to happen," Quinn was standing at the bow of the *Sapphire II* in Miami. She was talking to Gail. "I didn't mean for any of this to happen."

"Yeah, right, Quinn," Gail was laughing. "You're so holier than thou. Thought you weren't going to do like I did. Remember? *Crewing not screwing?*"

Quinn could faintly hear Noah singing. *"Rum goat liver, good to make mannish water; mix it up sweet, you make it for your daughter."*

She tried to climb aboard the *Sapphire II* but the yacht was rearing and plunging like a stallion out of control. Gail's laughter grew louder and almost maniacal. "You screw, too. You screwed the crew!" She kept repeating in a singsong voice that was driving Quinn mad.

"Stop it! Stop!" Quinn covered her ears. She had to fight a strong urge to push Gail into the roiling ocean. Noah's voice faded away and Quinn felt such a sudden sense of loss it was as though she was drowning. Frantic, she began to flail her arms and kick her legs. Quinn woke up with her heart pounding so hard in her chest she thought she might possibly have a heart attack. A burst of fresh air flooded the cabin as the overhead hatch flew open with violent force.

Startled, Quinn looked up and found she was staring down the barrel of an automatic weapon. A dark shadow dropped into the cabin. *"Arriba!"* The grating, raspy voice commanding her to rise was as cold and hard as the weapon that was now digging painfully into the base of her throat. Too shocked to do more than obey, Quinn swung her legs over the side of the bunk and shakily stood up.

123

The intruder grunted and motioned for her to precede him up the steps and onto the deck. The *Vanora* was bobbing aimlessly in the ocean. The spreader and mast lights were on. Quinn could see the silhouettes of too many people in the wheelhouse. She stumbled over something at the base of the mast. Reality washed over her with the coldness of a subterranean ocean current. In the yellow glow cast by the two large overhead lamps, Quinn could see the motionless body of Marcus. A stain as dark as chocolate covered half of his face. Her brain registered the fact that it was blood. Then, her mind shut down like a steel trap.

When Quinn and her captor entered the wheelhouse, Yoshua walked over and grabbed a handful of her hair. Pulling her behind him, he went over to where Marnie and Diego were sitting. Roughly, he pushed Quinn down next to the captain. Diego, too, had blood stains on his face and on the front of his once immaculate white shirt. Marnie sat ramrod straight. The look on her face was grim, but her eyes seemed lit from within. An angry looking welt ran almost the entire length of her cheek.

"Look who has joined the party."

A heavyset man rose from the far corner of the stifling cabin. He walked over and cocked his head slightly to one side. "Diego tells me you are very special to Rafael Santiago, a man of much importance in Mexico."

He reached out and caressed Quinn's cheek with his palm. Her skin crawled at his touch. His hand was soft and fleshy. As if sensing her utter disgust, he pulled his hand back, then slapped Quinn with such force that for hours after her face felt like one big toothache.

Marnie flew off the couch. She was hissing and spitting like a cat whose tail had been stepped on. Diego half rose and caught her by the waist of her pants. The man with the Uzzi stepped forward and with one swift movement hit the enraged woman on the side of the head with the butt of his gun. Marnie crumpled to the ground. Her spiky dark hair matted instantly with blood.

The man who had struck Quinn lifted one heavily bejeweled hand and slowly waved his forefinger back and forth. "No, no, no. We must stay in control."

He signaled for the gunman to retreat, then made a small formal bow as he introduced himself to the crew of the *Vanora*. Quinn remembered instantly hearing about him. This was Luiz Montoya; the man of shadows, the drug-dealing overlord of Cozumel. He was the man skulking around the island with Diego some months back. She noticed a pale white scar that neatly bisected his thick nose. Luiz was the passenger who had gone through the windshield during the accident with Diego near the ruins of San Gervasio. *Too bad it didn't kill him,* Quinn thought with a coldness she'd never suspected she had in her.

"What did you do to Marcus? Is he dead or alive?" Quinn was now kneeling beside Marnie. "We need some ice here."

Quinn was relieved that her voice was steady. She didn't want the loathsome man standing over her to be aware that she was feeling extremely vulnerable at the moment. Quinn was still in the scanty two-piece pajamas she'd worn to bed earlier. Her bare legs prickled with gooseflesh and she wasn't wearing a bra beneath the cotton sleeveless top.

"So far, both your friends will be suffering only major headaches. Go ahead, get your ice."

Diego rose and offered to go to the galley instead of Quinn.

"No! You sit right there. Let the woman do it." Luiz glared at the captain. "You are no longer in command of this ship, Diego."

Quinn sensed the men's eyes on her as she rose and walked unsteadily across the salon to the galley. Her ears were still ringing from the hard blow. She put ice in a large baggie. She was grateful she could carry it in such a way as to block the men from further ogling her breasts. When Quinn gently put the bag alongside of Marnie's head, the stricken sailor moaned and fluttered her eyes.

The companionway door opened and Marcus stumbled in, followed by two hulking figures. The muscular men had bald heads and were heavily tattooed. They looked and acted like professional body guards. Their eyes were as cold and distant as their expressionless faces. To Quinn they looked almost inhuman; *these people are cold-blooded mercenaries or worse,* she thought. The first tendrils of real fear began to uncurl in her stomach. *I think we're in seriously deep* shit, *as Marnie would say.*

"Now that we are all here," Luiz clasped his manicured fingers together, "shall we get down to business?"

He motioned for the crew members to sit side by side on the salon couch. Marcus seemed dazed. He had a nasty gash on his head. Marnie was in obvious pain but it didn't stop her from snarling at one of the bald hulks when he put his hand on her arm to push her onto the couch. Diego sat tensely beside Quinn. He kept darting looks at Yoshua with eyes full of murderous rage.

"Luiz, I had no idea that this *peon*, this *pendajo*, was trying to cut in on your trade." Diego's tone was conciliatory, yet he still retained an air of superiority.

"I'm not cutting in on anyone!" Yoshua smiled ingratiatingly at Luiz. "I saw the moment to make some money and get out of Panama. One kilo of *cocaina* is nothing to a man of your stature, *Senor* Montoya."

"Yes, that part is true," Luiz chuckled. He had a pocketknife in one hand and was picking at his polished nails. "However, *amigo*, you are a liar."

He motioned to the meaner-looking of the two men who had shepherded Marcus into the cabin. "Jose, please bring to me the 'kilo' of *cocaina* this man is talking about."

Quinn looked sideways at Diego and hissed under her breath, "You're smuggling drugs on this boat? Are you insane?" She could scarcely believe what was happening. To her surprise, Diego shook his head. "No. Not me. Not drugs, *cocinera*."

Jose returned with a large black bag in one hand and a smaller, odd-looking object in the other. Quinn suddenly understood Diego's bizarre shopping request in Cozumel for ten rolls of duct tape. Whatever Jose was holding looked like it was wrapped in newspaper, then sealed with the heavy sticky silver tape.

Marnie muttered, "I knew it. I just knew it."

"So, what we have here," Luiz took the black bag and dropped it at Yoshua's feet, "is not a kilo of cocaina, my sly friend. Rather, it is *six* kilos." He smiled at the look of alarm on the line handler's face. "Yes, we have found all of your stash places." Luiz looked suddenly menacing and for the second time on the voyage Yoshua was looking directly at the pointed end of a knife. "Or have we?"

Yoshua sputtered and looked wildly around. His nervous eyes seemed about ready to twirl right out of his head. He began speaking in rapid Spanish. Quinn could tell he was trying to desperately reassure the drug lord that he wasn't holding anything back. Luiz eyed Yoshua with contempt. "You think I would not hear of such a quantity being moved without my knowledge and permission? Or that I would not track you down?

"Take him below and tie him up," he ordered Jose. "We'll deal with him later."

Quinn was startled when the engines rumbled to life. Apparently, Luiz had even more men onboard then she'd been aware of. "Where are you taking us? What are you going to do with us?" Quinn decided to confront the cold-hearted man who was holding them captive.

Luiz picked up the odd package and turned it over carefully in his meaty hands.

"Diego has a delivery to make, don't you, *el capitán*?"

Marcus spoke up. "Why don't you tell us what in the hell is going on? If Diego isn't smuggling drugs, what's in that package?"

"What we have here is a piece of Mexico's heart and soul. Your esteemed, or perhaps not so esteemed, captain is on a mission to rob the government that betrayed his brother." Luiz chuckled in a sly knowing fashion.

Diego had been sitting tensely on the edge of the couch. His hands were balled up into fists. When he spoke his voice sounded thin and strained. "Luiz, no one needs to know what our business is. You and I had an agreement. I can swear to you on the head of my mother that I had no idea Yoshua came onboard to smuggle drugs."

Marnie snapped to attention. "Much as I hate to defend Diego, I have to admit I believe he's innocent of that at least. Now that I think about it, Diego getting mugged must have been planned to keep him off of the boat so that this little pimp could hide his stash. Yoshua fooled us all."

Quinn was shivering in her thin pajamas. She glanced at the brass clock over the nav station. It was four in the morning. "Mr. Montoya, if you don't mind, I'd like to make some coffee and breakfast for everyone. I need to go to my cabin for some warm clothes first. I can promise you I won't jump overboard."

Luiz looked at her appraisingly. "That would be a tragedy. Such sweet flesh for the sharks?" Quinn squirmed inside. *He looks like a shark*, she thought. *Especially with that weird scar on his nose.*

"You may go, but I will send Adolfo with you." The man who'd entered her cabin motioned for Quinn to get up and precede him. He hadn't removed his hood nor spoken another word; he seemed almost like a phantom.

When they reached the forepeak cabin, Quinn protested as the man followed her down the stairs. "I'd like some privacy, please." He ignored her. Quinn hastily pulled out a pair of jeans and a sweatshirt, then went into the head to change. She moved as quickly as she could for fear the menacing figure would either burst through the door or shoot it open if she took too much time.

When she emerged, Adolfo cradled the gun in one arm and pushed Quinn against the bulkhead. She shut her eyes and for one long horrible moment, Quinn thought the man was going to rape her. Instead, he quickly and professionally patted her down. Quinn let out the breath she was holding and opened her eyes.

For the first time, she got a good look at her captor's face. He was an older man; she could see strands of grey at his temples beneath the black hooded jacket. His face was deeply lined. His eyes so dark brown they looked almost black. Wordlessly he motioned for her to climb the stairs, then he followed her back to the main cabin and the galley.

Marcus and Marnie were still on the couch, being guarded by the two mercenaries. Diego and Luiz were nowhere in sight. Quinn got busy making a large pot of coffee and breakfast for ten. Her mind was as busy as her hands. Obviously, Diego and Luiz Montoya were engaged in some illegal smuggling activity but it wasn't drugs.

Along with Marnie, Quinn believed Diego wasn't in cahoots with Yoshua. The squirrely line handler however, must be working for someone of Luiz's ilk, Quinn reasoned. She'd heard and read enough about drug cartel rivalry to make her afraid enough to be willing to do something desperate to get her and her friends out of this situation. But what? Quinn whisked a big bowl of egg yolks.

The radio began to sputter. The static seemed worse than usual. Quinn froze when she heard the distinctive tenor of Rafael Santiago's voice.

"Calling the *Vanora*, calling the *Vanora,* come in *Vanora*."

Diego came flying down the steps from the cockpit. Luiz Montoya huffing right behind him. Diego had reached the microphone when Luiz yelled, *"Alto!"*

The defiant captain simply glared at him. "This is the *Vanora*, over." He barked into the hand piece. Moving swiftly, Alfonso leaped to the nav station and swung the heavy butt of his gun down on the console. There was a loud screeching sound, then a buzzing like a swarm of angry hornets. He swung again, then again. Everyone, including Luiz looked on in stunned silence.

"Amigo, what have you done?" Luiz was shaking his head. There was no answer from the mute mercenary.

Diego clutched his head in his hands. "Luiz, Luiz, do you understand that now Rafael will become concerned? Do you understand that he sent an airplane to search for his ship during the hurricane?"

Diego turned to look into the galley where Quinn stood immobile; thick egg yolk dripping from the whisk onto the fiberglass floor. "He seems more concerned about *her* than his multi-million dollar yacht. He will come looking."

Luiz spoke rapidly in Spanish to Diego. Diego looked thoughtfully at Quinn. "Finish what you are doing, *cocinera*." He smiled. "Perhaps you may come in handy to your captain, after all."

It was a quiet group that sat eating a hot meal of scrambled eggs, bacon and toast. The rising sun was turning the cloud bank and marine layer surrounding the *Vanora* from deep black to a sullen, heavy gray. The armed men sat apart from Luiz and the crew. Even while eating they seemed to be wary and alert. There was no sign of Yoshua and Quinn began to seriously entertain thoughts that he had been permanently silenced and maybe his body even dumped overboard.

"I wonder, Luiz, if your silent *caballero* understands that he also damaged the navigation and radar equipment." Diego said. "We could be in serious trouble if a fog should come in."

Luiz wiped his mouth fastidiously. "*I* wonder, amigo, if *you* understand that all former bets are now off. We are having a change of plans."

He looked around at the trio of Americans. "There are so many unscrupulous people in this world who think nothing of plundering, then sinking even such a fine vessel as this. An upstanding loyal crew also would think nothing of going down in defense of themselves and their ship." He raised a bushy eyebrow. "Don't all of you agree?"

As if on cue, Adolfo and Jose rose and advanced on the crew of the *Vanora*. Luiz's captain took the yacht off auto pilot and killed the engine. The third man they called Paco stood vigilant watch from the stern. Quinn had noticed earlier that a sleek-looking powerboat was rafted up alongside the *Vanora*.

"Take these two below and put them with Yoshua," Luiz motioned toward Marcus and Marnie. Quinn rose and made as if to follow her friends. Diego took her by the arm in a painful grip. "Not you. You stay with me." He dragged her up and out to the cockpit, toward the stern.

Quinn turned and watched her friends being escorted through the main cabin with eyes that were filled with dull horror and hopelessness. Then she turned on Diego with a sudden fury. "You animal! They're your crew, damn you!"

She flung herself at him, fists clenched. There was a loud and sudden reverberation in Quinn's ears. A sweetly acrid odor filled the air. Then everything went blank.

Chapter Eighteen

Shadows floated through the azure sea of the Pacific Ocean. Deep, dark, silent, the elongated shapes undulated within the underwater eddies. The motionless body of a young woman hung suspended in the water. Her thick dark hair moved like a shadow, too; long tendrils waving like sea anemones around her head.

One of the shadows rose and began to twist and turn, almost taking on a solid form as it wound itself in a ghostly embrace around the still figure. The apparition tightened its grip, squeezing Quinn's chest with such pressure that she awoke and tried to draw in a deep breath. Saltwater filled her mouth and her nose. Quinn began to struggle frantically to free herself. *Air,* she begged silently, *please God I need air!* She desperately needed oxygen.

Something gripped her hair and tugged so violently she could feel some of her roots ripping out from her scalp. The apparition loosened its grip, and Quinn was pulled by her hair to the surface. Gasping and spitting, she was dragged through the water and onto the transom of the *Vanora.*

"*Dios mio!* There is no water in her lungs. That is truly amazing. She was under for over five minutes. Lucky for you, Diego that she didn't drown."

"Lucky for us all, Luiz, that the bullet only grazed her head."

Quinn opened her eyes, squinting against the morning sun. Her vision was blurred, but she could tell it was Diego squatting beside her. Something warm was running down the side of her head and Quinn instinctively knew it was blood. She went to put her fingers to the wound, but Diego stopped her. "Be still," he said. His tone was almost gentle.

"Watch her," he ordered someone.

Quinn lay quietly, too dazed to move. She understood she'd been hit by a bullet, although she couldn't remember why. She also was aware the injury was on the same side of her head that had been struck by the main boom over a week ago. She closed her eyes and let herself drift away from the heat of the sun on her skin, and the deep murmuring of male voices in the background. "Shadows," she whispered. "There were shadows in the sea."

When Quinn regained consciousness she was lying in the cockpit. The sun was no longer shining directly on the yacht. The mellowing blue of the sky told her it must be late afternoon. Quinn's head ached terribly and she was nauseous. So nauseous, she could only groan when she realized someone had removed her wet clothes. She was dressed in her bra and panties and a man's button-down white shirt. She was covered in a light blanket and had a pillow under her head.

The *Vanora* was oddly quiet without the constant chatter of the marine band radio in the background, or the stream of music Marcus usually played on the state-of-the art sound system. Quinn raised her head slightly to look around. Apparently, she was no longer considered a flight risk or a threat. She was alone; even the transom sentinel was gone. A wave of dizziness caused her to lay her head back down.

Quinn was dreaming of the shadows she'd seen in the sea. Again, she could feel the subtle entwining of the one that had put pressure on her torso, like a woman's old fashioned corset, slowly squeezing her diaphragm and— *keeping the air* *and* *water out of my lungs*. Quinn's eyes flew open. *It saved me from drowning!*

"Ah, the maiden awakens," Diego's caustic tone jerked Quinn back to reality. They were alone.

"Where is everybody?" Cautiously, Quinn sat up, clutching the gray blanket to her chest.

"Our friend, Luiz, and his compradres are resting. Except for that one." He jerked his head toward the wheelhouse. "The silent but deadly one."

Quinn could see the outline of the hooded figure. Alfonso, the man who answered to no one. "What happened, Diego? I don't remember anything."

"Ah, *cocinera*, you attempted to rip my eyes from their very sockets. I believe you were about to kill me." Diego laughed. "How fitting that would be, don't you think? But, instead, that idiot Paco didn't have his safety on. When he tried to grab for you, his gun went off."

The mention of guns brought sudden tears to Quinn's eyes. "Marcus? Marnie? What have these madmen done to them?"

Diego held up his hand. "So far nothing has been done to them. And now we need to talk, Quinn, while we can."

There was a sober note in Diego's voice. For the first time since she'd met him, all traces of sarcasm and superiority were gone. Quinn glanced warily at the man she had come to distrust so completely. Diego Reyes's face was haggard in the deepening twilight. His eyes looked somber and haunted.

"You must understand, this is not of my doing. Yes, I engaged in a partnership with Luiz. But it was not to smuggle drugs. What I have is far more valuable than any drugs. It seems Yoshua found my treasure when he was hiding his drugs. He blackmailed me into letting him sail with us to San Diego. I truly did not know at first about the cocaine." Quinn knew that by "treasure" Diego was referring to the odd package Luiz had presented to the crew.

"As you may recall, I am a descendent of the ancient Mayans through my mother's blood. She was a proud woman, Maria Louisa Ixchel del Canto, and very beautiful." Again, Quinn noticed a look of utter sorrow on Diego's thin face.

Her ears perked up. "Wasn't Ixchel the name of the Maya fertility and moon goddess at the ruins in Cozumel?'

Diego nodded. The setting sun had turned the sky a flaming red. The glow seemed to reflect off the surface of Diego's eyes. Quinn was startled to realize his eyes were filled with unshed tears.

"I never knew my mother. Yes, there were many pictures of her. And one portrait painted by a famous artist in Mexico City." Diego looked at Quinn. "It was from her that I got my unusual eyes. In the portrait her eyes were most arresting. Striking. Many men were intrigued by *los ojos de Maria Louisa*. There is even a song a minstrel wrote about the eyes of Maria Ixchel del Canto Reyes."

Quinn immediately found herself caught up in Diego's story. He seemed completely unaware of the element of romance that already graced his narrative. She inched closer, not willing to miss one single word that fell from the captain's lips.

"I was born late to my parents. My brother, the first born son, was already at the University of Mexico for his first year when my mother gave birth to me. The sister I spoke of is from my father's second marriage to a much younger woman." Diego grimaced and Quinn got the impression he wasn't too fond of his stepmother.

"My mother adored her first son. I have seen it myself in the pictures of his childhood. She always looked like the Madonna when she was holding him in her arms. His name was Rogelio. It means "prayed for.' I think it was difficult for her to conceive. I think therefore I was something of a surprise to my parents."

Diego shut his eyes as though he was trying to conjure up images that no one else was privy to. When he opened them, Quinn could see that he no longer cared that he had an audience. He seemed oblivious to his surroundings. His eyes were fixed overhead where the North Star was making its nightly debut; alone, majestic, and dominating what had been the sun's arena before the moon could take away the bright star's brief glory.

"No one seems to remember the massacre at the *Plaza de las Tres Culturas* in Tlatelolco, Mexico City, on the night of October 2, 1968. The Olympics was scheduled for the twelfth day of October in Mexico City but there was much unrest that year. And the students of the National Autonomous University of Mexico where my brother attended wanted *libertad* for the Mexican people, not the Olympics. There was a riot. The soldiers began shooting at sunset and the killing went on throughout the night. Hundreds, maybe over a thousand, innocent people were murdered by the Mexican government. Students, bystanders. Men, women, children.

"Rogelio was one of them." Quinn surmised aloud.

"Yes." Diego's tone was bitter. "My mother never got over the death of her first born. She died they say, of a broken heart, only three months after the murder. I was still but an infant." He drew in a sharp breath. "There are no pictures of Maria Louisa holding her second child, Diego. My best memory of my mother is stained in oil on canvas.

"Your government is as responsible as mine, *cocinera*." The contempt and distain were back full force. "Your Pentagon supplied the weapons, the radios, the ammunitions. All in the name of security for the Olympics. The CIA in Mexico City was aware of the upcoming protests. They also were aware the minister of the interior, Luis Echeverría Álvarez, knew of the riot in advance and that he also knew the students were unarmed."

Quinn sat for a moment quietly digesting Diego's story. As twisted as his logic and reasoning was she finally understood the core from which his anger and hate radiated. He'd grown up without the love and adoration his beautiful mother had bestowed on his older brother. Quinn imagined Diego's father, too, had withdrawn after the loss of his wife so close upon the heels of the murder of his son.

Diego obviously had allowed his sense of betrayal and abandonment to translate into his apparent distain for women; he treated them in a manner that ensured none of them would stay for too long. While he must have longed for a mother's love, he also must have believed women would choose to leave him in much the same way his mother had. By choice and because of someone they loved far more than Diego Reyes.

"I can only imagine how horrible that was, Diego. To lose your brother and your mother because of some stupid political event. You're right. I had no idea that massacre ever occurred. I imagine your government must have hushed it up?"

Diego snorted. "According to their reports only four were dead and twenty wounded during the confrontation. Almost thirty years later, Alvarez was brought to trial in Mexico on charges of genocide in relation to the massacre. He was released after a few weeks of house arrest because the statute of limitations had expired."

The captain stirred restlessly. There were signs of life in the wheelhouse as Luiz Montoya's crew began turning on lights.

"I don't mean to sound lame, Diego, but what has any of this to do with that package you'd hidden onboard?"

Diego's eyes gleamed. "That package, *cocinera*, as Luiz so poetically described it, is truly a piece of the heart and soul of Mexico. It is a priceless, long lost Mayan artifact. It is a jade statue of the moon goddess Ixchel. It weighs almost ten pounds. Pirates raided the temple of Tulum on the mainland centuries ago. Often they would go to Cozumel to replenish their supplies and hide. Sometimes they would bury their plunder for retrieval at a later date. That is how I believe this relic found its way to the island. One of Luiz's people discovered the statue while hiding a vast quantity of heroin and cocaine in the jungle behind the ruins of San Gervasio. I made a deal with Luiz. In exchange for the statue, I paid him ten thousand dollars and agreed to smuggle some of his drugs in the future. He is a cautious man. He wished to see if I could get away with this first. "

Diego laughed, a high thin cackle that made Quinn afraid for his sanity. "It is only fitting that the namesake of my mother, Ixchel, will be used to punish the butchers who destroyed my family."

"What do you mean? How will you do that?"

"I will smuggle the statue into San Diego, *cocinera*. Then I will make it be known that the American government has been aware of its presence all these many years. Your government and mine will be at each other's throats over this. My people will not take lightly this sacrilege, nor the United States' perfidy. Just like during the Olympics, there is much unrest right now with Hispanics in *Los Estados Unidos*."

"Diego, that's crazy!" Quinn blurted out. "What could you possibly hope to accomplish by this? You could end up in prison for the rest of your life. And, for what?"

Diego leaped to his feet. "It is not crazy! You will see!" He shook his fist at the sky. "The lives of my brother and my mother will be avenged when *your* streets run with blood. When the parents of *your* youth weep themselves into an early grave."

Diego suddenly calmed down. "It is only fitting that the goddess Ixchel will be the avenger." Without so much as another glance at Quinn, Diego left the cockpit. He seemed to melt into the darkness along the gunnels of the *Vanora*, leaving Quinn sitting in stunned silence.

CHAPTER NINETEEN

D iego had no sooner disappeared, when Luiz came out of the main
salon. Quinn instinctively shrank away from the drug lord when he
lowered his hefty bulk beside her. He smiled and for the first time Quinn
noticed a gold inlay in one of his eyeteeth. "*Cara,* why is it every time I see
you, you are barely dressed? Not that I am complaining. Not at all."

Quinn had a queasy feeling in her stomach that Luiz had been present
when she was stripped of her wet clothes. She could see her jeans and
sweatshirt were still in a damp heap near the stern. She pulled the blanket
even closer around her.

"I was kind of out of it for awhile. I'm heading to my cabin now to get
some dry clothes." Quinn went to stand up but Luiz put a heavy hand on
her thigh.

"Not so fast, not so fast." He reached out and brushed a tendril of hair off
Quinn's neck. He dropped his hand and let it linger a beat on her shoulder.
Quinn couldn't control the shudder that went through her whole body at his
touch. It was like being caressed by a venomous snake. Luiz snickered.

"I confess I understand fully why Rafael Santiago so desires you. He
has always had an eye for only the finest women. Like his wife, Elise." The
smuggler made a sucking sound with his mouth, and Quinn's stomach rolled.
He made a motion as though to take Quinn's face into his hands, but bright
light suddenly flooded the cockpit. Luiz was breathing heavily through his
nose and he snarled at the man who stood before them.

"What is it you want?" He kept his hand on the side of Quinn's neck, his
grip tightening in anger.

"The prisoners, *el jefe*. The woman needs to go to the bathroom." Paco's face betrayed no emotion.

Luiz pushed Quinn away, then hauled himself up, using the binnacle for support. "That woman could use a lesson in patience, *amigo*. Perhaps you could give her one, no?" He laughed. "Too bad we have much work to do and so little time."

He looked down at Quinn. "You, go put your clothes on. The time has come to get serious. You will be leaving with us. You will be our insurance."

Quinn grabbed her discarded clothes and fled to the sanctity of her cabin. After dressing in white drawstring trousers, she deliberately chose a loose-fitting, long-sleeve blue shirt. She reached under her mattress and brought out the leather pouch Noah had Hank give to her. She tucked Rafael's note inside. Quinn got out her passport and wallet and put all three items in a waterproof bag that she tucked into the waistband of her trousers.

Her cell phone was in the same drawer as the passport. It was turned off but fully charged. Quinn hadn't used it since leaving Miami. However, she knew only too well from past experience there would be no reception. Too late, Quinn wished she'd bought an international phone. Silently, she vowed to never leave the country without one in the future. *If there is a future,* she thought grimly. She left the phone in the drawer and climbed the steps to the deck.

Much to Quinn's relief, Marnie and Marcus were in the main salon. So, was Yoshua. All three had their hands bound in front of them. Luiz tersely ordered Quinn to cook some food. He also issued orders in Spanish to his four henchmen. It was obvious to all that the smugglers were preparing to abandon ship. Paco hefted the black bag containing the cocaine in his arms and left the cabin.

"I am most happy to relieve you of the responsibility of your burden," Luiz sneered at Yoshua. "You should have known better than to try to swim with the big fish. Soon you will be swimming with the sharks."

Loud thumping on the deck and the sound of the automatic winch being deployed caused the original crew of the *Vanora* to look at one another in alarm. The life boats were being lowered into the sea. Alfonso and Jose were searching the cabin and cockpit. They were removing all the safety flotation devices. Jose entered the galley and unceremoniously dumped all the knives and flatware into a garbage bag. It suddenly dawned on Quinn what Luiz was planning to do.

The meal Quinn hurriedly put together reflected her state of mind. She simply opened cans of beef stew and heated them up. She buttered a loaf of wheat bread and set out plastic bowls and utensils. Luiz wouldn't allow the ropes to be removed from the three bound crewmembers' hands. They ate awkwardly and without much appetite. Quinn forced herself to eat; she had a feeling she would be needing all her strength.

Luiz's men ate standing up. It was obvious they were anxious to get off the yacht. Diego had joined the group in the cabin. He was cradling the bulky wrapped idol in his arms. He refused to eat. Reluctantly, Quinn retrieved the used bowls and spoons and placed them in the garbage. She didn't want this meal to end. It could very well be the final one for her and her crewmates.

Luiz stood up. *"Adios, amigos.* Time for us to be on our way."

"Aren't you going to at least untie us?" Marnie glared at him. "I see you've done away with the life rafts and the safety vests. Are you going to blow the boat up? Is that what you're planning?"

"Nothing so obvious, *senorita.* Already the *Vanora* is leaking from malfunctioning seacocks, compliments of Alfonso. Your bodies will never be found. We are twenty-five miles offshore in shark infested waters."

He strode across the salon and grabbed Quinn by the arm. "Rafael Santiago may mourn the loss of the *Vanora,* but not, I am sure, as much as he would mourn the loss of his lovely mistress."

"What about your plan?" Quinn yelled at Diego as Luiz tried to drag her rebellious body toward the cockpit. "How will you get Ixchel to the States, now? You need us, Diego!"

The captain seemed momentarily nonplussed. Then he smiled. "It is fate, *cocinera.*" He looked around at Marcus, Marnie, and back to Quinn. "None of you are worthy. Not one of you has shown loyalty to your captain. I could not trust you. I, and I alone, will finish this mission." He carried his burden up the companionway stairs without a backward glance.

Quinn was sobbing hopelessly as Luiz and Paco manhandled her into the thirty-five foot powerboat idling beside the *Vanora.* Diego was already onboard. Alfonso cast off the bow and stern lines and the boat leaped to life; speeding away into the increasingly choppy ocean. Through streaming eyes, Quinn could see where the stern of the luxury yacht they were abandoning was already lower than normal in the water.

A crescent moon seemed to bounce along the dark horizon as the powerboat dove bow first into three-foot swells. Luiz had tried to get Quinn to follow him into the cabin but she'd insisted she was getting seasick in the smaller boat. Quinn sat huddled in the aft port corner of the cockpit. She turned for one last look at the *Vanora*, whose lonely cabin lights grew more distant as each minute went by. Without thinking, Quinn abruptly stood up, then leaped from the boat and into the sea.

The water was surprisingly warm. Quinn could hear men shouting and the sound of engines throttling down. She began to swim with long, hard and sure strokes towards the sinking yacht. It would be a race against time; the time it took the captain to swing the powerboat around in the unruly ocean, then find her in the darkness, and how fast Quinn could make it to the *Vanora*.

Waves were slapping against the long white hull when Quinn reached the seventy-six foot yacht. From a short distance away, the spotlight from the powerboat began sweeping the length of the *Vanora*. Quinn had beaten her pursuers by mere minutes. She took a deep breath then dove beneath the water. Quinn fumbled and found the propeller shaft. *Shadows not sharks, shadows not sharks*, she repeated over and over in her mind. *The sea is filled with shadows not sharks*.

She clung to the cold steel for a minute or two, until her lungs began to ache for oxygen. Dimly she saw a distorted beam of light as the powerboat circled the *Vanora*. Quinn shot to the surface for air, and was prepared to dive again when, much to her relief, she heard Luiz's angry command. "Leave her! We must go. Let her drown along with her crew."

Quinn swam to the dive platform, which was already swamped. She found she was too exhausted to climb over the transom. The beam of a flashlight momentarily blinded her, then Marcus was lifting her onto the deck. Quinn clung to the broad shoulders of her Italian buddy and cried tears of relief. He held her tightly for a long moment. "You came back, Quinn. By God you came back." His voice was thick.

"Hurry, we've got to either stop the leaks or jury-rig a raft." Marcus pulled Quinn along with him toward the main cabin. The floor boards were pulled open and Marcus disappeared into the engine room. Quinn could hear Marnie ripping through compartments. She knew it was Marnie because Yoshua was still tied up and sitting on the couch.

"Let me loose, let me loose. You can't leave me." He whined. Quinn walked over and slapped him. Not too hard, but with contempt.

"Shut your mouth, you little worm. You've caused enough trouble. Unless you stay put and don't cause any more trouble, we *will* leave you. Rest assured of that."

Marnie appeared looking disheveled. "They ditched everything floatable. And the EPIRBs. Everything."

She managed a grin. "My good ole rigging knife came in handy, though. They didn't find it in my dirty clothes hamper. We'd really be sunk if it weren't for that. And for you." She hugged Quinn briefly. "I figured you wouldn't desert us."

Marcus hauled himself up into the cabin. "Those pricks," he said bitterly. "They sliced the rubber o-rings on the seacock valves. We're taking on water fast. I don't think the bilge pumps can keep up much longer. We've got to abandon ship somehow and *soon*."

The thought of leaving the comfort and safety of the *Vanora* and trying to keep afloat for God only knew how long in the unruly and unpredictable seas surrounding them made Quinn's face blanche. She'd already had a taste of that. As strong a swimmer as she was, Quinn doubted she could last for too long. She was also aware that even in temperate waters hypothermia would set in after only a few hours.

"Wait a minute! Did anyone check in the forepeak locker?"

"Check for what, Quinn? The only things in there are sails, lines, and tackle gear." Marcus sounded irritated.

"No, there's a jumble of stuff. I could have sworn I saw an extra lifeguard ring in there. There's a drogue, too. Maybe we could rig something at least for us to hang on to."

"Let's go," Marcus led the way.

There was a spare lifeguard ring. There were also two semi-deflated fenders. The working ones had been jettisoned by Luiz's henchmen in the effort to strand the crew on the sinking yacht. Yards of line were hanging neatly coiled on hooks lining the inside of the locker. The three friends hurriedly dragged the equipment up to the foredeck.

"Marnie and I'll figure something out here, Quinn. You go round up as much water and food as you can. Mostly water. Better grab that rat, Yoshua, while you're at it. We'll abandon ship amidships." Marcus was busy at work even as he spoke.

Surprisingly, Yoshua was still where the crew had left him. He watched Quinn with his nervous eyes as she put food, cans of soda, and bottled water into the mesh bags she normally hung fresh produce in. Quinn even had enough presence of mind to grab a couple bottles of sunscreen. Finally, she was ready to leave the *Vanora*.

"We've got to get moving," she said to the line handler cum drug smuggler in a voice thick with emotion. The enormity of what was about to happen had washed over her. It wasn't so much that Quinn was aware their chances of survival in the open sea were slim. The fact that the lovely and majestic *Vanora* was being sacrificed to a lonely grave; that her undeserved and undignified death was masterminded by a greedy, unscrupulous drug dealer and an insane captain made Quinn's very soul fill with a fierce hurt at the injustice of it all. At that moment she would have gladly traded the lives of Luiz Montoya and Captain Diego Reyes for the life of the graceful, true-hearted and once seaworthy *Vanora*.

Quinn slung two of the full bags over her shoulders. Then she placed two around Yoshua's neck. "Now you're a mule for real, huh," she said without a trace of humor, as she motioned for him to precede her to the foredeck.

The contraption Marcus and Marnie had put together was a work of pure ingenuity. The drogue was positioned between the chewed up but still usable Styrofoam life ring and the two fenders. PCV pipe formed a rigid frame and sturdy dock lines had been threaded through the drogue's grommets to secure a canvas floor made from one of the smaller storm jib sails. The reasoning, Marcus explained, was the conical drogue, which normally acted as a sea anchor that would fill with water to slow or stabilize a boat, would now act as a canopy and even a primitive sort of sail.

"We can put the food and water inside the drogue or we can tie the bags onto the sides and let the stuff float in the water." Marcus and Marnie began dragging their invention to the side of the deck.

"What about us?" Quinn asked. "Where do we sit?"

Marcus curtly replied. "We don't sit. We float. And we hang on for dear life."

The seas were still choppy. A squall was clearly eminent. The *Vanora* was beginning to take on water rapidly, stern first. Marcus cut the ropes binding Yoshua's hands. Without warning, he pushed the squealing line handler over the side before leaping off the yacht himself. Marnie and Quinn tossed the bags of provisions over, then awkwardly lowered the makeshift raft to the men in the water. The two women clasped hands—and together jumped into the sea.

No one had to tell Quinn how important it was to get as far away from the sinking vessel as soon as possible. All four survivors began to paddle and kick their legs, driving the raft away from the suction that was bound to happen when the *Vanora* finally succumbed to the tons of water that would soon be flooding her decks. Fifteen minutes later, the breathless crew paused. For all their combined exertion, Quinn noticed with a bleak sense of detachment the four of them hadn't made all that much progress. Still, they were a safe distance away from the distressed sailboat. But not far enough away that they couldn't hear what had struck fear and sorrow into the hearts of sailors immemorial.

There was a hissing, then a deep rumbling that to Quinn's overly stimulated imagination sounded like the moaning of hundreds of sailors lost at sea. She let go of the raft, covered her ears with her hands and buried her face in Marcus's chest. She simply couldn't take any more. Marcus held Quinn's shuddering body afloat in one arm and silently watched the proud white bow of the *Vanora* disappear into the dark, timeless embrace of the sea.

CHAPTER TWENTY

*T*ime is truly relative, Quinn thought tiredly. She was aware she was adrift at sea with the crew of the *Vanora*. She was also aware it was still dark. *Time isn't measured by a clock. Five minutes on the* Vanora *at dinner goes by like magic. Five minutes of pleasure is spent before you can even enjoy it. Five minutes in the ocean waiting to drown or get eaten by sharks feels like an eternity. How long have we been here? Forever. Forever.*

"Time isn't fair," Quinn spoke out loud. "How long have we been here?"

"Hours. Maybe four hours." Marcus's normally deep voice sounded weak and faded. The sea was still restless, tossing and turning the beaten foursome around and up and down like passengers on a berserk theme park ride. Even Yoshua was silent now. He'd almost driven everyone mad with his frantic attempts to crawl onto the canvas base that was keeping them afloat. "Sharks, sharks!" He kept screaming, as he tried to claw his way out of the water.

Marcus had finally locked Yoshua around the neck in a death grip. "You shut your mouth or I'll cut you loose. I swear to God I will."

It had been Marcus's idea to tie everyone to the floatation device with some of the spare line he'd taken from the *Vanora*. Without flares, without electronic homing devices, the crew's chances of being spotted in the vast expanse of water were next to none. Quinn still clung to the hope that Diego's prediction would come true; Rafael would certainly have called the coast guard by now. She recalled there had been another boat somewhere in the vicinity the last time anyone had checked the working radar. With any luck and a lot of prayer, maybe they would sail close enough to see the tiny raft.

The squall had passed, leaving the seas much calmer in the first light of dawn. The rising sun was turning the clouds on the horizon into purple, red and pink blossoms. An old adage came into Quinn's mind: *Red sky at morning, sailors take warning. Red sky at night, sailors delight.* There was no doubt in her mind they couldn't survive a storm. She doubted they could even survive another squall. The raft was slowly coming apart. All of them were shivering from a loss of body heat. Everyone was exhausted.

Quinn was semi-conscious. The night's exertion had taken its toll and the gentle rolling swells were hypnotic. The others were silent, too, each lost in their own reverie, trying to escape the horrible reality of their situation. Quinn was dimly aware that she was beginning to slide slowly into the water. *But, that's not so bad, is it? I can sleep down there. The currents will rock me like a baby in a cradle.*

She'd resolved earlier that the shadows she'd seen in the sea were figments of her imagination. She'd discussed the odd experience with Marnie and Marcus. How when she'd been pulled back onboard the *Vanora* after Paco grazed her head with a bullet, there was no water in her lungs. How she'd been aware of a shadowy life form that had squeezed her chest and kept her from inhaling a deathly lungful of saltwater.

"It was your subconscious keeping you alive," Marnie had assured her. Now Quinn's mind began to play tricks on her again. She knew she was losing her grip on reality—and on life. *I can relax now. There's no point in hanging on. The shadows will caress me and stay with me until I'm gone. They say drowning isn't really such a bad way to go...*

Quinn stirred. There was a humming in her ears that slowly began to grow louder and louder and more annoying. She shook her head weakly from side to side but the noise wouldn't go away; it actually increased in volume. Suddenly, Marcus jerked, rocking the dilapidated raft. Floating next to Quinn, Marnie groaned, causing Quinn to open her eyes.

Marcus was looking into the sky, a wide grin on his cracked lips. He began to frantically wave his arms. Quinn followed the direction of his gaze. She could scarcely believe her eyes. A small airplane was fast approaching, so low it appeared to be skimming the top of the ocean. She began to wave her arms, too, and was joined by the now fully conscious Marnie and Yoshua.

The sound of twin propellers spinning grew into a thunderous roar as the plane swept over the four joyful survivors. Quinn could see right into the cockpit. Rafael waved to her from his seat beside Donald. The plane swooped up, then circled from a higher altitude. It made one more pass, wings waggling as it sped off to the east.

"I imagine the coast guard will be here soon," Marcus was the first to speak.

"Maybe sooner than you think. Look!" Quinn pointed to the smoking trail of a flare in the distant ocean. "They want us to know they're coming for us." Tears streamed down her face.

"What's going to happen to me?" Yoshua spoke for the first time in hours. "Are you going to send me to jail?"

Quinn and Marcus exchanged looks. "Personally, I don't care what happens to you," Quinn was the one to answer. "Your precious cocaine is long gone. If I were you, I'd be more worried about running into Luiz again."

In celebration if their imminent rescue, Marcus handed out bottles of Gatorade and snack bars. Within the hour, the crew could see the thin white stick of a sailboat on the horizon. "That must be the other blip you saw on the radar, Marcus." Quinn shook her head. "Was that only the night before last?"

He nodded. "I imagine Rafael figured they were closer than trying to get a cutter out here. I wonder how far from shore we are? You'd think they'd send a helicopter and get us out of these waters."

Quinn scanned the area around the raft uneasily. *That would be the perfect irony*, she thought, *if we got attacked by sharks before the boat reaches us.* Apparently, Yoshua was thinking the same thing. He began his paranoid litany again, only this time Marnie pulled out her rigging knife and without warning or fanfare, cut the line securing him to the raft. Yoshua grabbed onto one of the fenders and stared at her in disbelief.

"Shut up or the next thing I'm going to cut is your throat. I've had it with you."

The boat approaching them must have been under full throttle. Quinn squinted as it got closer. There was something familiar about the outline. Someone was standing near the mast. Quinn watched as the oversized figure raised a flag on the halyard. It was several minutes before she could decipher the pattern. It was the flag of Jamaica.

"The *Icarus?* I don't believe this. That's got to be Dr. Felix on the *Icarus.* He's signaling to me with the Jamaican flag." She placed her head into the crook of the arm that was balancing her on the raft. Quinn squeezed her eyes shut. Her heart seemed about to burst with love and gratitude. *Thank you, dear Lord in heaven, thank you.*

The sailboat finally reached the exhausted and waterlogged quartet. Quinn was physically and emotionally numb; she was in shock. The hot sun had risen behind the dark clouds forming in the west; her face and head felt like they were on fire. From her shoulders down she felt disembodied. Eyes closed, she could visualize her torso and legs hanging silently and motionless in the water; *I'm becoming a shadow, too.*

There was a loud splash, followed by a second one. "Ahoy, sailors!" The loud, sonorous voice of Dr. Felix Templeton carried over the ocean. Strong arms grasped Quinn around her waist: Someone was cutting her free of the derelict raft. Then she was being pulled in a rescue grip to the waiting yacht. Through half-open eyes she could see Marcus, Marnie and Yoshua were being cut loose and assisted through the water.

She could hear Dr. Felix urging everyone on from the deck of the *Icarus*. Her rescuer reached the transom of the yacht where the burly doctor was waiting, arms outstretched. He pulled Quinn's limp body up as easily and swiftly as he would a lightweight fender. "Go help with the others," he called to the man who had saved her.

"Now this is a surprise, my dear," Felix wrapped Quinn in a blanket. "I've been following the *Vanora* hoping to catch up with you for a margarita. I never expected to be pulling you from the sea."

Quinn tried to speak, but Dr. Felix put a broad but gentle hand over her mouth. "You could probably use some hot soup and a nice warm shower for now. We can talk later."

A commotion from the stern caused him to sit Quinn down as he moved to help haul Marnie, then Marcus, then Yoshua onto the *Icarus:* each of whom was immediately given a blanket from the stack on the deck. Quinn was so beyond exhaustion all she could do after smiling weakly at her mates was lean her head back against the fiberglass coaming. She closed her eyes against the glare of the sun.

Quinn's stomach was growling. The welcome aroma of chicken noodle soup permeated her nostrils. Her mouth watered and she opened bleary eyes to see Dr. Felix's beaming face. "That a girl," he encouraged her to swallow the spoonful of broth he was holding up to her lips.

"I must be dreaming," Quinn sat up and took the bowl from his hands. She was in the dimly lit interior of the *Icarus*. Quinn finished the soup quickly. "Where is everybody?"

"My crew has gotten your crew showered and fed. They're asleep. You nearly scared me to death, Quinn." Dr. Felix frowned. "You appear to have a multiple contusion on your left temple. There's a slight indentation and a raw, recent laceration. What in the world has been going on with you?"

Quinn was about to answer when a puff of air, a zephyr wind, blew over the stern of the *Icarus* and down into the main cabin. She froze and her nostrils flared. Her eyes were huge when she looked at Dr. Felix. "Noah? Is Noah onboard?"

He nodded. "He's at the helm right now. Another one of your friends came along, too." A shadow filled the open companionway hatch. Quinn recognized the long scrawny outline and bushy head immediately. "Chip!"

"Quinn Anne, what's up?" He strode over, sat down and enveloped Quinn in a long bear hug, rocking her back and forth. "Girl, you just can't seem to stay out of trouble, can you?" Her reply was muffled in another long hug.

Felix rose and asked Quinn if she'd like to take a hot shower. "We're about running out of spare clothes for the four of you, but maybe Chip has something he can donate." He laughed. "So far nobody's fit into anything of mine. Although, Quinn, one of my shirts would amply fit you as an over-size nightgown if you're interested."

Quinn was bone-weary and she hurried through the shower. Chip had loaned her a pair of shorts and a t-shirt. She rinsed the saltwater out of the clothes she'd been wearing while she showered. Once dry, they would be wearable again. Her passport and other items had safely survived the entire ordeal. Quinn removed her passport and wallet, then placed the plastic bag with Noah's mojo and Rafael's note in a locker under the sink for the time being. The thought of seeing Noah again had her trembling as she dressed. She could hardly button the waistband of the denim shorts.

The *Icarus* was a forty-five-foot Columbia motor sailer. The sturdy and dependable yacht had a freeboard of almost eight feet. The gutters and deck were flat and roomy. The interior floor plan was simple; a master cabin and head aft, the main salon, galley and nav station amidships and guest/crew quarters forward along with a tiny head and shower.

The *Icarus* was roomier and more spacious than the *Zephyr*, but comparing her to the *Vanora* was like trying to compare a minnow to a whale. The *Icarus* was outfitted to comfortably accommodate four; seven passengers was pushing it.

When Quinn stepped out of the head, Dr. Felix was sitting only a few feet away at the chart table that also served as the dinner table. He motioned for her to take a seat. "I imagine you're eager to go say hello to our helmsman." Quinn nodded, and swallowed hard.

"You need a good solid eight hours of sleep," Felix went on. "I'd like to better examine your head wounds, then I can give you a sedative to make sure you get some rest. After you see Noah, that is."

As if in a dream, Quinn walked the short distance to the wooden steps at the base of the companionway. She looked up and saw Noah's silhouette at the wheel. Quinn grasped the handrails and pulled herself up and into the open cockpit. She was standing face to face with Noah, separated only by the binnacle. A green and white bandana covered his head and was tied in the back; its tails fluttering in the wind.

He was wearing sunglasses, so Quinn couldn't see Noah's trademark and fabulously sexy eyes. She knew he was looking intently at her, though, she could feel his scrutiny. *He knows about Rafael,* Quinn thought with a sinking feeling in the pit of her stomach. As if reading her mind Noah set the wheel on autopilot, then stretched out his hand.

"Come, Quinn. Come talk with me."

She took his hand and silently followed him to the foredeck of the *Icarus.* Noah pulled her down along with him as he sat in front of the wooden dingy strapped on the deck before the mast. Holding Quinn on his lap, Noah began stroking her hair. Quinn closed her eyes and drew deep breaths of Noah's scent. She could feel the strong steady throb of his heart beating in his chest.

"We thought you were lost." Noah's voice startled Quinn. She'd been in a state of semi-sleep, safe in the arms of her Caribbean lover. "When the call came through from the owner of the *Vanora* that his yacht was missing somewhere in our vicinity, we were fearing the worst." Noah sighed, and pulling Quinn even closer, he nuzzled her hair. "It is a long story how Chip and I came to be sailing after you with Dr. Felix.

"You should be resting, Quinn-nay, but I am a selfish mon." He tilted her head back and kissed her softly yet lingeringly on her lips. "After so much time without you, I had to have some moments with you by myself."

So he doesn't know about Rafael, Quinn was giddy with relief. So giddy, that when she stood up alongside of Noah, her knees wobbled. Quinn would have fallen if Noah didn't have his arm around her waist. "Come. To bed with you." Noah helped her along the gutter and down to the main cabin. The duo passed Chip in the cockpit and he smiled broadly and wished Quinn a good sleep. Dr. Felix was waiting below to check Quinn's head injury. He didn't seem to be too worried, and he gave her a sleeping pill.

Snug and secure in the forward starboard berth Quinn realized she must be sleeping in Noah's bunk. His scent was all around her. Quinn had no doubt that soon her two universes were about to collide. It was inevitable. Rafael Santiago had every right to hear firsthand from his crew what exactly happened onboard the *Vanora*. Just as Noah had every right to hear firsthand from Quinn that she had stepped outside the boundaries of their relationship.

Quinn fell asleep and didn't wake up until eight hours later. Night had fallen. It was dark in the forepeak. Someone had drawn the curtain separating the small cabin from the main salon. For a moment, Quinn was disoriented. She thought she was back on the *Zephyr*. She could hear Chip laughing, then the deep rumbling voice of Dr. Felix. She stretched long and hard, the scent of Noah lingering in her nostrils.

"Somebody better wake Quinn up and feed her," Marnie's voice jolted Quinn back to the present. Quinn sat up abruptly as scenes from the past two weeks washed over her. Captain Diego's leering face, the horror of the hurricane. Making love with Rafael in his study in Guadalajara, riding horses and making love in the stables. The tension of having Yoshua onboard and the menacing arrival of Luiz Montoya and his band of thugs. And most vivid and horrible of all, the dying moans of the sinking *Vanora*.

Quinn leaped from the bunk and pulled open the curtain. Four faces turned to look at her. Felix, Marnie, Chip and Noah were sitting at the dinette. Noah patted the seat beside him and moved closer to Chip so Quinn could join the group. Her heart was pounding and her chest was moving rapidly up and down. Quinn sank down beside Noah.

"You look pale. Are you all right?" Felix's voice was full of concern. "Let me get you something to eat." He rose and went to the stovetop. The whole area of the galley, dining area and main salon of the *Icarus* was only slightly bigger than the galley of the *Vanora*.

Noah put a protective arm around Quinn's shoulders and squeezed.

"We've all been through hell, huh, Quinn?' Marnie looked at her in sympathy. "I was telling these guys about it. They were in the outskirts of Cecelia, too. And let's not forget Luiz Montoya."

Felix had returned to the table with a platter of fried chicken, mashed potatoes and peas. "Here's some comfort food, my dear. Eat up. Doctor's orders."

Quinn was ravenous. She ate every morsel on her plate and drank two glasses of iced tea along with the meal. While she ate, Dr. Felix clued her in on how it came to be that the *Icarus* was trailing behind the *Vanora*.

"After the conversations we had while you were still in Miami, Quinn, I started getting a bit of wanderlust again. Chip here wasn't in the best of shape for any racing. Tommy got a replacement for him on the Pineapple Cup race. Got one for Noah, too." Tactfully, the doctor didn't make any references to Noah's drug and alcohol problem. Nor his problem with Lydia and the unborn child.

"I've always wanted to sail my way around the world and I was getting too damn comfortable in the West Indies. I got thinking I could bring the *Icarus* to San Diego. Trade her in for a bigger boat, then head to the Hawaiian Islands on my way to New Zealand, Australia, then Asia."

He looked around the table. "Course I would need a good crew. People I'm genuinely fond of and that I can trust. I feel like I'm looking at them. With the *Vanora* gone, technically you're not bound to any contract."

There were murmurs around the table. Marnie's face was lit up. The pressure of Noah's arm around Quinn's shoulder increased considerably. Chip was nodding, a big grin on his face. "Just like old times," he chuckled.

"What about Marcus?' Quinn wanted to know. Even as her mind raced. *What about Rafael? And how will Noah feel about me after he does find out about Rafael? I don't even know how I feel anymore!*

"Marcus is more than welcome." Felix assured her. "We need a solid crew of six, I'm thinking."

No one made mention of Yoshua. And until the crew of the *Icarus* could drop him off at a port in Mexico, he may as well have been a ghost. A bad spirit. One that none of the crew ever cared to encounter again.

CHAPTER TWENTY-ONE

————◆•◆•◆————

The *Icarus* was off the pacific coast of southern Mexico. Felix knew of a small village, San Mateo Del Mar, in the state of Oaxaca. The natives there, he said, spoke an indigenous language, Huave. The crew anchored right after dawn in the sandy roadstead near the village. Quinn was making breakfast when the radio began transmitting. Felix had quietly pulled Quinn aside the day before to let her know Rafael Santiago was desperate to talk to her.

With seven people on the yacht, it was nearly impossible to find any privacy. Quinn had been wracking her brain trying to think of a way to call Rafael without Noah or Chip overhearing the conversation. When Felix announced they would be anchoring off the village, Quinn assumed everyone would want to go ashore. Felix had charmed them all at dinner with stories about the Huave.

"The Huave call themselves Ikoots, meaning 'us.' They refer to their language as ombeayiiüts, meaning 'our language.' The term Huave is loosely translated as meaning 'people of the sea.' When you go into the village I suggest you buy some of the hand woven goods. The Huave weave traditional costumes called huipil using a dyed purple brocade. Originally they used a dye made from sea snails, but even after a number of washings the snail smell remained."

The *Icarus* was low on water which was the main reason Felix decided to stop over at San Mateo del Mar. With the extra people onboard, he was worried the water maker might not be able to keep up with the demand for fresh water. The crew sleeping arrangements were interesting. Chip and Noah had made room for Marcus in the forepeak, simply adding a v-board to enlarge the berth. Felix had insisted Quinn and Marnie share the larger master cabin in the stern. He and Yoshua were sleeping in the main salon.

In the early morning light Quinn had noticed only one other rather decrepit looking sailboat anchored offshore. It appeared no one was onboard. The sizzling bacon and sputtering radio competed with her attention. She could hear Rafael's voice but the reception was bad and he kept cutting out. The radio was mounted close by in the little seating area and chart table. Felix's bulky body filled the entire companionway as he lumbered down the steps.

He fiddled with the radio, then raised a brow and looked at Quinn. "When do you want to talk to this fellow, young lady?"

Quinn could feel her cheeks turn bright red. "I was thinking that maybe when everyone went ashore would be the best time. I know Rafael wants to know everything that happened on the *Vanora*. I don't want Yoshua around when I talk to him." *Nor Noah*, she thought guiltily. Felix nodded.

Everyone ate with gusto. Quinn had made chile relleno omelets with sour cream and salsa, bacon, and warm corn tortillas. She served coffee and orange juice along with the meal. Quinn was happy to be the unofficial cook on the boat. She certainly didn't miss Diego's condescending label of "*cocinera*," either. All seven of the crew ate topside. The climate in that area was very arid. The sun was already scorching hot and it wasn't even eight a.m.

Marnie helped Quinn clean up the galley while the men unstrapped the wooden sabot from the deck and lowered it into the water. "This is certainly going to get interesting," Marnie was drying the plastic plates.

"What is?" Quinn knew what Marnie was alluding to but she didn't feel like going there.

"You know, Noah and Rafael. There's bound to be a reckoning of sorts, Quinn. I have no doubt Rafael is going to want to see you again—and soon. And here's Noah. Damn, he *is* good looking. If I weren't gay, sister, I'd be all over him like white on rice."

Quinn sighed in exasperation. "Noah has unresolved issues, remember? He may be changing diapers in a few months and paying child support." She set the scoured frying pan down with a thump. "I have no idea what Rafael's planning. Jeez, Marnie, he just lost a couple million dollars with the sinking of the *Vanora*. I'm sure he has more pressing things on his mind than me."

Marnie snickered. "Well, you know as well as I do what body part men think with. You're going to have your hands full." She tossed the towel on the counter. "I'm sure the *Vanora* was insured, Quinn. Too bad there's no insurance for the heart. Someone's bound to get hurt in this little romantic triangle. I certainly hope it's not you."

Marnie left Quinn muttering to herself in the galley. Noah and Marcus came through on the way to their lockers. "You coming into town with us, Quinn?" Chip grabbed a leftover piece of cold bacon.

"I'd better not right now. I've got some things to do and I have to call my mom and dad."

Noah immediately offered to stay with her on the *Icarus*. The longing in his amber eyes was obvious. Neither of them had been able to find any time together since Quinn first boarded the *Icarus*, which was fine with Quinn. She didn't think she would bear up well under any close scrutiny.

"Noah, why don't I meet you later on? Dr. Felix thinks I'd better start preparing a written statement about what happened to the *Vanora*. The coast guard and police are going to want names and details."

There was a loud thump from the open overhead hatch. Quinn heard Felix's familiar rumble, then Yoshua's squeaky voice. Noah was obviously disappointed. He had a troubled frown on his face. Without another word he went to the forepeak and began rummaging in his locker.

An hour later only Quinn and Dr. Felix were onboard. Felix raised Rafael on the radio, then left Quinn to talk in privacy with the owner of the lost *Vanora*. Quinn had to squeeze her eyes shut to keep the tears from spilling out. She would never be able to completely put out of her mind the trauma that was associated with the sinking of the beautiful yacht.

"*Querida*, what in the name of *Dios* has happened? Your friend, the doctor, assures me you and your friends are uninjured. But, the *Vanora* is gone. I could not believe my eyes when I saw the little speck of your raft and not my yacht. Who is responsible for this?"

Quinn managed to suppress her tears. "It's not a simple story, Rafael. The line handler we hired in Cristobal had smuggled cocaine onboard while I was in Guadalajara with you. Diego it seems has some Mayan artifact he was trying to sneak into San Diego. Then, this Luiz Montoya and his thugs came out of nowhere.

"They were going to kill Marnie, Marcus and Yoshua. They tied them up, then damaged the sea cocks. They figured the police would think pirates had scuttled the *Vanora*. I can go into more detail when we talk to the police and coast guard."

For a long moment there was only the crackling of static on the radio. Finally, Rafael spoke. "Don't talk to anyone, Quinn. Tell your *amigos* to do the same. This is a private matter. I need to speak to my insurance company and my attorneys before we go any further. Do you understand?"

Quinn understood the steely tone of her lover's voice. Rafael was talking to her much in the same commanding manner he used with his employees. He fully expected to be obeyed.

"Did anyone harm you, *querida?*" The steel was gone; the multi-millionaire's voice was concerned and as soft and caressing as a kid glove. "Were you tied up and left to drown along with your *compadres?*"

Quinn hesitated, not sure how to explain Diego and Luiz's intent to hold her hostage on the assumption Rafael would be more concerned about her than the *Vanora*.

"No. They tried to take me with them. I guess kind of like insurance. A hostage thing if the authorities stopped them." Quinn's story sounded lame even to her own ears.

"They tried?" Rafael sounded slightly amused. "You managed to stop them?"

"I jumped from their boat and swam back to the *Vanora*."

There was another long pause. "*Muy bien, querida. Muy bien.*"

Before signing off, Rafael informed Quinn that he would be meeting her in Acapulco. He'd already discussed the itinerary of the *Icarus* with Felix. "I have missed you, *querida*. More than you may know. Remember the three recommendations I have given to you." With that the connection ended.

Quinn went topside and found Felix sitting in the cockpit sipping on a Red Stripe beer. She sat down across from him with a heavy sigh. "So we're meeting with Rafael in Acapulco?"

"We don't have to, Quinn. However, the man would like some answers to what happened on his boat and I can't fault him for that." Felix eyed her steadily. "Is there something you want to tell me?"

Quinn looked at her trusted friend and confidante. Dr. Felix already knew more about her love life than most of her female friends. He was discreet and Quinn knew he only had her best interest at heart.

"Rafael and I had—we're *having* an affair," she confessed. "At least I think we are. I spent a few days with Rafael in Guadalajara. It's been, so, I don't know, like magic when I'm around him. It's almost unreal, in a way. Maybe surreal is a better word for it." Quinn stood up and walked to the rear hatch over the master stateroom. She was gazing at the little village on the shore. Felix got up, lumbered over and placed a hand on her shoulder.

"So you're feeling guilty. Understandable. I'm sure you didn't expect to be seeing Noah for awhile. You *are* allowed to sow some wild oats, Quinn. Noah still hasn't got his act together by any means. I don't see a ring on your finger, or in your nose, either." He laughed at his small joke.

"Let's take the Avon into the village and find the others. We can talk about Noah on the way."

San Mateo del Mar was a village in the true sense of the word. It was small and quaint. Open stalls lined the dusty streets where natives sold the unusual and colorful weaving indigenous to the area. It wasn't too hard to find the crew from the *Icarus*. There were few cantinas or restaurants in town. Marnie, Noah, Marcus and Chip were eating tacos and drinking beer in a small but clean one-room eatery.

"Where's Yoshua," Quinn wanted to know as she sat beside Noah. He shrugged. "He is off doing his own thing. You are right, mon, he be giving me the creeps. His eyes are all wrong."

There was a murmur of general assent. The single waiter came over and Quinn and Felix asked for the same as their crewmates; tacos and beer. The food was good and cheap but right before they left the waiter warned them about eating anything from the street vendors, including the fresh fruit.

All six crew members spent several hours shopping together. Noah stayed close to Quinn the entire time; carrying her packages and taking every opportunity to touch her arm, her hand, and occasionally caressing her back. Chip was his usual comic self. He even offered to show her the scars on his behind at one point.

"Right here in broad daylight? I don't think the townspeople would appreciate it." Quinn gave him a mock frown.

"Ah, 'fess up, Quinn. You're just waiting for a private showing."

"It seems to me I've seen your privates showing, remember? I helped put your butt back together when your stitches ripped open." The whole group got a good laugh out of that. Everyone was still in good spirits when they went down to the sandy beach to the two tenders.

"What about Yoshua?" Marnie asked Felix who was looking at the Avon with a small frown on his lips.

"I'll leave the wooden boat for him. We can all fit in the Avon. I could have sworn I left this raft much higher on the sand because of the tide." Felix motioned for Chip to help him launch the heavy rubber Avon into the surf.

Back onboard the *Icarus,* Felix suggested everyone get ready for a sunset sail. He explained that because of the location of San Mateo del Mar gale winds were known to spring up unexpectedly. "The Isthmus of Tehuantepec behind the village is quite narrow and there's a gap in the Sierra Madres which accounts for a funneling effect when the trade winds blow from the Gulf of Mexico to the Pacific." Felix elaborated.

Quinn hurriedly stowed the woven items and trinkets she'd purchased in the master cabin. She'd also bought several pairs of shorts, pants and tee shirts, a bra and some cotton panties in lieu of the clothing she'd lost on the *Vanora.* She felt a twinge of guilt for having deprived Dr. Felix of his sleeping quarters, although the kindly doctor insisted she and Marnie occupy the stateroom throughout the rest of the journey.

Quinn was rummaging in the well-stocked galley for something special to cook to celebrate the sunset sailing when, Dr. Felix came out of the aft cabin with a troubled frown on his face. He asked Quinn to pass him a soft drink from the recessed refrigerator. After a long swallow, he wiped his mouth, then said, "I have reason to believe Yoshua won't be bothering any of you from here on out."

"Why do you say that?"

"Because I had an uneasy feeling that he'd come back onboard while we were in the village. Something about the way the Avon had been moved."

"And?" Quinn braced herself for what she knew was going to be bad news.

"And the shifty little fellow found my money belt. He took all my cash and my traveler's checks."

"Oh, no!"

"Oh, yes. I'm just grateful he didn't take my passport as well."

"What is a lot of money?"

"Several thousand dollars all in all." Felix grunted. "Strange as it may sound, maybe it's worth it just to get him off my boat. He gave me the willies, too, you know."

Felix called to Chip and Marcus to take the Avon back to the beach and retrieve the wooden sabot. When he told them about the theft, Marcus asked if the doctor would like them to search the village for Yoshua. Felix declined the offer. He told them to make haste since the wind appeared to be picking up. The two men were back and had both boats stowed on deck within the hour. The *Icarus* was ready to set sail.

Chapter Twenty-Two

The few days onboard the *Icarus* before arriving in Acapulco were ones of heartbreak and discovery for Quinn and Noah. With Yoshua gone, the remaining crew as a whole had fallen into an easy, bantering relationship. Felix regaled his small crew with humorous tales of his adventures in the Caribbean. Quinn kept up her duties as ship's cook. Marcus had moved from Chip and Noah's quarters into the main salon with the doctor. Marnie was intent on becoming the navigator. She spent hours poring over charts and books, and picking Dr. Felix's brain.

Quinn would long regret she'd forgotten about the waterproof bag she'd so hastily stored in a locker beneath the sink in the forepeak head. She was sitting in the main salon checking off the list of supplies from a record Dr. Felix kept. The water pump had been busy all morning. Marnie and Chip had showered after their watch, then Noah had taken his turn. Felix, Marcus and Quinn showered at night.

The wooden flooring creaked. Quinn looked up and smiled. Noah was looking down at her. A light, clean scent emanated from him. His dark golden skin seemed to shine in the late morning light. He rubbed his freshly shaven jaw, amber eyes locked on Quinn's face. Quinn was about to speak when Noah held out one hand, then slowly opened his clenched fist. He was holding the black bag and the crumpled note from Rafael.

"Love the eagle? Do you love this 'eagle', Quinn-nay? What is Rafael Santiago? Half man, half bird?" Noah squatted down in front of Quinn so that they were eye level. "Did you make love with him? Is that why he tells you to save your 'ooohs' for him? Is he the reason you no longer want to be

157

with me? That you make excuses to not be alone with me? Tell me the truth, woman!"

Quinn moaned as she looked into Noah's tortured and beseeching eyes. "I can explain the note, Noah. It's not as though I knew he was going to write it." Noah's eyes were riveted on hers. Quinn dropped her head and broke eye contact with him. "Rafael was on the *Vanora* for a few days in Cozumel and we were all partying one night. Drinking and dancing. It was the night before he had to leave for Guadalajara."

Quinn looked up. "We danced. He was teaching me the tango. It was a beautiful night; the moon, the stars, the music. I got carried away in the moment, I guess. But, I didn't even kiss him, Noah. I said something lame like 'oooooh that was wonderful.' The next day, he'd left that note for me with Marnie."

Noah stood up. "I am not a stupid man, Quinn. I know there is more to this story than you are telling me. I feel it in my bones. Why would you even save this note from him? When you are ready to truly talk, *you* come to *me*." He dropped the note and the bag at her feet, and left Quinn sitting with her head in her hands. Marnie had been so right when she'd warned Quinn the time would come for a reckoning. Quinn just wished it hadn't come so soon.

Even on such a crowded boat, Noah managed to make himself scarce most of that day and the next. If Quinn went topside, he went below. If she went forward, he went aft. He wouldn't make eye contact during meals. The rest of the crew appeared not to notice the distance between Quinn and Noah. Quinn sensed it in every cell of her body. When the ache inside grew to be almost unbearable, she asked Dr. Felix if she and Noah could have the midnight to four watch that night.

"You most certainly can." The big bear of a man grinned at Quinn. "It's about time you two decided to square things up." He put a comforting arm around her shoulders. "Follow your heart, my dear, but use your head as well."

The dinner Quinn made that night reflected her state of mind. For the first time since she was twelve years old, Quinn almost ruined a meal. The pork roast was underdone, the noodles were overcooked and she scorched the garlic bread. Quinn ended up tossing out the noodles and bread. She sliced the medium rare meat and pan seared it, then let it simmer in a raspberry, chipotle, garlic and red wine reduction until it was cooked through. She ended up serving the pork on corn tortillas along with refried beans.

"Now that was quite a save."

Marnie had been a witness to Quinn's culinary crisis. She was helping set out shredded cabbage, sour cream, and salsa to compliment the entrée. "Noah getting on your nerves or something?"

"So you noticed." Quinn was setting the chart table so everyone could serve themselves, then go topside to eat.

"Duh oh. The tension between you two is thick as a brick wall. Have you decided what, or *who*, you're going to do yet?"

"Marnie!" Quinn glared at her. "Don't be so crude!"

"Aw, come on. Actually, have you ever thought you could have the best of both worlds?"

"What do you mean?" Quinn was completely flustered again by Marnie's bluntness.

"You could have them both, I bet, if you wanted." Marnie winked. "That's what I'd do if I were in your shoes."

"Well, you're not in my shoes. So shut up and count your blessings."

Marnie shrugged, then fixed a plate of food and went topside. Chip and Marcus came into the galley followed by Dr. Felix. The three men heaped their plates and complimented Quinn on how delicious the aroma of the impromptu tacos was. Quinn put one taco and a dab of beans on her plate. Noah was nowhere to be seen. However, shortly after Quinn seated herself in the cockpit, he showed up. The amount of food on his plate was as sparse as hers. It was apparent neither of them had much of an appetite.

The weather had been ideal. Even though the *Icarus* was beating against the strong Pacific current, the winds had been kindly. The crew was able to keep the boat on an even keel, tacking routinely as they made their way to Acapulco. By midnight, the *Icarus* was on a starboard tack and on the last leg of the journey. A dazzling astral display of stars and constellations was being eclipsed by a full moon that seemed to be traveling across the midnight sky in tandem with the cruising yacht.

Noah had made no comment when Felix announced a change in the watches after dinner. He merely grunted, then disappeared into the forward cabin for a few hours. Quinn showered after the dishes were done. She found herself fussing over her lack of wardrobe. Her hair seemed more unruly than usual. She sighed in exasperation as she slammed Felix's blow dryer down.

Chip was at the helm when Quinn went up to begin her watch. They chatted lightly for a few minutes before he bid her goodnight. "I'll get Noah's lazy ass up, Quinn. He's late. See you *manana*."

Now Quinn stood anxiously at the wheel waiting for the arrival of Noah. The moon was so bright she could see schools of mating squid leaping out of the water. Several actually flopped onto the deck. Quinn set the autopilot so she could rescue the hapless creatures. Noah suddenly appeared in the companionway and Quinn froze; a large squid wriggling in her hand.

The illumination from the giant orb trailing the *Icarus* was such that Quinn could see every aspect of Noah's features. He raised a brow, and with a hint of a smile on his full lips, said, "Sorry, mon. Am I interrupting something?" His eyes traveled to the writhing cephalopod in Quinn's grasp.

Quinn flung the squid over the side. Wiping her hand on her pants, she said, "Well, there went dinner." Quinn began to giggle, then to laugh. Noah began to laugh too, and soon both of them were clutching their stomachs. After they'd regained some composure, Noah went to the stern and motioned for Quinn to join him.

Similar to Tommy's ice chest on the *Zephyr*, Felix had a Coast Guard approved life raft in a fiberglass container strapped to the transom that made a perfect seat for two. Noah sat down and Quinn sat beside him. Leaning back against the lifelines, Quinn and Noah looked out over the silver-shadowed billows of the ocean.

With a sigh, Noah broke the silence. "I have been thinking deeply, Quinn. I am being too harsh with you. I am asking too much." Gently he took her hand in his. "I have nothing to offer to you. Not like that man. The *eagle man*." There was a note of bitterness in his voice.

Quinn went to speak but Noah put his free hand up to stop her. "No. You must listen to me first." Noah closed his eyes. "I have lived a life of irresponsibility. Yes. Always life was fun to me. Women were easy. I have had many." He turned to look at Quinn. She could see in the bright clarity of the moon the shades of light and dark in his eyes. "I have enjoyed them all. Until the *skettle*, Lydia came upon me.

"She is determined to be my ruination. I still swear to you the child will prove to not be mine. It was spoken to me by the obeah."

Quinn shivered at his superstitious reference. Sensing her distress, Noah released her hand and put his arm around her. "You must hear me out. Other things were spoken to me during the cleansing. Much I don't remember. I was very sick from the purification rite for weeks after, so much is still a mystery to me."

"Noah," Quinn interrupted. "You seriously can't believe in all of that voodoo stuff!" She sat up and shrugged his arm off her shoulder. "It's creepy and it isn't real. Either the baby *is* yours, or it *isn't.* Only DNA testing will prove the paternity. You were having sex with her, you know!"

"Yes, but sex with her was nothing like making love to you. That is what I am trying to say. You know something so special passed between us in the lagoon in Jamaica. Something I have never felt before. You felt it, too. The obeah spoke about it."

Quinn would have bolted right then and there but Noah put his arm across her waist, pinning her against the lifeline. He was leaning all his weight into her. Quinn could feel Noah's heated breath on her face, the hard muscles of his torso pressing against her. Her thigh was pinioned between his strong legs. Noah pressed closer and closer. They were eye to eye and mouth to mouth. Quinn's hair flowed restlessly in the breeze off the stern. For one horrible moment, Quinn imagined the very demons of hell were going to crawl up her long tresses, over the transom, then onto the *Icarus.*

"Noah, stop it! Please just stop the with obeah business. Let's talk about us. Plain and simple us." Quinn struggled to break Noah's embrace. She couldn't control the tremor of fear in her voice.

Noah jerked. "You are afraid of me, Quinn? This I cannot—do not—believe."

"I'm not afraid of *you,* Noah. That whole obeah thing simply freaks me out. Same thing with you thinking Lydia put a curse on you. This is the twenty-first century, not the Middle Ages. You should be thinking about reality. Such as, there is a possibility you could become a father in the near future. Like it or not. With or without curses or voodoo."

Noah looked at Quinn as if he'd never seen her before. Then he shook his head. "Obeah is not voodoo. No. It is my heritage. It is in my blood." He stood up and turned his face to the moon. "The priesthood of my uncle uses obeah to heal and ward off evil. I have seen this myself. He was a great priest and his followers are many."

Noah looked down at Quinn. The moon was reflecting off the water into his light colored eyes, giving them an eerie cast. "I myself am considering learning the craft. Mi auntie believes I have the calling."

Quinn was stumped. In all her wildest imaginings of what would be the outcome of spending a four-hour watch with Noah, what he was sharing with her certainly hadn't even been in the peripheral. Her mind was spinning. If Noah were to become a priest, and their relationship survived, what role would Quinn play in his world? Quinn was aware of how lax she had been in the religious department since leaving her parents' home. Still, she considered herself a Christian and had an innate dislike of witchcraft and superstitions.

"This is all news to me, Noah. I don't know what to say. I was all set to defend myself and hopefully set things straight with us. I've been thinking a lot the past couple of days, too. About you. About you and me. About Rafael. My life is so upside down right now it's a wonder I can think at all."

Noah started to speak but Quinn put her finger on his lips. "I have to say something before I lose my courage. We both need to realize we only knew each other for one week—one week, Noah—and look at us. We had a very special moment in the lagoon. It rocked my world, that's for sure. It also scared the hell out of me when I realized I could have gotten pregnant."

Noah took Quinn by the arms and shook her lightly. "Would that have been so bad? Would you have suffered so much if I was the father of your child? It is because I am a Jamaican man? Is it?"

"That has nothing to do with it and you know that!" Quinn was furious now. "You're just being pig headed, Noah. And immature to boot. I don't want my child to be born like that. I want my child to be welcomed and born into a secure and loving home. I want to live a little, too, before I even *think* about having a baby. And so should you."

Quinn stopped her tirade and put her hand to her mouth. "I'm sorry. I realize the predicament you're in with Lydia. I shouldn't be carrying on like this. Please forgive me."

Noah sighed. "I forgive you because I love you. Maybe you don't realize it yet, Quinn, but you love me, too. We are one. Someday you will understand. I am a patient man, you will see."

"There is one other thing," Quinn was determined to get all her issues out in the open. "The night before I left the *Zephyr,* Tommy and I took a walk on the beach in Negril. We found you wrestling with a young girl. Do you remember, Noah?"

He shook his head. "No. I was too wasted."

"So was she. She wasn't wearing any panties and there were long welts down your back. Scratch marks." Quinn held up her hands. "We were together in the lagoon that afternoon, but I didn't make those marks—not with these nails."

"What are you saying?"

"I'm saying I think you had sex with her. After you had sex with me no less."

Again, Noah shook his head.

"No, no. Why would I do that? How could I do that?"

"That's what I've been asking myself all these weeks. I don't understand how you could do that."

Noah grabbed Quinn by the waist. "If something happened it was the drugs and the alcohol. They are like demons to me. Those demons have been cast aside, Quinn. You must believe me."

The moon had sailed past the *Icarus*, yet still cast its luminescence over the rippling water. A trail of glowing phosphorous danced in the wake of the yacht. Quinn told Noah she was going below to check the radar. Reluctantly, he released her. Without a backward glance Quinn left.

Felix was snoring loudly on the converted couch. Marcus had taken Noah's berth since he had the following watch. After scanning the radar and seeing nothing out of the ordinary, Quinn went into the master stateroom to use the head. She tried to pump the toilet as quietly as possible so as not to awaken Marnie.

After washing her hands and turning out the light, Quinn opened the door and stepped into the cabin. There was a rustling from the double berth. Marnie sat up.

"I couldn't help but eavesdrop," she whispered, pointing to the open hatch directly above her head.

Quinn rolled her eyes, then perched on the end of the bunk. "And?" She was whispering too.

Marnie made a slicing motion across her throat. "The dude has got some real issues, baby doll. I'm not so sure you should start anything back up with him. I mean, *I* was even getting spooked listening to him talk about demons and all that obeah stuff."

Quinn nodded in the semi-darkness. "We'll talk more tomorrow, okay?"

Marnie agreed and lay back down. Quinn went to the galley and gathered some snacks and Gatorade to take up on deck with her. Noah seemed to have withdrawn into his own world. He thanked her for the refreshments, then went forward to the bow where he stayed until Marcus and Marnie came up to relieve him and Quinn. Upon their arrival, Noah simply dropped down through the forepeak hatch into his cabin.

Quinn didn't see him again until the *Icarus* was approaching Acapulco. She was pretty certain, however, that Noah heard the hurried radio transmission early the next morning from Rafael. He was speaking to Felix and, rather than talk to Quinn directly, he asked the doctor to relay a message.

"Please tell Quinn I have reserved a villa for us at Las Brisas. There she can relax and recover from her harrowing experience. Tell her I am counting each minute until then. I look forward to meeting you, Doctor, and your crew as well. I must go now. *Hasta manana.*"

The squawk and sputter of the radio didn't mask the slamming of a forepeak locker. Quinn had overheard the transmission, too. She was making the bunk up in the aft cabin. Quinn sat down, put her head in her hands and began to rock back and forth. *No, Rafael, I really don't think you want to meet this crew. I really don't think so at all.*

CHAPTER TWENTY-THREE

A capulco was stunning from the water. The pink, white and multi-faceted resort hotels eclipsed the lesser buildings and residential areas. From a mile or two out, the crew could see the crystal blue of the Pacific Ocean end in a frothy and dazzling white surf at the base of the cliffs along the sandy shoreline. The Bay of Acapulco seemed to be spreading huge arms in a welcoming embrace as the *Icarus* motored steadily inside.

Rafael had been thoughtful in his selection of a villa. The exclusive property boasted a small marina where the multimillionaire had managed to secure a slip, much to Dr. Felix's delight. "The man must have some serious connections to score that." He was beaming.

The closer the Columbia 45 got to port, the more Quinn's nerves unraveled. *What if Rafael is waiting at the dock? How would Noah handle that? Will Rafael be able to tell Noah and I were once lovers? How and why did I get myself into this?* Fortunately, there was no one to greet the *Icarus* when the crew brought her in. It was high noon and blistering hot with a touch of humidity. Felix asked Quinn if she wanted to accompany him to the marina office. She was more than glad to get off the *Icarus* and away from Noah's brooding presence.

The marina master, Javier, greeted Felix and Quinn with great enthusiasm. He bowed as he handed a note addressed to Quinn on the familiar stationary of Rafael Santiago. The heavyset man casually examined the papers Dr. Felix handed to him and said there was no need to see their passports. The remaining crew could check in with him any time before four that afternoon.

While Felix chatted with Javier, Quinn sat on a bench outside and looked thoughtfully at the note before opening it. Rafael was supremely self-assured and confident. He had briefly explained his philosophy to her one afternoon when they were horseback riding.

"There are those who are born to serve, *querida*, and those who are born to be served." His world was made of black and white. He was born to be served.

Quinn had a feeling Rafael would always be in control—at the helm—of their relationship. He certainly wasn't a man who liked to be crossed. *I'm surprised his wife managed to get away from him. I wonder why she wanted to get away and take the children.*

If a confrontation were to develop between Rafael and Noah, Quinn had to believe the man of steel would triumph over the emotional and superstitious Jamaican. She said a silent prayer that no such thing would happen, then she opened the small envelope. A key slid out onto her lap. There was a tag with an address attached to it.

Querida, ("*mistress*" *echoed faintly in Quinn's mind*),

Your villa awaits you. #346. And I await you. See you at 6.

Besos,

Rafael

Quinn had never been in such an awkward position in her life. If she went to the hotel there would be no doubt in Noah's mind she was sleeping with Rafael. If she didn't go, she was pretty sure that would be the end of whatever the relationship was that she had with the handsome Mexican. With the *Vanora* gone, she wasn't bound by contract to Rafael, or Hank, for that matter. Dr. Felix had offered his crew decent salaries, but would Noah be included on the long trans-pacific voyage to Australia?

Dr. Felix came out and a thought popped into Quinn's head. "Hey, have you heard any news from Hank? Somebody needs to call him and tell him what happened to the *Vanora*. I don't know if Rafael has or not."

"Well, young lady, there's only one way to find out. We'd better give the man a ring. Let's walk over to the marine store and see if there's a pay phone in the area. Do you have his phone number?"

Quinn slapped her forehead. "No. I lost my address book among other things when the ship went down. I imagine Chip and Noah would have it."

The two friends went back to the *Icarus*. All three crew were on deck washing the fiberglass boat down. Chip knew Hank's phone number by heart and volunteered to go with Quinn to the marine store and call him. Noah only glanced at Quinn, a sad and questioning look in his eyes. She shrugged and shook her head, then followed Chip off the yacht.

Hank's phone went straight into voice mail. Quinn left him a short but detailed message; the *Vanora* had been boarded off the coast of Central America by smugglers who where in cahoots with Diego. They'd scuttled the big yacht and left the crew to die. Rafael had masterminded a rescue and the *Icarus* had fortunately been in the area. Quinn ended with a promise to call back in the near future.

"That should certainly get his attention," Quinn said to Chip. He agreed. As they strolled back to the dock, Chip took advantage of this rare moment of privacy with Quinn to ask her about the situation between her and Noah. "You two still don't seem to have resolved any issues since Jamaica. The poor guy's been through hell, Quinn. I thought you'd be a little more sympathetic."

Quinn stopped dead in her tracks. "Sympathetic? What about me? I've been through a few kinds of hell myself in the past month. First of all, Noah needs to get real and deal with his issue with Lydia before either of us can go forward."

"Lydia? What's she got to do with it? She's so history it isn't even funny."

Quinn suddenly realized Chip didn't have a clue about what was haunting her and Noah.

"She's not history by a long shot, old buddy. She may very well be his future. She says she's having his baby." Quinn had resumed walking again. It was a full minute before she realized Chip wasn't following behind her. She turned. The gangly sailor stood rooted to the same spot.

"What? *She* is having his baby? Lydia is pregnant?"

"I'm surprised you didn't know about it, Chip. Anyway, that's what she says. She's had her detective dad hounding Noah for prenatal expenses and, of course, when the child is born, child support."

Chip looked like he was going to be sick. "Poor Noah," he groaned. "I had no idea. God, this is awful."

"Tell me about it. Now do you understand why everything is such a mess? There are other issues, too, but I don't want to go into them right now."

The two walked the rest of the way to the boat in silence. Right before they boarded, Chip asked if Quinn knew when the baby was due. She did a quick calculation in her head, then said, "I'm not sure. I think maybe in November. She had to have gotten pregnant on that trip from hell with you and Noah, remember? The one from Mexico where she weirded out on you guys? You do the math." Quinn left Chip shaking his head and muttering.

Marnie was excited about being in Acapulco. She was urging everyone to go with her to watch the famous cliff-diving at La Quebrada. "These guys timing has to be perfect since they have to land in a little ten-foot inlet. If they miss a wave, they're toast." A dive was scheduled for one o'clock, she said, and there would be four more in the evening when the divers carried torches during the 136-ft drop into the thundering ocean.

"We could grab a bite of lunch at the hotel right there and watch the show." Felix, Marcus and Noah agreed to go. Chip said he wasn't feeling well, and went to take a nap. Quinn wanted to take a shower and she desperately needed some time to think, so she excused herself from the excursion. Noah seemed to take her refusal to go personally. He vaulted over the side of the *Icarus* and strode down the dock ahead of the rest of the group.

"I'm not going to be able to live like this for very long," Quinn grumbled as she stripped, then stepped into the shower. "I may as well pack it in and stay with Rafael or go home to Miami if Noah plans on keeping up his *baditude.*"

She took her time in the shower; shaving her legs and washing her hair twice. There would be plenty of water while they were docked. Quinn had decided she would meet Rafael at the villa, but she wouldn't be spending the night there. She'd have dinner with him, then make the excuse that she was needed back on the *Icarus*.

Quinn groaned when she realized the only clothes she had were the casual outfits she'd bought in San Mateo del Mar. She had cash and credit cards, however. There was still time to take a taxi into town and buy a dress or a skirt and blouse, and a pair of decent shoes. She tied her damp hair back, dressed in shorts and a t-shirt and hurried down the dock. She didn't have to hire a taxi as Javier hailed her and asked where she was going.

Javier offered to take Quinn to the city center but she didn't feel there would be enough time if she was expected at Rafael's rented villa at six.

The cluster of exclusive villas sat about fifteen minutes outside of Acapulco proper. Instead, Javier drove Quinn to the outskirts of the city. Along the way the jovial man had nothing but praise for Rafael Santiago.

"Senor Santiago has rented the villa many times over the years. He would bring his children and they would play with my children. Always he was giving the little ones treats and buying them gifts. He would buy gifts for me and my wife, too." Javier was quiet for a moment. "He doesn't bring the children anymore."

Quinn would have liked to get more information out of the marina master, but they had reached a clothing store. Javier said he would be across the street at the cantina having a beer. Quinn poked around, then emerged a little over an hour later with several bags in her hands. Luckily, she'd found a black cocktail dress with a pair of matching high-heels.

She also bought a white skirt with a white peasant blouse and beaded sandals. A heavy silver and turquoise belt complimented the ensemble. Quinn didn't have time to select accessories for the outfits. She was lucky to have purchased what she did. She crossed the street and went into the smoke-filled bar looking for Javier. Before long, he was dropping her off at the marina office.

The group of private villas was within walking distance of the marina, Javier pointed out. There was also a beach bar and grill on the property for guests and owners. He assured Quinn she would enjoy the private pool and Jacuzzi, outdoor wet bar, and personal maid and butler service that went with each villa. The view of the bay, he promised, was spectacular.

It was getting late. Quinn raced to the *Icarus* to get ready to meet Rafael.

CHAPTER TWENTY-FOUR

The same moon that had witnessed Noah and Quinn's confessions at sea now hovered over a couple sipping Napoleon brandy on the patio of the private villa overlooking the bay of Acapulco. Rafael had his arm around Quinn and they both were gazing at the huge orb hanging in the sky. They were laying on an over-sized chaise lounge. Their bare bodies gleamed in the pellucid moonlight.

Much to Quinn's dismay when she'd left the *Icarus* earlier that evening in her new dress, Noah, Marcus, Marnie and Felix were on the way back to the yacht. Quinn was unaware of how the simplicity of the black off-the-shoulder cotton/rayon dress made her own natural beauty more apparent. Without the distraction of earrings, necklace, bracelets or other adornments, the shimmering garment drew the eye to her figure. Long tendrils of hair along her bare shoulder, the deep green of her eyes, and the subtle rose of her lips were all the accoutrements any woman would need.

The returning crew of the *Icarus* stopped as a whole at the sight of Quinn stepping off the yacht. She was holding her new high heels in one hand. Her bare legs shimmered with freshly applied body lotion in the setting sun. Marcus actually whistled before he could stop himself.

Felix gave Quinn a half-bow and said, "You look simply lovely, my dear. A vision."

Noah's head was tilted to one side. His pushed his sunglasses on top of his habitual bandana. Quinn could see his amber eyes travel from her head to her toes—and to her empty right hand. Then he looked directly at her. A small smile hovered on his lips.

"Damn, baby doll. You're in the wrong business." Marnie said. "You'd better get your butt to Hollywood before all the sun and sea ruins your skin. You should be a model."

Quinn winced at the memory of how difficult and embarrassing her previous modeling experience had been. "Thanks, but trust me, I prefer life at sea. I'll see you guys later."

She glanced over her shoulder on her way down the dock. Noah was standing alone by the *Icarus*. He raised a hand in a half-salute. Quinn saluted him back. Fifteen minutes later, Quinn slid the key into a slot and opened the door of the villa marked 346. The interior was cool and the air filled with the scent of fresh flowers. Quinn rounded the corner of the short tiled entry way, then stopped short in amazement.

Like a panoramic 3-d picture the far hills and the bright blue bay of Acapulco stretched the length of the Saltillo tiled open-air living room. An infinity pool began at the edge of the area and extended to the end of the outdoor patio. Quinn was momentarily mesmerized. She ventured deeper into the villa. To the left was a recessed bar that was as big as Quinn's studio apartment bedroom. The skylight over the bar was made of blown glass depicting a seabed in blue, green and yellow.

Ceramic ollas laden with riotous bouquets of freshly cut flowers were scattered about the spacious room. Quinn stepped down into the sunken sitting area in front of the pool. A crystal vase filled with yellow roses sat in the middle of the glass coffee table. A card addressed to her was leaning against it. A bottle of champagne sat in a silver ice bucket. Two long-stemmed crystal flutes were on the table beside a platter of hors d'oeuvres. The sensuous strains of a tenor saxophone floated lazily around the room.

"Welcome to *Casa Sol de Mar,*" Rafael's voice startled Quinn. She spun around. Her heart sped up even more at the sight of him. *Oh, this man looks good in anything*, she couldn't help but think. Rafael was wearing a simple white muslin shirt, open at the neck; dark brown linen slacks, and he was barefoot.

Before Quinn could utter a word, Rafael leaped lightly over the back of the long sofa and took her in his arms. For one long moment, he looked searchingly into her eyes. Rafael must have noticed her rapid heartbeat. He smiled. Quinn half shut her eyes, expecting one of Rafael's earth-moving kisses. Instead, he kissed her lightly on the neck, then on her bare shoulder.

"You look ravishing," Rafael held Quinn at arm's length. His smoldering green eyes traveled up and down the length of her body. "Please, let's sit down and enjoy this fine champagne."

Rafael continually caressed Quinn's arm, shoulder, and her face as they sipped the chilled Charles Krug. Quinn had never tasted anything like it before. The champagne was cold and sparkling on her tongue, yet it seemed to expand as she swallowed, spreading a warm fuzzy feeling down her throat and into her stomach. It was heavenly. Just like the setting; and the breathtaking sunset unfolding over the bay.

"*Querida*," Rafael's lips were close to her ear. "I have anticipated this night for too long. There is much we need to talk about, but do we not agree that it will wait until the morning?" His hand was on her knee. Softly, slowly, Rafael began to stroke her inner thigh. Quinn wanted to explain that she wasn't able to spend the night. Rafael pressed his mouth over hers, stifling her protests.

Rafael was moaning, his tongue tracing the soft oval outline of Quinn's lips. He took her around the waist, laid back and pulled her on top of him. Rafael nipped Quinn's lower lip with his teeth, then grasped her heavy knot of hair and pulled her head back so her throat was exposed to him. He pressed his mouth against the throbbing base of her neck.

"I feel the beating of your heart," Rafael whispered. His pelvis began moving in a slow gyrating motion. Rafael released Quinn's hair and put both hands on her hips, pressing her harder and harder against him. His head was thrown back, his eyes half closed. Quinn couldn't help but respond to the heat and intensity of his desire. She began kissing Rafael on the neck, his shoulder, his chest. His skin was hot against her lips. Her body began to move in tempo with his.

Just when Quinn thought she was going to completely lose all control, Rafael laughed softly and rolled her onto her side. He was stroking her; from her neck to her thighs. "Tonight we feast on love and life. All night. Tomorrow we will let in the light of reality. Do you agree, *querida*?"

Before Quinn could respond there was a discreet knocking on the door. Rafael stood and pulled his shirt out of his trousers to conceal his arousal. With a wink at Quinn, he called out, "*Entrada, por favor.*"

Quinn sat up and hurriedly composed herself. A man and woman entered. Smiling and nodding at the tousled lovers, the man went to the bar and the woman carried the heavy tray in her arms out onto the patio. Rafael issued rapid fire directives in Spanish to the servants. Flustered, Quinn asked where the bathroom was, and following Rafael's' directions, she fled to the master bedroom.

Quinn leaned against the oak door in the ornate bathroom and tried to catch her breath. *How am I going to get out of this? He's determined I'm going to spend the night. Oh, God help me, I DO want to spend the night. Rafael must be the devil incarnate.* Quinn caught a glimpse of her disheveled self in the mirrors lining the walls. Her hair was tumbling down over her shoulders. Her dress was wrinkled and she was missing one shoe. Her lipstick was smeared and there was a red mark at the base of her throat.

"A hickey?" Quinn rubbed at the discoloration. "How am I going to explain this?" She asked her reflection. She grabbed a towel, ran it under cold water and pressed it against her neck. *I should leave right now,* her head was buzzing from the heady champagne. *I've got to get out of here. Gracefully, if I can.*

When Quinn emerged, Rafael was waiting for her. He held out his arm and led her outside to the patio. The sun was only a crescent sliver of red that quickly slipped beneath the rim of the western horizon. The succulent aroma of broiled lobster reminded Quinn that she hadn't eaten since breakfast. She sank weakly into the cushioned wicker chair that Rafael was holding out for her.

The dinner the concierge and his wife served to Quinn and Rafael was five-star and presented in such a manner it would have put many resort hotel restaurants to shame. Rafael had even arranged for a trio of mariachi's to serenade the couple as they dined al fresco. Each of the seven courses was served with a libation that complimented and enhanced the palate. By the time the flaming dessert was served, Quinn was almost narcotic.

Abruptly, Rafael stood up and clapped his hands. The service staff and musicians disappeared like magic. He pulled Quinn up from her chair and walked her over to the edge of the patio. "You see all of this, *querida*?" Rafael had his arm around her waist. Quinn nodded. Rafael turned her so she was pressed against him. He was holding Quinn so tight she could barely breathe.

"I can give you this, and more. So much more. You would take the Jamaican man on that boat before you would take this?"

Stunned and dizzy, Quinn shook her head. "What are you talking about, Rafael?"

"Felicia told me about your love affair with that Jamaican man, Noah. I know he is onboard the *Icarus*."

Rafael's grip on Quinn tightened. She began to struggle. "I can't breathe."

Rafael took Quinn's wrist and pulled her over to the large divan by the Jacuzzi. He pushed her down, then sat beside her. "You are young, *querida*. You are innocent." Rafael pulled the flimsy strap of her gown off her shoulder. "You do not want to make a mistake of which you will regret."

Quinn was seeing double moons behind Rafael's head. She was vaguely aware of him tugging on the side zipper that held her gown together. Quinn shut her eyes and heard the whisper of nylon fabric as Rafael undressed her. She could feel the soft cool breeze of the ocean move across her bare and over-heated body. Then the weight and warmth of Rafael was covering her.

Scent, sound, sight, all became a smorgasbord of sensuality as Rafael took possession of Quinn. From head to toe her nerve endings tingled. When Rafael's grip tightened in her hair she could feel the repercussions down to the tips of her toes. When he pressed his mouth against the soft skin between her breast and the hollow under her arm and began to lave her with his tongue, she almost passed out. No man had ever explored that part of her body with such intensity.

Rafael didn't stop even when Quinn begged him to. He was relentless in his pursuit of her. Rafael turned Quinn over and began kneading the muscles of her back, then he was on his knees and inside of her. He was murmuring his pleasure and taking his time, moving in tempo to the lazy, sexy beat of the recorded music that floated over the patio.

The moon was cresting over the villa when Quinn finally pushed herself away from the man who was dominating her. She was on her back and Rafael was poised above her "Stop, please stop, Rafael." His hair, his face, his chest were glistening in the moonlight.

The scent of sex competed with the salt air and the fragrant flowers in the villa. Rafael's chest was heaving. Drops of sweat fell on Quinn's face; the salty taste bitter on her lips.

"Stop now, *querida*? Or stop...soon." He thrust himself deep inside of her. And held her there while his hips writhed in spasm after spasm. Mindlessly, Quinn responded to the heat flooding her womb. Careless, knowing Rafael posed no threat, no fear of an unwanted pregnancy, Quinn let herself be carried away again on the tide of Rafael's hunger.

Hours later, the lovers lay spent, sipping on cognac. A lone ship sounded its horn in the distance. Quinn sat up and Rafael stirred beside her. The sun was beginning to make its ascent; Quinn could tell by the faint glow in the eastern sky over the hills that surrounded Acapulco.

"Oh no!" Quinn crossed her arms over her breasts.

"What, what?" Rafael took Quinn by the neck and pulled her back down. He was already rolling over on top of her when she began to struggle. "I have to go home, I have to go home."

"You are home, *querida*. This is your life. Your home. You are with the eagle." Rafael pushed himself inside of her. "There is no place else you will want to be."

Quinn could feel the world beginning to spin. She could sense Noah waiting for her on the deck of the *Icarus*. He may as well have been on the lounge with her and Rafael. But it was too late for her and Noah, Quinn realized, as her Latin lover pumped, then gasped in pleasure and went limp, his body weighing her down.

The next conscious thing she knew the sun was full upon her. Quinn woke up aware it was time to make some adult decisions. The nagging concern was that she'd gotten herself into waters way over her head. She was now dealing with a man obsessed and issues far beyond her experience. With Rafael's hand covetously on her belly, and Noah's voodoo predictions fresh in her mind, Quinn knew she had to get a serious grip and start charting courses of her own design.

CHAPTER TWENTY-FIVE

There was no one aboard the *Icarus* when Quinn showed up after a brief brunch with Rafael. She'd only nibbled at the lavish spread the servants set out. She was hung over. And her body ached from the passions of the night before. There were other marks on her body aside from the hickey on her neck. Light bruises on her thighs where Rafael had grasped her during the heat of the moment, and on her buttocks.

There was a note on the chart table from Dr. Felix explaining that he'd rented a car and he and the crew were sightseeing and buying supplies. He had to pick up the money he'd had wired to him, too. There was a cryptic post script at the bottom: *Talked to Hank. Big trouble in little china.* Quinn mulled that over as she changed clothes. Rafael had insisted they shower together in the sumptuous master bathroom at the villa. Quinn's face infused with color at the memory. The man's sexual appetite was insatiable. She pulled a crew neck t-shirt over her head. The high neckline would hide the hickey on her throat.

Quinn wasn't sure how she was going to deal with Noah. There would be no point in lying. She'd thought up a story about drinking too much and having to spend the night. *Well, I really did drink too much,* Quinn thought as she gulped down two aspirin to relieve her aching head. And what about Rafael? His parting words to her had been that Felicia and her husband would be arriving later that evening. He expected Quinn back at the villa at seven so the two couples could go out for dinner and dancing.

"He didn't even *ask* me, he *told* me." Quinn spoke out loud. She wandered around the unoccupied yacht, straightening cushions and washing the dishes she found in the sink. Quinn sighed in exasperation as she tried to stuff a cast iron skillet into the over-crowded cabinet next to the sink. "Time to do a little rearranging around here." She knew from past experience that there were deep recessed lockers beneath all of the bunks on most yachts.

She stepped into the forepeak and lifted the cushion of the port bunk. Sure enough, the compartment beneath had plenty of room for excess pots and pans. Quinn sorted out the utensils in the galley and soon had a pile sitting on the starboard berth. She finished stowing the utensils and was repositioning the cushion when she spotted the corner of what looked like a black ledger beneath the adjacent cushion.

Curious, she pulled it out. It was actually a black leather-bound notebook. Feeling a little guilty, Quinn opened it. Chip's name and address were neatly printed on the inside cover. Quinn fanned the pages. It was obviously Chip's journal. Each page was filled with neat entries, all dated. Quinn knew she should put the notebook back and not intrude on her crewmate's privacy. She actually did tuck it back under the cushion.

I wonder what he's had to say about me? The need to know was irresistible. *I'll only read passages if my name is mentioned*, Quinn reasoned as she pulled the black book out again. *I promise.* She took the journal topside where she could keep an eye out if Chip and the crew returned and began to leaf through the pages.

Half an hour later, Quinn sat in shock, one finger earmarking a page of the journal. She had been scanning the entries and was patting herself on the back for not intruding on Chip's innermost thoughts. She was truly on the alert only for the mention of her name. However, midway through, when Noah and Lydia's names leaped out at her, she couldn't help but read what Chip had written.

His annoyance with Noah and Lydia's sexual exploits was obvious on the fated delivery from Mexico. *You'd think they'd be a bit more discreet,* Chip had written. *I came up for watch and they were going at in the cockpit. Noah has no self-control. I've seen it time and time again!*

Quinn had frowned. Another affirmation that Noah was a wild card in the romance department. But the following entries were what rocked her universe.

I had a talk with Noah. He seems to be coming to his senses and agreed with me that he needs to cool it with Lydia. Of course, she doesn't seem to like that one bit. She blames me. The woman obviously can't handle rejection!

There was a blank page, then Chip wrote; *I can't believe what happened tonight. After Noah stormed off to bed, Lydia came up with a mug of hot chocolate for me. She was acting all solicitous until she spilled the damn liquid all over me. Then, consummate actress that she is, she acted all contrite. She went below and came back with towels and began patting me down. My chest, my stomach, my privates. She was crooning in my ear the whole time. I just couldn't help it. She was rubbing me and pushing those huge breasts of hers in my face. There was so much sexual tension in the air. Watching her and Noah going at it all over the boat. When she bared her breasts, then unzipped my pants I felt hypnotized. I don't remember putting the boat on auto-pilot and I didn't even think that Noah could have woken up and caught us in the act. She straddled me. It was wild and crazy. I hate to say it, but it was the most erotic sex I've ever had. I thought I was literally going to explode. She was merciless. Relentless. She was pain and pleasure. No wonder Noah went for it.*

There was more, but Quinn was too dazed to do more than skim over it; Chip's guilt and how hard it was to maintain an air of innocence for the rest of the delivery. His resolve to keep Lydia at a distance so there could be no repeat performance. His stab of jealously when she and Noah resumed their sexual relationship. She'd made an impact on the homely sailor that was for sure.

"No wonder Chip got sick yesterday after I told him about Lydia's pregnancy. He could very well be the father of her baby—not Noah!" Quinn shook her head slowly from side to side. "This puts a whole new spin on *everything.*" Noah's words about being sure he wasn't the father echoed in her head. *"I still swear to you the child will prove to not be mine. It was spoken to me by the obeah."*

Quinn shivered. *This is getting way too freaky. Noah's obeah may well be right, after all.* She slammed the notebook shut. "What a soap opera!" She said out loud. "Should I tell Noah? Should I confront Chip?" She frowned. Short of confessing that she'd read Chip's journal, there was no way she could confront anybody. Quinn jumped up and took the notebook to the forepeak where she carefully replaced it under the cushion.

The humidity, her hangover, and the overwhelming revelation that Noah might possibly be off the hook with Lydia, made Quinn dizzy. She went into the master stateroom, turned on the fan, and crawled onto the wide berth. Her thoughts were a jumbled mass of confusion; Rafael vied with Noah in her mind.

Where Noah could be considerate and patient, Rafael was demanding and determined to be in total control. Quinn couldn't even fathom what the multi-millionaire's plans were for her. She was having a hard time picturing herself in Rafael Santiago's life on a permanent basis.

Life with Noah on the other hand, could prove to be a roller-coaster ride. Voodoo, superstition, and still the lurking possibility he could prove to be the father of Lydia's unborn child. Noah or Chip? Who was the father? It was all too much to absorb. Quinn pushed all three men out of her thoughts and fell asleep to the gentle rocking of the *Icarus*.

The pitching of the boat and the sound of voices awakened Quinn three hours later. Her crewmates were back. She stretched, then sat up as Marnie entered the cabin, her arms laden with plastic shopping bags. "I see you finally made it home." She set the packages down on her half of the berth. "I doubt Noah slept a wink last night. I could hear him pacing around on the deck. Hardly got any sleep myself."

Quinn groaned. "What am I going to do? What should I say?"

"Nothing for now. You're off the hook. He stayed in town with Marcus and some guys from one of the racing yachts. There's practically an entire regatta of sailboats in the main harbor."

Quinn sighed in relief and sat up. "When is he coming back?'

Marnie shrugged. "How should I know? They're drinking and partying already. Tons of boat groupies in town, too. He might never come back."

Seeing the look of hurt that passed over Quinn's face, Marnie was immediately contrite. "Sorry 'bout that, baby doll. But, I can't help but feel kind of sorry for Noah, ya know?"

Quinn nodded. "I can't blame you for that, Marnie. Did Chip stay with them, too?"

"Nope. Dr. Felix wants to take us all out to dinner tonight. Noah and Marcus said they might meet us but the way they were putting away the shots of tequila, I don't see that happening."

"Noah shouldn't be drinking. He told me he gave it up again. For good this time."

Marnie snorted. "Certain things will drive any man to drink. Noah's no exception."

Quinn climbed off the berth. "I can't go to dinner tonight, either. Rafael made plans with another couple for us to go out." She thought for a moment. "Hey, maybe we can all go out together?"

"Sure, why not? But what if Noah *does* show up?"

Quinn left the cabin without answering. Marnie had her dander up. Quinn knew she'd cool off quickly if left alone. Dr. Felix greeted Quinn with a wide grin and a raised brow.

"Too much to drink last night?" He asked tactfully. Quinn answered yes and took the diet soda he offered her. Chip called down from the cockpit. "Anybody got a beer down there?"

Quinn went topside and handed him a cold can of Tecate. Chip chose to ignore the fact that Quinn hadn't spent the night on the *Icarus*. He seemed excited about the race boats in the harbor. He rattled off names; *Christine*, *Windward Passage*, *Merlin*, *Sweet Okole*, *Primavera*. Chip knew the names of the owners, the captains, and most of the crews.

"It doesn't get any better than these, Quinn. We're talking millions of dollars and a ton of racing history."

Felix and Marnie joined them in the cockpit. Chip entertained everyone for almost an hour. It was obvious he was aching to go racing again. When there was finally a lull in the conversation, Quinn brought up the idea of the crew of the *Icarus* going to dinner with Rafael and company. Felix didn't seem to mind, but he expressed doubt that Rafael would agree to the arrangement. "A foursome sounds more intimate than a crowd like us."

"I think Javier has his number. I'm sure he'll let me use the phone to call Rafael. I'll be back in a jiffy." Quinn hopped off the *Icarus*. Marnie wanted to go, too, so both women strolled down to the marina office. Javier was only too happy to let Quinn call Rafael. He even dialed the number for her. Rafael answered almost immediately. If he was surprised to hear Quinn's voice he didn't show it. He sounded delighted that she'd called.

When Quinn asked if he and his guests would object to joining the crew of the *Icarus* for dinner there was a lengthy pause. Finally, he spoke. "Whatever you wish, *querida*. The more the merrier, as they say. Will your friend, Noah, be joining us as well?"

Quinn stumbled over her words in her haste to assure Rafael that he would not. Her hands were shaking when she hung up the phone. She'd been hoping Rafael had put Noah out of his mind. She'd assured him last night that her relationship with Noah was on hold—maybe permanently. Rafael seemed easily convinced that Quinn was utterly incapable of resisting him and the lifestyle he was so eager to offer her.

Rafael had given Quinn the name of the restaurant where he'd already made reservations. He was confident there would be no problem adding four more people. Just as he was confident no one would object to him selecting the restaurant. Just as he was confident he had Quinn in the palm of his hand: At his beck and call and to do with as he wished.

Marnie was looking askance at Quinn as they made their way back to the *Icarus*. "Jeez, does he always affect you like that? Make you stutter and shake? Some romance that is, Quinn."

Quinn shook her head. "It's not what you think. He knows about my fling with Noah. I made the mistake of telling his friend, Felicia, about it when I was in Guadalajara. I don't want the two of them in some kind of confrontation. Rafael is used to power, control and treating people like subordinates.

"I've seen Noah get hot. He won't back down from anybody. I get a bad feeling when I think of the two of them meeting. I can almost guarantee it would get ugly."

"Well, if I were Rafael, I'd be a little worried."

"About what?"

"I'd be worried Noah might slap some nasty old curse on me."

"Oh, Marnie!"

Marnie laughed, then Quinn joined her. By the time they got back on the *Icarus* they barely had time to get ready for dinner. Quinn's only wardrobe choice was the skirt, peasant blouse and sandals she'd purchased the day before. She was regretting the loss of the costume jewelry that went down with the *Vanora* along with everything else. The mark at the base of her throat was obvious and neither she nor Marnie had any cosmetics to conceal it.

Quinn was standing in front of the vanity area combing out her hair when the pouch Noah had given her caught her eye. She undid the leather straps and shook the contents out onto the counter. Her initial revulsion had faded over time. One of the objects was round and flat. There were silver-inlaid hash marks on it and around the sides triangular shapes had been cut out. It was actually kind of an artsy piece. Quinn had a sudden inspiration. She withdrew the leather thong from the hem of the pouch and threaded it through one of the triangles. When she tied the strap around her neck, the amulet hung perfectly; it covered the red welt on her neck.

"Who would have thunked?" She smiled at her image in the mirror. "Obeah to the rescue." Quinn was humming under her breath as she clasped the heavy turquoise belt around her waist. *You never know, there may be something to this obeah stuff. Maybe this charm will ward off any evil spirits.*

She hurried on deck to join her shipmates. The sun was setting and directly off the marina the shimmering rays cast a swath of rainbow colors through the placid ocean. *It looks like a pathway to heaven or something,* Quinn thought as Felix helped her climb off the yacht. Feeling somewhat comforted, Quinn climbed into the jeep with her friends. In a deep baritone, Felix began to sing Otis Redding's "Sitting on the Dock of the Bay." The crew joined in with gusto. The foursome laughed and sang a medley of songs as the jeep bounced along the dusty road leading into Acapulco.

CHAPTER TWENTY-SIX

Quinn groaned inwardly when she and her friends walked into the five-star restaurant. She was completely underdressed and so was the rest of her group. Marnie looked fresh and pert in her usual trousers and button down shirt. Felix and Chip were dressed in slacks, aloha shirts and sandals. On the other hand, Rafael and Felicia's husband, Eduardo, were immaculate in silk suits. Felicia was wearing a stunning red, strapless gown. Her dark, luxuriant hair was upswept; dazzling diamonds on her ears and at her throat.

Following the introductions, Quinn whispered into Rafael's ear. "You should have told me this was formal attire."

He laughed and patted her on the back. "It is nothing, *querida*. A simple misunderstanding. We can dine in private if that would suit you." He motioned to the maitre 'd. Soon the entire group was being led upstairs to an intimate balcony with a stunning view of Acapulco Bay.

Felicia was her usual charming self and her husband was actually quite funny and down to earth. After cocktails, Rafael insisted on ordering the wine. The group as a whole was relaxed. Dr. Felix and the Mexican millionaire got engrossed in an in depth discussion of medicine and pharmaceuticals. Quinn had blanched when she saw the menu. There were no prices on any items and from past experience, she knew what that meant. Without doubt the bill would be in excess of a thousand dollars for a party of seven.

The six-course meal was stellar. Each subsequent dish seemed to outdo the one before. The wines flowed; champagne, mellow red, floral white. There was much laughter and general camaraderie all around. The only sour note was when the check was brought to the table. Rafael was reaching for his wallet when Dr. Felix put his big hand on top of the silver tray.

"Allow me."

Rafael immediately protested. He even placed his slender hand on top of the doctor's. Felix didn't budge. He smiled and slid the tray to the side of his dessert plate. "I promised my crew a night out, Rafael. And thanks to you and your good friends here, it's been much more than I could have possible given them. I insist. And the pleasure is absolutely mine, I assure you."

Rafael nodded graciously but Quinn detected a slight stiffness in his demeanor. *It's like he doesn't appreciate being upstaged*, she realized. *That must be one of the perks of having so much money. Being able to lord it over people.* Quinn was immediately ashamed of her petty thinking. *He means well*, she chided herself. *He has every right to assume none of us has his kind of money.* Quinn stifled a giggle. *Well, none of us do that's for damn sure!*

Rafael suggested the group go to a popular nightclub for after-dinner drinks and dancing. "My treat," he winked at Dr. Felix. At the valet station, Rafael took Quinn by the hand. "Your friends can follow us, *si?*" He helped her into a Mercedes sedan and shut the door.

The club was packed. Quinn had to give her host and his friends credit. Felicia let down her hair and the men removed their ties and jackets. The entire group blended into the crowd. Dr. Felix amazed everyone when he bowed to Felicia then swept her onto the dance floor. The big man who lumbered around his forty-five foot yacht making floorboards creak and moan seemed to sprout wings. Felix Templeton moved with the grace of a toreador. Felicia floated in and out of his arms as they swirled and dipped to the Latin rhythms.

The doctor was sweating when he returned his dance partner to her admiring husband. The table of five applauded. Then Rafael excused himself to take Quinn on the floor.

"Your doctor friend is quite something," Rafael's lips were close to Quinn's ear.

She agreed. "He's a wonderful man. A kind man and a very dear and special friend. He's like a father to me."

Quinn decided it was time to make certain things clear to the handsome, sexy man who was moving her expertly through the intricate moves of the mamba. When Rafael pulled her body into his, she paused and leaned back to look into his smoky green eyes.

"Felix has hired all of us to help him sail to Australia and New Zealand."

For one split second, Rafael froze, almost missing a beat. He recovered and smoothly moved to the edge of the dance floor, then pulled Quinn out a side door. "What are you saying to me?" Rafael took Quinn by the elbows and shook her slightly. "What has possessed you, Quinn? You want to be a *marinera*? A galley slave when you could be a queen? *Mi reina?*"

"I want to sail, Rafael. It's that simple. Really, it is. I want to explore the world."

Rafael laughed and let go his hold on her. "I am the world, *querida*. If you wish to sail, I will buy another *Vanora*. I will buy you captains and deckhands. I will chart a course for you around the world."

Quinn was silent as she tried to gather her thoughts. She needed to convey to Rafael that it wouldn't be the same if he chartered her every course. If anyone charted her course. What she'd learned in her short time at sea was that life was capricious at best. Like the wind and the water; restlessly at odds one moment, then in perfect harmony the next. Deadly and threatening with a certain overwhelming power and majesty like she'd witnessed in the hurricane; then serene and pacific; two elements at peace, all differences forgotten in a common quest. *Unite, go with the flow. Follow the universe. All storms cease, all fair days have their space in time.*

Rafael's harsh voice jerked Quinn back to the moment. "It's because of him, the Jamaican, isn't it? You wish to follow him."

Wordlessly, Quinn shook her head. Her eyes when she looked at Rafael were glistening with tears. When she could finally speak she said, "No. It has nothing to do with him. It has nothing to do with you."

"Then, what is it, *querida*? Don't you understand that you have made me feel? Feel love. Feel my senses and my life again."

Tenderly, Rafael caressed Quinn's cheek. "You ask nothing. You give me everything. I had already lost more than I thought I could bear."

He turned so his back was to her. "My wife lied to me. Time and time again. She took my children away from me. I should have been a smarter man. I should have seen her master plan."

When Rafael turned around, Quinn shrank back at the naked pain in his eyes.

"Elise was obsessed with rank and breeding. Her family could trace their lineage back to Cortez. She wanted children with a pedigree, but she did not want the bindings of marriage."

Rafael closed his eyes. "My father is Lebanese. His bloodline goes back to ancient kings. My mother, a Spanish noblewoman.

"Yet my son and my daughter are being brought up as wealthy and spoiled *gringo* brats. My wife lords it over her echelon in San Diego. She, of course, is dating a senator. She is ambitious and wants the best of both worlds.

"I pay her the child support. I keep a home in La Jolla for my children. They are not allowed to come to Mexico. She is afraid I will not let them return to her false existence."

Quinn placed her hands on Rafael's bowed shoulders. "I had no idea. Felicia told me a little bit about your divorce." Quinn's heart literally ached for the man before her. "But, Rafael, what is it you expect from me?"

Rafael looked up to the stars that competed against the bright city lights. "I'm not sure anymore. I thought perhaps of some uncomplicated love. You have no artifice about you, Quinn. I sense you are confused. I respect your desire to see what life has to offer you. I tell you again, I would gladly give you all that a man can give. When I make love to you I feel as though the world is calling to me. That there is hope. And real passion. That there is reason."

He took her face in his hands. "I have a feeling in my heart that you might know what love really is." Rafael kissed Quinn gently on her forehead.

"It is also true, *querida*, that I am unable to give you children. When Elise took my babies, my children, I vowed I would never again be in a position to have my children taken from me. I had a vasectomy."

Rafael took Quinn's hand. "Let's rejoin the party. The future is uncertain for both of us."

It was past midnight when Rafael suggested the group move the party to the villa. Felicia had brought several bathing suits and soon the four men and three women were in the outdoor Jacuzzi drinking, laughing, and telling stories. Finally, Quinn and Marnie were able to tell in detail the circumstances leading up to the crew of the *Vanora* having to abandon ship.

It was a somber Rafael who broke the silence following their story. "I know Diego's father. He and my father went to the university together. I grew up hearing romanticized stories of the death of his mother and the martyrdom of Rogelio. I had no idea Diego's soul was so poisoned by his loss."

He turned to Quinn. "You say he vowed he would still carry out this crazy plan to smuggle the statue into the United States?"

Quinn nodded. "He's obsessed with the idea. I think his mind has unraveled. The way he acted. And his harping on loyalty. That everyone should be more loyal to him, the captain, than to anyone else." Quinn got a bad taste in her mouth when she thought of Diego's demeaning attitude toward women. She set her glass carefully on the edge of the hot tub.

"This Luiz Montoya is big trouble," Rafael laid his hand caressingly on Quinn's neck. "His ego must be damaged. He, too, must feel betrayed. I'm surprised he didn't order Yoshua killed immediately. He is known for his creatively cruel ways to eliminate any competition. The more vile the death, the less he has to worry about others muscling in on his territory. He is greatly feared in the illegal drug circles."

"What are you saying?" Marnie leaned forward. "You don't think he's going to come after us do you?"

"You are witnesses to his participation in," Rafael ticked off the offenses on his fingers, "Piracy. Drug smuggling. Attempted murder. Stealing a national treasure from the Mexican government."

"Jeez!" Chip spoke up. "You two better be watching your backs. Marcus, too. Come to think of it, maybe he shouldn't be drinking and carousing in town. Maybe Luiz already has a hit out on him. On all you."

Dr. Felix coughed. "Maybe it's not a bad idea to get a move on up the coast. We could talk to the Coast Guard and police once we get to the port of San Diego. We can leave first thing in the morning. If Noah and Marcus make it back, that is."

"It almost is morning," Rafael pointed out. "You're all welcome to stay here for the remainder of the night. There are security guards all around the villa twenty-four hours a day. If you wish I can send a man into town to look for your friends. I have no doubt what district they will be having their fun in. All the sailors and hard-core partiers seem to find their way to that section of Acapulco."

Felix declined the offer to search for Marcus and Noah. He also declined the offer to spend the night. "You three," he looked at Quinn, Chip, and Marnie, "should definitely stay here. I'd feel more comfortable on the *Icarus*, keeping an eye on her."

It was a solemn group that climbed out of the Jacuzzi. Chip decided to go with Felix to the boat. Rafael showed his guests and Marnie to their respective suites. Wrapped in a towel, Quinn waited on the patio for his return. Rafael took Quinn in his arms and held her close to him in the moonlight. It was several moments before he spoke. When he did, his voice came out in a sigh.

"It is best that you go onward with your crew, *querida*. I need time to sort things out and take care of the situation with Diego and Luiz. Diego has much to answer for. He will answer to me, that I can promise you."

He tilted her chin so they were eye to eye. "I would like to ask you to promise me one thing, Quinn. One small thing."

Rafael kissed Quinn softly on the lips. "I ask you to give some serious thought to the course of your life. Give some serious thought to me. I believe you that you and this Noah have reached an impasse of sorts in your relationship. The best advice I can give you is to leave it as such. You are young and beautiful. There will be time for wise decisions, not impetuous ones."

Rafael took Quinn's hand and led her to the master suite. He pulled down the silk sheets, then tugged the fluffy towel off of Quinn's body. The love they made that night was sweet, tender and poignant. Quinn fell asleep in Rafael's arms; a deep, untroubled slumber. Whatever the daylight might bring, Quinn knew she had a solid friend in her new lover. She knew she would always be able to count on Rafael Santiago to be there for her. Whether she chose to remain his lover—or not.

CHAPTER TWENTY-SEVEN

Noah and Marcus didn't stumble their way onto the *Icarus* until almost noon. Both men were bleary-eyed and reeked of alcohol. Quinn and Marnie had left the villa early in the morning. Along with Chip and Dr. Felix, they'd worked hard at refueling the boat, topping off the water tanks, and securing the *Icarus* to set sail. The two drunken sailors were surprised to find the rest of the crew waiting to head out to sea. Rather than explain, Felix told them to shower and catch a nap. Neither man was in any shape to do anything other than get in the way.

Singing an off-key bar song the two drinking buddies made their way below. Chip cast the dock lines to Quinn and Marnie, then hopped onboard as the *Icarus* backed out of the slip. The sun was burning hot but once the Columbia 45 got well into the bay a breeze sprang up, cooling off the crew and calling for Felix to have the women raise the mainsail.

Once the *Icarus* was comfortably underway on a starboard tack, Quinn went below to make some lunch. She checked on Marcus and Noah in the forepeak bunks. Both were out like lights. The overhead hatch was open for ventilation, but the smell of tequila was still strong. Quinn wrinkled her nose and shook her head. Gazing at the two buddies lying there, Quinn's thoughts turned to Lydia. *I wonder if she understands there is a chance, a very good chance, that* Chip *not* Noah *is the father of her baby. Wonder how she and detective dad would handle that? I wonder how Chip would handle that.*

Quinn returned to the small galley. Dr. Felix had provisioned well. The epicurean doctor obviously liked to eat. Quinn had been pleased beyond words when she'd seen his well-stocked herb and spice rack. The older model sailboat had a recessed icebox instead of an upright refrigerator. However, there was plenty of storage room inside. Quinn had pretty well explored most of the contents during her time onboard. She was thawing a corn beef for dinner. Dr. Felix had a pressure cooker onboard and Quinn was looking forward to using it.

For lunch, Quinn decided she'd make Monte Cristo sandwiches. *Kind of a compromise for missing breakfast,* she mused. It took some time to prepare the layered indulgences. She beat eggs with water, then whisked in flour, salt, pepper, and baking powder. Quinn set the batter aside, then layered ham, turkey and Swiss cheese between thick slices of French bread. After dunking the sandwiches in the batter, Quinn fried them in butter evenly on both sides in an iron skillet. She dusted the golden-brown bread tops with confectioner's sugar and set out a bottle of maple syrup.

"Fit for a king, indeed!" Dr. Felix beamed. The four wakeful sailors were sitting in the cockpit eating the mouth-watering sandwiches.

"This is absolutely delicious," Marnie agreed. "I've never had one of these before. Think I'll have another."

Quinn passed her the platter she'd brought on deck. She'd quartered each sandwich and there was plenty to go around. Chip snagged two more for himself as the tray went by.

"So, Felix, what was the news with Hank?" Quinn took a sip of her orange juice, then selected another Monte Cristo.

"His knickers are in a twist. Loomis Grady apparently has been making Hank give him cash kickbacks for any referrals. It's not that big of a deal but Loomis, it turns out, has a shady background. Not to mention, Hank and Noah got into some trouble together awhile back. A minor drug thing, he says.

"Hank didn't have time to go into detail but he thinks it's a good idea for him to cool it with Loomis. Also, he thinks Noah might be better off going back to Jamaica until the investigative dust settles, so to speak. I was up front with him about my plans for us all sailing to the South Pacific. Although, that could take some time to put into place. I need to find a bigger boat just for starters."

And Noah can't go fleeing to the other side of the world until the baby issue is settled. Chip, either, whether he knows it or not. Quinn was mulling over the new information. *And, what am I to do in the meantime? Go back to Cyndi and Joey? Go home to Boston? Get another cocktail waitress job?* None of her options were appealing. Quinn set her uneaten sandwich down.

"How long until we get to San Diego?" She asked Felix.

"That depends. How soon do all of you want to get there? Anybody in a hurry?"

Quinn and Marnie both shook their heads. Chip remained silent.

"As long as we keep a low profile and our eyes peeled for that Luiz guy and his henchmen, I wouldn't mind stopping at a few Mexican ports along the way. Manzanillo, Puerto Vallarta. Maybe Mazatlan, and certainly Cabo San Lucas. You're all welcome to stay on as long as I own the *Icarus*. Who knows? I may find the perfect boat sooner than I expect."

It was late afternoon before first Marcus, then Noah finally woke up. Marcus was ashen-faced and shaky. Quinn took one look at him, then made him sit down in the cockpit while she went below to get him some Alka-Seltzer. "You're the poster boy for someone who's turning green, dude." Quinn told him with genuine sympathy.

Noah was coming out of the tiny forward head when Quinn went to the galley. He was shaking his head. When he spoke his voice sounded thick, and he spoke carefully as if each word hurt as it came out of his mouth.

"You must now think me a liar, Quinn."

"Not at all, Noah." Quinn decided she had better prepare two doses of Alka Seltzer.

"I think you needed to blow off some steam. I'm glad Marcus was with you. He's a good guy."

With a sheepish grin, Noah took the fizzing beverage Quinn was holding out to him. "Perhaps I'm not as cleansed or prepared for obeah priesthood as I want to believe I am."

"Perhaps not. But, we've both got plenty of time to let things sort themselves out."

Quinn decided to leave it up to Dr. Felix to clue Noah and Marcus in on the upcoming itinerary and even the turmoil brewing in Miami with Hank. What was festering in her mind was, should she let on to Chip that she knew he was a candidate as the father of Lydia's baby. Didn't Noah have a right to know? *But what right did I have to snoop in Chip's diary?*

Maybe Chip's conscience will start to bother him. He must know the dread in Noah's heart over this. He also knows it's been a real roadblock between Noah and me. Maybe if he has a couple days to think it over? I'll wait and see. If Chip doesn't fess up, I'm going to have to let Noah know. It's not fair for him to carry this alone when the odds are so evenly split.

The corned beef and cabbage dinner was a success all around. Quinn was impressed with the pressure cooker. Dr. Felix told her she could even make sourdough bread in it. He had a starter sourdough. The crew of the *Icarus* ate heartily under the starlit sky that night. Cornbread and beer accompanied the meal. Since Marcus and Noah had slept most of the day, Felix assigned them the midnight to four watch. Technically, Chip and Marnie had the eight until midnight. Quinn and Felix would take the early morning four until eight watch.

Sea conditions were ideal as the *Icarus* sailed through easy swells on a full main. Felix turned on the spreader lights and brought out a backgammon board and a checker board. The exquisite concertos and sonatas of Mozart, Beethoven and Vivaldi flowed from outside speakers. Felix Templeton had a passion for classical music, the masters, and opera. The studio-perfect sound system was one of his few luxury indulgences aside from fine food and spirits.

As the blended notes of piano, violin, and French horns filled the air in a silken symphonic embrace, an aura of peace settled over the *Icarus*. Six heads bent in concentration over the game boards. On occasion, one of the players would get up, stretch and look around at the expanse of water and the sparkling canopy of stars above the western hemisphere. It was a night of such beauty, harmony and serenity that the entire crew would remember it for a long, long time.

It hardly seemed possible it was nearly midnight when Dr. Felix called it quits. "I've got the early watch, gang. I'm going to bed." Quinn decided she'd better get some shut eye, too. She'd had only a few hours of sleep at the villa. She left Marnie, Marcus, Chip and Noah on deck and followed the doctor below.

"I see things have settled down a bit between you and Noah," Felix was pulling out the sofa bed in the main salon. Quinn nodded.

"I can't help but like Rafael, Quinn. He's to the manor born, obviously, but he seems to take the family business seriously. I was surprised at how far-sighted he is. He takes his position as president of the pharmaceutical corporation to heart. He's also concerned with maintaining quality control. He's not into just making the big bucks. He's got a good marketing mind."

Quinn was tired. "Your point being?" The question seemed to hang in the air before Felix responded.

"Point being, I advise you to not give up on the man. Not yet, anyway. Noah's going to be pretty busy the next few months. He needs to get out of harm's way *and* deal with little miss whacko.

"I advise you to stay busy as well. Idle hands are truly the devil's workshop. I can keep you and maybe Marcus or Marnie employed until I find the right boat. I'm not sure about Chip. If we plan on circumnavigating the globe, I'll have to conserve my shekels."

Quinn was sorely tempted to enlighten her physician friend right then to the reality that Chip could very well be the one about to have a major comeuppance with regards to Lydia. Not Noah. She was too tired, so instead, she thanked the big teddy bear of a man for his concern, hugged him, and wished him a good night's sleep.

Quinn was determined to give Chip a chance to prove his mettle. If he had a true sense of loyalty to his friends and shipmates, he would confess his culpability. He would share with Noah the burden of Lydia's duplicity. He would speak to Noah of his own accord.

But, if Chip doesn't talk soon, I'll talk it over with Dr. Felix. I'll follow his recommendation. Quinn prepared to get into bed. *Felix is the most sane and normal person I've met since I started this whole yacht delivery business.* She hopped onto the bunk. *Still,* a wide grin spread over Quinn's face as she laid her tired body down, *psycho cooks, demented captains, drug smugglers, randy sailors, lesbian deckhands, lordly yacht owners, and hurricanes. I know what I'm going to have as my epitaph:* **I'd rather be sailing.**

CHAPTER TWENTY-EIGHT

The hushed whisperings and movements of crewmembers changing the early morning watch woke Quinn at four in the morning. She could hear the rumblings of Dr. Felix. His voice was as big as he was and even when he tried to subdue it the timber seemed to reverberate in the air around him. The clanking of the coffeepot on the stove, the sound of Marcus and Noah making their way to the forepeak cabin, all impinged on Quinn's consciousness. Marnie was sound asleep beside her. Quinn had no memory of her bunkmate getting into bed.

She stretched, then climbed off the berth. When Quinn emerged from the cabin, the inviting aroma of coffee and fresh baked popovers was in the air. Soon she was on deck in the cool pre-dawn air. Felix was manually steering the *Icarus* along her course. Quinn noticed they were on a different tack; leaning to the port. The air seemed thick with moisture. The moon had long hidden its face below the mysterious and far off horizon. A patchwork of stars showed through the cloud cover overhead.

Quinn settled in the cockpit, cup of coffee and pastry in hand. Dr. Felix remarked that they were heading to Manzanillo, Mexico. The Las Hadas Resort Hotel there had a decent marina. "I sailed a few times to Mexico before I decided to head to Jamaica," he explained.

"You may not know this but the resort was the backdrop for the movie '10.' I imagine you don't know who Bo Derek is either."

"Oh, yes I do! I've seen the movie. I love the seventies. The fashions, the art deco. TV shows like Sonny and Cher, Laugh-in, and all those quirky sit-coms."

Felix was nodding his head, smiling.

"My mom still has some memorabilia from those days. She doesn't know I'm aware of what a rebel she was. But my dad's told me bits and pieces about their college years."

"Hmm, wonder if I may have run into Viviane and Harold during my wild hippie days in Negril."

Quinn burst out laughing. "Now, that I seriously doubt."

The mention of her parents brought a troubled frown to Quinn's face. She had no doubt her father had followed through with having his attorney's law firm investigate the backgrounds of Loomis, Hank and Noah. *Well, they'd be in for the shock of a lifetime if they found out about Luiz and Diego. Not that they'll ever find out if I can help it. I'll just tell them Dr. Felix made me a better offer and that I didn't like the captain of the Vanora; that part a least isn't a lie.*

"What are you thinking, Quinn?" Felix's deep voice interrupted her train of thought.

As briefly as she could, she told him about Harold and Viviane's interference.

"Parents are like that. You're always going to be their little girl. I wouldn't let it upset you too much. I doubt either Hank or Noah has much to hide. Loomis, yes. The way the guys talk about him, sounds like he's not real popular with anyone. And especially not with Marnie."

"She doesn't like him because he calls her a dyke."

"Oh, that's not the sole reason for her dislike. She and I discussed it on watch one night."

"Really? Do you mind telling me about it?"

"Loomis is responsible for that drug mark on the guys' records. Unbeknownst to Hank, a deckhand Loomis recommended was actually a mule for some marijuana Loomis wanted brought from Jamaica to Miami. At Loomis's behest, Hank and Noah brought this not so smart fellow along on a delivery from Kingston, Jamaica."

Felix liked nothing better than telling a good story. He settled himself on the seat, his coffee cup nearly obscured by his big hand.

"Nathan, I believe his name was, had a midnight watch. Marnie didn't say whether he'd been sampling the stuff in his duffle bag, but when Hank came up around two in the morning to relieve himself over the side, he checked on their bearings. I can only imagine the panic he felt when he realized Nathan had steered them off course. They were in Cuban waters."

Quinn had heard stories about how tough the Cuban authorities were about alien boats in their waters. She too, could only imagine the panic Hank must have been feeling. The boat could have been confiscated and all three of them could end up languishing in a Cuban jail cell for God only knew how long.

"Hank yelled for Noah and told Nathan to get the hell out of the way. When Noah came up and assessed the situation, he pointed out lights that were fast approaching them over the water. Hank already had the engine full throttle. That's when it dawned on Nathan that he, all of them, were about to get busted for smuggling drugs in Cuba. He wasn't so stupid he didn't realize that would mean prison for life. And in a prison from hell, not like American institutions.

"He disappeared below and came back up with a duffle bag in hand. Probably had a kilo in there. He was about to toss it over when Hank grabbed his arm. 'What the hell are you doing?' Nathan was stuttering he was so scared. 'It's pot, man! We gotta ditch it!' Hank must have cursed soundly at that, I'm thinking. The way Marnie told the story, it was Noah who was still thinking rationally. 'It won't sink right away. We have to put in a weight to take it straight to the bottom of the sea.' Everyone began frantically looking around. Hank was trying to steer the boat; the lights of the other vessel were nigh upon them. In desperation, Noah cut loose the lunch hook. You know, the light anchor we use in shallow waters. He tied it to the duffle bag and dropped it overboard. And none too soon, as a huge beam of light swept the boat from bow to stern."

Quinn was so caught up in the story she was sitting on the edge of her seat. She could tell Felix was relishing the attention.

"The sea gods must have been with those three. It was an American Coast Guard cutter. Three officers boarded the small sailboat. Hank explained that Nathan was a rookie sailor and that he, Hank, would take full responsibility for any maritime infractions since he was the one who left the idiot alone on watch.

"I guess the commander must have liked Hank, or appreciated his candor. When one of the officers came up from searching the interior, he was holding a small bud of marijuana in his hand. I have no doubt Hank's stomach turned to ice."

"I have no doubt, either!" Quinn was shaking her head.

"After a private talk between the commander and the officer, the commander asked Hank who slept in the forepeak cabin. Before Hank could respond, Noah spoke up and said he and Nathan did. With his dreadlocks and Jamaican accent, I'm amazed that the officials simply didn't cart Noah off.

"Hank would have none of that. 'I can, and will, speak for Noah. We're professionals. Our livelihood is delivering yachts. Noah would never, ever jeopardize that.' He shoved Nathan forward. 'But, I can't speak for this one. I hired him as a favor for someone in Miami. I can't tell you how much I regret it. Not just for this, but for his uselessness at the helm.'

"There was more discussion. Bottom line is, they cited them for a misdemeanor of possession of non-prescription drugs, not smuggling." Felix laughed. "I had no idea there was a misdemeanor possession at sea. I guess the Coast Guard decided they had to slap them on the wrist."

"Now that explains a lot." Quinn said. "I overheard a comment Hank made to Loomis in Miami that made me wonder if there was more to their relationship then meets the eye. Still, I don't understand why Hank would remain friends and in a business relationship with Loomis when the man practically almost threw Hank and Noah's lives away."

Felix shrugged. "Whatever the connection, you don't have to worry about it anymore. If you're serious about sailing with me, that is. Which I sincerely hope you still are."

Quinn held her palm up for a quick slap. "You bet I am, Captain Felix."

Two days later, the *Icarus* motored into the marina at Las Hadas, Manzanillo. The bay they'd entered was much smaller than Acapulco and far more scenic. From the marina Quinn could see across the water to a small city. There were dozens of boats tied up at the docks. The vessels ranged in size from under twenty-five feet to over sixty. It appeared most of the owners and the crews were American. It was late in the afternoon by the time the crew secured the *Icarus*. Felix suggested everyone do their own thing for the rest of the day and night. Quinn was eager to explore the grounds of the hotel. Everyone but Felix freshened up and left the yacht as a group.

Felix had gotten lucky with the slip. The *Icarus* was tied up on the first dock leading to the hotel. She was the seventh boat from land. Quinn observed several men and women her age either working on the yachts they passed or sitting on the decks. Everyone waved and called a friendly hello as she and her group passed by. Quinn was struck again at how closely knit the sailing community was. The dock turned into a broad walkway that led to a sparkling blue pool. The white spires of the famous golf resort and hotel seemed to cover the entire side of a hill. Red bougainvillea and lush palm trees were everywhere.

A restaurant and bar overlooked the huge pool with a little island in the middle. Marnie's suggestion they stop for a cocktail was greeted with a hearty affirmative by all. When Marcus went to pay for the first round of drinks, the waiter smiled and said it had been taken care of. He motioned with his head to a couple who waved from the other side of the bar. Marcus motioned for the couple to join them. "Welcome to Manzanillo," the man greeted the table. "Word travels fast on the dock."

The man introduced himself as Bobby. He was tall, thin, and appeared to be in his early fifties. He had a thinning patch of red hair and the blotchy complexion of a fair-skinned man who'd spent most of his life in the sun. His wife, Sandy, was in her thirties. She was an attractive, petite and busty blonde

Sandy laughed. "And sound travels, too, just to warn you. There's a couple two docks inside who fight a lot. So far, that's been the only drawback the two weeks we've been here."

Bobby and Sandy were cruising out of Dana Point, California. They made an annual run down the Mexican Riviera aboard their thirty-five-foot sloop, *Odyssey*. "We've been coming three years in a row," Sandy said. "There are quite a few repeaters here that I'm sure you'll meet sooner or later."

Marcus offered to buy the couple a drink but they declined. "We're expected at a barbeque on dock E. I'm sure the Harris's wouldn't mind if you came. They're really good people."

The crew of the *Icarus* thanked their new found friends but declined. Bobby made them promise to come to the next dock barbeque. "Probably be tomorrow night. Everybody barbeques so damn much around here I'm surprised I'm not crapping briquettes." Sandy hit her husband on the arm and the Californians departed laughing.

"Sounds like this is going to be a fun spot," Quinn raised her glass. "Here's to Manzanillo."

As it turned out, Manzanillo was a fun respite. Quinn fell in love with the spirals, domes and marble decor of the Las Hadas Hotel. At night the hotel took on a truly exotic appearance as craftily placed lighting lit up the statues that adorned the property. People were friendly and the crew of the *Icarus* made friendships among their fellow yachties that would most likely last a lifetime.

Felix hadn't planned on tarrying too long out of concern for the drug cartel lord, Luiz. However, much to the amusement of his crew, he met the sister of the owner of a neighboring yacht who was visiting from Michigan. Anna Hartley was a slender, middle-age schoolteacher. She had jet-black hair streaked with gray and blue eyes. She was attractive and easy going. Anna seemed to always have a gentle smile on her face.

"I do believe our over-sized captain has found himself a girlfriend," Marnie said. Felix and Anna were strolling down the dock arm-in-arm after an afternoon in Manzanillo.

"Yes indeed," Quinn sighed. "The guys seem to be scoring left and right, too." Chip and Marcus hadn't come back to the yacht until nearly dawn for the three nights since the *Icarus* had reached the marina. Noah would accompany them out, but he was usually back onboard by midnight. He was still keeping his distance from Quinn, but he was polite about it.

Quinn and Marnie spent their days shopping in Manzanillo. Although on a limited budget, Quinn managed to scrounge up a semi-decent wardrobe to replace some of what she lost when the *Vanora* went down. Marnie was so low-maintenance, Quinn had to snicker as they shopped. "You really don't care what you wear, do you, Marnie, as long as it's not a skirt or has any ruffles, lace or frills on it."

"It makes life easier that way. Think about it. The less you have, the less you have to lose."

Quinn laughed outright at Marnie's backwards philosophy. "Let's get back to the boat and get ready. Everybody's meeting at the Las Hadas lounge tonight after dinner for some dancing and drinking."

The lounge Quinn referred to had become a favorite night spot. Chip, Marcus and usually Noah, preferred to take a taxi into town to party. Quinn was happy staying close to home, the *Icarus*. There were plenty of tourists staying at the resort and every night, Quinn found herself dancing with a plethora of different partners. Marnie seemed to be doing okay in the partner department, too. She'd been hanging out with the same blonde woman two consecutive nights in a row.

Quinn was kind of smitten with a blonde of her own. A soccer player from England named Lee. He was actually a guest on one of the larger yachts in the marina. A 72-foot Dutch ketch. Quinn maintained a teasing, but hand's off relationship with him that only seemed to pique his interest. Lee claimed an average of every third dance with Quinn each night and her wineglass was never empty.

"You're an odd bird," Lee had followed Quinn outside for some fresh air. It was the third night, and Quinn was unaware it would be her last one in Manzanillo.

"Why do you say that?" Quinn was smiling, but her eyes were fastened on the splendor of the lit up resort below her.

"Because I know you're attracted to me. So, why do you keep trying to pretend that you're not? We're both bloody adults here, you know."

Quinn thought for a moment. What Lee was saying was true. She'd have to be blind and a nun to not be attracted to him. He was attractive, buff and had that charming accent. He had a quick wit and an obviously generous heart.

"I just got out of a relationship, Lee. A rather complicated one. I'm not sure it's really over forever, either."

"So? I'm not proposing marriage, luv. I'm proposing we have a bit of fun. Life is short. Seize the day and all that rot. What do you say?"

Lee turned Quinn around to face him. She was inches away from kissing him when Marnie and her gal pal walked out onto the balcony. Lee groaned, then greeted the two women. Marnie arched a brow at Quinn, who shook her head and followed Lee back into the nightclub.

When he offered to walk her home after midnight, she had to say no. There was no way she was going to hurt Noah any more than she already had. Lee let it be known he wasn't happy with her recalcitrance. He appeared somewhat mollified when she explained that her ex-lover was crewing on the *Icarus*.

"I see, luv. Well then, there's always tomorrow." Lee kissed Quinn lightly on the cheek and walked away.

Tomorrow wasn't in the stars for Quinn and Lee the soccer player. When Quinn climbed up onto the *Icarus*, Dr. Felix was sitting in the cockpit. Anna was at his side, holding his hand.

"Where are the others?" The doctor barked at her in an uncharacteristically harsh voice.

"I don't know. I last saw Marnie at the nightclub. I'm pretty sure Noah, Marcus and Chip are in town."

Felix passed a hand over his face. "Sorry to snipe at you like that, Quinn. I got a message from Rafael."

Quinn's heart seemed to stop beating for a moment at the mention of the Mexican millionaire's name. Before Felix could go on, her brain registered the fact that the only thing that could have Felix so flustered was that he'd gotten bad news. It had to concern Luiz Montoya.

"Rafael has done some snooping. The body of a certain Yoshua Hernandez was found. Near San Mateo del Mar, no less. The mutilated body of Yoshua Hernandez."

Quinn put her hand to her mouth. She was suddenly sick to her stomach. Images of Yoshua sprang to mind. As creepy and sneaky as he was, her heart ached for him. She shook her head to rid herself of the horrifying visions that were trying to crowd her brain.

"Is he sure it's our Yoshua?" Quinn's mouth was so dry she could barely speak the words.

"Yes, he's sure. What no one can know is if poor Yoshua was forced to spill his guts and tell his torturers about the *Icarus* plucking you guys out of the water."

"So, that's what you're so worried about." Quinn let out a big puff of air.

"I have a bad vibe about staying here any longer. Rafael agrees. Four days is way too long. We need to get moving. I don't mind hitting some other resorts along the way to San Diego as long as we only stay a day or two.

"We'll keep a low profile and radio transmissions to a minimum. The arms of Luiz's cartel from what Rafael has told me are long, deep and merciless. We need to impress on the guys to be discreet when they're out and about drinking. One word to the wrong person and there's no doubt it'll get back through the grapevine to Montoya."

Glumly, Quinn had to agree. She'd been having such a good time in Manzanillo, and she'd been looking forward to the same kind of experience in Puerto Vallarta and Cabo. Quinn had grown to love the people of Mexico. She was charmed with their traditions, their work ethic, their love of families and their obvious faith. However, Quinn could understand the reasoning behind Felix and Rafael's concern. It was time to move on.

"Better get some rest, my dear. Be prepared to cast off at a moment's notice. We'll be leaving as soon as everyone is onboard."

Quinn gave Felix a sad little salute, then Anna a big hug. Her eyes were tearing up as she went down the companionway steps. *None of this is fair. None of it. Dr. Felix gets a chance at love and because of me, us, he's going to be robbed of that. We're not the criminals here, yet, we're the ones who have to watch our backs and be on the run. Freaking drugs. God curse the people who run them. Why are people so blind? Why give power and money to lowlifes like Luiz and his crew?*

There's so much more to life then getting high, which is really nothing more than getting stupid. Quinn climbed onto her bunk; sad, discouraged, baffled and shaking her head.

Chapter Twenty-nine

The sound of the Perkins diesel engine rumbling to life at dawn awakened Quinn. Marnie was stumbling around in the darkened cabin, mumbling to herself. Quinn had changed from her evening wear into light sweatpants and a t-shirt before going to bed. She wanted to be prepared for the unexpected.

"Did you just get in?" Quinn got out of the berth.

"Yeah, yeah. It's all good." Marnie sounded a little bit high.

"Are the guys back, too?"

"Yup, they're on deck. Don't really think Felix needs the two of us right now."

"I'll make breakfast then." Quinn brushed her teeth and left the cabin.

The *Icarus* was out in the bay by the time Quinn finished making scrambled eggs, bacon and toast. She called for the men to come and get the food. Noah was first to respond. He had a day or two's stubble on his chin and his amber eyes were bloodshot. Quinn poured him a mug of orange juice and handed him a plate.

"Dude, you look like crap." Quinn smiled to take the sting out of her observation.

"I feel like such, I certainly do." Noah's hand shook as he raised the mug to his lips. "Come, let's you and I eat in the bow so we can talk together."

Quinn agreed. She nodded at Chip and Marcus as they passed her in the main cabin. Felix was at the wheel and he winked as Quinn and Noah went by.

Perched on the sabot strapped to the deck, the duo ate in silence as they watched the sun come up. For once Noah didn't have his trademark bandana wrapped around his head. His hair seemed to be growing back in rather quickly. Quinn had to fight a sudden urge to run her hand over the new growth covering his well-shaped skull.

Noah set his plate down on the deck between his feet. Quinn followed suit. She'd eaten every scrap of food on her plate. When Noah finally turned to face her, she was struck by the bleak look in his eyes. He seemed at a loss for words. When he finally spoke, his words cut to her very heart.

"I need to move on. You already are moving on, Quinn. I'm sliding backwards. Into a pit of absolute darkness. I have kept secrets from you. At least you have tried to be honest with me." Noah was speaking seriously and with care, no lilt of patois in his voice. He took her right hand in his. Smiling, he stroked the lightly scarred palm; deliberately evoking memories of the seven days they'd shared on the *Zephyr*.

"There is a storm brewing. It blows on the wind that moves us along in life. I choose to not retreat to Jamaica and wait it out. I would sink even deeper into the darkness there. I'm signing on for the Transpac race this year. I need to keep my mind full and my hands busy."

Quinn remembered her first meeting with Hank when he'd explained how he and Noah met on the biannual race from San Pedro, California, to Diamond Head, Hawaii.

"What do you mean a storm is brewing?"

"We are entangled in a series of events that can only explode. First there was you and me. Then, Lydia reentered my life and with vengeance in her heart. The eagle man appeared and came between us. You innocently became involved with a drug cartel. My demons came back to possess me."

Noah waved his hand in a circle in the air. "This is all bad mojo. Really bad. We need to keep our distances. All of us from each other, so the power doesn't feed from our energy. Me away from you. Away from Lydia. You away from the man who believes he is an eagle. The drug lord is somehow attached to this Rafael. I feel it."

Quinn sighed in exasperation. "Noah, you're acting on superstition again, not rationale." She wanted to grab him and shake some sense into him. Sensing her frustration, Noah stood up.

"Perhaps we are not meant to ever be. Our worlds are too far apart. The obeah could have been wrong in that regard."

"Oh, obeah be damned!" Quinn jumped to her feet. "Why can't you think for yourself, Noah? Instead of depending on some fortune teller?

No one can predict the future. We have to make our own futures by our decisions. By our actions. By how we chose to live each day."

Noah sighed and shook his head. He was preparing to walk away when Quinn grabbed his arm.

"I have something to tell you."

Noah turned and the look on his face was hopeful.

In a rush, before she could change her mind, Quinn blurted out.

"There's a good chance you're not the father of Lydia's baby. Actually, a fifty-fifty chance that you're not."

Noah stared blankly at Quinn, then his body swayed. For a moment Quinn thought he was going to topple over. Instead, he grabbed her roughly by the arms. "What is this? What are you saying? Are you trying to torture me?" He shook her.

"Noah, please. Sit down for a moment and let me explain."

Noah sat down abruptly as though all the strength had been drained from his body. His chest heaved as he drew in deep, harsh breaths. Quinn sat beside him and put her hand on his knee. When his breathing returned to near normal, she continued.

"I was alone on the boat the day after we arrived in Acapulco. All of you had gone into town. I was rearranging the galley and decided to stow some utensils in the forepeak. By accident, I stumbled on a journal underneath the bunk cushions. Chip's journal."

Noah sat rigidly, his eyes locked on Quinn. She could see the muscles bunch up under his skin. He was so still, he looked like a statue. Only his eyes were alive; alive with a deep smoldering glow of dawning awareness.

Quinn hurried on with her story. "Don't jump to any conclusions, Noah. Chip didn't even know Lydia was threatening you with a paternity suit until we were in Acapulco. He was as shocked as any of us were. I think it made him physically ill when I told him about it." She paused to catch her breath.

"Go on," Noah said in a voice of steel.

"I didn't mean to read the journal," Quinn's face flushed with shame. "I thought I'd just skim it and only read entries he'd made mentioning you and me. When I saw your name along with Lydia's, I couldn't help myself. I guess I was feeling some jealousy or something."

That small confession seemed to please Noah, even in his present state.

"The night before Lydia faked her suicide—you know—the night you'd decided to cool it with her, I guess she decided to take out her frustration and revenge on Chip. She spilled hot chocolate all over him, then acted all contrite and began to mop it up off of him."

Quinn became even more embarrassed as she related Chip's description of Lydia's seduction of him. When she finished, Noah didn't say a word. Finally, Quinn couldn't take the silence any longer and rising to her feet, she looked down and said, "I have no doubt, Noah, absolutely no doubt, that Chip would have told you about this himself, given time."

Noah did something Quinn had never seen him do before. He spat on the deck. "Chip has had five days to confess to me. And all the nights when we were out drinking, sharing our thoughts and feelings." Noah stood up, back rigid. His eyes shimmered in the mid-morning sun.

Unshed tears? Quinn thought with an aching heart. "Noah, Noah, can't you be glad that you might be off the hook? You can't blame Chip. Only Lydia is to blame. Think about it. She has to know the baby could be Chip's. She's just out to get *you*."

Noah spat again, then stalked away. Quinn crumpled onto the deck in a heap of misery, self-loathing and despair. *Oh God, what have I done? What have I done? Oh, please forgive me. Please help Chip and Noah get through this. Please don't make me the one to have ruined their friendship forever.*

A seagull lit on the deck near Quinn. It looked at her out of knowing, ancient eyes. The bird preened, long neck stretched out as it ruffled its feathers with its beak. With a hop, and a squawk, the seagull took wing and soared gracefully into the air, only to hang on a current parallel to the *Icarus*, before banking off over the deep cerulean water.

Quinn stayed where she was for over two hours. When the sun reached its zenith she got up and made her way back to the cockpit. Noah was at the wheel. He gave her the briefest of nods as she moved past him to go below and prepare lunch. Marnie was still asleep in the aft cabin. Dr. Felix was snoring on the couch in the main salon. The curtain between the forepeak and the galley was closed. Quinn assumed Chip was napping, too.

Everyone's schedule was off, so Quinn made a tray of sandwiches and set out condiments and chips. *They can all fend for themselves*, Quinn thought. For the first time, she wanted off a boat. Not even in Hurricane Cecelia had Quinn wanted to be somewhere else, anywhere but onboard, with such intensity. She wished wholeheartedly that she could call a helicopter to take her off the *Icarus*. *Enough is too much. I need a place to hide and lick my wounds and it's like all the air and space is taken.* The only solace Quinn had was that according to Dr. Felix' reckoning, they'd be arriving at Yelapa, a small cove in Banderas Bay near the port city of Puerto Vallarta, late tomorrow.

Quinn managed to eat half a sandwich. The plate she'd carried up to Noah remained untouched. She knew because when Marnie emerged from the aft cabin, Quinn helped carry her lunch up on deck. The normally agile woman was dropping chips and pickles all over the place before Quinn came to the rescue.

"I think that broad drugged me," Marnie sat in the cockpit gobbling a BLT sandwich. "I don't remember a freaking thing about last night. Nothing, zilch, nada. I barely remember boarding the yacht this morning." She stopped in mid bite and look of alarm passed over her face. "That *was* this morning, wasn't it?"

"Jeez, Marnie! Yes, it was. You should be more careful about the company you keep." Quinn's nerves were frayed. "Shouldn't we all," she added, glaring pointedly Noah. As Quinn stomped down the companionway stairs, she heard the bewildered Marnie say to Noah, "Hot damn. What's gotten into *her?*"

Not caring if Noah bothered to reply, Quinn went into the master stateroom, slammed the door shut, and flung herself onto the bunk. *Who needs the drama?* Quinn fumed to herself as she lay on her back looking at the ceiling. *Everybody's got issues, dammit. Life, even on a yacht, isn't perfect. Hell, I'm not the one who got Lydia pregnant. I'm not Marnie's babysitter, either.*

Quinn punched the pillow next to her. Even with the overhead hatch wide open, it was hot and stifling in the cabin. Quinn tossed and turned before finally willing herself to lay still and hopefully let sleep overtake her. She would have put money on it that fireworks were about to go off on the *Icarus* when Noah and Chip confronted each other. She had no doubt the impulsive, emotional Jamaican wouldn't be able to contain himself for any length of time.

In Quinn's opinion, Chip really didn't have a leg to stand on, either.

CHAPTER THIRTY

D r. Felix was grumbling. Quinn had slept from one in the afternoon until almost seven in the evening. The doctor wasn't grumbling that she'd overslept and hadn't cooked dinner. He'd actually cooked, and the spaghetti with meatballs was delicious. He was warming up a heaping plate for Quinn.

"I was on the radio briefly this afternoon and raised an old sailing acquaintance of mine." He set the plate down in front of Quinn, then eased himself into the seat across from her. "You know how I've been raving about Yelapa. What a secluded little cove it is. How we would throw down a lunch hook, skinny dip, drink and carry on back in the Day?"

Quinn nodded, her mouth full of a bite of meatball that was redolent of garlic.

"Well, my buddy informed me Yelapa's like a tourist destination nowadays. Crowded. You can still only get to it by boat but the fishing village is fairly commercial and the cruise ships bring in daily tours to the beach." Felix sighed. "Same damn thing with Cabo. I remember when the biggest attraction there was the *panderia*—the bakery. That and the Hotel Finisterra that sits on a private beach. Once Hollywood got wind of Cabo, the developers came flocking in. I understand it's more like Dana Point on steroids now."

Quinn had to laugh. Dr. Felix's mood lightened as the two friends cleaned up the galley. Marnie, Marcus, and Chip were in the cockpit playing poker when Quinn went up.

"Where's Noah?" Quinn looked forward along the deck of the *Icarus* but didn't see him.

"He's keeping to himself, again." Chip sounded uneasy. "I don't know what's bugging him on this leg of the trip. But something sure is."

He looked at Quinn. "You seem to have patched things up with him. I couldn't help but notice the two of you this morning on the foredeck popping up and down like Jack-in-the-boxes."

Marcus and Marnie laughed at Chip's droll analogy, then invited Quinn to join in on the card game. Marcus suggested they play strip poker.

"You wish," Quinn said.

Dr. Felix had remained below to go over some charts and paperwork. When he came up a couple hours later he was holding a bag of chocolate chip cookies. "Who wants which watch tonight?" The doctor wanted to know as he passed the bag around.

Quinn immediately claimed the midnight to four. After her long nap she wasn't in the least bit tired. "I'll take the same," Chip offered. Marcus and Marnie were left with the four-to-eight watch.

"Good enough, then. I'm going to get some shuteye." Dr. Felix walked the length of the deck of the *Icarus* before going below to make his bed in the main salon. It wasn't long before Quinn and Chip were alone in the cockpit. Quinn couldn't hide her nervousness. She knew too much and her conscience was bothering her.

Chip picked up on her unease. "What gives, Quinn? Are you PMSing or something?"

Quinn swatted him on the arm. "Don't be rude."

"Sorry. You just don't seem your usual self. Care to share with your old buddy?"

Quinn looked at her sailing companion. She and Chip had been through a lot together during the seven day crossing to Jamaica onboard the *Zephyr,* and the following three days in Negril. She'd helped nurse and comfort Chip through one of his darkest hours after the black fin shark had taken a chunk out of his backside. She'd also confided to him certain aspects about her unexpected romance with Noah. Chip had always been there to lend an ear and an understanding shoulder.

How am I going to tell him I read his journal? What will he think of me after that? Worse, how will he react if I tell him I told Noah about him having sex with Lydia? I wonder if Chip has it in him to forgive me for betraying him. Because, that's what I've done, betray him.

Quinn's head began to ache. Chip remained silent. He was staring out over the transom of the boat, a mournful look on his long, horsey face. It was almost as if he already knew the secret Quinn had been keeping inside of her. He was the one to break the silence.

"Quinn, I consider you a really good friend. We've been through a lot together in the short time we've known each other. There's really nothing you can't tell me or confide in me that would damage our friendship, I hope you know that."

Quinn groaned inside. She knew it was now or never. For a moment she debated whether it would be better for Chip to hear the news from Noah. *No, I have a feeling it would be best if Chip confessed to Noah, rather than Noah having to confront him.* Her mind made up, Quinn drew a deep breath.

"Chip," she began, "as you now know that whole deal with Lydia claiming she's pregnant with Noah's child is driving him crazy." Even in the faint light cast by the instrument panel on the binnacle, Quinn could see Chip's body stiffen. "It's caused a lot of strain on our already strained relationship. We've decided to cool it for awhile. Has Noah told you he signed up for Transpac?"

Chip shook his head. Quinn remained silent for a few minutes half hoping Chip would step up to the bat. When the silence grew too awkward, Quinn went on.

"Chip, the way I see it, the baby is due probably in November. You can bet your life Noah is going to insist on a DNA test. If Noah isn't the father, Lydia's still going to want the man who got her pregnant to be on the hook for child support for eighteen years."

"I don't understand why she's trying to put the rap on Noah." Chip finally spoke up. "That chick is a nymphomaniac *and* a psycho. Hell, any number of men in Miami could be the father."

Quinn flashed to Marcus. He, too, had bedded Lydia, but the timeline was too far off to cause him any concern. Marcus knew a bit about Quinn's romance with Noah. During watches crossing the Gulf, Quinn had told him pretty much every detail about the adventures onboard the *Zephyr*. He'd already known about her Miami modeling disaster and how it was that Quinn met Gail, then Hank. Quinn had prudently decided not to mention to Marcus that both Noah and Chip knew Lydia. What would Marcus's reaction be if he knew two of his current mates had known Lydia intimately, as in the Biblical sense of the word? Even more so, how would he handle it when he found out one or the other of those crewmates was most likely the father to her child?

As far as Quinn knew, Marnie had no clue about the drama brewing on the *Icarus*. She'd overhead parts of Quinn's heart-to-heart discussion with Noah on watch one night, but Marnie had made no mention of the pending baby and paternity suit. Quinn made a silent resolve; *once we reach San Diego and Noah leaves for San Pedro and the Transpac, I'll explain everything to Marnie and Marcus.*

As close as the quarters were on the *Icarus*, it caused a moment of wonder for Quinn at how six people could know so little about what was going on in each other's lives. *It must be the watch scheduling and our hopping from port to port*, she rationalized. *Whatever it is, thank God!*

Chip's restless pacing brought Quinn back to reality. He stopped beside the raft strapped on the transom. She stood and went to stand by him. *It's now or never*, Quinn put an arm around Chip's lean waist.

"I have a confession to make, Chippers. This is really going to be hard for me so please be patient and at least hear me out. And, please, whatever you do, *please* try to not judge me."

All in one breath, Quinn blurted out, "I was organizing the galley and when I used the stowage space under your bunk, I found your journal."

There was no immediate response from Chip.

"I knew it was wrong to invade your privacy. I even took it out then put it back. But, I was consumed with curiosity about what you might have written about me. Your perception of me, I guess. I swear I meant to only read parts where my name was mentioned. I didn't read the whole thing."

Chip finally spoke. "Well, that was right damn nice of you, Quinn." He pushed her arm off his waist. "Let me guess what else you read, do you want me to?"

Quinn was too miserable to answer. She was trying to hold back the tears that were threatening to run down her cheeks.

"You read what happened between me and Lydia, didn't you? That's what this whole little sermon about Noah is about, right?"

"I'm sorry, I'm so sorry, Chip." The tears would no longer be restrained and ran freely down Quinn's face. "It was so wrong of me to do that. I don't blame you if you can't forgive me."

Chip shook his head slowly back and forth, back and forth. He put a hand up to cover his eyes, then spoke in such a soft voice, Quinn had to lean in to hear him.

"Don't be sorry, Quinn. Yeah, it was wrong of you to read my journal. Maybe you won't believe me but I've been waiting for the opportune moment to tell Noah what happened that night between me and Lydia. It's just been hard for me to wrap my mind around all of this."

He dropped his hand, and without looking at Quinn, said, "I couldn't believe it when you told me Lydia was pregnant. It's taken me days to absorb the ramifications of that. I certainly hope you don't think I'd leave Noah hanging on a limb over it. I just don't know *how* to tell him. He's going to think I'm the scum of the earth. Lecturing him about banging the cook and shirking his duties, then when he makes an effort to do the right thing, *I* end up banging her."

"Chip," Quinn put her hand on his arm. He flinched at her touch and it cut her to the quick. "Lydia is the wild card in this scenario. The woman is evil. She's known all along it could be one or the other of you. She sicced her detective daddy on Noah right off the bat for prenatal expenses and child support."

Chip barked a laugh. "Yeah, of course. If you had your choice, who would you want to be the father of your baby? The heartthrob stud Noah? Or me, good ole homely, boring Chip?"

"Stop it! That kind of thinking isn't fair to anyone. None of this is fair, Chip."

"Life isn't fair, Quinn." Chip spat over the side of the yacht. *Lydia obviously leaves a bad taste in everyone's mouth,* Quinn thought with a grim stab of humor. She was tempted to spit over the side herself.

"Chip, I'm going to tell you something that Noah doesn't even know. I actually met Lydia at a party in Miami." Quinn could tell she had Chip's interest even though he still wouldn't look at her. "I was with Marcus, Cyndi and Joey. Lydia was modeling swimwear for Cyndi's boss, Olga. There were all these gorgeous models parading about, then Lydia came down the catwalk. Dude, I can't blame you for succumbing to her. I have to admit she's positively gorgeous. Almost impossibly so."

Chip was nodding his head, a faraway look on his face. At that moment Quinn felt so sorry for him, it seemed her heart would burst. She recalled how Chip had mentioned two lovers in his life; both had left him for other men. Chip was physically unattractive but he was also one of the sweetest, most good-hearted men she'd ever met. *Life's not fair, not fair. We've all come to learn that hard lesson.*

"Marcus has no clue about Noah and Lydia, or you and Lydia for that matter. But Marcus knows Lydia very well. He had an affair with her last year."

Quinn finally had Chip's full attention. "Yup, Marcus was sleeping with Lydia until she met her captain boyfriend. She dumped Marcus like a hot potato and went crewing with the new guy on a one-hundred-five-foot luxury yacht. When that gig ended, she dumped *him*, to go sailing with you and Noah."

"The plot thickens," Chip almost sounded like his normal self.

"Yes, it does indeed. I know I'm in no position to ask you a favor, Chip, but I'd like you to please keep that little bit of info to yourself until I get a chance to clue Noah in. And also Marcus."

Chip nodded. "I certainly have no problem with that. Keeping secrets, that is." He smiled in self-depreciation. "We truly are a ship of fools, aren't we, Quinn Anne?"

"There's one other thing," Quinn shrank back into the shadows.

"What's that?"

"Chip, I've already told Noah about the journal."

"You did *what?*" For the first time since the entire unpleasant subject had been brought up, Chip's voice rang with sincere and honest anger.

Quinn cringed.

"I had to, Chip. He was in emotional agony. I'd been waiting for you to say something. But you didn't."

"So that's why Noah's acting as if I have leprosy or something. Jeez, Quinn, how could you do that?"

Quinn didn't have an answer. She went below and began to brew a pot of coffee. Chip was at the helm when she came back up with two mugs and a couple of cream puff pastries. He took a mug and a pastry without a word. Time dragged on before Chip finally spoke.

"I'll talk to Noah tomorrow, Quinn. I hope he understands I've been trying to digest this. I hope he understands I wasn't going to stay quiet until the baby was born. I hope you both understand I've felt guilty about Lydia ever since it happened. I know Noah wasn't anywhere near in love with her, but still, it wasn't right for me to have sex with her on the heels of her having sex with Noah."

Quinn nodded. There was only an hour and a half left on the watch, but when Chip told Quinn it was all right by him if she took an early out and went to bed, she went without argument. She figured Chip could use some time to absorb everything she'd dumped on him in just a few short hours. The next day or two on the *Icarus* were sure to be interesting. Quinn hoped she still had friends left onboard. Only tomorrow would tell.

CHAPTER THIRTY-ONE

The cove at Yelapa was small—and crowded. Dr. Felix couldn't hide his disgust as the *Icarus* motored slowly along the outskirts. The strip of beach was packed with sunburned tourists and colorful umbrellas. Boats and catamarans were already anchored in the shallows, making it impossible for the *Icarus* to find a decent mooring.

"Maybe this is a good thing," he said, turning the wheel to steer the Colombia 45 back into Banderas Bay. "We might be better off among all the boats in the marina at Puerto Vallarta. Give us some anonymity. There are over five hundred slips there. Not to mention other spots where we can hide out."

Quinn grinned humorlessly. "You'd think we were the *banditos,* having to hide out. If they can use force, torture and intimidation, why can't we? Too bad you don't have any guns onboard, Felix."

"Oh, but I do, my dear, I do."

Quinn looked surprised. "I haven't seen any."

"They're safely hidden away. If the need should arise, rest assured we stand a good chance of defending ourselves."

Banderas Bay, "bay of flags," was huge. Felix informed the crew it was the second largest natural bay in North America, boasting over one hundred miles of coast line. The recreational activities were endless, he pointed out; ranging from snorkeling, scuba diving, kayaking and saltwater fishing, to exploring the jungles, rivers, and waterfalls in the Sierra Madre Mountains via hiking, horseback riding or mountain biking.

The sun-drenched beaches, fine dining, glitzy nightlife and shopping had turned Puerto Vallarta from a sleepy Mexican village into one of Mexico's top vacation destinations.

"I believe Chesapeake Bay has the record overall as the largest natural bay in North America," he'd added as an afterthought.

Felix also informed the crew they would only be staying overnight. He was antsy about the drug dealer situation but he was also eager to get to Cabo, he confessed to Quinn, because Anna was flying in to join the *Icarus* on the last leg of the journey to San Diego.

Quinn gave the big man a hug. "That's fabulous. She's a wonderful woman. Congratulations."

Felix had selected a slip in an out of the way corner of the marina. It was only accessible by a small inlet of water or by a long, narrow dock. It would also be easy to get back out into the bay from that location. With not much time to explore, the crew quickly secured the *Icarus* and washed her down. Then they split up into two groups. Marnie, Quinn and Marcus were interested in the souvenir shops; Noah and Chip expressed interest in the less touristy section of town and the cantinas.

Felix warned everyone to stay alert. He handed each group a walkie talkie. "Stay in touch with each other." He advised them. "If anyone smells something rotten in Denmark, all of you skedaddle back here as fast as you can. Try to make sure no one is following you, either."

With that warning ringing in her ears, Quinn set out with her two buddies to explore Puerto Vallarta. The tropical city was beautiful, lush, and colorful. "I bet Felix would be surprised if I told him I knew a famous movie, *Night of the Iguana,* starring Richard Burton, Ava Gardner, and Deborah Kerr was filmed here way back in the sixties," Quinn said.

"My, aren't you a fount of movie trivia." Marnie patted Quinn on the back.

Two hours passed with surprising speed as the trio moved among the crowded streets and shops looking for souvenirs for their loved ones back home. Quinn was harboring a secret hope that Noah and Chip were finally going to be able to talk privately and honestly about their common concern; paternity. *Maybe, their tongues will loosen up over a couple beers and tequila chasers.*

Quinn was smiling at a mental picture of the two buddies, arms draped over each other's shoulders, earnest expressions on their faces as they downed beer after beer. Suddenly, a hand clasped around her upper arm with a grip of steel that immediately cut off her circulation. A spurt of adrenalin coursed through Quinn's body with such sudden intensity that she was momentarily not only paralyzed but she couldn't see; her vision went blurry.

Quinn had been browsing inside a small, overcrowded kiosk for some cotton dresses. She was fairly certain Marnie was close by, but the store was so packed with inventory Quinn couldn't see over the colorful racks of clothing. She knew Marcus was at a curio shop next door. She opened her mouth to scream, but a rough hand immediately covered her mouth and nose.

"Do not scream. Listen to me." The familiar guttural and raspy voice sent chills rippling over Quinn's body. It was the quiet man. The silent one. The one on the *Vanora* who had rousted Quinn at gunpoint from her cabin. She remembered his eyes. Dark, almost black and completely without expression. His deeply-lined face. It was Adolfo, holding her prisoner again. *He's come to kill me,* Quinn realized with a hollow feeling in the pit of her stomach. *I'll never see mom or dad again. Or my brother, Greg. Or my nieces and nephews.*

A feeling of such deep sorrow washed over Quinn that she went limp and stopped struggling. Adolfo released his hold on Quinn's mouth and turned her around to face him.

"You must leave now. Go back to your boat and leave Vallarta immediately." He spoke in the same guttural whisper. In a daze, Quinn noticed the terrible scar at the base of the man's throat. It looked like someone had tried to slice his head off with a dull, serrated blade. She lifted her green eyes to his dark unfathomable ones.

"You're letting me go? You're not going to kill me?" Quinn whispered too. It took all the resources at her command to do even that.

"I do not shed innocent blood. You are in grave danger. All of you. Now, go." He pushed her. Quinn almost fell down her legs were so devoid of strength. When she recovered, he was gone. Dazed, Quinn stood there for a moment, wondering if the incident had really happened.

"Quinn, what's wrong? You look like you've seen a ghost or something." Marnie's voice brought Quinn out of her trance.

"Give me that walkie talkie. We've got to find Marcus, and Noah and Chip. We've got to get back to the boat and warn Dr. Felix."

Bewildered, Marnie dug the gray unit out of her purse. "Warn him? About what? Are you okay, Quinn?

"Come with me," Quinn grabbed Marnie by the arm. With her other hand she was already calling for Chip and Noah on the walkie talkie. Outside, Quinn's eyes darted fearfully around. She pushed Marnie toward the curio shop. "Get Marcus." Several taxis went by before Quinn could finally flag one down. Marcus and Marnie joined Quinn, and all three sailors climbed into the vehicle.

There'd been no response yet from Chip or Noah and Quinn was getting desperate when the mini radio squawked into life. "Chip?" Quinn's voice broke. "Thank God."

"Hey, Quinn, what's the matter?"

"Get back to the *Icarus* as quick as you can."

"What? Why?"

Marcus and Marnie were looking at Quinn in perplexity. Quinn held up her arm. The mottled and distinct outline of four fingers was clearly visible. Marnie covered her mouth with her hand and looked at Quinn in dismay. Quinn pointed at the taxi driver's back, put her finger to her lips, then shook her head.

"Chip, there's been an emergency onboard. You and Noah need to get back immediately. Do you understand? Remember what the doctor said to do in an emergency."

There was only a moment of silence, then Chip said, "I read you loud and clear. Over." He clicked off.

Quinn was panting as the three crewmembers raced along the docks leading to the *Icarus*. Between breaths, she told Marcus and Marnie about her encounter with Alfonso. She repeated her story in more detail to Dr. Felix once she was onboard. The doctor had obviously been hard at work on the *Icarus* while the crew was gone. He was sweating and had pieces of canvas and caulking stuck in the hair on his bare chest and back.

"Chip and Noah are on their way, Felix. I got a hold of them with this." She handed the walkie talkie over.

"Let's get ready to rock, then," Felix started the engine. Less than ten minutes later, Quinn saw Chip and Noah sprinting down the dock. Marcus had the springer lines undone and all three men leaped on the *Icarus* at the same time. Dr. Felix backed the yacht up, then headed down the narrow channel toward the bay.

Wearily, Quinn had to repeat her story in front of Chip and Noah. Marcus and Marnie exchanged glances.

"Alfonso struck me as being one really bad ass hombre." Marnie said. "Why would he warn you, us?"

"He struck me as more like a professional soldier. Not like the rest of that bunch." Marcus speculated. "That comment about innocent blood. I bet he doesn't mind doing in the likes of Yoshua, but when it comes to two gorgeous babes like you?" He grinned at Quinn and Marnie.

The entire crew was on deck. All eyes searching for any suspicious activity. No boats appeared to be following the *Icarus*. There was hardly any activity on the water except for a scattering of kayaks and jet skis. It was late afternoon and most of the commercial and recreational vessels were out on tours.

Once Felix was confident they'd gotten away from the marina undetected, he put the boat on autopilot. "I wasn't exactly idle while the five of you were ashore." He motioned for everyone to follow him to the transom of the boat.

"Check it out," he pointed with pride. It took Quinn a minute or two to figure out what Felix was showing them, then she laughed. "I don't believe it! How did you do that?"

Across the broad fiberglass beam where once the name *Icarus* had been stenciled, there now was a different name, *Illusion*. Felix grinned. "It won't hold up under close examination, but I stenciled a new moniker on some spare canvas. I figured from a distance no one would notice it's not authentic. I attached the top here." He pointed to the aft stanchions.

"The bottom of the banner was a bit more difficult. I had to get in the water and work some magic using the windvane. Providing we don't get any rough seas or weather, our cover should last all the way to San Diego."

Felix sobered up. "We're skipping Cabo. The sooner we get out of Mexican waters the better."

"No, Felix! You don't need to do that. What about Anna?" Quinn grabbed him by the hand. "Come on, you two had it planned."

Felix looked at Quinn. "I fault myself for this incident. An incident, by the way that could have gotten at least three of you murdered—or worse. I should never have made radio contact with another yacht and announced where we were going.

"I wasn't thinking. Even though the conversation only lasted five minutes, obviously someone is constantly monitoring the airwaves. I may as well have simply handed your lives over to Luiz Montoya."

Quinn took Felix by the arms. "But you've fixed it. We have a different name now. We just won't use the radio. How could they possibly know our itinerary? At least meet Anna and pick her up. We don't have to stay. She can sail with us like you planned. Think about how she's had to rearrange her schedule to do this. She wants to be with you, Felix."

The doctor shook his head. "No. I can see her anytime once you all are safe and sound. I don't want to put her in jeopardy, either."

There was a glum silence all around.

"Well, isn't this hunky dory." Marnie broke the silence. "What are we? Criminals? Cowards? Do we really have to run like hunted animals with our tails between our legs because of some two-bit piece of shit drug dealer?"

She glared at the group surrounding her. "I say *no*. Hell no! I say let's carry on and beat those assholes at their own game." She looked pointedly at Quinn. "And yes I said shit and asshole."

Quinn looked at Marnie, then burst out laughing. "Well, shit yes, then. I agree. Let's beat those assholes at their own game. We already have a boat alias thanks to Dr. Felix."

The tension of the past hour melted as the crew of the former *Icarus* enjoyed a communal moment of lightheartedness.

"Hey, big guy, I have an idea." Chip had a thoughtful look on his face.

All eyes turned to the lanky sailor.

"How about we send out some false radio transmissions? We shouldn't be too obvious. Felix, you could let slip into another conversation with that buddy of yours that we're heading straight to San Pedro, California. Think of some excuse for us to not even go to San Diego. Then, we can slip into Cabo as the *Illusion*, pick up Anna and take our own sweet time cruising to San Diego."

Chip received a resounding round of applause. Noah clapped him on the back and said, "You be one smart mon, my friend. All who agree say aye!"

The ayes had it.

CHAPTER THIRTY-TWO

I t was obvious to Quinn that Noah and Chip had reached an understanding. Despite the threat of Luiz Montoya, the spirits of the crew of the *Icarus/ Illusion* were near euphoric as the yacht sailed out of Banderas Bay into the sparkling, deep blue Pacific Ocean. Perhaps because the crew was living on the edge, the air seemed sweeter, the sails crisper. The twice-named boat seemed to belie her tonnage and her years as she leaped gracefully through the frothy whitecaps.

"Isn't it bad luck to rename a boat?" Quinn and Felix had taken the sunset watch.

"So it's said." Felix pushed his trademark captain's hat back off of his forehead. "I prefer to think we haven't renamed the *Icarus*. We've given her a middle name, that's all."

Quinn nodded. "It fits. Icarus was the Greek god who had an illusion that he could fly, wasn't he? Or, was that a delusion."

"Icarus wasn't a god, Quinn; he was a teenage boy in ancient Greece. He followed his father, Daedalus, who had devised wings made of feathers and wax to escape the prison he'd been placed into by King Minos of Greece, into the sky. Unfortunately, Icarus decided he could out fly the master. He disregarded his father's advice and flew too close to the sun."

Neither of the sailors could keep their eyes off the sunset that was unfolding before them. Quinn was so entranced, she was almost afraid to blink. The red orb of the sun seemed gigantic. There wasn't a cloud in the sky, no marine layer obscuring the horizon. The sea was a bed of molten silver. It was as though the sun was absorbing all the color from the water's surface; daring any earthly element to interfere with its descent. The huge shimmering globe seemed to melt into the horizon. Quinn had to avert her eyes a couple of times, the rays were so bright.

"Keep your eyes on the top of the sun as it sets, Quinn." Felix said. "There's a good chance you might get a surprise."

Quinn did as she was told; the sun's power had lessened considerably as it sank below the horizon. Just as the upper rim of the sun disappeared, there was a quick bluish green flash of light. Quinn clapped her hands in delight. Felix beamed.

"Was that your first green flash?"

Quinn nodded. She'd only heard about the atmospheric phenomenon. She knew conditions had to be just right for it to happen. Most people considered the green flash a sign of good luck.

"We're all due for some good luck, that's for sure." Quinn was unaware she'd spoken out loud.

Dr. Felix patted her on the knee. "Wait until Captain Tommy gets wind of all the drama and high seas adventure you've been through. It's certain to blow his mind."

"I'd love to see Tommy again. He's a good man. It's amazing how in one week we four became so bonded. I feel like Chip and Tommy are family." Quinn didn't include Noah in the equation only because her relationship with Noah was definitely not that of a sibling. Felix, of course, understood that completely.

"We may be seeing Tommy once we're stateside. You never know." Felix predicted.

Quinn excused herself to go make dinner. Chip and Noah were sitting at the chart table playing a game of chess. It made Quinn's heart swell with joy to see the two old friends sitting companionably across from one another; their faces reflecting how deep they were in concentration. Quinn started singing an old Crosby, Stills and Nash song, *Southern Cross*, as she began browning stew meat for a beef stroganoff.

Over dinner in the cockpit, Felix outlined their course. "We're going to tack our way across to Cabo rather than hug the coast of Mexico. We'll be crossing the Gulf of California, or Sea of Cortez as it's more commonly known. Unless that is, anyone really has the hots to see Mazatlan."

Nobody did. According to Felix's reckoning the *Icarus/Illusion* would reach the bitter end of Baja California some time later the following night. "We may have to stay two days. I don't dare radio Anna about our arrival. I'm going to have to call her from shore. She can catch the next available flight."

"Marnie and I will move into the main salon tomorrow night," Quinn said. She grinned at the flush that spread over the doctor's cheeks.

"Now, now, there's no need for that," he said.

"Sure there is." Marnie winked at him.

"You gals move to the forepeak," Noah spoke up. "I and Marcus will sleep in the salon along with Chip."

The leg over to Cabo was routine except for a midnight alarm. Quinn and Marnie had taken the first watch. Quinn had been nervously keeping an eye on a big container ship. She'd first spotted it as a blip on the radar earlier in the evening. Freighters and commercial vessels were a common sight but generally they kept their distance. This one seemed to be bearing straight down on the Columbia 45.

Quinn tried raising the vessel on the radio, but all she got was static. She also was using a fabricated set of call signals. If the Coast Guard caught them doing that Quinn wasn't sure what the penalty would be. Felix hadn't seemed too concerned about it. "Click the button here and there so you cut out strategically. We can say they must have missed a letter or two because of static," he'd told Quinn earlier.

The ship seemed to be looming larger and larger off the stern. Alarmed, Quinn went below and woke up Felix. He was up and on deck before Quinn could get the whole story out of her mouth.

"Bring the main sheet in." He ordered Marnie as he started the engine. Felix steered the *Icarus* hard to starboard. He began to push the control lever of the engine to almost full throttle. "Take the wheel, Quinn, while I go below and try to raise these jokers on the radio. We've plenty of leeway so just get out of their way."

Quinn half-expected the huge ship to change course and deliberately run down the *Icarus*. It was a chilling sight to see a ship that size so close. Quinn could make out the portholes along the side and the huge containers on its deck. Dr. Felix must have raised someone on the radio, she could hear him talking. It seemed like it took forever for the monstrous length of the vessel to go by. The hair on Quinn's arms prickled as the *Icarus* lifted on the big swell of the passing wake.

"Good grief, what was that all about?" Quinn asked Felix when he came up.

"I'm not sure. I got the captain on the radio. He said they'd been asked to keep a lookout for a missing sloop. That's a new one. He wouldn't give any particulars, either."

"The long arm of Luiz Montoya, wanna bet?"

"I'm fairly confident I handled it well, so not to worry. Why don't you two girls get some rest? I'll finish the watch."

Felix's reckoning proved to be right on. At three o'clock in the morning of the following night, the crew of the *Icarus* was dropping anchor in the roadstead in front of the formerly tiny village of Cabo San Lucas. Once Felix secured the anchor he ordered everyone to bed. "We'll take the Avon ashore at seven. I need to call Anna as soon as possible."

The ride to shore in the morning was a bit wet and bumpy. The bay at Cabo faced the Sea of Cortez and the current was fairly strong. To the west Quinn could see the famous El Arco de Cabo San Lucas, a distinctive, arched rock formation rising out of the ocean. Felix chose to take the Avon into the marina rather than land it on the beach. Tourists were lined up waiting to get on charted powerboats to go sword fishing. The first thing Felix did was head for a payphone.

"Quinn, don't you think you should give Rafael a ring? I have his numbers here in my book. I've no doubt he's anxious to see how you're doing."

Quinn agreed and after Felix hung up from talking to Anna, she placed a call to Rafael's cell. There was no mistaking the genuine affection in the multi-millionaire's voice.

"*Querida!* I am so happy to hear from you. How are things? Are you well? Are you happy?'

As always, Rafael's concern for her security and happiness tugged at Quinn's heart. She assured him all was well and they chatted for a few minutes. Rafael asked when the *Icarus* would be arriving in San Diego. "I have business there. Remember the couple who drank all that tequila?" Quinn did and she laughed. She got a warm rush remembering that was also the first night she and Rafael made love.

"Perhaps, *querida*, we could go out and have a nice dinner while I'm in town."

"I'd love to, Rafael. I really would."

Rafael asked if Dr. Felix was available. Before handing the phone to the doctor, Quinn asked Rafael about the *Vanora*. "Did you try to have her salvaged? Will your insurance company pay for her?"

"We never had time to discuss that, Quinn. We'll do so over dinner in San Diego, *bien?*"

Quinn bid Rafael goodbye and handed the phone to Felix. She walked over to where Marcus, Marnie, Noah and Chip were waiting impatiently by a railing overlooking the many sword fishing boats in the marina. "Anna will be in on a seven o'clock flight tonight. It's a half hour ride from the airport, so Felix wants to buy us all dinner in town. Anna will take a cab to the restaurant."

Felix was off the phone and he waved for the group to join him. As they walked toward what Felix remembered as the heart of town, he brought up his conversation with Rafael.

"I think all of us owe *Senor* Santiago a big debt of gratitude. Apparently, he got contacted by Luiz Montoya."

Everyone collectively stopped in their tracks. "What happened? What did Luiz want?" Quinn's heart was pounding. Marcus and Marnie were looking at Dr. Felix in alarm.

"Not to worry. What happened is Rafael has ransomed your three heads." He pointed at each former crewmember of the *Vanora*.

"He's done *what*?" Quinn couldn't believe her ears.

"He paid Luiz off—well off—I might add, to leave you three alone. To forget about all of you. He also guaranteed Luiz that none of you would ever disclose what happened on the *Vanora*. Not the drugs, not the statue, not even the scuttling of the ship."

Marcus and Marnie were staring at Quinn.

"What?" Quinn stared back. She was perplexed and upset. How could Rafael buy her silence and that of her friends without even consulting them?

"Insurance, remember?" Marcus said. "That's why Luiz tried taking you away with him. He knew Rafael would barter for your life. How cool is that?"

"Yeah, Quinn," Marnie sounded very impressed. "Not only that, he got our asses out of the same sling. What a guy!"

Noah had stayed silent throughout the whole exchange. So had Chip. Noah grabbed Quinn by the arm and pulled her aside. "Do not let this man buy you, Quinn. Do not let him buy your silence, your tongue, your soul. Who is he to give your word to another man?"

Quinn looked into Noah's earnest amber eyes. "I agree, Noah. I have to appreciate what he's done. But, I think it just goes to show he feels entitled to barter with not only my life, but the lives of my friends, too."

Noah let go of Quinn's arm. "I see you are not completely taken by this man. This man who thinks he is an eagle and the rest of us are doves." He gave her a hug. "I trust you to do right. I have faith in you, Quinn-nay."

Cabo proved to be, while not the dreamy quiet fishing village Felix remembered, an interesting blend of old charm and contemporary attractions. By the time Anna arrived at the ocean view restaurant Felix had selected, the crew of the *Icarus* was footsore and, as Marcus said, two and three-quarter-sheets to the wind. The sweet-natured school teacher took everything in stride: Even Felix's baritone and garbled operatic singing on the way back to the Avon at the marina.

Quinn had never seen the burly doctor inebriated. She secretly assumed the fact that he was teetering on the brink of being in love with the petite dark-haired woman holding him steady as they walked the uneven street to the dock, had something to do with his lightheadedness. Back onboard, the party carried on until the wee hours of the morning. A man had motored over in a dinghy from a neighboring yacht in the roadstead to inquire if there was any spare Vermouth on the *Icarus*. Felix invited him not only to stay but to go back and get his crew as well. That whole night the air rang with music and laughter.

It was one of those evenings that made yachting worthwhile, Quinn would later reflect. It was a bonding of a diverse group of people who shared mutual goals and experiences. Experiences that at times could put one's life in jeopardy, but the rewards of life at sea far outweighed any of the inherent dangers such as hurricanes, tangled lines in propellers, and as in the unusual case of the lost *Vanora,* criminal activity and the loss of a ship.

It was a hung over crew that sailed away from Cabo. It was also a hard beat against the current up the coast of Baja. Quinn had to hand it to Anna, even though the woman looked pale as a ghost and pretty well hugged the stern most of the way, she never complained. Quinn had stumbled on a snack that seemed to help ease the queasiness of being seasick—or hung over. She kept passing around tortilla chips dipped in peanut butter. Everyone claimed it made their stomachs feel better.

It was a disheveled crew that pulled alongside the cement Coast Guard dock at Shelter Island, San Diego, days later. With seven people onboard the *Icarus*, who was proudly showing her name off the transom again, showering had been kept to a minimum. Quinn had gotten used to saltwater showers on the deck with a quick fresh water rinse below.

Reaching journey's end produced a maelstrom of emotions in Quinn. The Coast Guard boarded the *Icarus* and the yacht and the crew passed customs. Felix suggested everyone shower and freshen up in the public lockers. He knew of a local bar and restaurant not far from the dock, the Red Sails Inn Restaurant, that was popular with the San Diego boating crowd.

"How about we all go there and get a real American meal. Cheeseburgers and French fries, anyone?"

When the freshly scrubbed crew of the *Icarus* was finally seated together at a table on the patio of the bayside restaurant, Quinn looked around at her companions and did a mental accounting: *Noah is leaving to crew on Transpac. I may not see him for a long, long while. But I know I will see him again. Dr. Felix and Anna definitely have a thing going on. Marcus and Marnie aren't going anywhere as far as I can tell. Chip has announced he needs to go home to New York and spend some time with his widowed mother. He's signed on to continue on with us when the time is right. Rafael is waiting in the wings. I still have to resolve some issues with him.*

Quinn sighed and looked out over the uneven outlines of the powerboats and sailboats bobbing quietly at rest in the harbor. The heavy ocean air seemed to press in upon the group sitting on the darkened patio. Mentally Quinn tried to add up how many nautical miles she'd traveled with her companions. The ship's log book would have the details. It was the responsibility of each watch to record all coordinates and incidents during their shift.

Dr. Felix raised a wineglass. His hefty arm all but dwarfed the slender shoulders of the smiling woman sitting beside him. All eyes turned to the couple at the head of the table.

"Here's to a crew any captain would be proud of. I salute each and every one of you for your courage, endurance, valor, and loyalty." There was a chorus of cheers from the five sunburned, wind burned, and travel weary friends gathered around the table.

"Most of all," Felix continued, "I want to salute you for standing by me and my ship in pursuit of my lady love, Miss Anna Marie."

That brought down the house. Chip, Noah and Marcus pounded on the table with their beer mugs. Quinn and Marnie hugged each other in delight. The amused waiter began placing platters of food on the table. Quinn was sitting across from Noah, who was sitting beside Chip. The three seasoned deckhands looked at each other and a wave of mutual understanding passed between them.

Only time would tell what direction their lives were to follow. There would be no immediate resolution for Chip and Noah as to who was the father of Lydia Caballero's child. There was no insurance that Marnie,

Marcus and Quinn were truly free from the threat of Luiz Montoya until Quinn met with Rafael face to face; and maybe not even then.

The only assurance the seven souls sitting around an outdoor table on the edge of a marine harbor had was that all of them were willing to set sail again. To put their trust, their lives, their fate, in each other's hands. All were bound and wholeheartedly committed to carry on with their quest: Chart new courses, battle the elements, and explore the world like few souls would ever see it.

"Sail on, sailors." Dr. Felix said. "To Australia or bust!"

Seven arms rose in salute over the dimpled glass candle holder in the middle of the table. Seven sailors, including Noah, tipped their glasses in a pledge to stand before the mast. To answer the call of the sea, the waves, the wind, and the far flung shorelines that beckoned to each and every one of them. To spend their lives sailing over and through the shadows of the sea.

— THE END —

Dear Reader:

For those of you who have never felt the sting of the ocean's spray on your face while bracing yourself against the tilt of a boat under full sail, I can only hope that your imagination has taken you there while reading the *MsAdventures at Sea* series. Isn't that what fiction is all about? Imagination. Yours and mine.

I truly have wanderlust. Give me a working yacht, a cruise ship, an airplane ride to a foreign country, a winding road tapering off into an unknown horizon, oh, I'm there—in the moment and anticipating the unknown adventures that beckon along the path and at the end of the journey.

My restless wanderings stopped when I met my former husband and his two young boys. My true life journey began when I had our son. Being a mother is the greatest adventure of all, full of reward, constantly challenging, endlessly unfolding and for me it anchored my questing soul. Now that my son is grown and off to college, I'm off on one adventure after another.

I quote from my original draft of the nonfiction *MsAdventures at Sea* article published in *Latitude 38*, August of 1981: *I feel sad for those who have never experienced the heart-squeezing delight of flying through the water on a crisp, sparkling clear day at nine and a half knots with the sails straining to symmetry and the toe rail covered in frothing spray. How many would give years of their life for the ethereal beauty of a full moon on a cloudless night, watching Orion and the Big Dipper go wheeling by to the splashing melody of the hull as it hisses through the water?*

I remember all of that vividly; and so much more. I'm compelled to share the world of blue water sailing with anyone who's willing to read about it. Up to this point, I'd sailed in the past to every port and over every body of water I've written about. Book three, the last in the *MsAdventures at Sea* series, is taking me into uncharted waters. Now I'm heading to New Zealand and Australia. Therefore, I can't titillate you with what is to come. I have no idea until I (we) get there. Quinn and her friends are tagging along. I can't promise a publishing date, either. I can only say I've averaged a novel a year over the past three years, so....be patient. Keep the faith. One thing I can guarantee is there will be adventure, there will be love and passion, and we will *all* find out who is the father of Lydia Caballero's baby.

"When you see the Southern Cross for the first time, you understand now why you came this way." Crosby, Stills, Nash and Young- Southern Cross.

-Christine

Александр Ку Коммитри 5500мм (10км 45min)

About the Author

Christine McKellar is a resident of Las Vegas, Nevada, and a freelance writer. She is the author of three novels, A Port of No Return, The Shadows of the Sea, and The Devil's Valet. A freelance writer for over twenty-five years, she's written for Las Vegas CityLife, Latitude 38, Latitudes & Attitudes, Easy Rider, Trailer Life, Industrial Design Magazine, the Huntington Beach Independent and various other newspapers and periodicals. Her first crime fiction short story, Bits and Pieces, will be published (spring of 2008) in The Las Vegas Noir anthology (Akashic Books). The prolific author recently began to pen her fourth novel, The Winds of Whyalla—the final sequel to her three-book MsAdventures at Sea sailing adventure series. (The Devil's Valet, a mystery romance, was completed between books one and two of the sailing novels, says McKellar.) "I'd written non-fiction for years, but I was always encouraged to write about my real-life sailing adventures as a hired cook on yacht deliveries. In 2003, I decided to take up the challenge with A Port of No Return "(A sexy, thrilling ride"-Kirkus Reviews). I made the decision to fictionalize a series of contemporary, sexy books based loosely on my travels and experiences at sea. The Shadows of the Sea is the second book of the series." McKellar predicts her current project, The Winds of Whyalla, will be completed in the fall of 2008.

Printed in the United States
96537LV00004B/313-381/A